# Tessa's Dance

David Edward Walker

Thoughtful Publishing Company
Seattle

Copyright © 2011
David Edward Walker
All Rights Reserved.

No portion of this work may be reproduced, copied, or distributed in any form whatsoever without the expressed written permission of the author and publisher.

THOUGHTFUL PUBLISHING COMPANY
321 10TH AVENUE SOUTH, #711
SEATTLE, WASHINGTON 98104

info@tessasdance.com
www.tessasdance.com
www.tessasdance.blogspot.com
davidedwardwalker.tumblr.com/

DISCLAIMER:
This is a work of fiction. All of the characters, organizations, and events portrayed in this novel are products of the author's imagination except geographical and institutional place names, historical events, and public figures. Any similarity to persons living or dead is unintentional and coincidental.

Cover Design:
Seth Walker, seth@setherama.com

## With Gratitude

I am grateful to so many people for helping me and fear I would leave out someone important by trying to list everyone. Thank you for assuaging my insecurities and encouraging me to surrender to the Source of all creation. I especially wish to thank Levina Wilkins (Yakama), M.Ed., Program Manager and Cultural Specialist, Yakama Nation Language Program, and Marilyn Goudy (Yakama), M. Ed., Special Education Teacher, Stanley Smartlowit Education Center, Yakama Nation Tribal School, for their friendship and counsel over the years.

Certain ceremonies have been purposely obscured or creatively altered in order to protect their cultural integrity. I apologize in advance for any additional inaccuracies. This novel feels like a song which has been given to me but I haven't sung perfectly.

This story is my way of honoring the daughters and sons of the Yakama people.

# One

At the creation, Coyote was present,
the symbol of power—teacher of balance,
the creator of confusion . . .
*–Andrew George, Palouse*

"You should get over here. She started banging her head on the bars and we had to cuff her."

I do not have a fan club at the tribal jail. Last year, Rory, a 12-year-old 'inmate,' was brought to me in his underwear in a public hallway there. Female officers paraded by as he tried to cover himself. I asked Tork, the lead officer, if he might bring the boy his striped jail coveralls and slippers.

"This is jail. Those are optional."

He delivered them eventually, handing them to Rory, saying, "Here's your warm and fuzzies," ambiguously referencing the boy's anatomy, the coveralls, or my services. After he left, Rory explained how some other kid, not him, plugged the cell toilet with a roll of toilet paper and flooded the whole cell block. At 3 am, Tork ordered all seven boys stripped to their underwear and deprived of their mattresses and blankets. The bed frames are stainless steel, mind you, and this was mid-January.

After I finished with Rory, I drove to the state child welfare office and filed a child abuse complaint against tribal jail. Of course, the state was not about to investigate. Word got around about what I'd done, but I didn't care—shit like this comes from Indian boarding school days and has to stop. I did piss people off, and I haven't liked going around tribal jail unless I have to since then.

"She's been asking for you," said Rena, the youth probation officer.

"Yeah, OK. I'm coming."

The jail is only a couple of blocks away so I walked. A tricked-out blue Mercedes, sporty BMW coupe with darkened windows, and late model trucks and SUVs, all in pristine shape, sparkled across the Yakama Indian Health Clinic parking lot. Some Public Health Service Commissioned Corps colleagues pull down twice what I can make in the Civil Service. I'd have resented it, but a homeless Indian man limped across Fort Road with a cane and a prosthetic foot before I could get started.

The sky, mostly overcast, held a promising cut of blue above the foothills to the south as the winds shifted to a chilly whip. I pulled my flannel close, lighting a smoke, a bad habit I blame on the availability of single cigarettes for a dime at Yakamart. Inhaling deep, I strolled past the elder program office and vet center, housed in beat-up old modulars. Out of nervousness, I hotboxed my cigarette.

I recognized Ron among the several tribal cops standing next to the new unmarked Challenger, wearing dark wraparounds with his hair buzzed and military-like. We rode around together not long ago to give me a feel for the projects—Apus Goudy, Adams View, Wolf Point, Totus, and Momachut—mid-60s HUD developments in pastel blues and greens, run-down and some overcrowded with families of ten or more in two or three bedrooms, leaking roofs, broken windows, bad plumbing, and lots of kids running wild on the streets.

I said, "Hey," and he nodded. Unable to relight my overworked cigarette in the wind, he handed me his to use. A paucity of words followed— "How's it going?" and "Alright, 'n you?" and "Doin' alright." The wind kicked hard and stung. He turned to leave, and I crushed out the butt prematurely so I could follow him through the steel security door into the front waiting area. I thought maybe walking in with him would help.

It didn't. Tork glanced at me and looked back down, didn't say a word—as if I expected him to. He glimpsed at me again and his pitted, pock-marked face narrowed, a slightly-raised lip exuding contempt. He'd sighted a bug he'd squash if he could get away with it.

"What?" he asked finally.

"I'm here to see Tessa Miyanashatawit."

"So?"

"Yeah, so?"

He gets my dander up.

"So I am supposed to care about that?" His eyes stayed fixed on mine, testosterone and adrenalin blended, and I was fifteen years old wanting to shove a fist into his face.

Rena popped out from the back, and his facial expression changed only slightly. A clipboard slid hard along the counter at me.

"Sign in. And don't be giving any of these kids, including her, shitty little books that make 'em suicidal."

"Not sure what you mean," I bristled.

"Don't be stupid enough to give messed-up kids like these books about surviving child abuse- 'Boy Named It' or whatever you gave some little girl here last year who tried to hang herself."

"Not something I did. I'm not into stripping off what little armor these kids have," I shot back with clear implications.

His eyes narrowed. "Hell it wasn't you. And I'm the one cleaning up your messes."

"Tork, hush," said Rena.

"Yeah," I shifted to peacemaker for her sake. "OK. No books."

"And no outside food," he sneered, both hands flat on the counter and standing erect.

"OK," I gave a simple, acquiescent nod and looked away. I could feel his stare bore into me but didn't meet it.

"Wait around in back," he grunted finally.

I walked back to a small room, empty except for a grey government-issued desk chair in the middle of a grey linoleum floor. Kids often spin in it while they talk to me. I tugged in the chewed-up plastic chair outside next to the portable breathalyzer and sat down. The only décor, a dog-eared black and white poster, held on at a cockeyed angle, dropped a hair closer toward the floor as I passed. Two native youth dressed in regalia and on horseback trotted further downwards over the words: "We respect our traditions. Yakama Nation, buckle up and don't drink and drive."

Rena peered in. "Can you come back here with me? She won't come out. Maybe you can talk to her."

There are no juvenile detention facilities, just very old cells housing either adults or kids, whatever the need might be. I followed Rena's oversized posterior as she waddled through several security doors to the last block of jail cells. I'd never actually been inside one of the cells before—usually kids were brought out to me.

Bending around a corner, I inspected old-fashioned bars filthy black from gripping hands with greenish flecked paint revealing rust underneath them. Behind these lay the chipped concrete floor, dirty yellow walls, stainless steel toilet, and steel-frame bed compressing tightly together in a six by eight-foot space. Even the lighting had an odd yellow tint and was caged in wire, making it less dark but not more light. A mixture of sweat and mildew held in the air.

Rena tugged my shirt sleeve, mildly irritated at me for lagging behind and hoisting a huge set of keys from her belt. She is also key-keep. Her struggles with the lock echoed through the silent hallway. Tessa, her back against the wall, sat cross-legged on the floor with a moth-bitten surplus blanket draped over her from the front, her hands cuffed behind her back. Her pose looked like a Remington image of the Old West. The dim bulb over her head spoiled this effect, and she became a little Indian girl, alone in a jail cell, like her mother before her. There was a cut and bruise on her forehead.

"She won't eat," said Rena.

"I hate bologna sandwiches," she slurred.

"Then listen to your grandpa and behave," Rena chimed back.

"Fuck that."

"That kind of talk counts when you go before the children's court judge."

"I ain't a fucking child."

Rena ignored the expletive. "OK, we'll put you in adult court and you can have a longer stay with us."

Rena looked at me, shrugged slightly, and explained. "Arnold found her out in the orchard near his place with some boys."

She looked at Tessa, indirectly lecturing her. "These boys run around out there making trouble and aren't in school, don't have nothing going for them."

She shook her head and turned back to me, "Arnold told the officers he can't control her. She blew point one nine when she came in."

"I didn't know that. I should talk with him."

"Fuck that," Tessa said from somewhere beneath her garb, "You don't talk with my grandpa."

Except for a brief meeting with Arnold when we first began working together, contact had always been between Tessa and me.

"Come out and explain to me why."

"I like being in here instead."

"I was told you wanted to talk to me. Come on out and tell me why I can't talk to your grandpa."

She reluctantly struggled to her feet with Rena's help who then removed her cuffs. Tessa wrapped the blanket around her head, hiding in such a way that we couldn't see her face. I figured she was ashamed, a much better situation than if she'd had no regrets. Rena arched her eyebrows doubtingly at our tentative success in getting her this far and took us back to the little room before waddling back to her office.

Tessa's hand reached through the blanket and spun the government chair; then she thought better of playing, sat down, and didn't move at all except to cover her head more completely with the blanket.

"Why are you here?" I asked, sounding like a bit of a hard-ass.

"Why would you care?"

"I get paid to care."

"Paid to care, like a whore."

"Ha, good one," I countered. "I'm not paid enough to face down jailers who don't like me so I can visit with people who don't belong here."

I only got stony silence for that one.

"So who'd you get loaded with?" I continued.

"I didn't get loaded."

"You blew point one nine. You were loaded. How'd you get the bump on your head?" More silence. "Let's see . . . there's Miyanashatawits in ESPs, Westsiders, Southsiders, LVNs, right, and DVKs. I see them all over the place."

No response.

"Surenos, F13, Lower Valley Locos, who else? Whose bitch are you, Tessa?"

I'm way too old for gangster rap but kids find it so irksome; they'll start talking just to shut me up. Not Tessa.

"Oh, never mind," I sighed with mock impatience, pulling out a package of Hostess Twinkies, the ultimate tool for youth interrogation.

"Here." I held the package forward. I could see her trying to peer through a small hole in the blanket without letting me see.

"I don't want any."

"OK, gangbanger. I know you're hungry. Have something to eat."

I held the Twinkie package at the tip of my fingers with both hands. A hand finally crept slowly from beneath the blanket and took them into her private shelter.

"Just because I'm eating these don't mean I'm going to tell you shit."

"It's a gift. Indian way. No expectations," I said but knew differently. I could hear the package being opened beneath the blanket.

"Tork finds out you brought me these, he'll lock you up."

"I doubt it. He can't lock up white people here." Tork wouldn't want me in his jail.

"It's against jail rules. It's contraband."

"You might hold a Twinkie to his head and scare him." No laugh.

"Tork bounces people off locker doors," she said, eating while she mumbled.

"Impressive for a man of his size. So . . . not to change the subject but why are you here?"

"I told you I'm not talking about it."

Then, she dropped the blanket to her shoulders, a sign of real progress. Her forehead was swollen and bruised, and she looked dirty. She sat there, mouth filled with an entire Twinkie, chewing, staring blankly into the space above my head. I'd seen many kids in this jail fall under the Twinkie trance.

I bluffed as I stood up. "OK. I'll just ask your grandpa what's happened."

"Fuck that." She moved her mouthful aside and caught me eye to eye, "You don't talk to my grandpa."

I lowered back down. "I've got news for you, Tessa—you signed a release when we first met. I talk to him if I feel I need to."

Her Twinkie chewing stopped entirely, and she struggled to raise her voice. "I never signed anything! And, if I did, I take it back. I don't release you."

She continued chewing while she glared at me.

"Interesting," I purposely glanced at my open hand, "so you want to cancel your release for me to talk with your grandpa while you're putting yourself in danger." I stared her in the eyes, "And I don't roll that way—I'm not waiting until you're tweaking full-time and on the run."

"What's that supposed to mean?!"

She knew exactly what I meant, so I didn't answer but instead paused and looked around. Grey floor and greenish-yellow walls the color of puke, already terribly depressing before you put oppressed people in there.

No wonder kids tried to hang themselves in this place.

"Fine. I'll talk," she finally relented.

"Tell me why you're here."

"I got drunk."

"With who?"

"Whom. You don't know how to speak English. And not your business."

"Tell me or I'm leaving." I made to get up again.

"Tiller and James."

"Miyanashatawits?"

"Yeah. James is my cousin. Tiller is my uncle. They live in Medicine Valley."

"Oh, Tiller, the football guy from Wapato. He was good until he got jumped to East Side Pirus and tweak. Same guy?"

She shifted away sullenly, second Twinkie in hand as I spoke.

"I thought you told me you wouldn't be caught dead in that shit. Now you're hanging with the tweakers. So are Tiller and James your meth connection?"

"That's stupid. I don't do meth. And I hardly ever been around them."

"Probably got to know them through Parker Heslah."

This surprised her and she was incredulous. "No way you know Parker. He'd never talk to you."

I know most kids around here. "Is he still tagging 'Native Blood' on the viaducts?"

She gaped at me for a second, a little crème filling on the corner of her lip. I didn't seem so dumb now.

"Does your grandpa know about your new crew?"

This rankled her. "You're so stupid! I don't have a crew. I told him like I told you—I don't really know them."

"I'm sure he knows better," I said skeptically. "Geez, Tessa, so you were out drinking and tweaking with Parker and East Siders. Great."

"That's bullshit. I told you, I don't tweak," she flared, trying to look dangerous.

"So let's have Rena take you over to the clinic and run your blood right now and settle the question."

A subtle look of fear broke her tough demeanor. She couldn't detect the bluff—any methamphetamine she used was already through her system—yet her momentary anxiety was my own little drug test. I had little doubt she'd used meth now.

"We need to talk to Arnold and get you out of that shit right now," I concluded, and she knew I had her.

At this, her lips tightened in fury for a moment before she swung her head and spit the remainder of her Twinkie onto the floor right next to my feet.

"Fuck that!"

"Nice, Tessa. You really need to work on widening your language. Tork can mop that up. Your grandpa's got to know what's going on. Do you talk to him or do I?"

Now I got all the way up.

"No. He doesn't need to know!"

She leaned her head back to look up at me murderously.

"Don't expect me to ever talk to you again if you talk to him!"

It was the only card she had left.

"I'd feel sorry about that—we've been working hard together. But you can't expect me to sit by and watch you screw your life up tweaking and getting loaded. I don't want your grandpa or your sisters dealing with another funeral."

"Hah. I'm not going to die."

"Last words of a tweaker. Tessa, do what's right and talk to your grandpa. I won't if you will."

"No."

Her arms crossed, and she never looked up again.

"Yeah. OK." I put my jacket on. "I'm going back to the clinic. You can have them call me if you want."

I glanced down at her, immobilized and tiny in the chair.

"I'll even help you talk to him, Tessa. If I don't hear back from you in a couple of hours, I'm going to ask Rena to help me set up a meeting with him myself."

"God, I fucking hate you," she spun her chair all the way around and turned her back to me. "I don't know why I told them to call you. I'll never talk to you again."

"OK."

At this point, she jumped up, shot past me, tugged the door open, and shouted, "Take me back and lock me up!"

Tork appeared, gratified at my apparent incompetence.

"Sure," he reassured, "Not into talking to the doctor today, huh?" He nodded with an expression of feigned compassion. "You know, you don't have to, if you don't want. Just let me know."

A helpful guy, he glanced back at me smiling. I grinned back at him. We were pals forever.

I caught Gail, one of the night officers, as she walked by the door a few seconds later. I had worked with her rambunctious little sister, Cissy, a couple of years earlier after she'd punched out a tribal officer. Cissy had been doing much better since our sessions and had even earned her GED and started at the community college. I knew Cissy's turnaround would likely put me in good stead with older sister, Gail.

"Can you keep an eye on Tessa? I doubt she's suicidal but she's a cutter. Just keep an eye and let me know if anything comes up. Are you here later?"

"Sure. I'm here until midnight," she nodded affirmatively as I walked out.

Tork was back in his bull pen, muscular and uniformed, mace and baton hanging at his side and shaking his head as I strolled up to sign out, leafing through a book called "Vehicle Extraction, Suspect Pacification, and Handcuffing Manual."

"Um . . . somebody seems to have spit a goober on your floor back there," I nodded casually toward the white, mushy Twinkie mound on the floor just visible in the other room.

His eyes met mine as I opened the steel door and left. It wasn't the right thing to do, I admit.

I walked back with another cheap no-brand smoke dangling from my mouth, number three or four. Yakama Indian Health Clinic looks like a military bunker with its low, contemporary architecture. It's landscaped so that the lawn rises up to meet the building ledges on the Fort Road side as though it's partially built into the ground. We even have people working inside wearing military uniforms. The sign near the street reads, "United States Public Health Service, Indian Health Service,

Yakama Comprehensive Health Care Center." It's a federal government facility, neither Yakama nor Indian, a compulsory provision of the Treaty of 1855.

Nobody gets asked their Indian name when they check in. The clinic clock runs on federal, not Indian time; we're not open late or on weekends. If you're native and employed but happen to get sick, you'll have to take time off to come in. And you should consider yourself lucky to have a job on a rez with up to eighty percent unemployment. That doesn't mean people aren't working in ways that aren't counted—like fishing, hunting, root and berry gathering, making jewelry, off-the-books farm and ranch labor, hustling something, or running tobacco, weed, or crank.

In our clinic lobby, children run loose, elders struggle with walkers, sick people doze, caretakers and others whisper. Everybody's waiting to learn 'what's wrong,' waiting for diagnoses and recommendations for surgery, chemo, insulin, antibiotics, nutrients, anti-anxiety or anti-depressant pills, x-rays, health education, counseling, hearing evaluations, optometric exams, or physical therapy.

Although IHS pays my bills, I don't really fit in. I'm at least partially responsible for that.

We'd never been to Washington state before and didn't even know what it looked like. Neither Ruthie nor I had ever heard of Yakima (the city) or the Yakama people (as they spell their name in the treaty) when I was offered this job during the second phone interview. Being hired over the phone should have told me something.

After moving from Oklahoma on the federal government's dime, we bought a small ranch house on South 23rd Avenue in the city, situated in Upper Valley. Ruthie got a job with Yakima School District. Yakama reservation itself is in Lower Valley, south of Union Gap, just one of the many boundary lines I cross on any given work day.

My first day on the job, I noticed how being white or a Commissioned Corps officer got you an outer office with a window: being Indian did not. I was the only apparent exception to the rule—the new psychologist had been relegated to the 'Indian side' of the hall.

I opened my new office door using keys the personnel guy signed out to me and gazed at a totally empty room. I mean there weren't even chairs or a desk. I waited around expectantly—but no one brought me any furniture. I walked back to personnel and learned the key man went to an all-day training. My hiring manager was out sick.

I had no place to sit except for the little waiting area by Deborah, the mental health department receptionist. I worked on a massive packet of governmental 'new employee' paperwork until she casually mentioned I'd displaced a Yakama co-worker from the space she'd been using for nine years. There'd been no advance notice of my arrival; she had to move all her stuff out the day before I started. And there wasn't time to locate and deliver any furniture.

I felt awkward about displacing somebody from their office space, especially 'on the Indian side.' So I stopped by the refugee's new cubicle, where she sat on the floor unpacking boxes into a space that couldn't possibly contain her things. I introduced myself and apologized for what had happened. She was cordial and minimized the whole situation—"no big deal at all—you have to have a door that closes." I knew there was more than that—but I guess neither of us felt comfortable delving further into it.

Eventually, Jim, the custodian, rolled up to reception pushing a desk on a dolly, saw me, and said, "Hey, this is for you."

"Great, I'm going to need some chairs too."

He shrugged at the idea and didn't respond, huffing and puffing the desk into position. Then, he rolled back out and down the hall without another word.

I started unpacking boxes of books I'd brought in from my car. Ruthie would rather not have my technical books cluttering our limited shelving space. They were better displayed at work, she joked, to add another coat of varnish over my thin professional veneer. In these books, I can look up the effects of untreated diabetes on cognition and emotion, unusual facets of alcohol-induced dementia, or electrolyte imbalances and sensitivities in the elderly. I understand what I'm reading, others likely don't, and this reassures me I'll remain relevant and needed. Having no bookcase, I felt stupid lining all these books along the floor against the wall. I kept my door open while I did, just wanting to look busy. Several folks walking by glanced inside. A man and woman saw me hanging my framed diplomas on the wall but kept moving; the guy said "hello" in a deep and formal tone as he passed. She said nothing.

I had lunch sitting on top of my desk my first day. A nearby door opened at one point, and I stepped around the corner in anticipation of meeting somebody. A small Latina walked up to reception and whispered something to Deborah. She turned, smiled close-lipped at me, and I started to move in her direction. She continued back into her office and closed the door. So I read names on doors, hoping in the process that I might bring about some impromptu encounter. I paused in front of the Latina's office. What kind of name is Dominia? I wondered. Next was Leo, another dominant name. Deborah saw me perusing and waved me over.

I leaned over her counter, and she whispered to me:

"Try not to be offended. Your new colleagues aren't too thrilled about the creation of your position. They really don't want you here, so don't expect much. Dominia said to Kent a couple days back she don't care for psychologists. She's big on the medication. Try not to take it personal. Other people are very glad you're here." She winked.

I found some coffee in the clinic kitchen and also noticed two comfortable chairs and a small table. Here, at least, I could sit down normally and might even be noticed.

A family practice nurse in military uniform strolled in.

"Welcome to IHS," she said, appearing bemused as though she already knew welcome hadn't been part of the deal thus far.

"Thanks," I said. "My name's Ret Barlow."

"Dr. Barlow," she nodded. "Cheryl Lynn, FRNP, Army Reserve," she shook my hand firmly. Her eyes gleamed.

She reached back and opened the door, peering out to see if anyone was coming; then she spoke quietly, "Geez, at least they could give you furniture." She pointed to the chair and table. "Take them . . . don't make a big announcement about it. Take them."

She grinned at her subterfuge and helped me quickly push and pull the furniture down the hall and into my office. No one seemed to take notice as we passed a few open offices.

My first day at Yakama Indian Health Clinic, I pushed a Yakama woman from the space she'd called home for a decade on the Indian side of the hall into a much smaller, more boxed-in space. After that, I confiscated community property so as to make my claim habitable.

I figured this sort of thing had happened around here before.

## Two

> These remarks as to improvement
> do not apply to the "wild" Yakimas
> ... They say that when they were born
> they lived upon their mothers' breasts
> until they reached a certain age,
> then they lived off the things
> that come from mother earth,
> therefore it became their mother.
> They hold her sacred and declare that her bosom
> should not be scarred with section lines ...
> –L.T. Erwin, Indian Agent, 1895

*Walak'ikláama* was the first Yakama word I learned.

I picked it up from the first elder I ever met here, Elisi. She sounded it out and asked me to repeat exactly what she said, which I did very poorly. She then explained the word literally means 'a person who ties another up in bondage.'

*Walak'ikláama* is the Yakama word for police.

"We were free!" she explained, pausing to sip the cup of water I brought her.

As she spoke, she lowered pouched eyes to survey my books, still lying on the floor three weeks after my arrival. No bookshelf yet. They sat there for nearly six months.

"We were free . . . and we didn't have no need for police. That's the first thing you need to understand."

Her eyes swept my room.

"Why would we need them? We looked closely after our young. No youngster would ever think to bring shame on his family or community. We saw to that. Police came with the white people. They were very strange and frightening. They tied you up; they imprisoned you; they locked you up—this was torture for us because we had always been free. It is one thing when the police are part of your society. Can you imagine what that was like when we never had anything like them?"

"It had to be very hard," I reflected.

"Yes. That's why I'm asking you to explain what a psychologist does. Are you some sort of *walak'ikláama*?" she asked as she peered at me.

"No, Elisi, I am not *walak'ikláama*," I struggled to say. "At least, that's not something I would ever want to be to the people here."

"Well, that's good" she responded, and then succinctly: "I'd expect you'll refuse the request to do competency evaluations over at the BIA office when my nephew calls you."

"I'm sorry?"

"My nephew's been asked by his supervisor to call you after you started up here and get you to evaluate a variety of Indian people for the BIA. They want you to evaluate their competency to make appropriate decisions regarding their own money and their own land. Is that something you think you should do? If you truly mean what you say, I expect you'd refuse."

Her momentary stare carried frank intensity.

"I'm not interested in that kind of work . . ."

"Time will tell," she nodded as she got up to leave. Our entire first encounter lasted no more than five minutes.

The call came about an hour later from a soft-spoken young man wondering if I might help determine whether an elderly Yakama man, a "known alcoholic," was competent in refusing access to his land for construction of a cell phone tower. His relatives were very interested in seeing it built and thought he must be demented for refusing the money offered by the company.

I politely declined to be involved.

"Well, OK, we'll have to find someone else," he responded as though I'd given the exact answer he'd expected.

Tessa Miyanashatawit wasn't going to talk with her grandfather Arnold either with me or without me, Rena's husky voice distortedly announced on my voicemail. She had to be cuffed again after throwing a tray. Rena said it could help in Children's Court if I'd drive out to White Swan and visit with him.

White Swan is a straight shot twenty miles from the clinic out Fort Road, past Laterals A, B, C, Harrah Road, and the deep scent of huge spearmint fields. After that, it gradually turns into mostly sage, scrub, and range until you pass the Head Start, the old government housing, and the rodeo grounds. If you're still not quite sure, you're already there when you hit the combined high school and middle-school athletic fields.

Cougar Den, the Laundromat, and a gas station with a convenience store are toward the right. Totus housing project is up the road. St. Mary's Catholic Church has been around since before the treaty was signed, and Wilbur United Methodist and the post office are nearby. Dilapidated barnwood buildings with broken windows were stores fifty years ago; now they lean over, picked clean of paint by the wind. Small frame houses are scattered along dirt roads. When you don't have much, getting rid of a 1984 Ford Impala, a broken washing machine, or an old tractor costs money, and you might be able to pull some parts off to fix something else.

Two gutted deer hung from a tree branch next to a shack covered with a blue tarpaulin, and an old man laboriously pulled himself from beneath a rusted-out pickup truck. Kids were running down the street and throwing small stones at each other, spotting my car as I slowed down and waved, which I always do. A passing car can be a big deal. There's no playground, no community center, no movie theater, no parks. A couple of small stones popped off my fender as a little boy about seven or so waved back.

I kept driving. I'd been out in this direction before but not nearly so far. I continued through the expanse before seeing anything more than rocky, washed-out, green scrub and sage behind miles of range fence. Brush and tumbleweeds and small conifers began to spread out on either side of me. The gravel became heavy with larger stone—the cheap stuff. Every now and then, old cars or trucks passed by going the opposite direction. We also waved at each other even though I didn't recognize the drivers. That's rural good manners.

A forest harvest was being brought into the mill to process, load on rail, and send across the southern Cascades. Stacks of timber were being organized by yellow loaders and haulers; log trucks were parked at various spots. The train is on the job 24-7 with no crossing guard, just a stop sign—you have to watch carefully. I patched out as I crossed the tracks.

A couple of guys looked up from near a loader and one waved, but I didn't recognize him. People see my old Grand Fury and think I live around here. My shocks are very soft; she bounced up and down as I shot off into the foothills. I saw them laughing at me in my side mirror.

I got across what I thought was Arnold's property line for a few minutes and became a little nervous for no good reason. A hawk dove down and hoisted some unfortunate rodent as I rolled my window open. I made the decision to turn off one two-track onto another with the usual sense I couldn't possibly be going in the right direction.

The sky cleared rapidly and completely to a brilliant blue and the sun bore down unseasonably hard. I passed a few ancient wrecked cars in front of a hand-built house and small barn, drove through an open gate, and immediately heard a barking din rushing toward me.

Three ferocious rez dogs came crashing along, announcing my unfamiliarity. Rez dogs are deeply interbred, typically smart, and often semi-feral. I got their message—I could be chewed up and spit out easily. I opened the door and got out trying to maintain absolute disregard while my heart pounded out of my chest. The lab moved in close but scampered back when I put my hand out for him to sniff. The littler one, small, stocky, and ugly, pushed toward me and then jumped back.

The leader, however, growled deeply and bared his teeth, which were big. Doberman, Shepherd, and Rottweiler were all in those teeth. I didn't like them much.

This was how I was going to die, and it didn't seem fair.

"It's alright boys; it's alright," I whispered, keeping my trembling hand held out. "We're all going to get along."

Growler moved forward toward my hand, and I thought I might lose it. He took a brief sniff. Then he turned and walked away as though I was no longer of any interest at all. The others jumped over one another to follow him. I'd passed muster.

I had the smudge kit in the back of my car but was unsure of Arnold's beliefs. We would be talking about his worries about Tessa, and I usually have a smudge available even if the practice isn't truly a Yakama tradition. Some disapproved of this 'imported' Plains Indian tradition, others liked to bless themselves with sage smoke periodically while we talked. As I'd been taught many years earlier in Oklahoma, I kept the northern California sage I'd bought at Wapato Pawn and Trade inside a large abalone shell and wrapped in red cloth. Because it's considered medicine and sacred, it gets wrapped in red. I had a box of kitchen matches too and didn't want to drop this stuff and break the shell, so I gathered everything up carefully in my arms from the backseat.

You never see yellow jackets until June or July, I thought to myself, watching several of them scamper across my rear window. How is this even possible? I pondered local ecosystems for an instant before a truly critical thought occurred—I might get stung. A hot poker skewered me left of my navel at that very moment, then again to the right, and then a prolonged, searing pierce above both made me yelp loudly and obscenely. I jumped back, holding the shell and sage loose in either hand with the red cloth dangling. Bounding backwards, I almost fell, regained my balance and swerved sideways.

Many yellow jackets started swarming toward me. Where the hell were they all coming from?

Frantically, I pushed the red-wrapped shell and sage toward my chest, totally committed to not dropping them, holding them inside my elbow while desperately trying to unbutton, even rip the buttons off with the other hand. This was one of my good shirts too.

They pursued me as I turned rapid circles, fighting to get my goddamned shirt off. A yellow jacket peered back at me from inside and eased out as I got a button loose. He flew at my face and I almost dropped everything.

Were these killer bees? I have an unreasonable fear of hornets, built upon an early masculinity lesson spent cleaning out a live nest in daylight with a garden hose.

Somehow, I recollected having one remaining cheap smoke from Yakamart in my shirt pocket. I'd seen on TV how beekeepers used smoke to calm bees. Did it calm hornets? With painful, continuous movement, I managed to light the smoke with a kitchen match, twirling in circles and still grasping my smudge kit. I blew smoke all around me.

Fewer and fewer hornets came at me, and I began to sense some modicum of control and safety.

"I should have warned you about parking near the bee people, doc. They're out very early this year," Arnold said conversationally from a seat on the front porch about fifteen feet away from me. He startled the hell out of me.

"You parked where we toss the salmon guts for them to eat. I guess you made 'em kind of mad coming so near. Lucky it's still cool, and it rained recently or there'd be more of them."

"Yeah." I stopped spinning and blowing smoke. "Ouch. I got stung."

"Sorry about that too, doc," he said calmly, mostly unmoved. "Those yellow jackets bite too. I think that's worse." His tone indicated real men got stung, noted it, and got over it. They certainly didn't go on complaining.

"Yeah. I think I got bit too."

"Well, that's bad. Yeah, that's no good. Come on up and have a seat."

I set my heroically-defended smudge kit down on one chair while painfully easing myself onto the other. My belly felt like hot needles.

"How are you?" I struggled to be sociable.

He looked over at the smudge kit. "Fine as frog hair, thanks. Appreciate you bringing that—but we don't practice that way."

"Oh, OK. I wasn't sure." I looked down at it and decided against putting it back in the car.

"I know some younger ones like it. We're Indian Shakers. Not New England Shakers like your white tourists always think of. On occasion, we cross over to the Waashat way at the longhouse, and I go sweat with my brother or cousins from time to time. My grandfather was a longhouse drummer and my cousins are still. But we're Shakers here in this house and got no need for a smudge."

"OK. I hope I didn't offend. I just knew you're dealing with a lot with your granddaughter."

He pulled out a package of Pall Malls and lit one up, staring straight ahead toward the field. He paused, glanced at me, and saw the curious look on my face.

"Excuse me for smoking, doc. It's not the Shaker way as you may've heard. But I gave up drinking fifteen years ago, and this is one of my few remaining vices."

"No problem."

Bees continued circling at the edge of the porch. One of them began investigating my foot. I had thin socks on and I became preoccupied with the idea he might go up my pant leg. My heart rate was up, and I wondered if hornets can smell fear. I lifted my shirt a little. Three bright welts were forming and swelling.

"Got you good, didn't they?" He noted, sounding very serious as he leaned forward, his face turned slightly away. I suddenly realized he was doing his best to control his amusement.

"Yeah, Arnold . . . it does hurt, you know?"

"You're man enough, though, doctor," he observed. "Of course the *twáti*, the medicine people out this way, they get a little jealous if you IHS docs come around. Hardly ever happens we get one of you from the clinic come all this way. I don't doubt they put a little something out to get you dancing around and blowing smoke in the four directions. Ha ha!"

His laughter burst into a guffaw and then a coughing fit.

Less amused, I only grunted and watched the hornet at my feet closely.

"Can I bum a smoke from you, Arnold?"

"Sure, sure." He continued to struggle to suppress himself.

We sat and smoked together for a few minutes. Then, the screen door opened and a very small girl, no more than five or six years old, emerged carrying a big tray with a huge Mason jar filled with powdered lemonade.

"That's very good, Cecelia." Arnold reached down by his chair and picked up his own smaller Mason jar, half-filled.

"Thank you, Cecelia," I said as I quickly set my half-done cigarette down on the porch rail and reached out to grab the weighty jar and rescue her little hands from struggling to keep their grip without dumping lemonade in my lap. "You're a good helper. Thank you very much."

Her torn t-shirt was pink with 'Barbie' written across it in sparkles, and she was barefoot in the chilly shade. She said nothing, didn't even look at me and, as soon as her task was done, set the tray down on the floor by the door so she could run over to her grandfather's knee and hug it with all her might. She then burrowed her face into his shirt.

"Be a good girl and go on inside. *Tíla*'s going to talk to this man for a bit about your big sister. I'll be back inside in a little while." She didn't move. "Go on now." He gently pushed her away.

"She hasn't been close in to many white people, except just for a minute or two at the IHS or the Head Start. Never here, to home," he said. Cecelia picked the tray up off the porch floor, struggled over to the screen door, and raced inside without giving me as much as a sidelong glance.

I grabbed the smoldering butt and sat and smoked with him some more. I blew smoke toward the hornet and his friend by my foot, and they both drifted back. I could defend myself.

A northern mockingbird's song blended with the kip of the western kingbird, filling our silence. There was a long, peaceful repose with only those sounds and the quiet humming of bees. It was getting late in the afternoon and the distant clouds were turning slightly purple. Arnold will speak when he's ready, I thought. Through sometimes painful social correction, I'd learned to avoid speaking to elders until spoken to.

"Thanks for making your way out here, doc," he said after several minutes. "You been still visiting with Tessa over to the school's what I hear."

"I do my best to sit with her once a week or so."

"That's good. Easier than having her walk to the clinic. But she's not going to be to school for a while."

He stamped his butt out on the porch with his boot heel.

"This is the first time I've had to do something like this," he said, gazing across the scrub. "I hated doing it . . . I know some other people make a habit of locking their children in that jail when they feel disrespected. Tessa and I only had trouble like this over the past year or so . . ."

He glanced my way for a moment and then stared back toward the old orchard.

"Since her grandma died, I been needing her help with the little ones. But I don't keep her home, even though at times I wish I could with all these children . . . it was Georgina's wish that they would get their education. Tessa loved her a lot. Her *kála* was her only connection to being treated like a real child. With Tina and her addiction, Georgina couldn't do as much for the kids as she wanted. But she always tried to let them know they were loved . . ."

He pulled on his cigarette. "Tessa's come through a lot over the years with her mom getting locked up and her *kála* passing on. But I have to stop her from going around with those boys—especially that Heslah boy."

He glimpsed me again for a moment, his cheeks wrinkled and his brows smoothed by the wind, grey hair thinning and pulled tight into two braids tied together beneath his chin.

"Indian Indian" some might say. He lit another smoke.

"That young Heslah boy and Tiller and James Miyanashatawit—they grew up in a crooked way. No love, no teaching, don't know who they are.

He poked his cigarette hard at me. "You know Mr. Frank Mathis?"

"I've heard his name."

"He's sort of a friend of mine in a strange way, especially considering he shot one of my dogs last year after I couldn't stop him pissing and shitting around his garden. Stupid dog anyway—I tried to keep him tied. I wasn't so mad about it, really. Frank come and laid him all gentle right inside that gate down to where you came through," he pointed toward the two-track, "Others come up and sniff their buddy and got the message. They been a lot friendlier to our guests since that happened."

He smiled toward me knowingly. "Frank's got the same message for these little gangbangers. He warned everybody, especially Tiller, who he don't like. Tessa and I got food over to Cougar Den couple weeks back and watched Frank walk right up to Tiller, standing in front of us. Frank says, 'Stay off my land and I'm not saying anything more about it.' Tiller tried to stare him down not knowin' Frank don't stare down."

"I could see right then Tessa knew more about Tiller and his buddies than I wanted her too. She was batting her eyes at Parker Heslah sitting in that booth there and I told her, 'stay away from all them.' I told her, 'you don't get mixed up between Mathis and these kids.' It ain't about his trees, I told her, it's about what these boys get up to. He means what he says. You know, his wife got killed by a drunk and he don't like all that drinking and druggin' on his land."

A tussle broke out inside and two pre-teen girls ran out. Eloise bolted through the door chased by Emily, holding a training bra. I think I had the order right, although I had only seen them twice and might have confused who was who.

"I have it! I have it!" Eloise exclaimed. She dodged back and forth around Arnold's pickup as Emily shouted "Give it!"

Eloise shot toward the outhouse only to be tackled and pinned by Emily, who quickly pulled the bra free of her grasp and then began slapping Eloise in the face.

"Excuse me," Arnold said quietly to me as he jumped off the porch.

"That's enough!" Emily looked up at his raised voice. "Get off her now!"

At this, Emily jumped up, and Eloise struggled to her feet.

"Can you see we got company? What is wrong here?" Arnold continued.

Both girls looked down and said nothing.

"Come on over and apologize to the doctor here."

"Really, Arnold, that's not necessary," I pleaded.

Both girls ambled over to stand in front of me with their heads down.

"*Tmáakni* . . ." he said. "*Tmáakni.* You two know better than to act so disrespectful, especially in front of a *páshtin.*"

I felt very awkward.

"Sorry . . ." said Emily.

"Sorry . . ." repeated Eloise.

"It's quite alright," I answered, and they glanced at their *tíla.*

He looked them over disapprovingly for a few moments.

"Get back inside and clean up the kitchen. Tend your little sister and brothers . . ." Without speaking, they made their way back through the screen door. Neither of them looked at me during the entire interaction.

I felt embarrassed, uncertain how to behave.

"Arnold, it really was OK. They seemed to be just playing." He nodded, but I had to say more. "I'm sorry my white skin would make you feel you or your kids have to behave some certain way."

He sat back down and leaned back, staring straight ahead.

"I appreciate it, doctor. You didn't grow up here, I suppose. When I was little, my mama, she'd fly into a rage anytime the *páshtin* come near our home. She'd run around shouting and yelling, picking up and tossing things in the closet or the cupboard, convinced if there was a mess, we'd get taken away. That was the Christian thing to do, you know—save the Indian children from their mothers."

He flicked his cigarette and smiled. "Truth is, I usually don't like the white people too much." He squinted at me. "Present company excepted."

"I'm glad to be an exception."

"Another cig?" he offered apologetically.

"Sure."

I wasn't doing my health any favors chain-smoking with him, but I knew we were getting to know each other. After we lit up, he stood up at his chair and stretched.

"Sore from hoisting salmon at the fishery last two days; temp work down to Goldendale. I come home tired and told Tessa I didn't want her going out. I suspected, you know—anyway, she was not to visit with that Heslah boy. Then little Ce Ce come over and woke me in my chair telling me Tessa climbed out the bedroom window. This was about 11 pm. I got my boots on and followed her to the other side of Mathis' land. His old orchard is pretty big."

"How could you find her?"

"She'd only just left. People make more noise than animals, doc." He chuckled to himself and looked me over some more. "Not easy to slip an old Marine. I spotted her flashlight easy once I caught her sound. I crept along by her until she got to their little campfire. These orchard orphans sometimes build fires that are kind of hard to see until you get to a certain angle along the tree line. They hadn't a clue I was anywhere near."

"Were they smoking?"

"I saw something get lit and passed around a couple of times."

"I'm worried about methamphetamine."

He pointed. "Where I'm talking about, Frank Mathis' lives right over that rise and they were not too far out of view of his place. Being around there at night was stupid enough on those kids' part without the drink and drugs. People 'round here are nervous. Our house is the only one within miles hasn't been broke into. That's because there's usually somebody home here. We got little gangsters busting in all the time around here stealing guns, food, beer, and whatever else they can use or sell off from folks don't have much of nothing to lose. They get high on that Mexican poison and spray paint the gang graffiti whatnot all over barns, houses, fences, even my own truck at one point. Some of them boys would just as soon shoot or cut you as look at you. Parker Heslah's one. I remember trying to help his mother with him when he was littler. Now he's all grown, he's just another kid with no family and no direction."

He looked off toward the hills.

"So, anyways, I sat down and had a smoke in the dark. After a time, Tessa got up and started circling back but I made sure I got here first. I was sitting here on the front porch before she tried to sneak past toward the window. I called 'Ayee, Tessa.' She jumped like a rabbit then started acting like the devil was in her."

"She might have been high . . ."

"She was all jumpy and strange; you may be right. I said 'come sit with me' and she used the 'f' word and walked back off into the dark. I smelled alcohol too. I thought 'I can't stop her or reason with her, I think.' Never reason with a drunk, I always say and I should know. So I phoned the sheriff instead of tribal police because they're so slow. As soon as I hung up, she come slamming back in through the front door calling me a worthless bastard in my own home. Never seen her like that."

He paused for breath and took a drag instead. This was followed by a long fit of coughing, and he wiped his eyes overlong. The memory is traumatic for him, I thought to myself.

"Can't have the little ones listening to that kind of talk," he muttered. "They were all up and out of bed. She kicked the door and made a big dent in it and scared hell out of Ce Ce. The deputy, he never showed. So I called tribal and that Whitcomb boy, Charlie Whitcomb, their newer officer come out. He's from a good family. I told him what happened and he went and got her out of her room."

"She cooperated?"

He shook his head. "I thought he was going to have to mace her. She ran at him screaming and he threw her down on the bedroom floor, wrestling with her until she was cuffed. She was all sweaty and wild-eyed."

He coughed more and wiped his watering eyes again, obscuring for me whether he was weeping or not.

"It was an awful thing for the little ones to witness. I told them her spirit was sick and don't believe their sister would really act like that."

"I'm pretty sure she smoked meth from what you're describing."

"Yeah, I'm supposed to go down to Children's Court tomorrow. Whitcomb said he'd stop in and wouldn't make a big deal out of the wrestling match he had with her. But he did a breath test, and that's going to count for the judge."

"I heard that from Rena today. My guess is she's been struggling with some very bad memories," I confided.

"Jack Brie. Cowboy Jack Brie." He already knew.

"So is that guy really a cowboy?"

He waved his hand dismissively. "He's just a pumped-up *páshtin* hustling Indian women. I consider him a dangerous person. I haven't seen him since Tessa's mom went to prison and he got off without a mark."

He paused again as if contemplating sharing a confidence with me.

"We never had assaults or predation in our families before *páshtin* like that man turned up around here. Something like that happened on a rare occasion, families would look the other way and that person wouldn't see sunrise. That's our unwritten law. Since the white men come onto our land, we keep our young women out the way. There's white men who'll rape and kill them to this day."

He leaned back through the screen door.

"Emmy? Emmy? Get Ce Ce and Franklin on their chores; I got to get them up early tomorrow and want them down early."

He shifted towards me with a ponderous gaze. "You likely don't know how, back in Fort Simcoe days, the soldiers whored our women to humiliate our men. That was the brutality the ancestors suffered. White people get all puffed up in these little town councils complaining about drunks on our reservation. Well, *páshtin* brought the alcohol. *Páshtin* brought the rape and destruction," he flicked the glowing end of his cigarette off on the porch post, "I got some white blood, you know. My own great grandmother got raped by a *páshtin* soldier."

"I'm sorry such things happened. It makes me feel ashamed."

He laughed out loud. "Wasn't your grandpa, doc!"

"No but I . . ."

"Look, doctor," he said, "I don't often talk to a white man about such things but in your case, I'll make it different. You're helping my granddaughter and I feel a need to teach you. So just listen when I'm talking about such things in our history. *Páshtin* got to listen because they forget easy. Indian people, we got long memories. Besides, I heard from somebody you got some native heritage in your family."

"I'm part Cherokee."

He shook his head. "Ah, civilized," he chuckled. "White people don't claim so much to Apache or Comanche or Lakota."

I bristled slightly. "In my case, the Cherokee connection is true, Arnold."

He waved his hand in the way he'd done. "Well, I don't doubt it. But you either ain't or you're all Cherokee. Get that? If your blood runs red, own it. Learn what that Indian connection is all about, doctor, not to go dancin' with wolves, now," he chuckled. "You seen that? That's a pretty movie. Not so much about Indians as about white people wishing they were Indians. Careful what you wish for's what I say. Anyway, think about what I'm saying and learn about your bloodline. And you're always welcome here."

He glanced back inside to see if Emily was following his instructions, then leaned over to look under the porch overhang at the sky. "That's red-tailed hawks up there, looking out for us. As to that other man you mentioned, Jack Brie, I got my Marlin 30 odd 6 with a scope on it and a bullet with his name on it. I had that rifle with me since I gone to Dakota in the 70s."

Knowing a little about the American Indian Movement, I turned wonderingly at what he said, but his expression kept me quiet.

"I shot at more than *yámaash*, the mule deer, after I got back from Vietnam, doctor." He moved his chair a little closer to me to whisper. "I was an angry motherfucker and you didn't hear me say it. But Jack Brie is one man I will fuck up good if he comes anywhere near this house. All my kids know better than to go near my rifle. It's not for play. It's our survival and protection out here."

"Is it lever action?" I asked, having only that degree of vocabulary about rifles.

He frowned and squinted at me. "Doc, there's no such thing as a Marlin 30 ot 6 lever action. It's a bolt-action model 455 been treated like a baby since I was one myself. One of the best they ever made; cost my daddy two large coolers of fresh caught salmon and that was forty years ago."

I ate two hot dogs while Ce Ce, Franklin, and Samuel spied on me from the hallway near the kitchen or even came as close as the edge of the old sofa I was sitting on, refusing to respond to a word I said except to giggle and run away. I knew declining food when it was offered would be impolite. Arnold sat with me and told me his greatest wish for Tessa—to have her 'brushed off' at an Indian Shaker home gathering.

He gave me a little baggie of salmon jerky for the drive home, encouraging me to talk with Tessa even if she was angry with me.

"The old people say if she don't bring out what's on her heart with somebody she trusts, she'll get sicker."

"Not sure she trusts me much now."

He thought for a moment. "My granddaughter will grow past all that, doctor."

On the way back, I pulled in next to the 'White Swan Station' or annex, an IHS-owned building next door to Cougar Den to visit Marta. She works dispatch with a couple of EMTs. I picked up a double bacon cheeseburger and a diet Coke and salivated my way back across the parking lot. I was really hungry.

Parker Heslah was sitting in a rusty Corolla two spaces down from me. His long black hair was stuffed under a reversed Steelers cap and his jeans were ripped. His feet were half hidden under the steering column but I could just make out his nicked-up pair of steel-toed Caterpillars. Ass-kickers, we used to call them in my youth. He looked asleep. I wanted to eat but I knew I should try to talk to him. I leaned over his open passenger window and peered in.

"*Shíx kláawit*. What's up?"

"Just chillin', what's up wit you, doc?" His eyes were half-mast.

"I've got some business here," I said, nodding toward the annex.

"Hungry too," he said.

"That's so. You eat?"

"All set, doc."

I pulled some fries out anyway and handed them over. He pushed my hand back—meaning he didn't want anything to do with me.

"How's your sis?" I persisted.

After Florence overdosed on tricyclic antidepressants provided by my IHS colleagues just weeks after her first attempt, I did her bedside psych eval at Toppenish Community Hospital. I'd seen a different Parker there: stone cold sober, eyes rimmed red, up all night watching her.

"Flo's good. She's down to Chemawa."

That's Chemawa Boarding School in Salem, Oregon where, back in boarding school days, Indian kids forcibly removed from their family homes drilled daily at five am in uniforms before being reeducated as cobblers, woodworkers, cooks, and maids, civilized servants to the white people. Of course, it was more culturally correct now. But it was still a place where many misbehaving native youth got sent. I'd been down there myself doing evals right next door at Western Oregon Indian Health Clinic for about a week. Around the same time, a Yakama girl from a revered family suffocated in her own vomit on the Chemawa jail cell floor. She came in from partying, dead drunk, and the staff locked her up and forgot about her.

Chemawa—the modern Indian boarding school, still carried the pain of generations and still had its own dedicated jail and cemetery.

"Ah. Maybe that's a good thing," I wondered aloud, not knowing whether it was or not.

"Yeah. She's out of trouble."

"And you?"

"Me? I'm all good, doc." His eyes remained sleepy, his smile was closed, and I became sure he was ripped. "I'm just chillaxin'."

"Yeah," I observed doubtfully, "I'm not sure how you do that, Parker. I heard you might get shot at someday, maybe soon."

"Where'd you hear that?"

"People. I heard you're banging around with ESPs again, and somebody might shoot you."

There wasn't a flicker of concern on his face.

"I'm not into that kind of shit no more, doc. Those little ESPs are all pussies. I'm grown since you known me."

"You get shot," I continued, "that'll be a tragedy for your sis."

"Just talk, doc."

He stretched his arms out across the steering wheel, and I could still make out 'THUG,' the home-made tattoo he'd carved across his knuckles when he was sixteen.

"Not from what I hear. It's said you're stealing guns and selling them for tweak."

His eyes became steely, and his voice got mildly agitated.

"Tweak? Don't you mean crank? Sounds like a movie when you say it, shit. People are crazy 'round here. They got nothing to do so they're always gossiping."

"Tribal cops too? They gossip? I didn't know that."

"Oh yeah, doc. They're the worse. They're like the *áyat*, the women. I been working. I been clean. I know you don't believe me."

It was about then I noticed the bulge in his belt, under the sweatshirt. And he saw me looking.

"That what I think it is?" I asked.

He pushed himself upright and the bulge disappeared. Then he shook his head.

"Fuck that. Keep your own head down's what I say, doc. What I do's my business."

"Well, say 'hi' to your sis and Liberty for me."

"Laters," he muttered, and the paranoid gleam eased, his head easing back onto the headrest in an opiated stare.

Marta looked up and her dimples jumped, revealing imperfect, overcrowded teeth. She was wearing a "Yakama Firejumper" sweatshirt.

"Did you see Parker out there?" she smiled.

"He looked stoned. I think he's carrying too."

"Guns all over this town. Parker pulls in there almost every day like he owns that spot."

She set her book down and sat up. "I think he sleeps there some nights. Leon goes out every now and then and tells him to move along."

"He says he's working."

"Up to the mill for a while but he spiked a urine test and blew his probation, so they laid him off. Since then, I hear he's beating down little boys and enforcing for ESPs."

A call came in over the radio and she eased her palm onto a large button on an old dispatcher microphone. The technology is thirty years old but most cell phones don't work out there.

"37, service code 4, 31-A, possible 32."

"37, 10-4. Do you need an escort, Ricky?" she responded.

"Negative, Marta."

"Stay in touch." Sirens blared in the background of the radio and also in the distance outside. She turned back to me, nonplussed. I bit into my burger and told her I'd been out to visit Arnold. I didn't say what about.

"That's going to give you an early stroke," she smiled while I chewed. I wondered aloud about Tessa to her.

"That's a girl been moving sideways around here for the last year or so."

"You ever see her with Tiller and James too?"

"The wannabes? Tiller's just out from county, so no, I haven't. But he's never far away. James and him come as a package and Parker makes three. Now Tessa and Parker, they always kiss it up out there. I thought you maybe noticed them, coming around here for those big burgers so often." I shook my head. "That's her man."

"I must have missed their last session." I said as I chewed, and she laughed. "She's only fifteen to his what? Nineteen, twenty?"

"Parker likes the young ones who look up to him."

I finished eating, thanked her, and said goodbye, noting Parker had moved on as I got back in my car.

Dusk held long as a huge full moon floated up just above the horizon. In what remained of daylight, I drove to Fort Simcoe State Park, not exactly a major attraction. The park is where the original fort was once located. I walked around and smoked the Pall Mall Arnold offered me as I was leaving. I could have refused that one, but I didn't.

The governor's house still imposes over a wide meadow, and its shadows stretched toward me. If you were poor and Indian, you'd approach across the front lawn, reduced to begging—a 'fort Indian.' The *páshtin's* civilization glared back from the ornate, Swiss Gothic facade, built tall and stout to purposely contrast with your destitution and poverty—a place for the safety and privilege of white people, a mirror reflecting the domination of you and your children.

I strolled past three old mountain howitzers—1850 prairie-carriage 12-pounders, originals from the days of the Yakama Wars. They still bore down upon these families, I thought, even though it's been a very long time since they had to be kept loaded.

In the fading light, I could see pretty far—twenty-five miles, all Yakama land. I turned around 360 degrees to take in the grounds. Fort Simcoe Boarding School once stood to the right and, behind me, the jailhouse and stockade. A stretch of stockade fence behind the governor's house ended in a small, elevated guard station. Uncooperative men and women were pilloried in front of this spot and bullwhipped by the governor himself. Captive men were tied, forced to kneel with guns to their heads and watched as white soldiers compelled their women to have sex with them. A rope swung in the wind from that same nearby oak tree where bodies of Yakama warriors hung down.

The place I wanted to visit again came up in conversation with Arnold. Indian children, beaten with sticks, were locked inside a stockade by the school matrons and their helpers. There's no roof or much left to identify it, only a few stacked-up logs beneath imported elms.

I stood inside, smoking, and my mind recollected Tessa sitting on the tribal jail cell floor. Yakama people learned how to lock up their children out here.

I'd never noticed the latrine Arnold mentioned but found it now; its outline barely visible, a trench where little Indian boys and girls squatted before each other, no longer able to hold on. Some slept overnight in the squalor, having spoken their native language deliberately, just so as to be locked up rather than force-fed white man's ways. Cracks opened between the few timbers still stacked upon the ground. Nobody bothered to mortar them.

The wind still ripped over the ghosts of Yakama children huddling together there. They chose to stay there instead of inside the warmth of the school.

These fields were converted by white people into a picnic park, a 'heritage park' as the state of Washington called it, on the sovereign land of the Yakama people. I'd never seen a single Indian person out in this park when I visited.

There is a chain ring anchored in the ground near the back wall of the old stockade ruins.

"Someday, it will be gone," I told Arnold. I found it the first time I came out to the park. I knew instinctively what it was for.

So I bent down again and tugged hard. That was a little way I could know about what happened here viscerally—not by some book or what someone said, but by pulling on that old chain.

I told him I drove out there and did this from time to time, and he stared at me like I was crazy. But he didn't say a word about it, one way or another.

"Don't want to be *walak'ikláama*," I blurted out my explanation.

My diction wasn't so bad, but it took him a moment. Then his brows lifted and his broken, stained teeth opened into a knowing smile. He nodded but still said nothing.

It wasn't until I got back to my car that I noticed the spray paint on the passenger door. It said '187.' That was a newer language I hadn't learned much about.

At the time, it pissed me off more than scared me.

## Three

To Young Chinook, Coyote said,
"You can blow hardest only at night.
You will blow first upon the mountain ridges
as a warning to the people."
—*Yakama story*

Several days before Tessa went to jail, I met her for a session over at the school where I spend much of my work week. I won't provide the name but say it's halfway between Toppenish and Wapato across from the massive apple orchard, next to Four Corners Christian Church along SR 97 by Olden Way, downwind from the pig slop and chicken coop, unfortunately, and next to the donkey that never moves.

I'd been driving around town, making a few stops, holding a large cup of coffee between my legs while eating a bag of Chili Cheese Fritos and locally-produced pepperoni jerky. I was late, and I needed a toilet.

After quickly signing in with Ann, I charged over to the bathroom to liberate my bloated bladder. Peeling, pink paint petals floated down from the concrete brick where I braced my hand, dropping in flakes between my feet into the urinal floor drain. I decided to brush my teeth with a little travel toothbrush I keep stuffed in my binder. I stared at my reflection in the mirror, noting all the stall doors were either absent or wouldn't close. A young man sat on his throne watching me brush. The fluorescent lights buzzed over both of us.

I walked back and Mrs. Marshall, the wizened, black-eyed, Gila Indian principal, greeted me.

"You're here early. Tessa's still in Samuel's room."

I smiled wordlessly, and she eased back behind her desk quietly regarding a lanky, evidently irritated kid across from her, lodging some complaint, all hands and gestures. She looked very administrative to him, but I could see she had solitaire up on her computer screen as I passed behind.

I looked over what was going on in the classrooms for a few minutes. Eight young men gazed doe-eyed at Ms. Frank, the Scandinavian reading tutor in the first room on the left. A lone girl sat solemnly beside her as she tried to stimulate discussion but ended up stimulating more than that. Enthralled by her overdone cologne and regretting her openly proclaimed love of Jesus, the boys winked and shifted, their glances moving toward the top shelf of the black storage cabinet. They'd hidden her purse again. Her flustered reactions were the best part of class.

I passed Mr. Harris' room next; he was reading his newspaper with a bored expression, his students hunkering down over workbooks—'pass packets' from the state Office of Public Instruction. Stacks of additional packets awaited on tables behind them, a means of making up missed high school credits. Most kids drop out after a few months of pass packets. A young man with long, black, braided hair filled out a brochure offering a 'free' sitting for the "Armed Services Vocational Aptitude Battery."

Ms. Samuel waved at me from where she stood outside her classroom door, glancing back to admonish someone for leaning too hard on unstable cubicle walls. I walked into a room full of Indian kids working on the internet, computer lines draped over their heads. She continued coaching several in fluent Yakama—mixing words like 'password,' 'html,' and 'file' with the dialect of the Wiinatchapum. They flitted about her like moths on a screened porch door. She winked at me and tapped Tessa's shoulder as she sat staring at a screen full of emails. Tessa rose with utmost apathy and followed me back into the hallway.

As we walked back down the hall, Mr. Pilson's screeching voice jabbed words at an introverted young man who hadn't the slightest idea about something. Tessa paused to watch Pilson's thin fingers stretch high up on a whiteboard, reluctantly completing a quadratic expression.

"You should already know this," he snickered.

A notoriously-incomprehensible math teacher, kids only learn from him by making him angry.

"What an airhead," she noted aloud as we walked on.

The bell made me jump, and she stifled a laugh, wanting to maintain her sullenness. Brown, tan, and off-white young people merged in, some stopping to fraternize near doorways and lockers. I cocked my head at her, signaling her to keep up. She glared back at me. Four girls bunched up in front of the administrative offices where we headed, circling, primping and posturing. Three boys muttered in quiet teen code nearby, feigning discussion of video game cheats. Every eye suddenly moved toward Tessa.

One of the boys poked another, "What're you lookin' at, Alex?"

"Huh?" he responded, gawking. His two friends laughed uproariously and the tallest girl aimed a contemptuous expression Tessa's way.

I mistakenly took the broken chair, cramming in between a cheap computer desk and a couch crowding my feet.

The big picture window next to us rattled loudly as rainy wind blew the very late winter's endless clouds by, carried by a warm Chinook. Soon, the Plateau foothills would turn amber green with early bloom, and the sun would shine every day.

She climbed up behind the couch onto a wide windowsill, sat on the ledge, and wrapped her arms around her knees with her head cocked sideways, viewing the wind show outside as droplets trickled down the window.

She ignored me.

"Where are you today?"

Nothing. I stared in her direction on purpose until she noticed.

"What is your general problem?" she snapped at me. " . . . OK, I been thinking about something way back when. Now shut up. . . I'm sleepy."

She rested her face on pulled-up knees.

"Tessa, don't sleep."

Her head popped up slightly. "I . . . don't . . . want . . . to . . . talk. . . today." She sing-songed her words. "You are so *ayayásh*."

"Don't call me retarded," I replied. "Those are new laces."

"Yep." She ignored me again.

In September of the prior year, Tessa had called Ms. Frank a *shuyápo k'usík'usi*, two words she'd linked together from Ms. Samuel's tutelage meaning 'white dog/bitch', and earned a three-day suspension and a subsequent referral to Sherry, the part-time school district counselor, and a woman Tessa believes has no purpose. Sherry felt Tessa was too much of a handful and 'referred' her to me. At our first contact, Tessa concluded I had something to do with mental health, which meant I was alternately nosy, stupid, or arrogant.

I already knew defiance was family tradition for her. Miyanashatawits come from the old *Piitl'iyawilá* band, descendants of Owhi, Kamiakin, Qualchan, and Skloom, who once roared "No surrender!" in broken English at white militia bivouacked on the other side of the Columbia. Her great uncle was killed by U.S. Marshalls at the Wounded Knee siege at Pine

Ridge in February, 1973. Arnold was likely there too, I'd concluded.

Two generations later, Tessa was the kind of native girl I sometimes see at the school who is little different from the textbooks she used—important parts missing or marked over, hard to read, defaced of her identity, and ripped in certain places.

By Thanksgiving, she'd confided with me she was crushing and snorting her stimulant medication. That's when I first saw the substance abuse coming forward. Up until then, she might have gotten drunk a couple of times and smoked weed, which lots of kids do. This was different. I confronted her and asked her why she was expanding her horizons.

"It's all dope," she responded. "It's a cheap high, so who cares how you get it? At least it's a legal buzz. It's not like I'm huffing gas or anything."

We worked on that logic for quite a while before she finally gave up the idea. It was her own memory of her mother's willingness to sell several of her great-grandmother's baskets to get high that brought her around the corner. She didn't want to be that desperate to get high. And she didn't want to be anything like her mother.

Several weeks later, she told me about meeting with an Indian Health Service psychiatric nurse who wanted to up her dosage due to her 'school behavior issues.' Tessa told her she and I had decided she "didn't need to take pills anymore." She was already a strong-minded kid in her own right, but for some reason she felt she needed me in the equation. The conversation spiraled downward from that point forward.

"She told me that's not your role. She brought her supervisor in and he said I'm mentally unstable and if I stop taking meds she prescribes, he can lock me up in a mental ward. Can he do that?"

"He might try."

"Would you let him?"

"No doubt I'd try to stop him. But the truth is, I don't have any authority over him."

She accepted this response unquestioningly. I think she also wanted to know if I'd go to bat for her. The fact I would do so somehow put me in a select league of grown-ups, I guess. I wasn't so bad anymore.

"Cool," she answered with a nod. "Well, so I just went out and told Leila what she said and Leila came back with me and told her and the supervisor, 'it's Tessa's choice.'"

"I'll bet they liked that," I responded.

Despite our deepening rapport, she was often tentative at our weekly sessions. Sometimes she was chattier, other times she acted like we'd never met before. It was usually the latter rather than former that suggested she was thinking of opening up more with me about something.

Tessa started this particular morning's session in total silence, drawing a heart in the vast condensation taking up the bottom half of the picture window. So I knew something must be up.

"Is that broken?"

"Ha. I don't tell my shit to white people." We'd done this kind of conversation before.

"Hmm, well, I believe we talked quite a bit last week, despite my whiteness. What do you make of that?"

She didn't make anything of it.

Her long hair trembled like a curtain before her face as she paused to lean across the couch and, in one sweeping motion, grab a tissue from the box on the desk, blow her nose, and draw another heart. All this movement took place while she continued looking out at bending willow trees. She sneezed and hummed a little.

I pinched my thigh, trying to stay awake.

"Can we talk about not telling your shit to white people? I'm getting bored."

"Don't feel like talking is what I mean. So shut . . . up." she whispered, sing-songy again. To me, this meant I was being asked to provoke conversation rather than wait for it.

"Must be boy problems . . ."

"That's not your business."

"Sorry. I may have hit a nerve. Some BF around your neck of the woods must be bringing you down."

It was a stab in the dark based solely upon her attitude at the moment.

"That's not your business either." So I was right. Who might this boyfriend be?

But I decided I was moving too fast and decided not ask. Besides, I intuited there was something else going on.

"You have lots of nice hearts there."

"Maybe I'm a worm," she said.

I turned away to cough and caught her glance as I shifted, trying to ease the desk corner poking my back. She wondered what I made of what she'd said.

"A worm with many hearts or whatever—is that what you mean?"

"Whatever." Now she was backing up.

"Geez, I'm talking across a canyon with you today, Tessa. You hear my echo but you're way over there on the other side."

"My grandma used to say I'm asleep when I'm awake. I don't have anything I want to talk about. School is fucking boring. That's all."

"Do you have to say 'fucking'?"

"What do you care?"

"It's unbecoming."

"What does 'unbecoming' mean?" she stopped her drawing only for a second, inquisitive.

"Not dignified. You don't need to talk so harshly. Your grandma wouldn't have liked it."

She started drawing again. "That's stupid. You didn't know my grandma. She wouldn't care. And she's dead."

"Sorry, but I know she wouldn't have liked that kind of talk."

"I say 'fucking' all the time. Fucking. Fucking," she glanced at me to see the effect. "What's wrong with that? Everybody says it, Doc—tor Bar—low."

She wrote 'DB' in a circle and then drew a line through it.

"Hoh, well, at least I'm included in your art, even if I am crossed out," I observed.

She wrote 'Dumb Bitch' below it. "There. That's art too."

"Hmm, and so what's up with all this? Are you pissed off?"

Her voice mimicked officiousness. "Doctor Ret Bar—low, return to the urgent care clinic . . . Ret . . . what kind of name is that? Like Rhett in 'Gone With the Wind'?"

"That's a pretty old movie," I said, impressed she would know about it.

"Uh duh, my _kála_ used to watch it . . . it's also a famous book, dummy."

"Right. Well, Ret is short for Return."

I figured she'd eventually find out anyway. Most kids have something to say about it.

"Return! That's your real first name?" she stopped and looked at me incredulously. "Really? Return! . . . Why would your mother do that to you? How embarrassing! We should just call you Reet, then, not Ret . . ."

'Return'—from the disowned Cherokee half-breeds and quarter-breeds of my Ozark hillbilly side my great aunt called 'thieves, vagrants, and alcoholics.' I was teased about my name mercilessly as a kid. Tessa gleefully partook of this new opportunity for a minute or two.

"Tessa," I said, interrupting her fun. "I'm guessing there's something going on but you're having a hard time bringing it out so you're keeping us busy by picking on my name. So I say keep it up, and then we won't have any time left to talk about what's really going on."

She glanced at me, slid a little closer to a foggy spot offering more creative room, and spoke with self-satisfaction.

"OK, I will."

Then she drew a horse. The head and body were pretty well-executed, and I could tell it was galloping.

"Are you OK with that?" she asked with an overdose of saccharin.

"How do you mean?"

"'How do you mean?', same kind of question. 'Are you OK with that?' You ask shit like that all the time. 'What about that?'" she mimicked.

"Must be Pick-on-the-Therapist Day," I admitted. "At least you're paying attention." She'd zeroed in on my most cliché phrases.

"God, I know. It's so obvious. You think you can make me talk..."

"Talk if you want or don't. It's not my business."

That had an effect. She stopped her finger's movement in mid-execution. Then she restarted.

"If I decide to talk to you, it'll be because you're so *ishinwáy*, poor and pitiful. Aaaaaaz."

She held onto the Indian-English nuanced ending, signaling she was enjoying her own humor.

"Well, I think you could go back to class, Tessa, if you don't want to talk at all."

"Nah, I have Pilson this hour. Being here is better," she noted matter-of-factly.

Two horses galloped onto her scene. She used the side of her palm, pounding lightly to make spots on her second horse.

"How are those horses?" I asked, knowing how she adored them.

"Huh? These aren't good horses; these are shitters."

That's a derogatory term for wild horses of the Yakama back country—the bad ones, the ones who make a mess and won't be tamed.

"They're *k'úsi* . . . wild and free," I said with mock indignation.

"No, they're just old shitters. And what do you know about wild horses? You didn't grow up here."

"Fair enough. Somebody taught me."

"Who?"

"Whom, you mean. I thought you loved horses. Why do you call them shitters?"

She dusted her pant leg absently, shrugged, and looked at me for a moment.

"It's 'who.' You don't even know your own language, even though you're a doctor. And they're shitters because they have a shitty life."

"What's the life of a shitter?"

"Eaten by bears. Bit by snakes. Rez dogs pack after you. People shoot at you. Get the mange. Or they get corralled and broken . . . pushed into stupid races like at Indian rodeo."

"I don't know much about Indian rodeo."

"Or whatever else, right?" she said with mild delight. "They bring wild horses in and race around trying to saddle them and jump on their backs."

"You don't like it . . ."

She turned suddenly and looked right at me. "They should let them stay wild," she proclaimed.

"Yeah," I reflected emphatically. "But I've heard wild colts make the best horses."

She looked at me again, surprised that I would say something like that. For my part, I was hoping she'd work in the metaphor with me.

"Not this one," she concluded, looking back at her drawing. "She's going to be free forever. Nobody ever breaks her down."

She stopped drawing again and huddled up with her arms wrapped around her knees, head down; a small girl trying to be smaller. Maybe she's trying to sleep again, I thought.

"Hey, what just happened—we were talking about. Then you went away."

"Oh. That," she spoke from behind bent knees. "Just having a moment."

"About what?"

"Too embarrassing," said her knee-muffled voice.

"I won't even look your way." I moved my gaze toward the door. "Tell me."

"No."

And we both became very quiet for a while.

"OK," she sighed.

"OK . . ." I replied.

Another pause before she raised her head and spoke.

"OK, Barlow. If I show you something, you can't say anything to anyone anywhere, anytime, ever, or write anything down about it anywhere. And if you do, I'll find your little wonderbread white man's house over to West Valley or wherever. . ."

"No threats."

"I'm not kidding, Barlow . . ."

"I get it. I won't tell, Tessa."

"Here . . ." She fished from her pocket a small square of dirty notebook paper, wadded up into many folds, and written in loopy, cursive penmanship in a tight block on the page.

I unfolded it and ceremoniously put on my reading glasses, adding to the formality of our deeper dialogue. Her face changed as she watched me, and was now more earnest.

*"Your Little Girl"*
*I can't stop thinking about this picture*
*All the time, out of that time*
*It never goes away. I wake up with it.*
*I go to sleep with it.*
*Back when things were bad*
*When we lived on Larena Lane*
*Leila worked doubles paying your loans,*
*Your big sister took care of you.*
*I was still little and you were drinking and using*
*When Ce Ce wasn't even born yet*
*Just like when you had Emily and Eloise.*
*I stayed home or we all of us stayed at Oxford House.*
*I never can forget and you never can remember*
*That time when you bent down and cleaned*
*What he did off of my shirt*
*And I'm crying like someone threw up on me.*
*And you don't say anything,*
*You stagger around and bang into shit.*
*You say you didn't know what was going on.*
*When I was your baby,*
*you cleaned me like the carpet or the toilet,*
*But you don't remember.*
*I remember what was going on.*
*I never was your baby*
*And I will never be your little girl.*

My legs were up against the couch and partially blocked her path. Her legs kicked fast and hard as they hung down from the sill with unsaid anxiety. Through the corner of my eye, I saw her looking at the door like a caged animal. Confiding this poem with me was very trusting and also very difficult.

"She called you 'her little girl' again," I inferred aloud, referring to Tina Miyanashatawit, Tessa's mother, currently in prison for possession with intent to distribute. I'd never met her.

"Last Saturday. She said, 'my little girl, I never knew what you were going through' for the zillionth time. She said the same shit to me before we went to live with my *kála*. She wants me to act like it's true and I believe it."

She glanced back and away. Suddenly, she smacked her hand hard against the pulled-up blinds. It dawned on me she was crying, and I pushed a box of tissue down the sill toward her. She pushed it back vehemently and put her palm into her eye instead.

"Fuck," she muttered.

Witnessing the extremity of her aloneness and how she pushed away support, I welled up at the pain implied—an occupational hazard. To Tessa, men who act soft or mushy are either really gullible or looking for sex. So I cowboy'd up quickly— clearing my throat with a rattle like old guys are supposed to do.

She looked at the paper I still held and whispered, "I didn't show it to anybody . . ." so quietly behind her hair, I wasn't really sure that was what she said. "Not even my sisters."

"Oh," I whispered back and nodded.

She wiped tears I wasn't supposed to see on her sleeve.

"I'm sorry you're in pain."

"I'm not," she said.

"Oh," I responded simply, knowing I didn't have to differ.

A few minutes later, she told me something that was on her mind and wouldn't go away. It was a memory about dancing in the living room for two inebriated consorts of her mother's when she was very little. An implicit worry emerged on her face that she, the dancing little girl, invited them to consider her sexually.

"What's wrong with loving to dance?" I tried to ask reassuringly.

She stared at me for a moment but her thoughts were elsewhere. "My ma said 'stop dancing.' Like all harsh or whatever. I don't remember much from then but I can't stop remembering that. What's wrong with loving to dance?" She flung her hair back, daring me to explain.

"Yeah. You were just being a kid."

"Why would she say that? That I couldn't dance in front of them?"

"I'm thinking you already have some ideas."

Her pondering expression merged into contempt. "Because she's a whore and thinks I'm one too," she said. "She thinks I made the assholes she brought into our lives grab me."

"Maybe you think so too."

"Fuck off!"

She popped off the sill and stepped over the couch, almost tripping. Such was the power of this idea.

"Fuck off!" she said again. Rage still on her face, she climbed back up on the sill, facing the door on the opposite wall, her feet kicking hard enough on the wainscoting behind her legs to bruise her heels. We were very quiet for a while.

"It doesn't mean you can never dance again," I said. "All that shit from back then can't stop you from dancing forever."

"Yes, it can. That's just how it is. It's like that, Reet. I don't dance. Not ever. Not even in front of myself. I won't even dance in front of a mirror."

"But you would like to," I responded.

She didn't deny it but, as if in explanation, began telling me more than she ever had about Cowboy Jack Brie, Tina's boyfriend, who landed her mother in prison—his large, rough hands, brilliant blue eyes, and biker mustache. It was like she'd changed the subject from dancing but I didn't believe she had. She hated him instantly. Brie he owned a working Chevy K-20, which meant a lot to Tina, and he started coming around at a time when her mother's addiction was at its height and had pushed them all into moving in with Tina's sister, Leila, at Apus Goudy housing project on Larena Lane. Although she was still little, Tessa recalled how everything about Brie seemed to fill her Auntie Leila with dread. She tolerated Brie because he gave her money and she could make the bills that Tina brought with her.

Tessa stared outside at the willows before telling me in a very flat tone how she would become Brie's 'baby' if he tried to reach for Emily or Eloise. She would jump into his lap, her heart pounding, offering herself so as to distract him and protect her sisters. It's a mistake some therapists make—you don't need to ask questions when someone's flowing about trauma like this— just shut up and sit there. Maybe you'll murmur a caring 'hmph' from time to time. Otherwise, just stay out of the way. Tessa told me all this in her own way, and I was surprised by her directness and confidence, despite her frequent expressions of ambivalence during the times we'd met.

"'I'll kill them all; makes no never mind to me,' that's what he'd say," she whispered, imitating Brie's threats. Tessa was convinced Tina knew what Brie was doing to her but acted like she didn't. After a long while of living with her grandma Georgina, she'd told her what Brie had done. Jack's *wak'íshwit*, his spirit, was twisted, grandma held her and told her tearfully, "long gone down the wrong road," *chilwit wapasúx*, a devil. Now she and her sisters were safe from all that, she reassured, and she and Arnold were going to keep them safe forever. Then, she died.

Tessa gazed right at me for a moment more. "Jack Brie used to say 'Let's go read us a story about Jack and his beanstalk,'" and her eyes shifted toward the floor. "He'd say that to me right in front of my mother. And she knew what it meant but pretended she didn't. I know she knew. It was his signal of what he wanted to do. He'd wait until Leila was gone to work. His voice still gets in my head."

I only nodded and waited. When she didn't say anything more, I told her she'd probably been had to tune out just to get through those terrible days. I thought maybe this became a sort of a habit and might have given her trouble in school. I said I thought that she was still very bright anyway even if she tended to do that from time to time. I was trying to be supportive, I suppose.

"That's all psychology bullshit. I'm not bright, Barlow. I flunked fourth grade. I never did school any better since then and never could. I can't even do multiplication."

I said there was a difference between being educated and being bright and I knew people who were quite educated but very stupid. She just shook her head, looked outside, and stayed quiet.

I watched her sitting there and for the first time I think I finally began to put things together about what it must have really been like for her when she was younger—compelled to be truant from school, washing dishes and cleaning house, pitching cigarette butts, tugging her drunken mother out of bed, cleaning puke off the toilet so she and her little sisters could use it, hanging clothes outside, heating canned beef stew filched from the convenience store, and turning on cartoons for her baby sister. On top of all that she did to try to make what could never work somehow work anyway, Tessa had to sacrifice herself and allow herself to be violated in order to protect her sisters and mother from Jack, the resident pedophile and rapist. At this realization, I told her I thought she was a genius in the art of survival and asked her how a person who'd survived all she'd been through could ever be considered a failure. She didn't answer me but only shook her head again and kept her eyes on the willows.

And so our time was nearly gone, and I felt I had to find something more to say. I had to find some way to reach back to her the way she'd tried to reach out toward me because I knew what a risk it had been for her. I needed to reciprocate.

I held her crumpled paper poem up in the air.

"Tessa, you said you never showed this to anyone, not even your sisters. And so I want to know," I leaned toward her. "What's it been like for you to have taken a chance on showing it to me?"

Instantaneously, my question put a flame to the dried sage between us. She swung her head around from the window, and all in one exhaled breath she spoke:

"Like finally having a real true friend, I guess."

The remark was completely unexpected, I think, by both of us. During the next few seconds, her shifting black hair cleared a path toward a very open expression, arched eyebrows, and the slight, shy smile of a not-quite-woman. Her eyes lifted slightly upwards in surprise, tears forming—not in grief so much as in recognition of suddenly becoming more human. Just as quickly, what she'd actually said hit aloud her head-on with a dawning awareness that she'd never, ever say anything like this to anyone, especially to some *páshtin* psychologist. Her normally tough exterior struggled to reassert itself.

I'd somehow capitalized on her impulsiveness; my question had set her up and she'd said more to me than she ever meant to. Dread, embarrassment, and shame now began to enter her eyes as vulnerability and inpregnability fought it out. I had to help her save face and restore some modicum of distance and balance.

"Well, thanks, Tessa. I have to say I'm very honored by you taking me into your confidence." I intentionally made my tone just a little privileged.

"Don't let it go to your head . . ." she responded like lightning.

"Sure. OK."

"And don't start acting like you're my dad or anything. I don't need bullshit like that."

"Tessa . . . I won't act like I'm your dad. But I won't pretend a very brave spirit didn't write this poem, somebody who survived and made it through a whole lot of shit. I figure at some point somehow you're going to have to stop working so hard to convince everybody who tries to care about you in any way that you're a failure and not worth it."

She looked directly at me, blankly at first. The wind suddenly struck the window very hard and startled both of us.

"Shit!" she sparked too loudly, but it wasn't really for me. Her eyes were not altogether angry. The bell rang and she got up, trying to sustain a fake expression of annoyance as she exited.

Mrs. Marshall caught up with me in the hall while I looked for my next client.

"I saw Tess. She looked pretty irked," she said, likely worried she'd act up in class.

"Yeah," I responded. "Well, not really. It was just kind of hard for her—being seen today."

She squinted at me for a second, looking confused.

"I mean so clearly," I added. "Being seen so clearly."

She nodded at me uncertainly as I walked away.

Tessa was in jail five days later and I knew it wasn't coincidental. She was trying to prove that I was wrong about her. She was moving further into dangerous terrain.

## Four

I asked him why he thought the whites were all mad.
"They say what they think with their heads," he replied.
"Why, of course. What do you think with?"
I asked him in surprise.
"We think here," he said, indicating his heart.
I fell into a deep meditation.
For the first time in my life, so it seemed to me,
someone had drawn a picture of the real white man.
*-Carl Jung, after meeting with*
*Ochiaway Biano (Mountain Lake) of the Taos Pueblo*

Little Cecelia, that is, Ce Ce, bounded through the courtroom door like she was coming home from school. She spotted her older sister sitting with Rena at a table in the front and ran toward her.

"Tessa! Tessa! Can you come out now?" she shouted before someone shushed her loudly.

Tessa hugged her close.

"No, sister. Not right away, I don't think."

"You said we'd go fishing," Ce Ce protested.

"I know, Ce Ce, but I've still got to do some business here."

"Can I sit here too?"

"You sit right behind me, sweetie."

I watched her being a big sister, glad of Rena's willingness to let her help get Ce Ce settled. Arnold ambled in, carrying Samuel, about three or four years old, and towing Franklin, age eight. I'd done a developmental assessment with him out in White Swan a couple of years earlier. Arnold grimaced from his sore back and shoulders as he set Samuel down. Samuel immediately began to wander and climb on the benches.

"Why can't we stay in the truck?" Franklin whined at him.

Arnold gave no answer and shook his head disapprovingly. Franklin should have been in school; Arnold must have opted to keep him out for his sister's day in court. Maybe he'd learn something. Arnold might have put Samuel in Head Start but when he suddenly started coughing long and loud, I figured he must be sick. Emily and Eloise, friends again after the brassiere battle, looked shy in jeans and worn boots with matching t-shirts reading 'Native Daughter,' their eyes stayed fixed on the aisle floors while they tentatively found a bench together. I'd learned from Tessa that Eloise had many problems from Tina's alcohol abuse during pregnancy. One twin unaffected, the other born with numerous challenges—the outcome was always unpredictable. She leaned in close to Emily and reached over to take her hand. Emily shook it off irritably, but she didn't move away. Clearly, she looked after Eloise.

"Sit down," Arnold gruffly instructed Franklin and grabbed Samuel at the shoulder, pushing both toward a bench at the rear. "Don't move around. No noise or playing. Sit quiet while we're in here."

A bailiff strolled in.

"All rise."

"Get up," Arnold snapped. Both boys jumped up very enthusiastically and gazed inquisitively at the room around them. Ce Ce jumped up, too.

Leonora Waldrup, the Children's Court judge, strolled in wearing her robes. The bailiff called out:

"Children's Court of the Fourteen Confederated Tribes and Bands of the Yakama Nation, now in session . . . Honorable Leonora Waldrup, presiding. Please be seated."

Everyone sat back down. The judge strolled by me grasping a loose sheaf of papers and climbed up to her elevated bench. Her long black hair was pulled back in a tight bun held in place by a hand-beaded barrette in the design of the flag of Yakama Nation—fourteen feathers and stars shooting from golden rays behind Pahto, otherwise known as Mt. Adams, a spread-winged eagle hovering protectively above them all. The eagle's exceptional vision takes in the big picture, protecting the people below. Much more than her robes, this adornment identified Judge Waldrup as a leader.

"The People of Yakama Nation versus Ms. Tessa Miyanashatawit," she read from her papers. "Ms. Miyanashatawit, how do you do?"

"OK," said Tessa from her chair.

"'OK, your honor,' in here," Judge Waldrup said as she continued reading.

"Your honor," Rena stood, "the prosecutor and youth services are asking to forgo a trial provided Ms. Miyanashatawit complies with entering inpatient treatment for substance abuse."

Tessa cocked her head up at Rena at this.

"I want a trial, Rena."

"No, you don't," Rena countered knowingly.

"Young lady," said Judge Waldrup, easing her glasses down her nose and leafing through the papers, "You've been charged with defiance of authority, consumption of alcohol by a minor, and public intoxication."

For the first time, her eyes behind half-glasses looked up and swept carefully over Tessa sitting at the table.

"Oh, I forgot to mention: stand up while I'm addressing you."

Tessa looked at Rena and slowly rose up at the table. Judge Waldrup's gaze turned back to paper.

"You are entitled to have representation if you want a trial. We have an excellent attorney here who can help you. But you may want to remember I have a copy of a breathalyzer examination taken three nights ago with your name on it I'm looking at here. It says your breath was over two times the legal limit . . . for adults. You're not an adult. You don't get a jury here." Again, her gaze shifted directly toward Tessa for only a moment. "You're going to have to prove to me that this exam is incorrect."

Tessa looked confused.

"Can you do that?" demanded the judge. "Can you prove maybe this test got mixed up by the tribal officers and belongs to someone else? Can you show maybe the machine wasn't working right? Can you prove this test is wrong?"

"No," Tessa muttered.

The judge glared momentarily at her.

". . . your honor," Tessa finished.

The judge leaned forward.

"I have a statement from your grandfather here. Are you going to depose him?"

"What's that?" Tessa looked worried.

"'What's that, your honor?' . . ." Judge Waldrup shot back, leaning back in her chair, looking at the papers again. "That's where your attorney or you ask your *tíla* a bunch of questions about his charging you with defiance and try to show he's lying. Do you wish to examine your *tíla* and prove he's lying?"

"Oh." Tessa looked back at her grandfather sitting in the rear. He stared straight ahead with a scowl on his face. "No, your honor."

"Now the tribal prosecutor's office and Rena seem to think the best thing would be to get you some help with your alcohol abuse. Do you admit you abused alcohol three nights ago?"

Tessa hesitated and then her gaze fell to the floor.

"Yes."

"Yes, your honor."

"Your honor," and here a hint of the attitude with which I was quite familiar entered her demeanor, and I wondered if the judge would notice. The courtroom became very quiet for a second, and Emily smiled and covered her mouth at the same time.

"'Yes, your honor,' please try that again," said Judge Waldrup, still feigning that the papers before her deserved more attention.

"Yes, your honor," and now Tessa's response was even more accentuated. I knew she didn't like being pushed around by anyone, but I was still surprised she'd keep this up.

Judge Waldrup sighed, set her papers down, leaned forward, rested her chin in one palm, and stared at Tessa, almost affectionately but not quite.

"Young lady, I do believe you think you're tough. If you understood the seriousness of your situation, you would address this court respectfully. I want you to say, 'yes, your honor'. I want you to say it without the attitude and tone. Keep this crap up, and I'll just hold you in contempt of court and lock you in jail for three more nights. Are you *up* for that?"

Judge Waldrup's question carried just a hint of the same adolescence as Tessa's.

"Yes, your honor, I mean, no . . . your honor!" answered Tessa.

Emily burst out with a laugh, and Arnold snarled, "Hush!"

"OK, then," said the judge. "Now, Miyanashatawit is a name I know. I know your grandfather here. He served on our tribal council. I knew your grandmother and respected her. We went to high school together—and I took her to lunch over at the Heritage Inn a couple months before she passed on. Maybe you didn't know all that. Do you think she would be pleased to see you here with me today?"

"No, your honor." She started to sit down.

"I'm in charge here," muttered the judge quietly. "And if you decide to sit down before I tell you to; you'll be doing it back in jail."

Tessa rose back upright and her eyes darted quickly in several directions. She was quite out her element.

"Now, what I'd like to know is, are you supposed to be a Yakama?"

Tessa gazed at the judge for just a moment, and her face reddened with indignity.

"Yes . . . I am."

"That's 'yes, I am, your honor.' I won't give you another chance."

She squinted at Tessa.

"Because you've violated Article 9 of our Yakama Treaty of 1855 by obtaining and consuming alcohol illegally on our sacred land. Were you aware of that?"

"No, your honor."

Judge Waldrup raised her eyebrows.

"Ignorance of the law is no excuse. And I don't believe you didn't know you were breaking the law. And are you trying to encourage your friends and your Yakama brothers and sisters sitting in here watching you right now to follow the same path you're taking, that is, to get some alcohol, party down, get addicted, and then destroy themselves?"

Tessa glanced back at her *tíla*. He looked straight ahead with the same unpleasant scowl affixed to his face. She turned back to the judge, who was looking right at her.

"Answer me right away when I ask you a question," she demanded.

"No, your honor."

Judge Waldrup sifted through a couple more papers. Again, her brows lifted as she read, and her lip curled as she spoke to Tessa.

"And are you using foul language in my jail?"

"I, uh," Tessa stammered. She looked at Rena, who shook her head.

"I warned you," Rena said.

"Yes, she warned you," said Judge Waldrup. "But you figure you can just do what you want, don't you? We're going to sort that out for you, right now, this morning."

Judge Waldrup folded her hands on her raised desk and stared emotionless at Tessa. I wouldn't have crossed swords with her.

"No, your honor . . ." Tessa tried to explain. "I was upset."

The judge picked the stack of papers back up and shook them at her.

"Do not waste my time with excuses! Don't presume to try to teach me, your elder, when the 'f' word or any other such word is permissible. Do you talk that way in front of your little sister here?"

Judge Waldrup glanced down at Ce Ce, who squinted back at her with clear disapproval. The judge raised her eyebrows, mildly impressed, and turned back toward Tessa. Tessa's posture slipped a little, and she glanced around, stunned, I believe.

"Stand up straight and take hold of your dignity—right now!" Judge Waldrup thundered.

Tessa stood straighter, humiliated, struggling to hold back tears.

The door at the back slipped open very quietly, and Elisi took a seat in back. I didn't have any idea she'd be coming.

Judge Waldrup pointed to an older woman seated in front of a typing device. "Ms. Consuela here is my court stenographer. She's taking down what we're talking about while I talk to you on behalf of the Yakama people, your community. We don't want our young people falling into addictions, using ugly language, and running around in gangs. You better decide if you're part of this community or someone else."

Her eyes closed to slits, and she pointed a finger at Tessa who was now trying harder not to cry and not quite succeeding.

The judge's tone was blistering. "I don't have a care about your tears . . . don't look for sympathy from me. I don't care about your pity party. Oh poor me, I got myself caught and locked into the jail. Yes, you did, and coming in here in front of me is what that means. You don't want to meet up with me in here. Now isn't it true your own mother suffered from drug and alcohol addiction and is currently incarcerated?"

"Yes, your honor," Tessa slurred, looking at the floor.

"This must have brought much pain to your family. And it leaves me wondering why you are doing this?! You're using whatever brains the Creator gave you to try to wreck your life. Why?"

She turned to the sparse courtroom, mostly empty except for Rena, Arnold and the kids, Elisi, and me.

"We're going to stop your spiritual infection. I don't want you or your brothers and sisters to go this way. Many good people have died from alcohol and drugs on our reservation. I lost my own daughter and grandson. The pain of their deaths still hurts me. It never goes away. Look here!" She gestured Tessa's attention toward her family. "Every one of these children are watching us have our little talk here today. Your own grandfather is watching and praying for you because he knows what addiction can do."

Tessa stood silent, her head now aimed rigidly toward her feet. Shame is part of how things are done here, I thought to myself.

"You may be seated," said the judge, and Tessa lowered herself into her chair. Her hands then went to her face, and Rena passed her a tissue which she accepted, surprisingly.

"Dr. Barlow?"

I stood up. "Yes, your honor."

"I have a letter signed by you with a mental health diagnosis of Post-Colonial Stress Disorder and alcohol abuse." Judge Waldrup paused and chuckled. "Is that for real? Is there really such a disorder? Not the alcohol diagnosis, the other."

"I didn't make it up, your honor."

"I have another letter here from Dominia Garcia, your colleague. She's entered a mental health diagnosis of Childhood Bipolar Disorder. How am I supposed to think about these two labels?"

"Well, your Honor, Childhood Bipolar Disorder is not in the recognized system we use and isn't scientific at all really. It's a load of bunk, part of the European-American culture of today. Then again, Post-Colonial Stress seems more accurate, and far more culturally-appropriate. I don't like calling it a disorder, but the IHS insists on it."

Judge Leonora Waldrup and I went back a ways. She looked mildly amused. I helped her granddaughter get through a difficult divorce from a violent guy.

She turned to Rena. "Dominia wasn't able to come this morning?"

"As a general rule, we don't see the Indian Health mental health folks over here, your honor, except for Dr. Barlow."

"Well, I guess if I have any questions, I could call. I'm intrigued but I'm going to work with what I've got. You both agree on the alcohol abuse."

"Your honor," I went on, "Ms. Miyanashatawit has also been abusing her psychiatric medication. Additionally, she was likely fraternizing with young people known to use methamphetamine and appeared to be smoking an unknown substance."

Tessa's posture shot rigid from where I could see her. She stared ahead and didn't look back at me.

"I see. Thank you for that. I don't see anything on that in the documentation."

"I only mention it because Tessa has become a danger to herself by widening her experimentation with substances and intoxication."

Tessa's head spun around with a look of fury.

"Hello, Officer Whitcomb," said Judge Waldrup. We all looked back at the tall Yakama Nation Tribal Police officer standing at the rear of the courtroom. I hadn't heard him enter. "Thanks for stopping by. Do you have testimony to offer this preliminary hearing with respect to the charges against Tessa Miyanashatawit?"

"Yes, your honor."

He smiled knowingly at a formality both he and the judge had obviously gone through many times.

"I have a report from you here. Do you affirm the substance of this report is true?"

"Yes, your honor." Tessa watched him closely as he continued, "I attest that the report I submitted is true, accurate, and factual and am willing to testify as such should the court move this matter to trial."

"I suspect that won't be necessary, Charlie, but thanks for stopping by . . ." She looked at Tessa. "Ms. Miyanashatawit, I'm sending you through our Drug Court to a thirty-day treatment program at All Nations Center in Cle Elum."

Tessa turned toward Rena, who nodded her head affirmatively.

"Your honor?"

"The Court recognizes Mr. Miyanashatawit."

Arnold got up and limped slightly coming to the front of the room. He leaned hard on the banister, likely still sore from hoisting fishery salmon. They were obviously acquainted.

"I want to do what's best. But it's not an easy thing having her gone so long. I've got these little ones, and she's a big help. I can get more work when she's around to help."

Tessa covered her face again with both hands. I knew she was ashamed to hear her grandfather plead like this.

"IHS doc says Franklin's got the pertussis, the whooping cough. He's been keeping everybody up at night. He's pretty sick the last few days. I had to keep him back from school today but couldn't very well leave him home alone. Is there any shorter program she could go to?"

The judge looked down at Tessa. "Yes sir, this is hard on a family and I do understand. To be honest, thirty days is not really enough, Mr. Miyanashatawit. There's even less promise keeping her out of harm's way with less than that. I wish we had some alternative. I do appreciate sending her away for treatment is a burden. We need to do what's right. So that's my decision."

Arnold nodded quietly, shook his head slightly, and sat back down.

"Court adjourned."

"All rise," declared the bailiff. We all stood up as Judge Waldrup exited the room.

"Tessa, you're going away?" Tessa looked back at Ce Ce.

"Yes, Ce Ce, I guess I have to for awhile."

Rena touched Tessa gently on the arm.

"I won't go fishing until you come back . . ." Ce Ce's crestfallen look changed to one of resolve. The subtly was not lost on Tessa, and her eyes filled again with tears.

Rena muttered, "Time to go back."

"Ce Ce, I'm sorry."

Ce Ce wasn't going to cry in front of strangers like her sister. She watched Tessa exit in her black and white striped coveralls with a blank expression—a habit learned across generations, limiting public expression. She walked over to Arnold, and buried her unspoken feelings into his pant leg while he reached to grab Samuel, who was climbing on a bench again.

Arnold whispered something to Elisi and they both nodded at me as I got up to leave. I thought they wanted to talk but Elisi shook her head and mouthed "Not now . . ." as Arnold turned to deal with all those kids.

Tessa was still lingering with Rena just inside a far hallway that led back to the jail. By jail policy, she had to have cuffs back on her. Her eyes met mine for only a moment and I was pretty sure she hated me and everyone else everywhere. I was sorry it had to be that way.

I almost knocked into Officer Whitcomb opening the door; he was talking on his cell phone in the middle of the sidewalk. His hair was pulled back tight into a long braid and his brown face was smooth. From his linebacker shoulders and muscle mass, I guessed I'd have been the one pulling myself off the ground if I'd not seen him in time. I started to make my way around him, and he pulled the phone away from his ear.

"Dr. Barlow? Hold a second . . . I got to call you back," he concluded, snapped his cell shut, poked out his hand, and we shook in the very light-touched, traditional manner. "Charlie Whitcomb. I heard you were having some struggles working with Tessa."

"OK," I answered noncommittally. I could talk about her professionally in court but wasn't comfortable with informal chit-chat.

"Just thought I'd mention the heart of that girl's problems boils down to Parker Heslah. Get her away from that boy, and she'll straighten out."

"Thanks," I responded evenly, "It's not always easy to discourage the teens in that way once they've formed a little romance."

"Yeah," he nodded. "Well, whatever tricks you got. Parker's police business right now. I can't say much more as to why. He's bad medicine. I believe he may have put a bullet hole in one of our cruisers last week. I'll tell you what, he's not going to like you working with his girl."

His tone seemed strange to me—subtly discouraging and without hope. Between words, he seemed to suggest I was far out of my element; I was unwelcome. Truthfully, I couldn't exactly put my finger on it. I felt as though I'd been caught in some petty crime over which he had no jurisdiction. Even so, I'd never had such personal engagement about a client from a tribal cop before.

"Maybe you could tell me what '187' means?" I tried to appeal to his expertise in order to forge some sort of relationship. Besides, I wanted to know.

His expression hardened even more. "Where'd that come up?"

"Spray-painted on my passenger door while I was out around White Swan a few days ago."

"Where in White Swan? You file a report?"

"Out by the annex and then over at Fort Simcoe. I didn't report it." I hesitated to say anything about Parker.

He shook his head and looked down at the ground with his hands on his hips for a moment. He had better things to do.

"That's kind of what I'm saying. These little ESP bangers—well, Parker likes his tagging. My advice is leave him and all of them be, doctor."

"But what does it mean?"

"187? You never heard of that? 187 in the California Penal Code means 'murder with malicious intent'. It means you're not liked very much."

He watched for my reaction. I decided I didn't care to show him one.

"Yeah, right. Well, thanks for that. I hear you."

I reached out my hand to shake his and his cell rang at the same moment. He chose the cell, answered it, and turned away. I'd been briefed and dismissed. It wasn't a friendly interaction.

Cheryl Lynn, FRNP, met me in the hallway as I passed my magnetic ID through the lock and opened the back door of the clinic.

"Got a minute?" She looked left and right.

She swept her office door open and closed quickly as I walked in and sat down next to her computer station. Then she sat down in front of the screen, glancing at me for a few moments with mixed formality and kindness.

"I talked to my husband about you."

"You did?"

"Hah!" she giggled and became serious again. "I put that the wrong way . . . You and I seem to have opposite shifts of a sort—I'm always doing well-child check-ups when you're seeing clients and you seem to be gone when I'm around. My husband, Tom, and I, we're always talking about this place. That's what I meant." She smiled again. "He's a colonel out at Yakima Training Ground, career military."

"Not a man I'd want to annoy."

She sighed. "He's not your worry. You're kind of our special case, Dr. Barlow. The Portland IHS office created your position very reluctantly. Dominia was a major player in resisting having you here. It wasn't her idea and if it's not her idea, she won't like it. I wished I'd helped you more."

"You helped me get office furniture."

"Oh, yes."

She frowned, and that look of concern passed over her face again.

"You have a behavioral health meeting this morning with Gaillard?"

"In a minute—something about 'service integration'."

"Dominia, Leo, and Kent have been working something up for you." Her eyes were sympathetic. "Deborah told me. She has a lot of respect for you." She shook her head. "Look, Ret, Dr. Barlow..."

"Ret's fine."

"Don't ever forget Dominia pulls the strings over there in mental health. She felt threatened by a diabetes program I created and got me taken down a full-step in rank two years ago. She's big in the Commissioned Corps and knows lots of people. I didn't even know what she was doing until a friend of mine at Reserves forwarded me an email performance review of sorts she'd been copied in on. It was a note Dominia had written to one of my superiors. I had to provide all sorts of documentation to undo the poison. She has her fingers in everything at this clinic. Don't mess with her... Deborah told me this morning, Dominia and Leo wrote a formal complaint alleging you're interfering with some of their treatment plans."

Formal complaints are a big deal at Indian Health Service. They can end up in your employee record as evidence toward pushing you out of your position.

"I didn't know that." I admit I was a little shocked. "I guess they want a fight."

She relaxed and her eyes laughed at the crack.

"You'll be all right. You seem to be immunized from caring much about the impression you're making."

"My mother used to say the same thing." I suddenly recognized a friend in a place where I thought I didn't have any. "Well, thanks for warning me, Cheryl. Not sure what my strategy will be off-hand but I appreciate not having to go in totally blind-sided."

"I just wanted to make sure you knew. IHS hasn't had an appropriation increase in twenty years. We've got cuts in Basic Health, and management's always working in desperation mode for funding. Who gets the cash rules. Dominia's just an RN working under Leo's supervision to get her psychiatric credential. She's got no direct authority over you. But she can do three med management sessions an hour at 133 dollars per encounter. More money rolls through pharmacy mark-ups and charge backs. You talk to a client and that's one encounter. Do the math—administration doesn't like you pissing off the pill peddlers. We need to keep our Indians sedated."

I looked at the clock and got up. "Well, thanks for the heads up, Cheryl. I better get something going and I've only got three minutes."

My heart rate was accelerating as I exited and she said, "Be careful." Maybe I was going to lose my job.

The formal written complaint was in an envelope in my mailbox. It wasn't there earlier that morning. Deborah sent me a glance of warning.

"All good," I tried to reassure both of us as I opened the envelope. "And better late than never."

"And what's all that supposed to mean?" she gazed at me wonderingly. "What are you going to do? They're trying to get you, you know."

"I've only got one idea," I answered as I ran back to my office. "But at least I've got one."

I hurried inside to grab my planner and a file folder with some personnel-related materials I'd collected. I could only skim what they had written on them before walking over to the conference room.

# Five

When men oppress their fellow-men, the oppressor ever finds,
in the character of the oppressed, a full justification for his
oppression. Ignorance and depravity, and the inability to rise
from degradation to civilization and respectability,
are the most usual allegations against the oppressed.
–Frederick Douglass

"Dr. Barlow, glad you could make it. There are several things we need to discuss regarding your role and responsibilities."

"Is that right?" I feigned surprise, staying smooth as silk as I took my seat.

My several colleagues walked in not far behind me. They didn't look at me at all as sat down, somehow ascertaining how to keep at least three chairs between me and any of them. They whispered, grinned, and focused toward the other end of the long table as if they were about to watch a sporting event together.

William Gaillard, MD, a mostly reasonable man, stared down at a duplicate of the complaint letter I had in my planner, twirling his lengthy, gray mustache. I guessed he hadn't read it any sooner than I did. We both squirmed uncomfortably on our padded vinyl seats. Everybody else sat upright, backs straight.

The late arrival, Kent Williams, squeezed his beer belly around my neck, pausing to tug my short pony tail. He'd done this a couple of times in the past, and I'd let it go. He chortled at this mischief and others turned to look. They smiled, and I didn't because it wasn't funny.

"First off, I'm sure there are different opinions here, and we don't all have to agree," Gaillard began. "Second, I'd like to maintain a professional demeanor in our conversations."

Across from me sat the lead psychiatric nurse, Leo Aspen, ARNP, tapping his pen on his pad nervously. His glasses were dirty and there was scum on the inner rim of his coffee cup. Next to him sat his assistant-trainee, Dominia Garcia, RN, looking rosy and made-up in the Commissioned Corps uniform called "service dress blues" with a peaked white cap and her rank neatly embroidered on her shoulder. At least she didn't have regulation white gloves on. Her insignia read O-5 in the Corps, equivalent to a battalion commander in the Army.

Corps officers were required to wear their uniforms from time to time at our clinic, but there was nothing special about this day. Her power garb was letting me know where I stood. The two clinical social workers, Eileen Scoville and Kent, sat on my side of the table further down. They appeared stoic as Gaillard tried to open things up.

"Dr. Barlow, the main purpose we're here is to improve working relationships."

"I'm all for that," I offered, not really believing myself or him.

"A formal grievance has been entered regarding your tendency to practice independently from the clinic mental health department. We use a team approach here and there's a sense from Commander Garcia that you've encouraged one of the patients you share to go off her medication."

His effort to acknowledge Dominia by rank was not lost on me. I asked Commander Garcia, "Do you mean Tessa?"

Dominia flushed but didn't utter a word.

"Please address your questions to me, Dr. Barlow."

"I thought this meeting was informal."

"It's easier to have a few ground rules. So let's try that one."

"OK. I'm confused," I pulled out the file I'd scrambled to grab. Thank God, I'd spent some time familiarizing myself with its contents during a snowstorm last year.

"Is this a Stage 1 Grievance Procedure?"

"Yes, it is."

"Well, it'd be great if someone would say so. Now, the letter I have," I pulled it from the planner, "is addressing their grievance to you, Dr. Gaillard..."

He looked slightly perturbed.

"I'm the official with the authority over the matter grieved."

"I'm sorry to differ. You're not the authority as it's defined in the IHS manual's grievance procedure section."

Dr. Gaillard looked a little annoyed. "But I'm the medical director."

"Doesn't matter, Bill, sorry. As an independently-licensed psychologist, my 'duties' description in my written job definition states I have 'authority over matters pertaining to clinical psychological practice in the clinic.'"

I pulled out a copy from my folder and slid it down the table.

"If you'd like to see..."

He sat back, shocked that I had such an item at hand.

"Ret, I'm your boss," he protested.

"This is just his immature reaction to authority in general," Leo remarked.

I continued, "The manual clearly states that for Stage 1 administrative grievances, the official handling a grievance is," and I read, "'the official who made the decision or took the action about which the employee is dissatisfied.' That's me. But nobody in this room or involved in writing this complaint letter ever talked to me about their grievance. The letter's addressed to you, Dr. Gaillard, rather than me. So this isn't being done according to procedure."

Commander Garcia's eyes were the only thing that changed on her face. They looked darker.

"Well, whatever the procedures, Dr. Barlow," said Gaillard, "it appears we need to clear the air."

"Fine," I allowed, "Are minutes being taken?"

"I'll take minutes," said Gaillard, now more openly irritated.

"You're the chair and shouldn't have to." I looked around and, not surprisingly, no one volunteered.

"Well, OK," I said reluctantly, "but can I just ask that you note down what I've observed about the complaint letter and that we are deviating from procedure? Either that or here," I opened my planner, "I'll just note it to myself here as well."

I paused to write and spoke aloud as I wrote.

"Stage 1 grievance procedure not followed according to employee manual . . ."

"Very well," Gaillard was ascerbic. "Write whatever you like, Dr. Barlow, and I'll put in my notes that we've had to deviate from procedure."

"We didn't 'have to', Dr. Gaillard," I said. "I mean, we haven't followed procedure, have we? So that's what you should note down to be accurate. I want to note that," I jotted a bit more in my planner, scribbling really, but they couldn't see what I was doing, "because it could come to mean a lot later if I have to appeal the findings."

Dr. Bill Gaillard pursed his lips and frowned.

"Now," I purposely shifted my gaze to the several hateful expressions aimed my way, then looked back at Gaillard, "Am I to address all my questions to you? What about comments?"

Dr. Gaillard shifted in his seat as though a hemorrhoid was flaring.

"Gads, Barlow, let's see how things work out. Did you encourage this patient," he checked his notes, "Tessa Miyanashatawit, to discontinue her methylphenidate and sertraline?"

"Well, she reported to me she was abusing her Ritalin."

"Methylphenidate," chimed in Dominia.

"Whatever . . . she said she was crushing it up and snorting it."

"And you brought this to Dominia's attention?" asked Leo, now stepping into the inquisition.

"Let me think now," I pondered. "Tessa's trust of me was fragile at the time. Still is."

"She was endangering herself," remarked Eileen. Kent nodded.

"Not extensively," I countered. "I don't consider occasional low-level psychiatric drug abuse to be particularly endangering . . ."

"You don't . . ." Leo's tone was scathing. "He told her to go off her sertraline too."

"Dr. Barlow," Gaillard took an officer-like demeanor, "it's a medical call what's dangerous as far as abusing psychiatric substances."

"She was snorting the same dose Dominia prescribed. That might get you high, but it didn't seem to me likely to result in an overdose if it was prescribed correctly."

Dominia gave me a squint of smugness.

"I've been in recovery myself for twenty years," I said. "I'm pretty sure I can gage where Tessa was getting a buzz and where she might be crossing the line."

"Without alerting anyone else?" Leo pushed.

"As I recall, I mentioned something in my chart note."

Leo pounced, "Really. Where exactly?"

"I wrote something like 'may be reluctant to pursue her psychiatric regimen,' I suppose."

"There's nothing like that in the chart. And it's totally obscure, Barlow, and you know it," Leo seethed.

"It's doctor, Leo, if you don't mind," I said flatly, as though totally unperturbed. "I thought I wrote it in there . . ."

"But it means nothing! And it's not in there anyway!" Leo snapped.

"We can pull the chart and have a look if you're unhappy, Leo," offered Gaillard.

"So why didn't you come and talk to us directly?" Leo challenged.

"Why didn't you come and talk to me directly about a Stage 1 grievance? I don't report to you and am not accountable to you, Leo. Besides, Tessa reported you'd threatened to lock her up on a mental ward if she went off her meds." He sneered at me. "I figured if you did something that ridiculous, she'd probably hold me responsible for telling you about the medication abuse, and that would almost certainly disrupt any therapeutic work we'd done forever."

I turned to Gaillard. "She's not a kid who's easy to reach. And, as for the Zoloft, I never said a word to her about going off her anti-oppressants."

"I'm sorry," Gaillard looked perturbed, "what was that?"

"I didn't tell her to stop taking the anti-oppressants, the sertraline, the Zoloft. I would have told her to definitely talk to Dominia or Leo first. If she'd gone off that, I would have told her that even though the anti-oppressant isn't supposed to be addictive, she'd get a depressive crash if she went quit cold turkey."

I took a sip of water and let the words float around for a few moments. My mouth was a bit dry with anxiety anyway, but I wasn't about to let them know.

"Uh," Leo leaned forward with his arms crossed on the table. His blond hair was matted down and wavy and he parted it on the side, making him look even nerdier. His face was very red. "Am I hearing correctly? Are you saying anti-OPPressants?"

"Sure," I sipped my water, holding my cup up. "Anti-oppressants. It's just semantics."

I set my cup down, looking at him as blankly as possible.

"This is what we have to put up with!" Leo gestured wildly at Gaillard. "We try to stabilize an emotionally disturbed youth, and he has to import politics into the situation."

I took a whack at this. "Hmm, are you saying efforts to sedate emotional reactions to oppressed experience are not political?"

Not the brightest or most verbal of guys, he gaped, and we all watched the twists and turns on his face for a few seconds, except for Dominia, who looked out the window.

Gaillard finally remarked, "Dr. Barlow, can't you let the medical side treating this shared client deal with a medical situation?"

"This client was assigned to me. She sought my psychological services and recommendations. Her grandfather requested I meet with her. She's my client, in other words. She doesn't want to take meds. Why do I have to say more than that? The meetings with these other providers you're saying are part of my 'team' are forced. They're follow-ups to initial encounters with her pediatrician that happened years ago. She doesn't even know Leo or Dominia's names. They're just people who give her pills. Why should I call them my team if Tessa doesn't view them as part of her 'team'? I don't practice using your medical model. I don't accept its premises in relation to disturbing or dysfunctional behavior. Granted, a social, historical, and behavioral viewpoint has never been fashionable at Indian Health Service, but the world's changing. What you all call depression, I call oppression. Leo's saying I'm being political, and he's not. To me, our whole situation is political."

Gaillard sat back in his chair, dropped his pen onto his paper, and rubbed his eyes.

Kent now sidled in, "Well, speaking of which, did you happen to enter a diagnosis of 'post-colonial stress disorder' into Tessa's chart?"

"Yes, I did."

"That's not a recognized DSM diagnosis," Kent declared to Gaillard," nor ICD-9 for that matter. Also, it's a breach of diagnostic procedure as specified in the IHS behavioral health manual."

I glanced at Dominia and thought over the diagnostic label she'd affixed to Tessa for Judge Waldrup.

"Fine," I said. "It's more accurate, however. Childhood bipolar disorder is not a recognized DSM diagnosis either. With respect to the label I entered, I was just trying to cooperate. I realize there's some sort of actuarial philosophy coming into play here and I tried to come up with a DSM-type label we might all get along with."

I spoke to Gaillard: "The childhood bipolar label is ridiculous. It was created out of classist presumptions held by idiots out at Massachusetts General linked at the pockets with drug company money. But I thought the concept of post-colonial stress—proposed by esteemed health professionals who also happen to be native—one would think such ideas would work for the Indian Health Service."

"And since you're an Indian now, you know who's dealing with oppression and who isn't," Leo spit his sarcasm.

"Just an average white guy, Leo."

"With your hair getting longer and going to sweat lodge too," he nodded again, turning crimson with rage.

"That's not your business," I retorted.

"A lot of white people go Indian when they work at the IHS," came Kent's patronizing voice as he spoke to Gaillard, "Barlow going native is his business. But he's still refusing to comply with the IHS behavioral health treatment manual in his practices."

I responded, "So who at IHS has demonstrated scientifically, philosophically, or otherwise that Western psychiatric models and labels are more valid or superior for Yakama people than Yakama psychologies or Yakama beliefs and practices?"

"Indian Health Service has always used and always will use the medical model in provision of behavioral health services." Dominia finally spoke and with vehemence.

"You say so, Commander," I responded.

After this, we all sat there in silence for a long time. I just wanted to leave.

"This 'post-colonial stress disorder' thing is not a diagnosis billable under Medicaid, Dr. Barlow. We are dependent upon accepted terminology in order to access our funding stream. As medical director, I forbid you from using it."

"Fine, can we do that with Childhood Bipolar Disorder too? Also, can I enter posttraumatic stress disorder with intergenerational and oppressive features?"

"Why not write your own diagnostic system?" asked Kent provocatively.

"He doesn't even believe these Indian kids have ADHD," Leo said, and then he raised his finger exactly like my middle school homeroom teacher used to do. "And that's just one of the reasons why Dr. Barlow's a threat to every child on this reservation."

I stared at Leo and thought about Florence, Parker's sister, swallowing handfuls of pills someone there had given her. I took a sip of water to slow down.

"Dr. Gaillard," I finally said, "I'd appreciate it if you'd note how I have diplomatically but unsuccessfully attempted to guide this Stage 1 grievance toward following proper procedure. As to my views, I'd also appreciate it being noted that I brought up for many months the epidemic, faulty diagnosing of ADHD in every traumatized or misbehaving Indian kid coming through this clinic, including mentioning how a twenty-minute meeting and cursory interview is not a best practice for understanding a native child and his or her family, even for those working within the medical model."

Leo leaned in and opened his mouth. I held my hand up toward him.

"You've had your say in your letter. Dr. Gaillard, I've encouraged Kent on several occasions to come out with me to the schools and see what we've been doing with talking circles and other Yakama traditions integrated with behavioral approaches. I can show friendly emails and memos in which I provided him, Leo, and Eileen with pertinent copies of articles, readings, et cetera, supporting what I was doing."

I paused to survey all the players after my ass that day. Not one had made a single effort to befriend me or get to know me since I'd arrived. I'd never been on any of their lunch dates—not that I would have wanted to go when I look back, but it was rough in the beginning. All the peace-making efforts had come from me and were never reciprocated. I couldn't recall a single act of kindness or friendship from any of them since I'd arrived two years earlier. Then, I looked at Gaillard. At this point, I was completely done with my so-called 'team.'

"Despite this inappropriately handled grievance process, which I've offered right here and now to try to fix, I want it noted I've generally gone out of my way to work with my colleagues in the Yakama IHS mental health department."

"He considers himself an expert," Eileen bristled toward Gaillard. "As for me, I've only been working here for twenty years."

Now it was out there. "Eileen, no matter what you want to make of my ego, perhaps the truth is nobody has ever questioned the cultural validity of what you do."

"It's just arrogance that makes you think you're the one to do so," said Kent. And I finally understood what this had all been about.

Instead of answering, I spoke to Gaillard. "I'm not a supervisor for these people like Kent. But I think arrogance is reading John Grisham novels with your feet on your desk while kids across this rez drop-out, drink or drug, or kill themselves."

Grisham novels happened to be one of Kent's favorite pastimes while he waited for his government pension to vest.

"I'm done," said Kent, and the others got up with him. They all walked out.

"Well," I smiled falsely at Gaillard, "so much for service integration . . ."

He shook his head but said nothing as we both gathered our papers and left separately.

I leaned across the reception counter to check for messages in my mailbox next to Deborah.

"You had a couple of calls," she told me.

"Where?"

There were no notes or anything in my box. In fact, the little Dyno tape label with my name on it was gone, and I wasn't sure I had the right mailbox.

"Huh. Where'd they go?" she asked. "Where'd your name label go? I just put them in there about ten minutes ago."

She searched my face.

"Persona non grata," I responded to the question she didn't ask.

I'm supposed to keep my office locked but I don't like to. Elisi was sitting in the comfortable chair next to my desk. She likes to visit me most Wednesdays and Fridays.

"Dr. Barlow," she looked me over as I sat down, "If you grow your hair longer, you'll be called a wannabe."

"You're the one who told me to grow it longer, *kála*."

"You might not be wise to always follow my advice. What I really said is our people believe if your hair is short, it's harder for the Creator to see you and for your healing ways to work for us. Now your colleagues will say you're some old hippy wannabe."

"They already do."

Her head wobbled when she laughed. She continued working on beadwork.

"You're not your usual energetic self this morning."

"I got taken down a few notches."

"Trying to rehabilitate the IHS?" Onward she beaded knowingly, not looking up.

"Is nothing a secret here?"

She set down her project on my desk momentarily and looked me over again. "Moccasin telegraph," she explained. "You look tired and angry."

"I've been in a fight." I may have sounded too vehement. I know I was trying to get control of my temper after what I'd only just walked away from.

She stood up all in one motion, moved in front of me, placed her middle and ring finger in the center of my forehead and pushed long and hard. I sat there, stunned, never having had someone touch me in this way before, knowing better than to interrupt, although I hadn't the slightest idea what she was doing.

Her fingertips felt hot. After a few seconds, she pulled her hand away and clapped both hands, like you would to get something off them, as though there was dirt on them. She lifted both hands as she did this. The effect was as though she had absorbed something from my forehead onto her finger tips and then clapped it off into heaven. "Got rid of the hatefulness . . ." She spoke down at me with intensity. "You need to stop. We don't need no more warriors around here."

Great, I thought, out of a shitty meeting and into an elder scolding. Tessa's morning in Children's Court was only a few hours behind me. Now it was my turn to look down at the floor.

"Doctor Barlow, you've been having your little personal crusade. It's exactly what we don't need. Are you Kevin Costner or somebody?"

I laughed.

"That's not meant to be funny. This here isn't a dream or a movie. Stop acting all romantic about us. You've got much to learn, but I don't blame you for it. I'll teach you some. You need to know we've had all this hate and violence around here for more than a hundred fifty years. This is our land, and we live here. We've also had all sorts of educated do-gooders just like you come out, and what does it do for us? People like yourself come around here, try to help out, and then get all infected with the hate and anger. Then you eventually start fighting with each other and go on your merry way."

"White people," she shook her head, pausing to pick up her beading and continue. "The IHS is all we got for health problems among our people. You'll never make things better with them. You should give that idea up. You know, my grandniece sat with that Dominia a couple of times and thought she was nice."

This observation felt like a slap in the face and I broke the traditional protocol. "May I speak?"

"No, you may not. I'm talking right now. So you listen." She beaded some more. "OK, I'll try another way to teach you. Why did you come out here from Oklahoma to work at the Yakama IHS? Was it for our government pay here?"

"I already told you the story of how I came out here, *kála*," I answered with mild indignation. "That was the truth."

"Tell me again."

"I was praying to do better things in my life."

"I thought psychologists weren't religious."

"Well, I'm a spiritual person. I was meditating and praying."

"Hoh, the New Ager. The Buddhist. That's what you mean."

"*Kála*," I protested meekly. "I was in a suffering state at the time."

"Oh, sorry," she shrugged.

"I've told you this story before."

"It's more important for you to keep telling it than for me to hear it," she lifted her brows and chuckled. "But I'll remind you so you know I was listening. You had this friend. He passed on. This close friend you loved. I won't say his name."

"Ernie."

"Best not to say his name," she cautioned. "He hears you and walks toward you instead of where he's supposed to stay—in the Creator's presence. So it's best not to say his name. Anyway, that one'd been through much abuse in his family and gone runaway to Alaska to fish the salmon. You hadn't seen one another in a very long while. He had some sort of drug problem nobody knew about. And you were supposed to meet him in Arizona at some big wig event."

"That's right," I admitted. "A conference on the psychology of consciousness."

"Whatever big words you have is fine. You'd long forgotten all about those plans to meet him there. He'd died, and you put your grief away, like we do here. You put all memory of him away. Then you end up going down there to Scottsdale for other reasons. And you'd never ever been to Scottsdale before in your life. And that mike got passed around and everyone introduced themselves in the Indian way . . ."

"Yes, *kála,* thank you for listening to me."

She paused to glare at me. "That's no problem. Now you tell the next part of your own story back to me again."

I sighed audibly and knew she'd continue to sit there and insist until I complied.

"Everyone was Indian," I said, "and from all over. I was one of only maybe three white people. I felt very out of place. I couldn't think how I would introduce myself."

"You aren't all white, but you don't own that, do you? Anyway, you don't know yourself and why Creator sent you there and that made you nervous," she smiled as she beaded. "And then?"

"The mike finally came to me, and Ernie's death came into my mind all at once. And I remembered how we were going to meet right there at that same time of year and in that same place."

"Best not to say his name; don't do that because it makes his spirit suffer and want to come back to be near you to calm your hurt. The Creator sent you and sent his spirit there to Scottsdale already, that was enough. That got you crying in front of everybody when you were there."

"I never told you that."

"But I know it's true, don't I? That was a great teaching for you."

She set her beadwork down momentarily.

"Come to think of it, that's not very much like a white man. To follow the signs the Creator lays before you, allow your intuition to take you to a place you never been, not even knowing why you're there, and to open your heart in front of strangers. There has to be that kind of search for every human being. We used to send our young people up to sit on the mountains for days, you know." She picked up several beads. "And the Zuni man there heard you crying and visited you afterwards."

"How do you know he was Zuni?"

"Well, what did he say to you?"

"He said I'd need to 'be blackened' to work as a psychologist with Indian people out his way."

"He was Zuni. That's a Zuni way from out in the southwest, not a Yakama belief. Those Zunis are a good people. He meant you needed to have your mind completely cleared. He meant you needed to be cleaned out of all that negative learning you've had."

"Oh."

"And that's what we got here now in your debates with that Leo and Dominia, arguing about all that book learning and politics. White people like to do that. What difference does any of that make if you don't change your heart? Your arguments and conflicts come across the generations of your own ancestors' trying to dominate one another. It's just another form of the violence that's gone on. That don't have nothing to do with the path got opened up for you in Scottsdale. That was a more humble path. That was you giving in and letting something bigger run your life. So you need to back away from all these fights you get in around here. They're useless. Quit acting like a white man."

"My skin is white, *kála*."

She shook her head. "You know I heard one of your historical leaders called Chief John Ross led your Cherokee ancestors and fought in the Supreme Court to keep the white people from taking their lands, and he was mostly a Scottish by blood. But he spoke the indigenous language and knew all their ways. He'd been raised to them. Did you even know that?"

I shook my head.

"Skin color is not at all what I'm talking about when I say quit acting like a white man. I'm asking who are you in the history of your own people? Because that history's still being written, Dr. Barlow, right now as we speak."

With this, she struggled to her feet and packed her beading in her bag. I helped her to the door.

She turned to me. "You ought to go to the sweat lodge again."

In elder speech, this was akin to a command.

"Get this anger inside you purified. It don't help you. Ask your Creator to release you from it. Talk to your buddy Trick."

Trick is her nephew and a friend of mine. She smiled cryptically before meandering down the hall, carrying her bag and beadwork.

The next morning, there was an all-staff meeting on the topic of service integration which I found both irksome and ironic. I got in a little late, grabbed some coffee, sat down, and waited for it to begin or, really, be over. There are about sixty people working at our clinic, and we were spread around tables and in corners of the bigger lobby.

Two elder tribal staff members, Shirley and Janna, sat around the corner of a table, adjacent to me. I hold both in high esteem.

"*Ay shix máytski. Mish nam wá?*" I greeted them.

They nodded and grinned at me for trying to speak Yakama with them.

Janna responded, "*Shix máytski.* Doing fine, thanks." Good morning.

At this same moment, Kent eased behind me with his big belly toward a seat at the other end of the long table. He heard me speaking Yakama to them. Once again, he tugged on my hair, harder this time.

Hair is considered sacred. The two elders both looked first at him, then at me. They said nothing but stopped smiling immediately. Their faces became stone. From their perspective, I had been greatly affronted.

I felt my face turn hot, and my heart began pounding. I couldn't even hear what people were talking about for the next half hour.

The meeting broke up and Kent joked around with the deputy administrator before coming back in the same direction to leave. He placed both hands on my shoulders as he slipped by me again and bent down.

"Morning, wannabe," he whispered loudly.

I said nothing. Shirley and Janna heard what he said and watched me.

People got up and moved in various directions. I tried to hurry off through the crowd. Having successfully avoided smacking him down, I just wanted to get the hell out.

Shirley caught up with me at the door.

"Doctor Barlow. Are you Indian? Do you have Indian heritage?" she asked, looking straight ahead as she walked next to me.

"Why do you ask me that, Shirley?"

"Because I was watching you with your coworker there. You know, you swallow your anger like we do."

## Six

> There are a number of frankly psychotic children ... There are quite a number of severely neurotic children ... After a girl has run away from the boarding school and been brought back, she was almost immediately taken to the health service for a pelvic examination ... Many of the physicians, and to their credit, rebelled at making these examinations ...
> –Robert Leon, MD, *Mental health considerations in the Indian Boarding School Program, 1960*

Two days before Tessa left for the addiction recovery program in Cle Elum, Parker Heslah flipped his Corolla at the corner of Branch and Stevenson out near Harrah. There's nothing much out there except a few farms and vineyards. He was evidently stoned out of his mind.

I got the referral to go over to Toppenish Community Hospital to rule-out suicidal intent. He certainly didn't want to see me, but he was temporarily restrained by grogginess and an IV.

"What the fuck, doc?" was the greeting I was met with. I pulled up a chair next to him. "Don't feel like talking."

"Sorry about that. Were you trying to off yourself, Parker?"

He reached up with his free hand to wipe parched lips and noticed me eyeing the bandaged forearm.

"If I wanted to die, Barlow, I know better ways."

I told him he'd never be cleared to leave unless he answered my risk assessment questions. I was all done but didn't let him know and just used the question and answer format we had going already to call him out.

"So why do you want me dead, Parker?"

His eyes met mine in an instant.

"What gives you a stupid idea like that, doc?"

"187."

He frowned falsely. "I wouldn't know nothing about '187,' doc, 'cause like I already told you—I'm out of that shit. But if somebody's giving you the word, my advice is jump back before you get jumped. White Swan can be a dangerous place."

I hesitated as I thought about what he was trying to also say between the lines.

"Parker, come on, you don't like something about me and what I'm up to, so tell me. I don't have any plans to stop going out to White Swan."

He picked at his bandaged arm. "I got me a girl, and I take care of her. She don't need your help is what I'm saying. I help her."

"Two can be better than one in that kind of thing. Why not let's get you some treatment and straightened out too? That'd really help your girl right now."

"I wasn't high. I fell asleep."

"Right," I said as I leaned back in my chair and watched him. We sat and looked at one another for a minute.

"Are you done now?" he asked. "Can I go?"

"Not quite," I said and pulled out a white sheet of paper and a clipboard. I asked him do a drawing.

"I don't do no art," he said.

"I guess you do," I responded. "Because you want to leave this place. No stick figures. Draw you and your family or whoever you call family doing something together."

He paused with suspicion on his face.

"Fuck no. Why should I?"

For some reason, he finally took up the task. I guess he wanted to leave that bad. After a minute or so, he started to push back again.

"This is bullshit," he said as he drew.

I couldn't get him to complete it. He handed it back to me upside down.

"Don't look at it," his eyes carried more than a little malevolence so I decided to respect it. "Save it for later."

I wrote in the chart he should get set up with ADATSA, Alcohol and Drug Addiction Treatment Support Act, the Washington state law which is a funding resource program for low-income folks. Then I cleared him with the charge nurse and left the building.

I pulled out the clipboard in the car. He'd pictured himself next to a basketball hoop with two guys— 'Tiller' and 'James'. Each of them had a crudely-drawn pistol in hand. All around them were tags—Native Blood, etc. In the background was a quickly drawn outline of what looked something like my car. '187' was written on the passenger side door.

I tried hard to view it positively. After all, it was nice to be considered a part of the family.

It was still early morning, and I had time to drive all the way down to the river —the Columbia River, *Nch'i Wána* . I was intellectually jazzed about doing an actual network family therapy session, applying a model Delaware Indian psychologist Carolyn Attneave developed with her colleague, Dr. Ross Speck, a friend of R.D. Laing's. The two native pre-teen boys from Celilo Falls who'd broken into the longhouse freezer and stolen several items came from esteemed local families. Their behavior wasn't so much at issue as the disconnection from their culture that it signaled. One doesn't steal from the longhouse—it's just not done.

I planned to use Rock Creek community center and to make a spiral of chairs with the boys at the center. We'd put close relations nearer, moving as far out the spiral around them as we could, including cousins, friends, teachers, etc. and depending on how many people showed up. After all this was set up, we'd start at the outside of the spiral and work our way in toward these kids. Each person would speak about his or her desire to support them, commit to help resolve the problems they faced in growing up, and vow to keep them out of such trouble. A single network therapy session could offer such a revelation of support for kids who'd misbehaved that they never did so again—that is, provided people in the network followed through on what they said.

After leaving Parker, I got on state route 97, crossing over the wide Plateau until it veers southeast near Satus and heads up into the foothills. It gets wild in a hurry as the road winds up and down through folds of desert scrub, past small brooks and blown-out gullies, gradually countered by stands of cedar and pine approaching Satus Pass.

It was about three hours before I found the family's address where I was to check in and then follow folks over to Rock Creek. Only the grandmother was home. She leaned outside and looked left and right before telling me she was sorry but everyone had gone fishing. The decision was made based on the temperature, currents, and the insects. Several folks tried to call me but my cell was turned off. People have to eat and it was a good day for it, I responded. She nodded to me pleasantly as she closed the door.

It's a different culture, I told myself. I decided to take a break.

I stopped to hike around Maryhill Stonehenge, a World War I memorial and pacifist statement created by wealthy Quaker Samuel Hill configured exactly to the ancient site in England.

The winds blew chilly and strong, but I braved them, warmed by the sun baking through the big thunderheads and heating up my black windbreaker. Little blue wild flowers struggled against the scrabble along the gravel trail as I gazed across the Columbia Gorge, an overwhelming expanse.

The very wide river was dotted all along with barges and boats, railroads and highways lining the Oregon and Washington borders on either side, traffic winding inward and away from its banks and estuaries, slipping into tunnels dynamited in the 1930s out of solid granite, crossing suspension and draw bridges to places with names like the Dalles, Hood River, and White Salmon.

As the trains passed by, I called out 'Burlington Northern', 'Southern Central', 'Northern Pacific,' or 'B & O,' and an elderly couple huddled together as they headed back to their RV, no doubt commenting on my deviance. I was reminiscing about doing the same thing in reaction to my uncle's huge basement model railroad when I was a kid. The scene looked similar—the Gorge is so unreal, I lost my concept of distance, and the entire massive scene became miniaturized.

There are trails running behind the monument which have been there for thousands of years. I soon found myself creeping along the bottom reaches of the cliffs off the Plateau, well past where a sign stood reading, 'Danger! Loose rock!'

My friend Trick told me, "People go back that way all the time." This was a case of careful who you listen to.

Soon, the gravel edged away from the trail, and I began to climb up, finding myself on an incline of about forty-five degrees, and wondering what the hell I was doing. I had on worn-out running shoes and kept sliding sideways, losing my balance, and gaping at the steep slide to a sheer drop of about three hundred feet. If I lied down too far to compensate, I'd slide on the rock, yet if I stood up too tall, I was going to tumble backwards.

In my line of work, we might think of this as an existential crisis. I suddenly slid down hard about twenty feet, sure I was dead. True to my occasional tendency to overreact, I'd only scraped my knee and wrecked my jeans. I continued up a little higher to where I wanted to go.

On the rock before me, half faces gazed from distant horizons, multiple figures danced toward me from three thousand years earlier, sacred referents to visions and spiritual journeys, beyond photographs and duplication, television ads, or documentaries.

Elisi said I needed to see my place in history and make it real. Others were here long, long before you ever were, these cliff paintings told me. I wanted to think about that for a few minutes in light of recent experience.

After I climbed back down, I gave up two years of my life to a half-pound ground round smothered in onions at Sodbusters in Goldendale and drove home in the late twilight.

The outline of foothills expanded all around me, and the Milky Way was clearly visible, providing a glorious canopy. There were no city lights, not even the lights of remote farms or dwellings, only starlight, a rising moon, and my headlights.

I relaxed, singing loudly to stay awake with "More Than a Feeling" by Boston, a song I've always disliked, playing on the only station I could get to come in. I hadn't seen a car in over an hour. There was no traffic, nothing at all in sight, and I still had a couple hours ahead of me. I swayed back and forth across the double yellow line for no good reason, just being goofy.

At the moment I was belting out, "I closed my eyes and she slipped away," a brilliant all-white coyote with a huge bushy tail jumped out right in front of my headlights. I spun 360 degrees, cracked my left fender off the guardrail, and put my heart into my mouth.

I just sat there for a few seconds. The airbag did not deploy; I must be OK, I thought. Then I eased back into position and pulled to the curb to have a look. I fumbled my crummy wind-up ecoflashlight three times, fishing around on the dark floor for it over and over. I finally got out and got it shining on a big dent to the right rear, just above the painted '187'. Then I cursed mightily.

But my own voice alarmed me. I became completely still in response to its solitude. There was absolutely no noise—none at all. There was no wind. It was so quiet; I could hear my own heart beating in my ears.

A mournful howl lifted from low to high and penetrated the night. The hair on the back of my neck rose involuntarily. He was very near.

*Spilyáy*, coyote trickster-hero. Why have you stopped me in my tracks?

"Where have you been?" Ruthie came down from the lighted doorway as I got out of the car. "I tried to call you on your cell. Elisi's called twice, and I couldn't tell her where you were."

"Sorry," I said. "I was out in back country on the rez. Elisi called here?"

Elisi had never called me at home.

I tried to kiss her, but she pushed me backwards. She was pissed. She glared at me from a side of the car I didn't want her to see.

"God, do you think we live in a vacuum? I'm sitting here wondering for two hours if you're OK." Her eyes narrowed and focused on the door. And then, she noticed. "Oh my God, Ret! What happened to the car?!"

"Uh, a little vandalism."

"Vandalism? Who did this? Ret! Somebody wants to kill you. Did they kick the door too??"

"What? Calm down. No, the graffiti came before. I just had an accident on the way home."

"You just had an accident! Are you hurt??"

"I'm fine, Ruthie, I'm fine. I'm sorry I didn't call."

She shook her head slightly and crossed her arms. "Ret, that's a gang sign on our car and you absolutely know it. Do you think I don't?"

"What do you know about gang signs?"

She leaned down toward the door, felt the dent, and then ran her hand along the texture of the paint. Then she rose up, and faced me, feet spread. She was pretty mad.

"Ret, where do I work? I've had cross-training about this stuff since we moved out here. Quit acting like it's nothing. Tell me what happened"

"OK, a white coyote ran out in front of me and I smacked the guard rail. I'm sorry! I wasn't paying good attention. As to the tag, that was a separate thing. I've been working with some of the native kids near White Swan."

"You're closer in than just working with them. '187' means somebody really hates you. You've got to call the cops, Ret. God, look at this car!"

"Tribal cops already know. I'm fine. Some of the kids are gang-involved. You have to expect this kind of stuff. Don't worry."

I tried for some affection and distraction from the topic but she lifted my hand off her shoulder forcefully. "Expect this kind of stuff—no, I don't have to expect it! Take me seriously for once. You're scaring me. And you have to call Elisi."

"Why? I haven't even eaten yet. Geez, Ruthie, I'll call her in the morning."

"Because somebody died," she climbed up the porch stairs. "We're not done talking about this car, by the way."

"How do you know?"

"She told me! Ret, are you sure you're alright? You can't just keep driving around with that number painted on the car."

I followed her into the kitchen, barely succeeded in kissing her cheek, and earned another fiery glare for doing so.

"I'm sorry," I reiterated. "I should've called. I was in kind of strange place in my mind today." I pulled out some Andouille sausage I spotted on the top shelf of the fridge. "I'll take the car in tomorrow and get a quote to get it fixed."

"What strange place? And don't eat that. That's not yours. That's homemade for Henry from Delphine Ginderson." Mrs. Ginderson teaches with Ruthie at East Yakima Elementary. She's in her seventies and should retire. Henry's in his eighties and lives next door. Ruthie has been working on getting the two of them together for the last year. "Ret, what's the strange place?"

"Nothing, never mind," I said as I stuffed two slices of cheddar cheese and some pretzels in my mouth. "I went down to the River and didn't call ahead and should have. My appointment fell through and I decided not to go back to the clinic."

"You played hooky," she nodded knowingly. "So that's the strange place."

"Sort of. I did a bedside eval in the morning," I cut myself a hunk of salami and added it to my mix, watching her as I chewed.

"You're two hours late and don't call," she thought aloud. "You get vandalized and have an accident and don't call. And you're in a strange place in your mind. That's where you are." She walked out of the kitchen, obviously annoyed and hurt. She walked back into the kitchen appearing about the same.

"Ruthie, do I go down on my hands and knees? I didn't want to worry you. I really am sorry."

"Call Elisi, Ret," she started to walk back out. "And, oh, you might call me too whenever you think of it or can get around to it!"

I clearly had more to do to repair the damage and not just to the car. Returning Elisi's call would be a start because that's what she wanted me to do. I walked into the den looking for the phone, which is never on its base station.

"On the couch . . ." she said from the bedroom, dazzling me.

"That's what I was thinking," I responded, acting like I already knew, and now searching for the address book near the phone stand.

"On the coffee table . . ."

"God, how do you know?"

"You're very predictable," she said, lying on the bed, holding her Trollope novel, and watching me pace around looking for things. "Except, of course, when you're driving around on the rez."

"*Shix kláwit,*" said Elisi. "You keep late hours, doctor."

"Hi, *kála.* Ruthie wanted me to be sure to call."

"There's been another woman killed on the rez. My sister."

"Elisi . . . I'm so sorry . . ."

"She was a drinker, living up in a halfway house in the city, near Nob Hill and Fourth."

Her voice shook slightly as she spoke.

"I am very sorry."

"I need to come talk to you tomorrow morning."

"I'll have a time set aside."

"I don't want counseling, doctor. That's not what I'm meaning." She paused to get control of her emotions. "I want to talk to you about that girl in the children's court. You know."

"Ah. I can't really talk about my clients with other clients, *kála.*"

"You'll likely change your mind on that."

"I'd need a signed release from the client."

"Signatures on a piece of paper don't mean so much to Indian folks, doctor. Look at our history. I'll talk to you about that more in the morning. Now I needed to tell you something else, why I was asking your lovely *áyat* to be sure to have you call—you got to be aware of your spirit right now."

"Beware?"

"No, be aware. There's many things going on, unusual things for you, being raised a white man and not really knowing any better." Her voice became softer. "You're being brought to something you might not understand."

"There's a lot I don't understand."

"Good to notice. You're still a child and don't see the dangers. I want you to pay attention to anything unusual happens to you from here on out, especially in your dreams."

"You're being so mysterious, *kála*, and we psychologists get taught to pay attention to dreams."

"Not in the way I'm saying."

"*Kála*, do you have to be so cryptic? What do you mean?"

She bristled.

"Listen! This isn't some hippy-dippy crap. I hold onto fifteen thousand years of history coming through my grandma says you need to listen to me now. When I say you've been sent here, believe it. Get out of your books. Things are different now. My sister is dead. There's no more hope for her in this life." Her voice broke again, and she struggled to speak. I was sure what she was telling me was coming from a place of terrible shock and grief. "There is great meaning in her death. The Creator woke me up to this big spiritual change, and I now understand that you're caught up in it. So do what I say. Tell me as soon as possible about any dreams you remember." Her voice was more urgent than I'd ever heard before.

"OK, sure, *kála* . . . and again, I'm sorry for your loss."

"I appreciate that, *kála*," she said, addressing me as another of her many adopted grandchildren. "I'll see you later in the morning around 10 am. Goodnight."

"I have an appointment at 10."

"Noon, then."

Ruthie was already asleep and the room was dark. I kicked the underside of the chair and dropped onto the bed harder than I planned—holding my shin bone in agony.

"Mmmm," she murmured.

"Sorry . . ." I grunted. She turned over and began to snore loudly. I tried to fall asleep.

"Ret, Ret, wake up!"

"What?? What . . .?"

"You kicked me!"

"Huh?"

"You kicked me . . . owww," she moaned. "Really hard!"

"Oooh. Sorry."

I'd been in a very deep sleep and started to fade back there.

"Well, it hurt!" She rolled away, holding her leg.

"Sorry, sweets," I muttered, more awake.

"Don't 'sweets' me. Did you have a bad dream or something?"

"I don't remember."

"Well, go back to sleep." She massaged her thigh. "God, if you do that again, you can sleep out in the living room."

"Sorry. I didn't mean to hurt you."

"Go back to sleep."

In the morning, Ruthie came out limping slightly from the bathroom grimacing. As she poured her coffee, she observed with saccharin sweetness, "I have a big bruise on my thigh. Want to see?"

"I'm really sorry, sweets."

"No 'sweets.' God, what is going on? You're banging up the car, trying to get yourself killed, don't tell me anything, and then kick me as hard as you can in the middle of the night! It hurts, Ret."

"I am really sorry. Please don't put all that stuff together in one package, Ruthie. Now, should we get it looked at?"

"You look at it—right now . . . you're the one who did it. It wasn't just some sort of light kick, you know."

She lifted her robe, revealing her beautiful, white legs.

"Look . . ."

The red imprint on her right upper thigh was beginning to turn purple in the middle.

"I'm going to limp around the classroom all day."

"God, Ruthie, I did that? I really am sorry."

"You never did anything like that before. I mean you toss and turn sometimes, but you never attacked me."

"It wasn't like I wanted to attack you," I said defensively.

She pondered me for a second, putting her finger to her chin inquisitively.

"Some part of you does," she said finally, "you're angry with me and don't know it. You're subconsciously enraged. That's why you're not telling me things and kicking me while I sleep. I could have you locked up."

"Intriguing," I responded with a leer.

"Stop," came her feigned annoyance, limping back to the bathroom.

She was still grouchy when I left. Ruthie was always a little grouchy in the morning but I hadn't helped things.

"Those too . . ."

"Nail clippers?"

"Yes, all sharps," said the officer behind the Plexiglas window box I'd already shoved my little utility tool into.

"All right, doctor, please pull the door when I buzz it." I entered a vestibule with two cameras at opposite upper corners.

A speaker crackled. "Go through the next door when it buzzes." I grabbed the knob too late.

"Sorry. Try again." This time, I walked through.

A male officer patted me down with a wand and flipped through the planner I brought in. "And you're here to see . . ." He didn't bother to look at me—same training academy as Tork, I concluded.

"Tessa Miyanashatawit. She was transferred here from Yakama Nation Tribal Jail last night."

"OK, doctor. Have a seat."

He led me into a small, fluorescent-lit room with an overhead camera dome and a round table bolted into the floor. The chairs were those ubiquitous, all-plastic, white lawn chairs. Hard to hurt anybody seriously hitting them over the head with one of these, I thought to myself. But you might make a knife out of the plastic, I pondered.

"Wait here, sir."

I sat down across from an enclosed command center from which you could see everywhere across Yakima County Juvenile Detention Facility. That was the only interesting spot near me. I was on the outside of it, looking in.

My surrounding décor was pink, which I read somewhere is supposed to be calming, but I found it ugly and jarring. The little room I was in was in the back of some sort of day room or lunch room. The portable tables were all folded up.

Nothing was going on. No one was around. I spent fifteen minutes of nothingness doodling on my planner. I checked my voicemail. Gail from tribal jail left me a voice message that another girl had been brought in and somehow got the word about Parker's rollover to Tessa, still awaiting her transfer to the All Nations program in Cle Elum. She'd started cutting, and they'd had to call in the crisis folks. A female officer came out the door of the command center and clip-clopped officiously over to me. She leaned in the doorway.

"Dr. Barlow?" I nodded. "I'm sorry. There's been some mistake. Your client, Tessa, was transferred early this morning."

"Transferred?" I was unhappy.

"Yes," she explained, "we don't do psych watches here, at least, not for cutting or that sort of thing. She was sent over to the inpatient unit at Provincial Medical Center about three hours ago."

"Any idea how that came about?"

"Well, yes, we called the CDMHP," that's vernacular for 'county-designated mental health provider,' "early this morning. I was told they called you over at the clinic. I'm sorry that doesn't appear to have happened."

"I see. No, I didn't hear from anyone. The CDMHP said they spoke to someone at Yakama Indian Health clinic?" My voice had a certain vibration I was hoping wouldn't get taken the wrong way.

"Yes," she looked slightly flustered. I was grilling her a little. "I'm sorry. I'm the duty officer. I thought they'd called you."

"No. No one called me. Listen, it's all right. Perhaps they called someone, however. Do you keep a call log? It would help me follow up on my end."

"Sure," she raised her hand to her temple, thinking as she turned. "Give me a minute."

She returned promptly—which meant ten minutes later—and peered in again.

"Dr. Barlow, the log says a night officer spoke to Dominia Garcia, the on-call nurse. And the transfer note says the CDMHP talked for a while on the phone with Ms. Garcia before deciding to move Tessa over to inpatient at Provincial."

"Thanks so much for that."

It was 9 am, and Elisi wouldn't be in at the clinic for a few hours. I decided to head over to the hospital.

I wasn't in a hurry, but I drove fast. I was really angry, and I still had a bent fender which rattled as I sped along with '187' painted on my passenger door.

"I'm Dr. Barlow from IHS. Can I speak with Dr. Fitzsimmons, please?"

I gripped the front desk at Provincial hard after standing in line for several minutes.

"I'll just see if she's in," said the receptionist as he picked up the phone and leafed through a small booklet. He muttered as I stood simmering but I caught the gist.

"Yes, ma'am, a Dr. Barlow... Dr. Fitzsimmons... from Indian Health, no, not on the affiliated provider list that I can see. Yes, I can hold."

I got mad all over again.

"Tell her this is my patient, and I've been working with her for the last year."

He looked up at me without seeming to hear or understand. He muttered a few more words and put the phone down softly, smiling affably at me. It would've been stupid to tell them what I said anyway.

"Yes, Dr. Barlow, if you'll just have a seat, Dr. Fitzsimmons' nurse said she can talk to you after rounds."

"How long will that be?"

"I'm sorry. I'm not certain, sir."

It was half an hour.

My guess was that Fitzsimmons had no rounds or other commitments and was just enjoying her fun. We had a little history.

I saw her walking up from behind the receptionist with her put-on smile, upright, perfect hair and posture, and in heels, lab coat with matching pens, and her eyebrows lifted in slight deference to my frumpy jacket and jeans. She looked like one of the doctors you see endorsing women's skin products on an infomercial.

"Greetings, Ret! Great to see you," she began, holding out her hand.

I saluted casually instead of shaking, which she clearly noticed. Her smile drooped ever so slightly.

"Margaret, I need to see a patient you have, Tessa Miyanashatawit."

She feigned contemplation. She knew exactly who I was talking about.

"Oh yes. The bipolar Indian girl who's self-mutilating."

"So you say . . ."

"Ret, let's not go there. I've already consulted with Dominia. Come on down off the high horse and talk to the rest of us."

"Look, this is your turf, and I'm not here to challenge that or interfere. But I've been working with this girl and her family for quite a long while. She's not Dominia's client. She's mine. I need you to respect that."

"I really do doubt she'll be willing to see you. We've had to put her in the quiet room and she's decompensated."

"I might be able to help . . ."

"Or make it worse. Why not come back tomorrow? We're unlikely to hold her more than 48 hours."

"Margaret, please . . ."

Her eyebrows rose slightly, revealing the subtle strokes of my painful obsequiousness on her narcissism.

"OK. But one of my staff will have to be there," she said with slight sanctimony.

"I'm a licensed psychologist."

"Who has no provider privileges with Provincial. I'm allowing you access as a courtesy and nothing more. And since she's currently agitated, I can provide you with no more than 15 minutes."

"Come on . . ."

"Take it or leave it. I still believe she'll be in no mood. I'm trusting you're professional enough to back off. You do have inpatient experience?" Such a question was clearly intended to cut, but I let it slide.

"Four years of it. Would you like to see my resume? I have it on my thumb drive." I held it up on my keychain—the ultimate kiss-ass, I thought to myself.

"I'm sure that's unnecessary," she continued. "Follow me."

There was no small talk in the elevator. She ushered me through signing in at a number of places and then introduced me to a social worker named Sherman Jarvis who seemed nice enough. She made her polite goodbyes, resuming her plastic smile and cordiality by extending her hand again. This time I shook it, despite my better instincts, and she walked off. Sherman gestured for me to follow him.

"Dr. Fitzsimmons speaks highly of you . . ." he said.

"She does?" I asked with open skepticism.

"Well, yes, she has," continued Sherman with a glimmer in his eyes. "She described a unique diagnosis you had reportedly made. Something 'post-colonial.'"

"Stress disorder," I offered. "Where'd she learn about that?"

"She heard about it from her cousin, Dominia Garcia," he answered. Again, there was a slightly satirical look on his face, "She called it 'creative psycho-diagnosis' or something like that."

"Great. They're cousins," I responded. "I have my own in-house gossip columnist."

"Don't worry about Margaret and her foibles. You just adapt," he sighed. And then I knew he might not be her biggest fan.

"Can you fill me in more on Tessa?"

"Uh, from reading her chart, she's only been here for about 5 hours, but she's managed to get some attention. She was brought in for slicing and gouging her legs and making a mess over at the tribal jail. There's been two code 99s called on her so far." I looked confused. "Our language for behavioral crisis. That's why she's in the quiet room. She swung at another Indian girl in here and then cursed out a staff member."

He paused as we came up on the quiet room itself to look me in the eye. "She does that sort of thing again, doctor, and it won't be pretty. Margaret likes to carry around injections of haloperidol. She favors four-point restraints. She has no concept of psychotherapy and doesn't really believe in it—post-modern or otherwise." He winked. "Here we are."

He opened a special thickened door with acoustical tiles on both sides and a small window in its center.

"Tessa, you have a visitor . . ."

I peered into the room, and she was sitting in a hospital gown and bathrobe with her hands crossed in her lap on a single bed. Dark red lines of superficial cuts crossed both her thighs and mixed with two short troughs that had been sutured shut.

She swung her head toward me, only to say, "Fuck off."

"Hi, Tessa, and how are you? Can we talk?"

"No, I'm not in the mood."

"I can see that. But maybe we could try to talk a little."

"Leave me alone."

Sherman stood at the door.

"Dr. Barlow, listen," he said. "under the circumstances, I'm beginning to think . . ."

"I get it," I said, not without frustration. "If I had a chair and could just sit outside the door for a bit maybe . . ."

"I don't think Margaret would go for that."

As I moved away from the door, Tessa stood up and picked up her mattress.

"Tessa," I cautioned.

"Fuck off!" She screamed as she ran at the closing door with the mattress.

"Shit," I said as I turned toward Sherman.

"Damn," said Sherman, staring at the covered window.

"Take the mattress down from the window, Tessa," he said loudly. Nothing happened. Then he looked at me, "I can't have her do that. We have to be able to see her. There's no camera in there."

"Great," I recognized the implications.

He moved over to a nearby phone and punched several numbers. His own voice came over the speakers above us. "This is Mr. Jarvis. Code 99 in the quiet room."

I heard the sound of scampering feet before I saw three buff-looking white men and a buff-looking white woman running up. They were all young and had on matching blue polo shirts with the Provincial Medical Center logo embossed on their pockets.

Jarvis looked at me with reluctance all over his face. "She's got the mattress in the window and won't take it down," he said to a muscular guy in the front, keeping his eyes on me.

"Tessa," muscle man leaned against the door. "Tessa, you have to take down the mattress. You can't put the mattress in the window. We have to be able to see you."

"Fuck off," came a muffled reply. "Fuck all you white people! I want out of here! I want to go home! Get the fuck away!"

I stifled a laugh without any idea what was funny. The odds were better than four to one, and I knew who would win. Sometimes I laugh when I'm afraid and it can get me in trouble. I was afraid for her.

Muscle man scrunched his abundant eyebrows at my seemingly inappropriate laugh while he continued to 'intervene.' "Tessa, babe, if you can't control your behavior, we're going to have to help you."

With this, he pushed the quiet room door open. There didn't seem to be any resistance. The mattress just fell onto the floor. Tessa stood on the other side by the bed, rigid, with her fists clenched. "Don't come near me."

"Tessa, we can't have you putting the mattress up there like that, babe," said muscle man. "We're going to have to control your behavior for a time until you can do so yourself."

"Fuck you," she said. "You touch me, and I'll kick your ass."

Jarvis and I stood back from the door as muscle man moved forward with his three helpers behind him.

"I need you to move further back, Dr. Barlow," said Jarvis.

"No, thanks, I don't think I will." I had to witness what came next. His look transitioned from irritation to a modicum of understanding, and he nodded.

Muscle man moved forward more, still talking. "Tessa," he thumbed behind him to the girl who was holding several padded leather belts. I didn't notice them before; they seemed to appear out of nowhere. "Babe, we have to have you put these on you. I need you to cooperate with that. OK?"

"Fuck no. And I'm not your 'babe,' asshole."

Her eyes widened. She looked wild with rage and fear.

"We're not going to keep them on long," continued muscle man. Other than his voice, no one talked. The others moved only when he did. "Just until you can get control of yourself."

"No way," she licked her lips. I recognized what was happening—her heart rate was amping up; her mouth was terribly dry; she was threatened and had nowhere to go. She had been in this place many times before. I could see her beginning to crouch, ready to spring.

"Now," said muscle man and, surprisingly, the other three stopped moving forward behind him. Instead, they grabbed the mattress by the door. En masse, they moved toward Tessa. She jumped at them but they were too quick and shoved her against the wall, pinning her behind the mattress.

"Fuck!" she screamed. "Fucking assholes!"

My own heart rate accelerated, and my muscles tensed. I wanted to stop them; I wanted to fight. No one could stop what was happening. Her right fist struggled around the mattress and tried to swing at muscle man. He grabbed it deftly as the female helper moved in and attached one of the belts to her wrist. Tessa struggled to shake free, but she couldn't with all the weight coming on her.

"Careful, let her breathe," said muscle man.

"Motherfucker!" she yelled as she tried to double over low and slide under the mattress in order to escape. But the female had her other arm now and slipped the belt on it from above. She yanked on it while the other three continued to push her up against the wall.

"OW!" screamed Tessa. "You're breaking my fucking arm! OW!"

"Bag!" yelled muscle man.

One of the guys reached into his back pocket and pulled out a screened bag. They lowered the mattress enough to show her head, and she tried to spit. He dropped the bag down over her head all in one motion, and she couldn't take it off with both her wrists bound and held by the entire team.

"Move!" came a yell behind me as Dr. Margaret Fitzsimmons shoved me in the center of my back. "I knew this wasn't a good idea in the first place." Her glance shot mixed anger and contempt as she stepped in. "It's more trouble than it's worth to have you come in here and destabilize my patients, Barlow."

Muscle man wrestled Tessa on top of the mattress which was now on the floor. There wasn't much problem involved with four against one, and they knew exactly how to do this.

Restraints were attached quickly to her ankles as Fitzsimmons crouched over her.

"No," begged Tessa. "Please don't. Please don't." She was dissociating, lost in traumatic reenactment. Her mind was hardly with us. "Please don't."

"Please don't," I echoed, and Sherman touched me on the arm and shook his head.

"This is what happens, Tessa," said Fitzsimmons with mock gentleness, slightly out of breath, holding up a hypodermic she'd just produced from her lab coat pocket. "I didn't make this happen, you did. We can't have you acting unsafely. When you're in an acute bipolar episode, you have to take your medication to avoid this kind of situation. Listen to Dominia's advice. You wouldn't be in this situation if you'd followed medical advice."

"I'm not! I'm not in an episode! I'll be good!" yelled Tessa.

"This will calm you, dear," and she plunged the needle into her shoulder as Tessa screamed.

I continued standing there, knowing everyone wanted me out. I didn't care.

Minutes passed in silence, broken only by Tessa's inarticulate moans. Slowly the crisis team rose up from her as she went limp, her body soaked with sweat. They pulled the hood off. Her hair was ragged and her eyes rolled back in her head as they shifted the entire mattress with her on it onto the bed frame. They attached the restraints to the bed frame posts.

Fitzsimmons got up and walked out. Her phony smile was still there. "Post-colonial stress disorder, Barlow, really, what an insult to intelligence. You need to hit the books on what constitutes a bipolar crash."

I didn't respond. Then, I thought of something to say.

"*Walak'ikláama.*" A person who ties another up in bondage.

She glanced back at me as she continued down the hall. It was further evidence of my craziness. She kept walking.

A chair was brought in and one of the team came back and sat down with a magazine in hand next to Tessa.

Sherman Jarvis was still behind me, and I turned back toward him.

"I think you better go, Dr. Barlow."

I handed him my card. "Can you keep me advised of what happens with her?" I must have looked somewhat pitiful because his expression softened.

"Of course. She'll likely be fully-stabilized in a day or two and then be sent off to Cle Elum. Provided I can still put a good face on all this and persuade them to take her."

"Stabilized?"

"You know what I mean," he confessed.

"I do now."

## Seven

The worthless characters, known as liquor-sellers who infest this portion of our country have been a source of annoyance to me and to our Indians. When the Indian goes to the fishery, or the mountains to gather berries, or to the nearest town, these miserable wretches follow him and tempt him, and are bringing about his destruction . . .
-*A.A. Bancroft, Yakama Indian Agent, 1862*

"You're late," said Elisi, as I walked past reception. She was sitting in the small waiting area near my office.

"It's not like you to use the clock on me," I retorted. I was in a shitty mood.

"Let's go," she motioned. She followed me as I unlocked my office door and sat down as I took my coat off.

She asked immediately if I'd had any dreams. I was confused about why she was asking me this kind of question—I thought I was supposed to be the therapist. I told her about kicking Ruthie, and she found it pretty amusing.

She laughed quietly, "She mad? She should call the cops."

"Yeah, she mentioned that." I had an instant regret about not even remembering her sister's death after the experiences I'd had in the morning. "Are you alright, *kála*?" I asked.

I have a sandbox on my table with small stones and a little rake in it. She picked up the rake and neatened the sand.

Her eyes were red and glassy as she peered down at and then fiddled with the colored stones. After a few moments, she set the rake down absently and stared off into the corner. I don't have any window to look outside, being on the Indian side of the hallway. I switched off the glaring overhead fluorescent I sometimes use when I'm reading and turned on my desk and table lamps instead. It was the best I could do to set a warmer tone for us.

"Tribal police and the Yakima sheriff interviewed my brother and me yesterday. He identified her body. I just couldn't do it." Her eyes filled and, grabbing a tissue, she blew her nose. "We had lots of fights and arguments. I haven't seen her in twelve years or more, just argued with her on the phone. I'd say the same thing every time—get help, get sober, stop using, I'll take you to a program, all that." She paused and then sighed. "She was murdered. The coroner said she'd been strangled. She'd been out there about two weeks. A couple of boys found her. Third woman they've found dead out near Brownstown in as many years."

"*Kála*, that's an awful thing. It's just terrible. Ruthie's and my sympathies are with you and your family."

She pulled back hard from her tears and stuffed several tissues into her bag. "I appreciate it." She forced herself upright. "Funeral's tomorrow over at Satus Longhouse."

"Is the FBI involved?" I asked. Then she looked right at me and the anguish in her eyes made me instantly regret my question.

"I wouldn't know. Any felony crime on reservation land is an FBI responsibility. But they don't do anything."

Embarrassment combined with the stupid look on my face.

"You wouldn't know, doctor. FBI don't care about Indian people. Twenty deaths in the last fifteen years on this reservation, almost all Indian women; they never do anything.

Leonard Peltier and Wounded Knee and AIM in the 70s still sticks with them; not that they ever gave two cents for dead Indians before then."

She picked up her bag and stowed it next to her. Then she looked straight at me again with a clearer expression.

"Tessa is my grandniece."

Here, I slipped, knowing full well I should've avoided acknowledging the name of another client. It seemed stupid after all of us meeting up in children's court. "I never knew that."

"We could fill the Herke hop kiln with what you don't know, doctor. Tessa doesn't know either. Her grandma Georgina was my half-sister."

"How is it you're Georgina's sister?"

"My dad had an affair. In the days when he was a fisherman."

"Ah."

"We used to have a fish stand up U.S. 30 on the Oregon side. But when they flooded out Celilo Falls to open up John Day Dam, he went out of work." She tipped her head to her bag as though she would bead but didn't. "Oh, Corps of Engineers said they'd build seventy new fishing sites for us right they finished Bonneville. They built maybe ten or so over the next eighty years. Meantime, the river fishermen got all put out of work, our ancient resting places got all flooded out, and our way of life was destroyed. Not a federal government priority, right? The Corps made a very nice windsurfing park for all the German tourists, though. You don't see many Yakama windsurfers, do you?"

Now, she pulled out her beadwork and set to it.

"All those men and the rest of us ever since carry that great spiritual wound of the flooding out of our way of life. Before then, my dad never took a drink in his life. He was Shaker Indian through and through and only spoke our language. But with the flooding, he got ashamed before his wife and kids. There was hard times and we got so poor. He lost his way. He would wander looking for work. He'd drink and that's how the affair started whereby my half-sister, Georgina, was born. But he kept all that under his hat out of shame and we didn't know anything about it until years and years went by."

She looked into the distance and visited her memory for a moment. "My sister who they found; she was part of all that. She watched him come and go but she never knew he had another family until I found out. She was real close to our dad and didn't understand why he was gone so much. She used to go out fishing with him, you know. And then, after the Falls got flooded out, they made it whereas he had to get a license to fish where he'd always fished. The Fish and Game police started shooting real bullets at any Indians dipping nets or for hunting the *yámaash*. This was all in the late 1950s, early 1960s, termination days, the federal government trying to drive us off our own land and into the city."

My mind moved between my own painful morning and the difficult memories she described. There was something in the sequence of my life right then that demanded I understand how witnessing Tessa forcibly restrained and medicated and hearing about Elisi's father could possibly fit together. It was as though I knew there was some intrinsic connection between the two seemingly disparate events if I could only discern it. She stared at me while I thought, lifting her brows quizzically, waiting for me to say something, to explain what I was thinking about. But I didn't have anything to say. I just wanted to keep listening to her. I looked down and tried to recompose myself.

She continued, "We got to where our bones were brittle and our bellies were big as people say. And my dad, he just couldn't stand seeing his children like that. My mom would yell at him how she didn't have enough food for all us kids and why didn't he go to the city and get trained. She come up in Mission Boarding School, you know. She had my oldest brother when she was only fifteen and he was much lighter-skinned than my daddy. I was fifty years old before I figured out how desperate she must have been. She was a fighter. She'd never allow herself to become a drinker like my dad. She stayed a mother to us and his new catting-around made her furious."

Elisi started beading faster, her needle picking six or eight in one motion, stringing them together with amazing skill. It was her turn to tell a story she needed to hear. "Oh, he'd shout out how, goddamnit, he'd never leave the river. Then they'd fight and she'd run around smacking us kids with anything she could find. And my sister would hang on him when he tried to walk out and beg him to stay."

She got quiet but kept beading, tears beginning to stream down her cheeks. "Not my mother, but my sister—she'd beg him not to go. She couldn't have been more than six or seven. It hurt her more than the rest of us when he left. I believe that's the time in our growing up that sent her to the streets. She gave up and pushed her pain into alcohol just like he did when she got older. Only my dad turned himself around and she never could."

I sat wordlessly as she sipped her water. She wiped her eyes, and then dived back into the beading. A large and beautiful rose was taking form on a wide piece of deerskin.

"*Kála,* what are you making?" I asked gently.

"Just something for my grandniece," she responded quickly, offering no additional information. "Around then, I went off to Chemawa school and then to live with my grandma, which was fortunate for me. My sisters and brothers stayed with hard times, and I had a lot of guilt about it."

Her face pointed toward the beadwork but crisscrossed with micro-expressions, shifting lips, flickering eyebrows, eyes widening and squinting in response to her inner reflections.

"You might say the flooding of Celilo Falls wrecked my family, really. Of course, nobody knew those jobs in the city were more white man lies until my uncle came back and said there weren't any. All that yelling and rage in our lives for nothing. And that all happened long before I met Georgina at the stick game."

"Stick game?"

"Yes, yes," she became impatient, and I was sorry I'd interrupted. "Like you see at the pow wows where families band together and face off. It's a gambling game."

I had stood and watched this game on many occasions but never understood how it worked. She was in no place to explain now.

"I wasn't playing and neither was she. I was about eighteen or twenty, I just can't really remember exactly. We had just met there and were joking around. And my dad come walking by. He hadn't been living with us for a long while but would drop back home with some money or some fish sometimes. My mom wouldn't speak or look at him when he come around."

"There we were at this stick game and he's walking by and glances at me and then Georgina and turns and walks away without one word. And this was very confusing. We were standing right next to each other." She paused, caught up in the image. "I tell you the Creator is so mysterious and no one can ever understand Him. I just happened to say out loud to myself something like, 'now why'd my dad go and walk away like that?' and she, Georgina, who I'd only met a few minutes before, she heard me say that, and she turned right around to me and she said, 'that ain't your dad; that's my dad!'"

"Wow."

"And I said 'What are you talking about? I don't believe you.' It made me mad, really. I called her a liar actually. I didn't believe her at all."

She took another sip of water and set her cup back down.

"But pretty soon, we got to talking and I knew it must be true. I didn't want to accept it at first but eventually I had to. Here's a picture of me and Georgina back then."

She pulled out an old black and white photograph from her purse. Elisi looked young and svelte, dressed in a white cotton dress with her hair bobbed. She had her arm around a smaller woman, clearly younger than her, with darker skin, eager eyes, straight black hair, and the same wide smile as Tessa had in happier moments.

"Did your mother know about Georgina?"

"Oh, sure, she did. She loved my dad even if she kept pushing him away. Of course, she was very hurt about what he'd done. Eventually a couple of the *twáti*, you know, real ones, the old women, medicine women, they come around and said 'you got all these children and you need to straighten up and follow the Lord.' I think he took all that, just their coming to talk to him, very seriously—like a warning. He gave up drinking right then and there and went back to her. And my mother took him back too. It must have been eight or nine years they'd been apart."

I waited for more.

"I want you to take me to see Tessa," she said out of the blue.

"Take you to see her?"

"Yes. I called up there to that substance addiction program she's getting sent to over to Cle Elum and they won't let me see her. They don't know we're related and she doesn't know me, not yet. You can get me in."

"How do you know she's being sent there? There may have been a delay." I couldn't say more but she already knew.

"Oh, doctor, that's all done with. Leila went up to Provincial Hospital and got her signed out. They're going to have a little hearing and get her off to treatment."

"*Kála*, I can't be talking about one client to another client."

"Well, that's sort of stupid, doctor. I know all about her anyway."

"And what do you mean about me taking you to this program?"

"You can make me a cultural advisor to you. Take me in to see her when you visit."

"*Kála*, I can't do anything like that without Tessa's permission. And I wasn't actually planning on visiting her there. I don't generally do that when kids are off at chemical dependency treatment."

"You need to go visit in this case. And how will you get her permission?"

"I'm not sure I should."

"You'd stand in the way of her finding out about me?"

She lowered her beading to look at me, and then pulled it back up before her face. "Trust me . . . this is a spiritual thing for you, doctor. I know you have your codes of conduct and all that. This is more than that. This is about doing what's right."

"*Kála*, I'd have to have a very good rationale for doing something like this. I'm in enough trouble around the clinic as it is."

"That's why they let you wander. They don't like you in the building here so they don't care if you wander off. Isn't the Creator wonderful? You've been sent here just so you can help my family. You and I could go over to that All Nations Center and they wouldn't even miss you."

"*Kála*, Tessa hates me right now. She won't even see me, let alone you."

"Well, she sure isn't indifferent about you; I can see that in the courtroom. You've gotten through to her—and you a white man. Maybe you have some baby-talker in you from the Indian blood in your family, I don't know. Maybe she has a father complex about you or something. Arnold sees it or he wouldn't let you have nothing to do with her."

She leaned forward with an expression I'd seen a time or two before—that of an elder authoritarian. In Yakama ways, this look was not to be trifled with. She peered at me with skepticism. "Now you listen to me. Arnold also knows all about this sister connection and also what I'm asking you do to do for me here. This is a family matter—not just about you working with Tessa. This is a request for your services and it's about family. This is about healing a family, do you understand? Before Georgina died, I came to visit her inside the healing chapel over at Toppenish hospital at her last moments. She was really sick."

She reached over and grabbed my hand as she spoke. It was very warm. "Just before she passed, she grabbed my hand like this. She had one foot in the spirit land. You could see it. We hadn't had enough time together over the years but we were fast friends and only a few seconds were left. Georgina looked to me and she said . . ." Elisi's eyes watered, "She said 'Sister, please take care of my granddaughter. She doesn't know who she is. I couldn't teach her enough.' And she said, 'Please, please, Elisi.'"

At this, Elisi dropped my hand and covered her eyes. Then she lowered her hands and spoke to the wall. For the first time, I noticed how the sentiment of loss and longing had been primarily responsible for the lines of her face.

"She said, 'She's not been taught to use her *kápin* or learned about her womanhood. She doesn't have her Indian name.'" She grabbed a tissue and dabbed her eyes. "I said I would take care of this for her, just before she passed. I made that promise to her and you're going to help me keep it, doctor. Georgina was the one sister I could help. I could never help my sister who I won't name—who fell to alcohol and the streets. But I'm going to help Tessa for her own future and for the memory of both my sisters. That's part of the journey I'm on."

Elisi composed herself and resolve crossed her face as she got back to beading. "You are going to do this. I don't care about whatever code you got. You are taking me to see her. Now is the time for that. It's part of your journey too."

"What is a *kápin*?" I tried changing the subject, not knowing how to respond to her insistence.

"It's the digging stick our girls use when they gather the bitter root and wild potatoes. It's what signifies a girl is now a woman, an *áyat*."

"Oh," I tried to think of a way to let her down easy. "*Kála*, I've never been to All Nations Center. I don't know anybody there. Tessa hates me now. I don't know if they'd even let me come visit her, let alone you coming along with me, and I doubt Tessa will have anything to do with me."

She got up from her chair slowly and smiled in my direction without looking at me. "You're a good man for all your faults. You'll find a way, doctor. Pray and you'll be guided."

She picked up her beadwork and put it in her bag, smiling at my befuddled expression. She moved toward the door before turning back toward me.

"You see, there's some kind of battle going on now—and it's between living and dying and right and wrong. I've been asked by the Creator to do something and I know you're supposed to help me. That's the healing that's coming to us. That's the therapy, doctor. Think on that because it's not just for Tessa—it's also for you."

Maybe it was the mood I was in from the morning, but she was getting through to me in some way she never had before.

"I enjoy hearing about these spiritual things you're saying," I admitted. "I've just never had much belief in those kinds of things."

"No, that's not it. You just don't understand how you can believe in them. Isn't that more like it, doctor? You're not accustomed to a Great Mystery guiding you, something you can't name or study or comprehend."

She seemed to have found me out and nodded with certainty at me. "Faith is not part of the white man's science, is it, doctor? But it's what keeps scientists searching—you can't deny it, can you? I have to go to my sister's dressing now. Search your heart and try out praying, doctor. You don't have to act all Christian and guilty about it. My people were praying for many thousands of years before Jesus became the greatest rabbi of the Jews. Prayer is reaching as far into the universe as you can while holding tight to the very center of yourself. And remember your dreams. I need to know about them."

"I'll hear from you soon," she mouthed back at me as she made her way down the hall.

Ruthie and I met up right away with Trick outside Satus Longhouse the next morning. He smiled widely at us.

"What's up, doc?"

My response was ignored as he hugged Ruthie. Then he galloped away, giving us both a teasing look, flicking his hand slightly to signal us to follow, his long, thick braids flipping up from his back while he jogged.

He's nearly an elder himself, someone people turn to for advice. But he bounces around like a little kid. He leads two local sweat lodges every week, works as a counselor at the tribal chemical dependency program, and sponsors sobriety for many folks. He often jokes out loud about his several years beneath a bridge in Seattle, smoking crack, doing burglaries and stealing to feed his addiction. I think he may have done prison time, but I never had the courage to ask.

As we roved behind him, a little boy ran up holding an iPod, calling out to him.

"Trick, look at this! My grandpa got it for me."

"That's good, cousin, that's very good."

"There's things you need to know." He turned to Ruthie and me, and his expression changed from playful to serious as he motioned us closer and the little boy went on his way. We took up residence on a couple of lawn chairs near the pow wow pavilion with several of his aunties, uncles, and cousins. "Elisi being my auntie and this woman who died also being my auntie, we got a lot of relatives around. You two are considered family here with us."

Trick introduced us to several people. Ruthie expressed sympathies to an older woman holding back tears. She nodded without looking at either of us. Instead, she extended her hand, touching each of ours ever so lightly with hers, and then touching her own heart. I was quite moved by the gesture. Trick told us later she was one of Elisi's sisters. Elisi and she had helped bathe their deceased sister's decrepit body during the overnight dressing vigil, adorning her hair with numerous eagle feathers and wrapping otter fur around her braids, brought by family members from as far away as Seattle, Spokane, Warm Springs, and Umatilla.

The mortician, Mr. Esmond from Toppenish Funeral Home, was unusually kind, although I noticed a tremor in his hand when I shook it. A sallow-faced white man with an ill-fitting tan suit, southwestern bolo, and straw cowboy hat, he'd been serving Yakama families for over fifty years. He prepared the decayed body as best he could for free. We learned he'd done this for reasons only known to him and had also done so with two bodies found near Harrah a few years earlier. Mrs. Esmond, a rotund, red-faced woman, mentioned to Ruthie that they'd donated the many flowers they brought. She walked off to finish arranging them inside the longhouse.

The flowers installed and the body delivered and dressed, Mr. Esmond closed up their empty hearse and moved back toward the longhouse to join his wife. Trick, Ruthie, and I followed them inside. At the door, Trick introduced Ruthie to Cherry and Amy, his older and younger sister, respectively, who took her to the woman's side of the longhouse.

"I met Cherry before at your house," said Ruthie to Trick. He looked bewildered.

"Sweat lodge last fall," Cherry punched her brother in the shoulder. "Dummy."

After holding my hand over my heart in the doorway and turning completely around counterclockwise, I walked inside. The seven drummers were taking their positions as I entered, standing on the slightly-raised wood flooring encircling the dance area. I was near the wall on the men's side, north, facing the women at the south across the dance floor. Pendleton blankets had been placed on top of the casket, which was laid at the west end of the longhouse dirt dance floor.

I could see Ruthie stand up alongside Cherry and Amy on the other side. Elisi was sitting with other elders in the front.

The drums began to beat in unison. With my right hand closed in a loose fist held over my heart, I began waving my arm up and down ever so slightly in time with the rhythm just as many other people were doing. The plaintive, mourning voice of the singer soared over the drums and numerous close family members began stepping out from both sides of the longhouse and onto the dance floor. They formed a long line in front of the casket. Elisi was first, then her sisters and female cousins. She appeared to be accompanied by at least seven or eight women, in any case. Several men followed, possibly brothers, cousins, nephews; I didn't know. Two of them appeared quite young. Many more people began to follow suit. All of the family members distanced themselves slightly from one another as their numbers stretched more than half way down the sixty or so yards of floor length.

Without exception, everyone was dressed traditionally, women in dark and quiet cotton print dresses with or without wide sashes about their waists, their feet clad in wondrously hand-beaded moccasins, several with jet black hair sometimes so long as to be down to their ankles, braided and wound with otter fur, and men also in deerskin moccasins, some with buckskin breeches, others instead with plain, worn-out jeans, most wearing ribbon shirts, several with ornately-beaded buckskin shirts. Some of the women covered their heads with tight-woven grass hats that looked like small, inverted baskets; others had positioned several large eagle feathers in their hair, either sideways or straight up.

As for me, I wore my very own ribbon shirt for the first time, black with blue ribbons, which I had purchased at a pow wow about six months earlier. It's called a 'tear shirt' by the Cherokees, having once made them out of the torn remnants of surplus cloth, charitable discards channeled through the federal government. At least this was how it had been explained to me. I thought I would feel awkward about wearing it, but I didn't.

The songs and rhythm of the drums grew in intensity as the family began to dance, surging together sideways and in tandem, hands held loose at their sides, carefully crossing their left foot in front of their right with a certain loose unity, touching the toe, setting it down while easing the right one over from behind, bobbing downwards slightly, moving away from the rhythm of the drums at the west end of the longhouse. Their faces were expressionless, their eyes straight ahead, their attitude attuned in contemplation, prayerful, and matching the tragic solemnity of the occasion. When they reached the end of the longhouse floor, they reversed their movement and came back.

The drums slowly began to beat louder and slightly faster as the singers' voices became more plaintive, allied with tears emerging on some cheeks. There is nothing like Yakama singing in the world. What for me was initially an indiscernible dialect chanted across drums, sounding quite foreign and atonal, now brought me great comfort. As soaring yells and chants intermingled with a sort of modal and minor key and a simple melody, I began to understand why Trick whispered in my ear on the way inside, "Listen to the drums; the drums can heal, doc."

The longhouse leader's voice broke in over a small PA system addressing the attendees on each side of the longhouse who watched the family members dance. "This is not the time for crying. Those of you who are shedding tears need to pull back. There will be a point for crying later in the time set aside for that purpose. Stop your tears now."

Several drew out tissues and dried their tears while others assumed flinty looks, moving their hands up and down in front of their hearts with somewhat greater intensity, as I did, as we all were doing. The drums, the singing, the movement of the family, the leader's structure—shifted me from witness to participant. I abandoned temporarily what I knew from my own world about the observation of tragedy and blended in with a more ancient combination of rhythm, movement, song, and emotional reticence, all aimed toward letting go, toward saying goodbye.

Although the longhouse was closed at the eastern end with a wall just like any other side, it seemed to me as though it suddenly became entirely open to the sky. The dancers neared the end of the longhouse, raising their arms high and in unison, then back down, coaxing Elisi's sister's spirit from her coffin, encouraging her flight from a distorted earthly body, physically lifting their arms to transport her above her troubled life, setting her down upon the ceremonial pathway of their moving fingertips, all pointing in the direction of the Infinite.

As I met up with Ruthie afterwards, Trick came up and hugged us both. He whispered in my ear, "There's more to come. You need to stop by. The old people been talking."

I asked, "What do you mean?"

"It's dark times. Come to sweat with me. You been told to by your elder anyway. You don't get cleansed, it could cause you trouble."

Having just been through a rather profound experience, I looked over the mourners heading to their cars. "What do you mean? Cause me trouble?"

"Might give you bad dreams, doc. Might make you sick, you keep working with all that negativity and malfunction.

Anyway, call me," he laughed and shook his head, looking back over his shoulder and heading for his pickup truck.

Ruthie and I ate at Villa Senor, and I had my favorite—chorizo burritos smothered with cheese. Not exactly low cal, but I was famished. We talked about the funeral, IHS, then kids at school and the small city politics of Yakima, the poverty of the south side facing off with the wealth up on Scenic Drive, and the juxtaposition of abundant harvest and near starvation in the same community.

Our conclusion was that Yakima Valley was a microcosm of everything good and bad about human beings.

Having brought ourselves to this point of philosophic elevation, we stopped on the way home to sit on the sidelines and watch a bunch of kids play soccer, which happens in so many city parks and fields in the early spring. Later on, the chill of evening and the red sun's rapid descent kept us bundled together on the front porch, watching the neighborhood kids chalk up the sidewalk for hopscotch. We retreated inside, and I was too tired to lay my head on her lap while she watched TV. I went to bed and passed out.

*I am standing in front of a structure that looks like a simple shelter, not unlike the manger in a nativity scene. It has four poles with a roof covered in reeds and grasses and is only about six or eight feet square. Underneath, a baby sits upright, looking content and safe. He or she smiles up at me, perhaps holding something, I'm not sure. To the baby's left are a sheep and a rooster.*

*To the baby's right is a beautiful red panther. I say red because I know it is a panther and she isn't black. She is more reddish brown with eyes that are yellow green. As I look, the panther pads slowly over to me. I stroke her head between the ears. Then I rub her jowls with both hands. I am not afraid at all.*

*The panther is friendly to me and begins to purr. I feel very comfortable.*

I didn't want to wake up, but I did. I noticed the clock read 3:33 in the morning. Ruthie was snoring, and I got up and used the toilet. It takes me awhile to fall back to sleep when she's snoring so loud. I reached into the night stand drawer and put some little rubber plugs in my ears. Night fell behind my eyes again like a velvet curtain.

*I am walking down the street toward a woman sitting in an intersection in the middle of a Western ghost town. It's like an old movie. There are tumbleweeds rolling down the street, just as you'd expect. Dust kicks up as the winds blows. She is wearing a Victorian dress with a very high collar, sitting in the kind of chair I've heard called 'bentwood,' and holding an ancient looking, leather-bound book. She opens the book to the middle as I walk up to her, and she points to a page. The page looks like a ledger, like an accounting book. On the top of the page, a word is entered,* Dhladatsi gigage.

*She says, "Remember that word."*

*I ask, "Who are you?"*

*She responds, "I'm John Ross' daughter." Hmm, I think to myself, John Ross, chief of the Cherokees during the Trail of Tears. I didn't know he had a daughter.*

I woke up again, rolled over, and looked at the clock. It read 4:44. *Dhladatsi gigage,* I scrawled onto a scrap piece of paper near my dresser in the dark.

In the morning, Ruthie woke me up. I'd overslept. She was dressed completely to go to school. There was a delighted look on her face.

"Come on, get up! Get out of bed . . . come outside."

She pulled me out of bed in my underwear and tried to drag me through the front door.

"Hang on, Ruthie!" I said with sleepy irritation. "I've only got my undies on."

"Hurry up or you'll miss it."

"Miss what?"

She grabbed my arm while I was tugging my pants on. "Come on!"

I labored out into the vivid blue sunlight and down onto the steps of the front porch near where she stood.

"Look!" she grinned and squinted, pointing upward. It was so excruciatingly bright, I couldn't see anything.

"What?"

"Damn it, Ret, look up there!" She pointed again and stared. "It's amazing!"

I squinted and studied until my eyes adjusted, and I spotted them. There were three of them—red-tailed hawks, two adults and a juvenile. They were hovering over our house.

"They're dancing," said Ruthie.

"Huh?"

She cupped her hand above her brow as she watched. "They keep shifting in and out of the center. One goes to the middle and hovers there; the other two fly in semi-circles and stay on either side. Then they trade places with him. It's like they're dancing!"

I watched her watching them and then looked up at the brightness as best I could as they traded places just as she said. It was fascinating.

"I'll bet they're teaching their little one to hunt," I suggested.

"Why don't they dive down and try to catch something then, smarty pants? No, they're dancing."

We were both transfixed, watching the three hawks hover and circle in and out right above our house.

"Ret," she said, "does it mean something? Do you think it means something?"

Ruthie's eyes smiled in the way they did when we first met, like those of a child constantly enraptured by the world just as it is.

"Yes, I do."

"Because why would they choose our house to do this over, Ret? Why would they choose our house?"

"Because you have bats in the belfry."

And I tickled her until she fell. But she got up fast and chased me into the backyard. I was too smart for her and circled back to the front. She came rushing around to the front, and I sprinted back again in my bare feet. The hawks flew above us, circling, and we circled back and forth below, laughing and laughing. I hadn't laughed that hard in a long time.

They say red-tailed hawks mate for life.

# Eight

> Coyote will precede me by some little time;
> and when you see him, you will know
> that the time is at hand.
> When I return,
> the spirits of the dead will accompany me,
> and after that there will be no spirit-land.
> All the people will live together . . .
> Then will things be made right
> and there will be much happiness.
> –*James Teit, Nespelum*

I crossed the lengthy path, opened the heavy front door, and stepped across to the front desk. The receptionist looked up at me, "You're up early."

"Is Trick in yet?"

"He's here. Go on down."

He was reading the newspaper at his desk. I surprised him.

"Hey! Come on in and have a seat."

As soon as I sat down, I saw pictures of panthers everywhere on his wall, an observation I'd never made before.

"Trick, how come you have all these pictures of panthers?"

"Those? Been there all the time I known you. Geez, you need to be come visit me more. Panther's my animal, *xáy*. My *pawaat-łá.* You know? You're not really supposed to tell your animal. But I can tell you, huh?"

"Trick, it's very weird. I dreamed of panthers last night."

He looked quizzical, "You did, did you? Well, the old people would say pay attention to that, you know."

"And there were red-tailed hawks hovering over our house this morning and flying in all four directions."

"Seven, doc—north, south, east, west, up, down, and especially inside you. Especially inside you, doc . . . hawks, huh? Teaching the young one was what that was."

"To hunt?"

"Or to dance," he laughed. "You don't think the animals dance, do you, doc?"

I shook my head.

"Now panthers, they're special. We call them cougars or mountain lions, but I always like the word panthers, like you said. They protect their young, you know. A mother panther, her claws come out when her young are threatened. She'll fight to the death for her young. She'll never abandon them. That's why I like her."

"Trick, have you ever heard an Indian word like *dhladatsi gigage*?"

He laughed, "What'd you say, doc?"

"*Dhladatsi gigage.*"

"Sounds like Oklahoma talk, doc. You learned how to speak it?"

"I don't know anything about Cherokee language."

"Where'd you hear that then, doc?"

"I heard it in a dream. Not about the panther, about this woman."

"Maybe something you ate."

"Hah, right. Chorizo burrito."

He rubbed his belly, "*Coma ahora, pague después*, huh, doc?"

"She was sitting in a ghost town. She was saying I needed to remember that word. She came to me and talked to me in a dream. After I dreamed of the panther. She said I needed to remember that word. *Dhladatsi gigage.*"

"You go ask Wilma up front. She's from Oklahoma. She's one of your people. She's Cherokee."

"Oh no, Trick. I'm too self-conscious. I'm not enrolled Cherokee, just another white man with history."

"What's that supposed to mean?" he looked at me slightly cross. "Stop with this wannabe mumbo jumbo. Your blood runs red, better claim it instead of getting worried about whether the federal government says you're an official Indian. Your ancestors are trying to tell you something so be respectful. Geez, find out what that dream means."

He opened his paper and began to read.

"Hmm. Another ethics complaint among our leaders. Hmm. I got to read my paper now, doctor. I'm not a smart man like you. So go on now. I don't want to talk to you until you learn more. I got to read my paper. Go on now and talk to Wilma."

With that, he shut me out. I walked back down the hall.

I'd had a bad experience along these lines, meeting up with some enrolled Cherokees at a conference one time and mentioning we might be related. They completely snubbed me from that point forward. They wouldn't talk to me at all or even look at me. I fit the stereotype—another white guy claiming Cherokee. It hurt them to hear such things from white people. It hurt me to have them respond like that.

I continued strolling slowly toward the reception area where Wilma sat. I'll find out some other way or some other time, I said to myself, as I reached for the exit door.

"Doc Barlow."

"Huh?" I turned back toward Wilma, sitting there, looking at me and holding the phone.

"Trick said you had something you wanted to ask me about."

"Uh," I shook my head. Goddamn it, he's cornered me, I thought.

"Uh, well, I guess, yeah." I walked to the counter. "I heard a word and didn't know what it meant. I was told it's an Indian word. *Dhladatsi gigage.*"

"Say that again?"

I tried . . . awkwardly. "*Dhla dat si gi ga ge,*" I repeated slowly.

"That sounds like Cherokee language. Do you speak it?"

"Not at all."

"I don't know what it means; I've never heard it before."

"Oh . . . OK. Well, thanks for trying."

"No, wait a minute. Let me make a call." She picked up a phone and dialed. "Auntie Ida, hi, Auntie. Yes, how are you?" She paused again. "Yes, we're coming with the boys on Saturday. Now can you help me with something for a second? Yes. I have a gentleman here and he's saying a word or words I don't know from our language. Can you see if you know it? Yes, he's right here. Yes, he's a white man. No, I don't know how he knows it; I want to see if you know what he's saying. OK. I'll have him say it."

She leaned forward, handing me the phone, "Here. Say the word again just like you said it the second time, slowly. See if my auntie knows."

I held the phone to my ear, "*Dhla dat si gi ga ge.*"

There was a pause on the other end before a creaky female voice on the other end said, "Say that again?"

"*Dhla dat si gi ga ge.*"

"Do you know Cherokee language, young man?"

"No, I don't ma'am."

"Well, that's interesting. That's very interesting. What you're saying there is *red panther*. That's what you're saying."

As I walked back into the clinic, Deborah stopped me at the desk.

"Elisi called. She asked how long are you going to wait to set things up." She eyed me somewhat suspiciously, knowing all my business and wondering how I'd answer.

"Call her and tell her I'll try," I answered resignedly, and her nod carried more approval than assent.

It proved much easier than I anticipated. Yes, they permitted outside clinicians to visit on a limited basis. No, they could not say who was there or not there as I well knew, but they could fax me a request for a release of information. For adolescent clients, they were accustomed to occasional resistance to seeing a clinician with whom they were working; the clinical director was accustomed to approving visits in such cases, provided it made clinical sense. A guardian's signature would be required on the release in any case. Fax the release back and then call for an appointment at that point.

I picked up the fax from Deborah, and she called Arnold Miyanashatawit. He happened to be over at the agency on some business and stopped by and signed it that afternoon. She faxed it back, and I set up time for the next morning even though I was supposed to be over at the school. I called there and cancelled. Deborah got Elisi on the phone and transferred her back into me.

"Piece of cake, then" she said, "Come pick me up in the early morning." Only a few moments later, she asked, "And did you have any dreams?"

I told her briefly but had a client coming in soon. After I got off the phone, I sat and stared at my computer screen for the few minutes. It wasn't even turned on. I just sat there staring, my sense of reality fractured in several places.

The client was a DNKA ('did not keep appointment'). Eventually, I powered up and started taking care of some email. I had the door cracked slightly in case Deborah wanted to let me know she'd shown up late. I didn't have my overhead lights on because I hate the glare. I had my desk lamp on instead. A few months earlier, I had stepped up onto my chair, lifted the false ceiling tile, and pulled the wires off the overhead speaker. It was an easy operation; I was tired of blaring announcements, "Dr. Gaillard, line two please, Dr. Gaillard, line two," and being told nothing could be done. I knew facilities management would make a big deal about doing it, and I also knew how to disconnect a speaker. So there was nothing at all hooked up above me, and the computer and the table lights were the only things on. These electrical descriptions become relevant in a moment.

There I sat, typing away, minding my own business.

CRACK!

It sounded like someone had clapped their hands as loud as they could immediately above my head. I nearly jumped out of my skin, flying up out of my seat, and spinning around. There was no one there. I looked toward the door, out the door, and no one there either. I thought my spiteful colleagues were playing a practical joke. I got on the chair and examined overhead; the speaker was still disconnected. I checked behind and around the computer—there was no circuit popped; everything was working fine. There was nothing present to explain what happened right above my head. I peered out into the hall, my heart still not settled. My colleagues' doors were all closed. I walked down to Deborah who was just setting the phone back down.

"Hi."

"Hi," I said, "You OK?"

"Why wouldn't I be?"

"I just had something weird happen."

"What?"

"A bang in my office. Like a . . . bang! A crack, really loud, right over my head. But there was no one there."

She looked nonplussed, opened a file drawer, put a couple things away, and took a sip of her coffee.

"Things like that happen here sometimes."

"What do you mean?"

"You're not the first one." The phone rang, and she held up her finger as she picked it up. She finished writing the message, said goodbye, and looked back up at me.

"Gardenia. Buy a gardenia. It's a stinky plant. They like that."

"Who?"

She cocked her head at me. "Doctor Barlow, I don't know who. Someone."

My look of pronounced skepticism brought a slight laugh. "I don't believe in ghosts, Deborah."

"Oh, you will on this reservation. Buy a gardenia, that's what I did. If they're friendly, they'll appreciate it. If not, they won't like the smell and they'll back away. Also, get some clean tobacco like that 'Natural Spirit' brand, not Marlboro or Winston. Sprinkle some out on the floor in the 4 directions, then light one and blow smoke in the directions too. All the while, pray and ask to be helped. Smudge your office when you're done."

"Where do I get a gardenia?"

"Over to the Walmart's where I got mine," she said, pointing to a small flowering plant on top of one of the filing cabinets I'd never noticed. I must have still had a look on my face. "I'm just telling you; it helped me. I don't have weird stuff happening near as often. Remember, this clinic was built on top of an Indian burial ground."

"Deborah," I couldn't contain myself, "that's the plotline to 'Poltergeist.'"

"Maybe it is," she smiled. "Maybe it is . . ."

"Quit trying to be spooky."

"Wasn't me who was being spooky, doctor," she winked. "It was someone else. And you're the one who's spooked, not me." She had me there.

My two o'clock did show, a young girl named Lorine. Art helps her talk, and I had some paper and markers ready. She's only thirteen, lives in foster care, and was dropped off by her caseworker. Lorine has some mild problems, an earlier history of seizures which have cleared up as she's gotten older. She can be kind of spacy. Dominia medicates all the kids in that foster home (there's six or so) and deemed Lorine psychotic. She's currently on Seroquel.

I knew by her last name Lorine is from a 'medicine family' up in Browning, Montana. She's Blackfoot Piikáni. When we first met, she taught me to say *'ni kso ko wa,'* a phrase she'd learned from a great uncle up there, a great and compassionate man with whom I'd once had the honor to sweat. He'd taught that phrase to me too, but I let her teach me again. It means 'all my relatives,' that is, we are all related.

Lorine and I might never have found common ground if not through the shared connection to her uncle. She'd gone through terrible physical abuse before she was finally removed from her last placement which was eventually shut down. She sleeps poorly and still has flashbacks. She's very quiet and drawing helps bring out some of the implicit and painful memories in a safe way.

We sat together while she drew. I was telling her she was a really good artist, looking down at her grimy hands moving across the paper she focused on. She glanced across the room for a second and then continued drawing while she talked.

"There's someone in here," she said casually.

"What do you mean?"

"She's nice. She's standing by the door."

She continued drawing as if nothing was the matter. The hair on the back of my neck stood up for no apparent reason.

"Who is she?"

"Who knows? I never saw her before." Again, she just kept drawing. My mind dwelled momentarily on the noise I'd heard, but I instead decided Lorine was communicating in metaphor and trying to tell me something.

"What does she look like?"

"She has on an old-fashioned dress. She looks old."

"And you never saw her before?"

"She's been dead a long time." She moved her marker while she talked to me.

"Does she say anything?"

Lorine looked up from her drawing. Then she looked near the door.

"Nope. She's just standing there next to the door checking you out."

"To see if I'm trustworthy," I offered. This is a metaphor, I thought.

She shrugged as she drew, "No. You're trustworthy. I have no idea why she's checking you out."

"Do you see dead people often?"

"Used to happen to me more when I was little. My grandma told me not to worry about it." She glanced up again. "She's speaking now. She says you need to pay attention."

"She says what?"

Lorine lifted up her drawing and turned it around to show me. She'd finished the bright sun and clouds with which she'd started but had added a gravestone with "RB, RIP" written across the top in big block letters.

She looked at me and in a calm voice said, "That's for you. She says remember."

"What's for me?"

"Ret Barlow, rest in peace. She wants you to watch out. She was trying to scare you without hurting you. She just wants you to remember."

"Remember what?"

"How do I know? She says you'd know . . . she just says she wants you to remember what she said."

Ron, the tribal cop I rode around with, was pulled up behind my car in the parking lot as I walked out. My rear window was partially smashed in and spray-painted with the number '56'.

"It means 'gunnin' and runnin'' in Blood language," he observed. "East Side Piru." He ran his tight-gloved hand lightly over the obliterated window and shook his head. "Geez, doctor, I guess they don't like you much—you must be getting in their way. You want to make a report?"

I did. After that, I drove the car to the dealership and they said it would take a couple of days. Insurance wouldn't cover the windshield. I had a thousand-dollar deductible for the rest of it. So we'd have to pay out-of-pocket to avoid having our rates go up. I decided Ruthie already knew about the rest of the damage to the car—why have her lying awake at night along with me about this latest development? It'd all be fixed anyway.

What I would have liked was some sort of peace treaty with Parker and his associates. Yet I was pretty sure his conditions would include having me backing off from working with Tessa. He wanted to scare me away from my professional commitment to helping her—help she'd begun to open up to for a time. The violence I saw done to my car scared me at first. By the time I left the dealership, I was more angry than scared. Parker and crew were trying to push me around. People often consider shrinks to be all warm and fuzzy. They actually thought they could push me away from working with somebody.

I don't push very easy.

## Nine

> Since the time this *tahmahnawis* was given me,
> I have followed it just as I was told . . .
> I now wish that all my friends,
> as my brothers and sisters,
> would keep this ruling with me,
> stay by it as I have . . .
> -*Nah-schoot*

"She said she's not talking to you or any old woman . . . pardon me," said Millie, the program director, a tall, austere woman who happened to be Spokane Indian, her tone diffident before Elisi.

It rained the entire drive, and now I sat next to her in a small, plainly decorated office, bleary-eyed, and working on my third cup of very weak coffee.

"Did you tell her what I said?" asked Elisi, "Did you say I knew Georgina?"

"Yes, but she didn't budge. She seems pretty angry at you in particular," Millie shot a look at me as though I must be guilty. "She seems to blame you for having to be here."

"She would. How's she doing?" I asked.

"She complies with groups and sits with her CD counselor. That's about it. She's not engaged."

"Sorry to hear that." Thirty-day programs don't do much unless a kid is motivated.

"She did come once to the girls' sweat lodge. The leader said she opened up a little in there. She's up at all hours of the night too, doesn't seem to want to settle."

"Scared," said Elisi.

"I guess," said the counselor. "So many of these kids come off the rez and are fish out of water. She said something in sweat about worries for her boyfriend. Things we hear all the time, wouldn't go into detail. People don't understand him; he's a good person; they're going to get hitched up someday. He's in danger, all the boys these girls like, you know, bad boys—always in danger. Now with her though, the counselor wrote up what she said in sweat. It was something—let me think . . . Oh, yeah, something about stealing guns or some such."

"That'd be Parker," I said. "I hope she's not in that stuff too deep with him."

Elisi reached inside her Pendleton jacket pocket.

"Give her this," she said.

She handed the counselor a small piece of beadwork, a homemade pin, not particularly skilled in the making from what I could see. It was round and about two inches in diameter with a couple of rings of beads making outer bands like a target. In the middle was something like a horse but the beads were too large to make it clear.

"Tell her we'll wait."

"What was that?" I asked as the counselor went back through the door to the lobby.

"It's a pin she made."

I leaned back, impressed. "*Kála,* where'd you get that?"

"Georgina, she asked me to take it."

She looked at me momentarily as though I was suspicious about the circumstances.

"She wanted me to have it. Told me before she passed. She pointed to it; she was wearing it on her hospital gown. Tessa wouldn't come down to see her like that—all thinned down and her hair falling out and ready to pass on. Not that Georgina really even wanted her too. I think she understood whereas most people wouldn't. But she give me the pin and I guess it was her way of saying 'goodbye.' She just looked up at me and said 'give this to her when I'm gone.'"

The floor counselor returned. Behind her—head down—stood Tessa, hair uncombed, even somewhat matted, and wearing grey sweats and an oversized Gonzaga University sweatshirt. She looked to me like she'd just woken up. The fire I had once known in her manner seemed only a candle flame at that moment.

"Thank you," said Elisi, then she whispered to me, "let me handle this."

"Hi Tessa," she rose and stepped forward just a little toward her. "I'm your Aunt Elisi."

"I don't have no Aunt Elisi," she sulked quietly.

"I'm your *kála's* sister."

"Then how come I never heard her say one word about you?"

"For various reasons. I'm sure you have questions. Let's go sit somewhere."

Tessa glanced at me.

"Does he have to come?"

"Dr. Barlow? Sure, Tessa, I got to have him with me while I'm here. He won't say anything. That's the rules." She looked at me. "Right?"

"Right," I agreed, reluctantly.

We moved into an empty meeting room the counselor had pointed out to us.

"This is just fine," Elisi motioned Tess to a chair. "How's it going for you here?"

Tessa shrugged.

"No one likes being caged up, do they?" Elisi observed.

"Where'd you get my grandma's pin?"

"That you made for her . . . well, of course, it's not mine." Elisi sighed lightly. Tessa opened her hand just a little and looked at it. "I know it might make you sad too. But she told me she wanted you to have it back, Tessa. She wanted me to be the one to give it to you."

"She never said nothing to me about you."

"I understand that. To tell you about me, she would have to tell you about where I come from and where she come from. And she might have felt somewhat uncomfortable doing that. Do you know much about your family, Tessa?"

"Not really."

From where I sat, she looked terribly dejected and depressed. She stared solemnly at a spot on the floor.

"Can you help me get back home?" she muttered. "I miss my brother and sisters. I need to go home."

"I know Tessa . . . you miss your friend Parker too," Elisi spoke with a sigh again.

Her head snapped up at both of us. "How would you know that?" She glared at me with bullets in her eyes.

Elisi saw. "Oh, you think Dr. Barlow told me. He didn't. No, I found out from other people."

"I hate this place," said Tessa. Then she looked right at me again, "And I hate him too."

"That's a very strong word. Let's not worry about that right now."

Elisi began talking to me as though Tessa was now superfluous. "This child doesn't really know herself very well and I know what that's like—she really can't be blamed."

She looked back at her; you could see Tessa's eyes shifting focus.

"I'm not a child," Tessa snapped quietly.

"Oh, you are to me, dear," said Elisi, and it couldn't be denied. "I'm afraid you always will be. After all, I'm near seventy-five years old, and I've seen a lot more life than you have. Do you think I was always this old? I used to be a fiery girl like you myself."

Tessa glanced at the clock on the wall as though she was bored. Elisi ignored her and turned back to me.

"They couldn't handle me in school either, you know. I went to school in Wapato when it was just a train stop before they built it up into a town. They thought of all of us Indians as dirty back then, did you know that? They thought we were all backwards, the white kids and their parents and their teachers."

She sat up straighter in her chair and spoke to me with considerable emphasis, although the talk was clearly for Tessa.

"When I come to the school, I didn't speak English, I only spoke our native language. I didn't want to speak English either. Not at all. And I didn't want any part of school. I had to wear a dress my grandma made me out of burlap. Do you know what a burlap dress looks like, doctor?"

I shrugged. After all, I'd agreed not to talk.

"Well, it looks simple and poor. It's all rough—scratches your skin but you get used to it. I had my hair done up all in tight braids. The kids looked to me and laughed when I came to the classroom on my first day."

I noticed Tessa was paying attention.

"The teacher she laughed too. She said 'don't mind this little Indian girl; she's very backwards, children.' Oh, I understood English a little but I refused to speak it. I knew what she said all right." She glanced at Tessa and back at me. "We spoke only our native language at home you know, doctor."

I had become Elisi's prop.

"My grandmother would have no English in our house. She went to school out to Fort Simcoe. She'd had her mouth washed out with soap; she'd been locked in that stockade out there for speaking our beautiful words." She shifted her posture toward Tessa. "That's somewhat like you, dear, isn't it? You won't give in even if you don't like being locked up, will you?"

Tessa didn't answer but was clearly engaged with what she was hearing. She wasn't pretending to boredom anymore, at least.

"Why, yes, dear, that's you. This was a long time ago. And my grandma, she was a lot like you too, you know. All headstrong." She turned toward me again, the captive audience. "Yes... Yakama girls. We're discussing Yakama Indian girls."

Tessa's head went up slightly at this idea as Elisi continued.

"And I can understand a Yakama girl not wanting to be in a place like this. Especially a Miyanashatawit."

"Why 'especially'?" Tessa sat up in her chair, listening now.

"Oh, I've known many Miyanashatawits. I went to high school with Irene Miyanashatawit. You know her?"

"No."

"Your grandpa never mentioned Aunt Irene? No, I don't suppose he did. She's been gone these many years. About your size too. She had your eyes. Yes, Irene Miyanashatawit. She would likely be a great-great auntie of yours if she was still alive."

"I never heard of her," said Tessa, now trying to diminish the story. Elisi ran right over her. You couldn't stop her.

"Well, that's right, you couldn't have so don't you worry about that. I can teach you about her and then you'll know your family better and not have to worry. I remember one time, there was a little white girl, Aida Harwood, from Harwood Orchards. Her father was an orchard owner and Aida had lice, you know? Who knows how she got them. It was more common then, I suppose. And she was a bad one. Aida snuck over to Irene's purse. We carried purses or book bags in those days."

Elisi paused to sip her water, and neither Tessa nor I moved.

"This has to be around 1950, not too long after the war ended. After the boys came home, you know. Why, Irene's dad, he was a big man. He went in to buy a beer and that bartender he said 'no Indians allowed' which was the wrong thing to say to a returning Yakama warrior. I guess he threw him through the window when it was still closed, mind you. That man would be a great-great uncle of yours." She chuckled. "Anyway, I'm getting off track somewhat and he's not the best example. Well, there was Aida Harwood, and it was between classes, and she's snuck over to Irene's purse and grabbed a hair brush out of it. She brushed her hair all through. You know, she got the lice from her own hair on there. I saw her do it myself. And then she set it back into Irene's purse. Then she set back down.

"When the class was settled, Aida raised her hand up. 'Teacher,' she says, 'Irene's got lice. I seen them on her brush.' So the teacher walked over, I don't remember her name, Mrs. Janssen or something like it. She took a look in Irene's purse and pulled that brush out. 'Oh you dirty Indians,' she says, And she made the class move their desks all back from Irene, all except us Indian kids. She made us all bunch up around Irene. She said, 'Birds of a feather' or some such."

"I hate people like that," said Tessa, and by this I knew Elisi had her hooked.

"They're hearts are black with hate, aren't they, dear? And we must not be anything like them. Our people believe words make a difference, you know. Hate is a very strong word, and you have to be careful with it. You've used it for the second time. A word is like medicine. It can be for good or bad. So think about that. Now, you're right and I knew Irene Miyanashatawit was angry, no doubt. But she had a way about her. She was a Miyanashatawit, you know. I don't think she really hated Aida."

Tessa looked unsatisfied. "She should have knocked hell out of her."

"Hmm," said Elisi. "That might feel good, I suppose. But that's not what Irene did. She knew her ways."

Tessa looked at her blankly.

"I can see you don't quite understand. I'd have to tell you more about the Miyanashatawit family in those old days."

At this point, a counselor opened the door and leaned in.

"Are you all going to be much longer in here?"

"Oh no," said Elisi. "We can leave now if you need the room."

"No!" shouted Tessa, obviously surprised at the strength of her own outburst, putting her hand up to her mouth immediately afterwards. The counselor nodded and ignored the yell.

"No worries, Tessa, I can find another space," she said.

Elisi looked at Tessa somewhat sternly after the counselor left.

"Tessa, you mustn't yell like that. That lady was trying to do her job."

"I just wanted to hear more," Tessa said defensively.

"I understand that. But you need to be careful not to hurt others. *Itm'āāksha,* Tessa."

"What?"

"*Itm'āāksha.* It's a beautiful word. It means be cautious and careful in all things, be peaceful, be restrained and responsible with what you say. *Itm'āāksha.* It takes so many English words to explain. Try saying it. *Itm'āāksha.*"

"*Itm'āāksha,*" Tessa struggled to sound it out.

"Oh, very good. You said it first time."

"I don't know my language. Only a few words my grandpa taught me and what I learned in Ms. Sampson's class at school."

"Don't worry about that. After all, many Yakama people don't know their language. That's nothing to be ashamed of. Our language was taken away from us by the white missionaries and do-gooders. Why should we be ashamed if so many of us don't know it well anymore? We just need take it back, you see. That's what we do about that situation. So now you know a new word, *Itm'āāksha*."

And Elisi's gentleness began to weave a spell on Tessa.

"*Itm'āāksha*," repeated Tessa.

"Yes, be proud of that word. In that word is your dignity and bearing. How you carry yourself. That's a quality you have as a Yakama person, part of what makes you Yakama. You must not let yourself be brought down by the negative behavior or meanness of other people. That lady there, she meant no harm to you, you know that. She was expressing herself and didn't know the room was important to us right now. So *itm'āāksha*, we don't hurt her or anyone else, unless it's in self-protection. To do so is against our ways."

I became invisible at this point. Tessa was transfixed on Elisi.

"Now, dear, you know about what happened to Haller's troops when they come to attack the Yakama families and bands back in the old days."

"I don't know. I never heard anything like that."

"Well, it's in some of the books the white man made, but as I told the doctor here, there's a lot of hot air in those books. We have our own stories, don't we? Anyway, you see this 'Major Haller' come up to Toppenish with his militia men. These were the white soldiers on horseback and they traveled right through White Swan not far from your *tíla*'s place, where you been living but before it was a town, of course. To really understand your relative, Irene Miyanashatawit, who really knew our history, having schooled herself on it, to understand her response to the terrible thing Aida Harwood did to her, Tessa, you need to know what the Miyanashatawits and the many other families did when they met up with Haller and his troops. They were very effective at protecting themselves."

Tessa smiled at this. "How?"

"They kept to the high ground. They didn't have much for guns, you know, except for just a few muskets. Do you know what they are?" Tessa nodded affirmatively. "Well, they traded with the whites and got these muskets to hunt with. They didn't have much else to fight with."

Elisi paused and sipped some more water.

"Still, they used their minds and they knew their land. They were excellent horse people too. They could ride like the wind. They did not have the good kinds of guns to fight the fancier rifles the cavalry men were carrying. So they took the high ground. You know the ridges by Union Gap, just as you're coming through from Yakima and onto the reservation?"

"Yes." I'd never heard Tessa say 'yes' before in any of our conversations.

"They moved all the mothers and children to a far spot on one of those ridges. Then, they took timbers and made a rampart of sorts at the top of the west ridge."

Tessa looked uncertain but Elisi already knew her question.

"It's like a protective wall bullets can't go through. They made several of these ramparts. They made the most of their position. Kamiakin, Owhi, and Skloom, they were all united about doing this, no matter what you might read in the white people's books. This was a time of great crisis. They were protecting our land from the white soldiers. Those soldiers were coming—lots of them."

"And the families of the Klickitat come to help. And the Miyanashatawit family of the *Piitl'iyawilá* band were among those people, your ancestors. The danger pulled our people together, rather than ripping them apart like these days. And after they got all ready, they waited . . . they just waited. They had placed lookouts."

Elisi gestured, swinging her hands lightly into the air. "They called out to one another in the meadowlark's tongue. They spoke to each other in the hawk's language. At night, they communicated like owls. Haller and his men set their camp up nearby. There were these birds talking all around them, and they didn't know. They thought they were going to punish these Indians." Tessa's eyes had a gleam in them. "Do you have a question, dear?"

"I wanted to know what for? Why were the white people trying to punish them?"

"Why, for killing the Indian agent Andrew Bolon. That was what for."

"Who was he?"

"To tell you the sum of it, there was a Yakama elder named Mosheel, and he mistook this Indian agent, Andrew Bolon, for another white man who was called Nathan Olney. You see, Nathan Olney had hung Mosheel's three cousins and Mosheel would have liked to have revenged their deaths. These cousins of his were from a band down in what is now called Oregon. The whites called them 'Bannocks.' Now agent Bolon did hang numerous Indians in his time, but Mosheel thought he was this Nathan Olney, who was a devil of a man. So Mosheel killed Bolon thinking he was killing Olney. The killing was a case of mistaken identity."

"Olney is a Yakama name," Tessa remarked. "I have friends who are Olney."

"It's an honorable name, Tessa. Remember many Yakama people married in with the whites and have white ancestors, so many of us have white or Mexican names. That don't make us less Yakama."

"My name is hard to say," said Tessa.

"You have a good name. Miyanashatawit is a good name."

Tessa shook her head, "You may not have heard about my cousins."

"Yes, I know what gets said about your name nowadays," said Elisi, "but it doesn't matter what shame your cousins bring on themselves, Miyanashatawit will always be an honorable name. To finish up . . . our warriors were behind those ramparts on the high ground when Haller and his men came on horseback. They waited and took careful aim with their three muskets. They were well-prepared and shot from above down on those intruders. As soon as the shooting started, seven hundred of our men come down from the hill on their ponies. They gave them a kind of hell they never bargained for. Why, the soldiers were getting set to attack but quickly mounted back up and started to run."

"They chased them."

"The horse was on our land before we were and has always been friend to the Yakama people. They have *yaych'ū'nal. Yaych'ū'nal.* They shared this quality with us. It means courage. It means running toward trouble even if you're afraid, not running away. Can you say it?"

"*Yaych'ū'nal,*" said Tessa, who seemed to radiate warmth as she did so, "I love horses."

"Good. They love you . . . because you're Yakama. Horses work for other people because they make them work. But they carry Yakama people on their backs because they want to."

"I've seen Yakama people thrown by wild horses at the Indian rodeo," challenged Tessa, trying out an idea.

"Oh, as for that, the horse was trying to teach them how to ride right and, in horse ways, it's disrespectful to get on without permission. The horse has to teach the rider too, you know. No, no . . . no Yakama has ever been thrown from a horse unless they didn't really have permission to be on their back in the first place."

"I never heard of that," Tessa said skeptically. "How do you even know a horse is giving you permission?"

"Oh, you'll know that. They'll let you know," Elisi answered as if this was self-obvious. "They'll let you know in their own way. Now what was the other word I taught you?"

"Uh . . . *itm'āāksha,*" Tess recalled.

"And it means?"

"Uh, to be careful, to not hurt anybody."

"And the other word you know now."

"*Yaych'ū'nal,* courage."

"Yes," said Elisi, "yes, this way of speaking comes naturally to you. The ponies had *yaych'ū'nal* and they came thundering down from the hills sharing it with the warriors riding them, chasing down Haller and his men. And the Miyanashatawits were there and they led everyone. They were strong riders. All the way across Toppenish Creek, over the ridges, through what would one day be Fort Simcoe, and all the way to the Dalles. Those white soldiers came back to the Dalles with their horses all worn out, carrying dead and wounded men. Not a single Indian died that day. And you know why?" Tessa shook her head. "Because they had a strategy. They were very intelligent people. They weren't all polluted by the white man's alcohol and drugs. They stuck to the high ground."

"And that's what I wanted to tell you because that's exactly what your relative Irene Miyanashatawit did with Aida Harwood. Oh, Irene was a very tough girl and there's no doubt in my mind she could've hurt Aida physically. Aida was not so tough. But Irene had *itm'āāksha.* She kept the high ground."

"I don't understand."

"Why, Tessa, I thought you might know. Irene was the first Miyanashatawit to go to college. She was valedictorian of Wapato High School in 1951. No, I'm afraid Irene knew better than to try to beat down old Aida. No Indian girl would get away with beating down a white girl back then. Why, things are not so different now."

"Irene worked very hard. There was everything possible against an Indian student going to college back then. She picked the hops in season, doing that back-breaking work all the while keeping up with her studies. She never had it easy like Aida. There were many white people didn't want her up there on the stage at commencement time. There were even a few Indians told her she was acting all white just by getting herself educated. But Irene Miyanashatawit, she gave that valedictorian speech up at that podium and from where I sat, I could watch Aida Harwood's face while she did it."

Elisi shook her head and laughed suddenly and loudly as she remembered.

"Aida sat there, staring straight ahead on our graduation day, not too smart herself, you know. She cared a lot about class and prestige. For Irene, being the top student was an achievement to honor her family, an example she could set for her brothers and sisters. She was never jealous or envious. Irene was a gentle and strong person. She had that quality, *itm'āāksha*, Tessa, is what I'm trying to tell you."

"Aida, however, sat and suffered in her envy because the only thing mattered for her was to be better than other people. And here'd she'd lost prestige to an Indian girl by the name of Irene Miyanashatawit. I will tell you this much. Irene became a teacher and come back home after her studies, back to Yakama Nation. She worked her whole life on this reservation, teaching little children. She founded our own Head Start program. And that day, when she was giving her speech? I saw her lean forward from up there, and she winked at Aida Harwood sitting back in the rear. And I know Aida saw her. You know how?"

Elisi's face opened up with joy.

Tessa shook her head.

"Why, she literally fell right off her chair!" She broke out in laughter and Tessa smiled in a way I'd never seen. "Those flimsy folding chairs they rented before they built the gym. There was Aida leaning back in one and that wink from Irene hit her like a punch in the nose. She fell right out of her chair."

Elisi went on chuckling, "I was there. I never did forget that. I'll always remember that . . . but I see we're out of time and we have to go."

Tessa jumped up as Elisi struggled to her feet.

"Will you come back again?"

"Sure I will. I come up to see you, didn't I? I'll come back again."

"But don't bring him," said Tessa looking at me.

"Hmm, no, I better. I like Dr. Barlow."

"I don't."

"Well, that's somewhat impolite for you to say, but I know you're working on some new ideas about yourself. Anyway, he's my ride so you'll have to see him if you want to see me."

Tessa held the door for Elisi as she exited and closed it on my foot before I walked through behind her. Then she glared harshly at me.

I took this as a good sign.

"I wanted to talk with you for a second," Gaillard caught me in the clinic hallway a few weeks later as he was coming up to the nurse's station.

"Sure," I followed him.

"Step inside my office," he jested because his space is a cubicle. I sat down next to his desk.

"Well, I got a call . . ."

Oh no, I thought, another 'issue' about me, I thought, and wore it on my face.

"No, no, nothing bad. I got a call from that All Tribes Center. Millie, the program director, she called."

"Yes? You mean All Nations?"

I really didn't appreciate her calling my boss without telling me, especially at this point in time.

"Yeah, I just thought I'd tell you. She seemed quite pleased about that girl you and Dominia were having trouble about—Tessa Miyanashatawit. She said she's going to all her sessions and meetings there and has really turned a corner. She said you've been coming up there a few times, and it really helped."

"Well, not exactly. I was the driver, really. I go up there with an elder."

"That's good thinking. And it's good evidence-based practice. These kids do sometimes really connect with the elders—and, provided you're working with the right one, you can make some progress." He grinned slightly with about as much upbeat expression as I'd ever seen him muster. "Anyway, I thought I'd let you know that you've done some good work there, Ret."

"Well, thanks for that, Bill. But like I say . . ."

"Good treatment planning."

"Ahh. Well, I can't even take credit there. You know, the elder, Elisi . . ."

"Oh yeah, Elisi, I know her. Yeah, she's a good one. Listen, I've got some dictation to do. Don't be so self-effacing. You did a good job. I know it hasn't been easy to fit in here . . ."

I left him, having tacitly accepted credit for Tessa's progress where I felt I'd done nothing. I walked back to my office and discovered Arnold Miyanashatawit had called twice.

"Hello, doc." His rez cell phone was working. "Yes, well, we were hoping to have you come out for a Shaker meeting at our place this Monday night. Tessa's coming home and like I once mentioned, I been wanting to get her brushed down as she gets back on the good Red Road."

"Are you sure she'd want me there, Arnold?"

"I had a talk with her about it, see. She said it was OK for you to come. Elisi suggested it."

I called Ruthie, and we spoke briefly about it. I'd been gone a lot lately in the evenings doing work. I made it clear I was going to simmer down and what an honor it was to be invited—never having been to a home Shaker meeting before. In retrospect, I pushed on her about it and didn't really listen. She gave in. It never occurred to me to invite her.

## Ten

*When not engaged in action they will sit whole days in one posture without opening their lips, and wrapped up in their narrow thoughts. They usually march in Indian file, that is to say, in a long line, at some distance from each other, without exchanging a word. They keep the same profound silence in rowing a canoe, unless they happen to be excited by some extraneous cause. -Francis Galton, 1865*

I arrived too early as usual, not being fully acculturated to the community's sense of time. Arnold greeted me at the door and talked with me.

"Doctor, you're as welcome here as any member of my family," he explained. "But these ways haven't been stole yet by the plastic shamans and New Agers."

I sensed a subtle worry. "Arnold, I won't mention what I experience to anyone."

"I don't care if you do as long as you respect what you witness. Not that you as a white man can't benefit from what we do here. But you have to be Indian to be Indian is what I'm saying." His remark seemed to have a double entendre for me in particular but I wasn't sure what to make of it.

I was escorted to the living room by Ce Ce where much of the furniture had been moved either out or up against the walls. Franklin's loud and lengthy cough culminated in a painful 'whoop!' from a bedroom in the rear. Leila, Tessa's aunt, waved at me as she opened the bedroom door and went inside. Arnold and several older women I didn't know were taking all the pictures down and turned two mirrors around to face the wall. I asked if I could help and was told to relax.

I sat in a folding chair forming part of a large circle. In the middle of the circle was another folding chair, and I theorized this would be for Tessa. There were many large candles lit and placed on a small table toward the edge of the room. Tessa rounded the corner carrying two more and set them on the table. She didn't look at me.

"Hello," she said to the air, and I realized there was no one else but me in the room.

"Hi, Tessa, welcome home."

"Thanks," she said and bounded back out of the room toward the kitchen.

Emily and Eloise came in, moving nearly in unison as they picked up toys and odds and ends and carried them out of the room. Eloise came back around the corner a second later, and I returned her silent wave.

As people began to arrive, they moved counterclockwise around those of us already seated and reached out to shake hands. We only lightly touched hands and then touched our hearts, like Elisi's sister had done with Ruthie and me at the funeral. Once again, I found the gesture emotionally powerful. After a guest rounded the circle doing this, he or she would sit down.

Eventually the room was full and several chairs had to be set up behind the circle. There were no white people present besides me. What I'd been invited to be a part of was technically illegal on Indian reservations until 1972 when Nixon signed the Native American Religious Freedom Act. There was no one there to explain anything to me, which was better because I wanted to participate in what was happening to the extent I could. I felt honored, but also alone and awkward.

The service began with several individuals rising and moving to the front of the room to speak and say prayers. Some told stories of being helped or saved from their own proclivities by holy forces. Some talked in English and others in Yakama. Between the speeches and prayers, long, mournful songs would be sung in Yakama. Three or four men and women eventually stood up and began to ring handbells, which were large and all in the same key. The volume of multiple handbells ringing in rhythm is very loud. The pitch was at the high end of mid-range, and I wasn't sure I could stand it for long at first, but I began to acclimate to their wide, true pitch resonating through me after a minute or so.

Eventually, Tessa came forward and sat in the chair, looking solemn and humble. The lights were made dim, and the room lit only by the candles. More bell ringers joined the others. Now the ringing became very, very loud. The rhythm seemed to synchronize with my heart rate. Over the top of the ringing, the participants sang mournful songs. I could not understand the words and assumed they were in Yakama.

A circle of people gradually formed around Tessa, seated with her back straight, eyes closed, palms resting on her knees, and both feet flat on the floor. They began to move in a slow dance around her. The bells rang and singing continued. My ears rang too.

Several people, including me, did not join in with this dance. For my part, I felt uncertain what to do. I followed the lead of others who weren't dancing, and we stood and held our right hands curled in a loose fist in front of our hearts, waving them slightly up and down to the rhythm of the bells, like I'd done in the longhouse. The bells rang, the dancing and song went on; we stood and waved up and down. The ringing, singing, and dancing continued without pause and, during all this time, the little children of the Miyanashatawit family sat on the sidelines, sometimes jumping up and moving their own little half-closed fists to the rhythm, then sitting back down and patiently waiting and watching their elders. Tessa, looking relaxed as she sat too, hardly moving or shifting the entire time as a mass of loved ones and friends circled continually around her to the bells.

I was told later the songs and dance are considered prayer; movement and singing formed the same healing prayers over and over. I glanced at my watch a couple of times in the candle glow. After two hours, the ceremony was still continuing, and I began wondering how long this might go for and regretting the estimated time I gave Ruthie. With nothing I could do about that, I soon dropped away from concerns about time, becoming slowly and subtly immersed in the endless singing, moving, ringing, and rhythm.

A woman I'd never seen strolled in from the rear of the home. She was the leader, a minister of sorts, dressed in vestments consisting of a white alb tied with a simple tan cincture. Accompanying her were two other women dressed in white nurse's dresses and wearing old-fashioned white nurse's caps. They broached the dancing circle which continued to sing, ring, and move. Now many people began to shake bodily while they danced. Within the circle, the minister stood in front of Tessa as the trembling nurses gently lifted her out of her chair to stand. As Tessa stood, the minister and nurses shook and trembled before her. They soon began laying their hands on her, gently moving them modestly over her body from her shoulders downward, raising them up and clapping them together upwards as if to remove what they had brushed off and send it to Heaven. Their motion was the same as what Elisi had done to me when I was angry after the contentious mental health 'service integration' meeting. Elisi soon walked in from the rear and began participating in brushing off her grandniece.

The dancing began to subside as everyone present began to be drawn into the activity of lightly brushing off Tessa's shoulders, back, arms, or hands and clapping negativity up toward Heaven. Someone came to us and tugged me and others along the edge into the circle. As the bells continued to sound and the songs to be sung, I was encouraged to reach out and lightly run my hand along Tessa's back.

Her eyes were still closed, and she stood relaxed, swaying slightly. I was terribly reluctant about this. I wondered deeply at the moment if I, as her white male therapist, should be touching her back. Absolutely positively no, all my training told me. One of the nurses smiled, grabbed my wrist, and gently but insistently pulled my hand forward. Soon I'd been compelled to join what everyone was engaged in and was clapping the negativity I drew off Tessa into the skies. This activity may have gone on for another quarter or half an hour; I lost track.

By the time the singing finally ceased, the voices sounded hoarse. As the bells stopped, my ears rang like I had been front row of a rock concert. A final mournful song was sung and the lights turned back on. The candles were extinguished one by one, the pictures replaced, and the mirrors turned back around. Several large folding tables were brought into the room and set up. I helped in moving all the folding chairs forward and in bringing food out.

There were traditional foods of salmon, venison, elk stew, elk jerky, wild potatoes, camas root, bitter root, and huckleberries. There was also fried chicken, baked beans, potato salads, huckleberry and cherry pie, ice cream, chips, and all sorts of soda pop. Paperware was placed all around the table and cups were filled with water.

I was directed to take a seat at the head of the table which was a complete shock. Arnold Miyanashatawit sat near the far end, and Leila sat at the opposite end smiling toward me. Elisi was on my right. She met my insecure expression with a Cheshire cat grin. I had no idea what was about to happen. At least thirty Indian people looked directly down the table at me expectantly. I felt my pale face going red at the public scrutiny.

"*Chiish!*" said Arnold, and everyone lifted their cups and took a sip of water.

Then we took a nibble of a little piece of salmon on our plates. Arnold spoke to me directly as if to explain what everyone else present already knew.

"In this way, we celebrate the water that brings us the salmon, doctor." He looked across the table and then, in a most mundane voice, noted, "Dr. Barlow will now offer a blessing for us . . ."

In my life, I'd never done such a thing. I had read a simple grace from a book my mother kept at Thanksgiving a couple of times as a boy, but I had no idea what to do. My professional role was completely shot. The room held silent. Everyone's eyes were closed, waiting for me.

"I'm not quite sure . . ." I stammered.

"Just say what's on your heart, doctor," said Elisi encouragingly. "Speak to your Creator, and we'll bear witness to your words."

She lowered her head and grabbed my right hand underneath the table. A woman I'd never met sitting on the other side grabbed my left hand. Eyes stayed closed, and now all hands were clasped around the table.

I had to speak. "Lord . . ." I wasn't sure where the words would come from. I hesitated but all of the sudden felt surprisingly moved and then my lips could not form words for a few moments.

"Creator . . . who we know by many names . . . we have come to this moment from many, many places . . . trying to understand this Great Mystery through which we suddenly find ourselves at the same table sharing food with one another, grateful to be brought together and cared for. There is such peace and love and kindness with us here right now; help us hold ourselves close to that in our lives from here on out. Thank you for allowing our paths to cross and helping us to find this circle of relatives, sisters and brothers and friends tonight. We are very grateful. I am very grateful." Again, I hesitated, overwhelmed by very warm hands holding mine, the circle itself, or some wider circle extending beyond me. "Please bless this home and family, particularly Tessa, who has been through so many difficulties and trials. She has returned home safely with her health returned. She's walking on a very good path now. Protect and safeguard her and her family and all of us gathered here. Thank you. Thank you."

Where these words came from, I did not know. They seemed to emerge rather than be composed by me. I heard several 'amens' as I raised my head, relieved to have made it through. The hands holding mine gently fell away. Elisi looked at me approvingly.

I noticed James, a middle-aged client of mine, sitting about in the middle and reaching for a roll as many dishes were passed around. I had just prayed fervently in front of him which I hadn't thought through at all. I had no informed consent in place to even say 'hello.' It was at his initiation if he wanted to acknowledge any contact with me, not mine. These are the predicaments of a psychologist inside the community, I thought to myself.

He passed the basket across to a guy across from him and said loudly, "Geez, cuz, you should get in for some counseling with doc there. He's helped me some. Since you and Zelda broke up, you probably have some things to talk about."

James turned toward me and smiled warmly as his cousin and fifteen other people leaned in to look me over again. Several people nodded with friendly expressions. Some people squinted. Some faces had no expression at all.

I waved and smiled back as nonchalantly as possible.

About 11 pm, after the last bite of huckleberry pie had been consumed, Arnold asked, "Everybody—if you don't mind, could you come outside for a few minutes?"

I didn't have cell phone reception and couldn't call Ruthie to tell her how long this was stretching out. I had no idea what to expect but still felt it might be rude to leave.

As soon as we stepped out the door, the dogs ran up, not barking but sniffing and following, excited at having twenty-five or so people moving across the yard by the light of the full moon following Arnold.

Tessa, Arnold, and Elisi were in the very front with children scampering back and forth but staying fairly close to them. We continued to wander further back through the brush near an old shed and then turned the corner.

I stumbled walking out in the dark, falling flat on my face, causing commotion and some giggling, embarrassing myself but without real injury. At the moment I tripped, I was trying to make out a couple of flashlights and two silhouettes standing next to a pickup truck with a horse trailer.

Tessa stopped dead in her tracks, parting company from Arnold and Elisi who continued moving forward. She stood staring ahead at an unfamiliar site: portable corral fencing stretching across the space behind the pickup. Arnold turned around, reached a gnarled hand out, and gently drew her forward, his arm now on her shoulder, bringing her up next to Elisi who stood at the fence with the kids. The two men with flashlights strolled up as Arnold spoke:

"Tessa, these are two more new relatives for you and your brothers and sisters to meet on your Auntie Elisi's side. This is Edward and Leon, uncles of yours. I known them both from some fishing we used to do together at the River, but we haven't seen one another in too long. That right, Ed? These men are both horsechasers. They're Yakama horsechasers and come from your own family. I'll bet you never thought of that . . ."

The two men shifted into the light of Leon's flashlight to reveal big smiles of limited teeth that had a brotherly similarity. Edward stepped forward.

"Hi." Tessa spoke shyly, glanced at them, distracted, trying to be polite, but her eyes stayed fixed on the rear of the corral.

"Is that a horse?" she asked them both.

"That is a horse," answered Leon to everyone's sudden burst of laughter as he moved his flashlight toward the small, muscular, deep brown animal grazing at the rear.

The moment the flashlight hit her, she backed onto her heels, then ran full gallop straight at all of us. We surged backwards; she kicked the fence hard, almost knocking it and us over. Her nostrils shot steam, and I thought of horsepower as an early expression of the locomotive. That's how hard she came at us.

We retreated involuntarily while she tried to jump up, swinging left and right, whinnying and neighing with her long tangled black mane flashing in the moonlight. Edward cooed softly at her, trying to calm her, as he and Leon braced the fence. I thought she would leap right over the corral but she backed away, charging around in circles, then back toward us threateningly. She was a very powerful animal, and we all stayed well away from the fence line.

"That is a she and she is your horse," Edward announced. Tessa appeared completely dazzled at this idea. "Now she's a little skittish and irritated with all these people and the noise . . . Your *tíla* and your auntie Elisi asked us to bring her by . . ."

"We all worked on the corral while you were gone to treatment," Arnold broke in. "We thought you might need something to help you on your way down that good Red Road when you come back home."

"She's what we call a Cayuse or Mustang, Tessa," continued Leon, "Or rather, she's what we call *k'úsi* in our language. She ain't gentled much but she's settled a bit. She's just a filly. She's been cooped up over to our place near Granger for a week." Several of us looked on, incredulous. If this was settled, what was she like before? "She might have a little mange, too. But you can't ask for a healthier horse overall then one bred to these hills here."

Tessa continued to watch, alternating stunned glances at Leon and Arnold, then fixating on this wild animal blasting back and forth against the moonlit shadows of tall grass and shrubs.

"How will I train her? I don't know how." She turned to Arnold, "How will we feed her? I don't know how to take care of her."

"Well, that's just the thing," said Elisi, coming forward, "These uncles, they're going to help you work with her. But when I say work, dear, you'll have to work every day if you want to ever be able to ride her. Right now, she's wild as can be, and she don't know you yet."

"As to feeding her," said Arnold, "we've got some here for her to graze and we can keep her watered for now."

"We brought a bale of alfalfa and a bag of oats," Leon added.

"But if we're going to get hay and feed and get the vet to look her over eventually, you're going to have to make that happen, Tessa," noted Arnold. "I can't afford it . . ."

He looked up and around when he said it.

"Can I ride her?" Eloise's voice cut in.

"Sure," Arnold said, "once your sister's got her to that point."

"Can I have a horse?" asked Ce Ce.

"You all can ride her," said Tessa, "if I can just keep her. But I don't have a job, though."

"Well," said Leila, "that's not entirely so. I talked to Mel, and he's got a need for a part-time hostess and table bus. I told him I thought you might be interested."

"I'll do it," said Tessa.

"Don't you want to hear what's involved? It's hard work and minimum wage with no hope of advancement . . ." smiled Leila.

"I'll do it."

"You have to keep your grades up, Tessa," said Arnold.

"I'll do that too."

Arnold turned back towards Elisi as I stepped up to see a little better. I saw him wink and nod. Several people came forward to congratulate Tessa and admire the filly.

"What you going to call her, Tessa?" asked Samuel.

"I'll call her . . . I'll call her. I don't know what to call her," she stared at the barely visible creature at the rear corner of the corral, alternating between grazing momentarily, running back and forth, and tossing her head toward the moon. "I want her to have a Yakama name. I want to call her something in our language."

"What would you call her in English?" asked Elisi.

Tessa gazed at the moon as the filly tossed her head again. "I'd call her Moon Child," Tessa responded.

"Moon Child, hmm . . ." Elisi thought for a moment. "Why not call her *Ámashitum?* That means Owl Child . . . owls favor the moon and the night."

"*Ámashitum . . . Ámashitum,*" Tessa moved tentatively toward the darker edge of the fence, "*Ámashitum.*"

The rest of us were quieter now. Leila whispered to several women. Edward lit a cigarette and, of course, I borrowed one. Leon, he, and I and several other men stood in the moonlight in a short circle. The children were tired. Ce Ce clung to her grandfather's leg.

"*Ámashitum . . .*" we heard Tessa softly calling.

"Tessa . . ." said Arnold, "we got to get these children settled."

Beneath dim flashlights and layers of crickets chirping, Arnold said, "It'd be good if some of you were to come back out when Leon and Edward'll be back out. Right?"

Edward explained, "What we want to do is get the filly here . . ." he turned to glance at Elisi, "*Ámash . . . Ámashitum,* gentled up . . . Some of you may have heard 'broken.' But that's not really Indian way, you know. We don't break a horse's spirit. We like saying 'gentled up' better. That's how we were raised . . . to make friends with the wild horse. We're going to gentle her up like a woman likes to be . . ." He chuckled, looking at Leila—who didn't chuckle at all—and his tone got more serious. "We're going to help her bond with niece Tessa here."

Arnold and Elisi turned back toward the house, and everyone followed. There was new energy in Elisi's seventy-five-year-old step. Unlike me, she never stumbled once on the way back, at least that I could see.

Ruthie joined me at breakfast after my three hours of sleep.

"I stayed up really late waiting for you to come home," she said. "I wanted to talk to you about my contract next year. They want me to teach 3$^{rd}$ grade."

"Ruthie, I'm sorry. I couldn't get cell reception out there. I couldn't leave."

"And you didn't want me tagging along."

"Well, it was sort of like the funeral and I knew you wouldn't really know anyone."

"I knew Cherry at the funeral."

"Yes, but not very well."

"Does 'not well' include going stark naked into sweat lodge with somebody?"

"Well, right, I'd forgotten that," I acknowledged lightly, chewing my toast, and not really understanding.

"Hmm," she gazed at me. "When you were at the Shaker meeting alone last night did you feel uncomfortable like you thought I would? Or is it like now you're less white than me so it's not really a problem?"

She scooped another mouthful of yogurt while I contemplated this perilous question.

"I'm not sure how to answer that . . . "

"Well, your wife is white. I don't have any Indian blood. I'm not on an ethnic identity search either. Maybe it's more comfortable to not have me with you when you're out on your rambles."

"I'm glad to have you with me anytime," I answered with mild defensiveness.

"Doesn't seem that way. . ." She shook her head. "And I'm wondering when you might start coming home on time occasionally like you use to do so we can at least talk about how our days went. I've been getting pretty sick of being single."

"I'm sorry, Ruthie . . ."

"Yes, you are. But it gets a little lonely even so. Even when you're here, you're staring off and unresponsive to half the things I say."

Her tone mixed frustration and hurt.

"I don't understand what you mean."

"What did I want to talk to you about last night?"

I paused and thought. We sat there looking at each other.

"Is this a test?" I asked.

"No, it's an example. You asked what I meant."

"Well, I'm sorry. I can't really remember what you said. It was something about school."

"Good. You heard the word 'school.'" Her eyes looked sad. "What else?"

"Um, I don't know," I set my fork down and sipped my coffee very quietly.

"No, you don't really know," she said and her eyes looked sad.

I struggled to say something. "Ruthie, there's some things that have been happening to me I don't really understand; I can't really explain . . ."

"I'd just like to know why you go off into outer space even when you're here with me. It's like I'm living alone in the same house with you."

She sat looking at me and waiting, but I could think of nothing more to say. I was tongue-tied, emotionally paralyzed—trained as a psychologist and now completely at a loss for words. So I just watched her while she watched me until her expression became angry and she got up from the table. She walked over and dropped her cup in the sink somewhat forcefully, moved slowly to the doorway with her eyes still on me, and looked me over one more time, giving me plenty of time to express myself. But I didn't. The silence between us became deafening.

Finally, she lifted her hands upward, shrugged deeply, and mouthed, "What??"

I still couldn't answer. I managed to mutter, "I don't know what to say. I've got a lot on my mind."

"Like what, Ret? Like what?" That was not a question I could figure out how to answer. She shook her head, spun back around, and stormed away, muttering, "OK, don't talk to me," slamming the bathroom door shut.

It's what makes her the most upset—when I shut down like that—and for me, fighting with Ruthie is truly an awful thing. We were in a fight about my emotional distance and it was my emotional distance which made it difficult for me to resolve our conflict. Our silent preparations for the day only further depressed me. I said "goodbye" and heard her quiet "bye" as I closed the door. No kiss, no hug.

Upset and estranged, I stormed down to a convenience store, bought a pack of Marlboro Reds, and drove fast on my way to work. My morning passed routinely with two clients and a brief visit to the school. At lunchtime, I sat on the edge of my front bumper, chain-smoked four cigarettes, wondered about my apparently urgent need to charge up my dopamine system, and tried to analyze why I was acting so distant from my wife.

A minor crisis regarding an overdue assessment report needed for a kid in juvenile detention set me back down typing at my desk at 4:30. I'd spaced out on getting it done; I was forgetting my regular duties. I got home about 9 pm, late again, feeling terribly guilty. I could tell right away she was already in bed. All the lights except the one in the front hall were off.

I opened the front door quietly, shut it even quieter, and stripped to my underwear in the dark. I crept into the bathroom and brushed my teeth. She hates it when I smoke and has a great sense of smell. I slipped into bed, lying down next to her as she either slept or pretended to sleep, I couldn't tell. The ceiling fan spun slowly overhead and the bedroom window just above my head was cracked open slightly. I could hear distant sirens.

I'd made myself so disconnected from her and felt very selfish. She was openly telling me she needed me, and I was lost to her. I reached out in the dark to touch her and couldn't bring myself to risk it.

I placed my right hand over my heart, feeling the heat of my own palm, marking my breath in my mind for a while, quieting my thoughts. And I asked the universe for help. I really felt the need for help. I guess I prayed, if that's what one might call it.

Then the night seemed to spin, and I could no longer keep my eyes open.

*I am at work near the clinic in a building that is very old and made out of barn wood. The Casino Events Center is across the street, and all the Indian Health departments are speaking at a conference there, including my mental health colleagues. I feel I should get over there. But I wasn't invited and don't even know what the conference is about. I am very concerned about Dominia and what she'll say. Two Indian guys drive up to where I'm standing and want me to ride with them. I go with them but don't understand what we're doing or where we're going.*

*We pull into a housing project with many small frame houses. I cross the street to get to one of them, and there is a tiny squirrel near my feet following me. Indian people and the guys I came with are cooing at the squirrel from the other side of the street. One says, "Can you bring her over?" And I respond, "Sure," but I don't pick her up, I don't want to. I think she might bite me. But she stays right alongside me as I cross. We get to the other side, and I stand on the lawn of this little house with a white picket fence. There are giant piles of shit all over the lawn. At first, I think, 'What is all this shit?' But then I look and see someone has a pet bear. That is, I realize there's a bear there, and it belongs to someone. So that must be where all these piles of shit came from, I think.*

*Right next to the bear is a black baby panther. The bear and the baby panther start wrestling. They're not really fighting, just wrestling.*

"Goddamn it, Ret!!"

"Wha?"

"You kicked me again."

"Shit."

"Oh, owwww." She writhed a little and turned on the light. "Shit."

"I'm so sorry."

"God, Ret. Shit. You kicked me in the same spot on the same leg. Why are you doing that??"

"Honest, Ruthie. I didn't mean to do it."

"Well, that helps. Oww."

"Here, let me rub it," I offered.

"Don't touch me. If you're really sorry, go sleep on the couch so I don't get kicked again."

She flipped off the light, grabbed all the covers, pulled them over her head, and rolled hard away from me. I struggled to disentangle myself from the sheets, grabbed my pillow, pulled a quilt from the closet, and took up residence on the living room couch. It has a sprung spring right in the middle, so I spent the rest of the night tossing and turning. I got up to pee four times.

She was sitting in the kitchen, drinking coffee and reading the paper. I overslept, fell off the couch onto the floor as I awoke, and then stumbled in, squinting at the clock.

"Are you OK?" she asked.

"I should be asking you that."

She nodded and then her lip folded downward which meant she was going to cry. And I felt really sorry then because she hardly ever cries.

"Ruthie, goddamn it, I don't know what's wrong. I didn't mean to hurt you."

She lifted her bathrobe and said, "Yes, you did. Look." Another rosy bruise was superimposed over the first one.

"God. I am so sorry, I just am so sorry. Maybe I'm going psychotic . . ."

"Well, figure it out so you can stop kicking me. Honest to God."

I looked down at her feet, curled into sheepskin slippers I'd given her for Christmas.

"Just figure this out, Ret, and stop kicking me . . . Maybe it's hard for you being an outsider with the Yakamas, but please don't get so hooked in with your friends I can't find you . . . and what do I have to do to get you to come home earlier and more often?"

She smiled slightly, her eyes showing tears again, and took another spoonful of yogurt with her eyes on me, glancing at her paper before I realized the gratitude I felt.

I moved over and hugged her from behind where she sat. She didn't push away.

## Eleven

> Now be careful!
> Where you are stepping!
> Step on the back of the little bird.
> It will bring [you] up to this new world,
> which you have never seen before.
> Then will you be rejoiced over.
> *-Song overheard during*
> *Quas-Ki Ta' Chens' death vision*

"*Kála*, I need to talk to you about something. You know, I don't take notes about our sessions."

Elisi sat next to me sipping a latte she'd brought from the stand over at the cultural center.

"That's nice. I have cousins in medical records."

"What I mean is it seems you're so often helping me understand how things are around here. I've been learning about family and culture, and I really appreciate it. But I'm really starting to worry about how we're working together. As a psychologist, I have an ethical duty to avoid multiple relationships. We've never talked about all this, you know."

"What do you mean?" she said, frowning at her cup and reading the side.

"I mean, I need to start being clearer about certain boundaries with my Indian clients."

"You want to talk about boundaries. Of course. White men been doing that with us for a long time. And who said I was your client?"

"Well, we've been meeting for an hour once or twice a week for a long time. I thought . . ."

Elisi set her cup on my desk next to her and leaned forward to look at me. She scrunched her face up, accentuating her wrinkles.

"Do you think I'm crazy?" she demanded, sniffing the air as though I smelled bad.

"No, *kála*, not at all. But I would never say that about any . . ."

Her stare stopped me.

"I asked you, do you think I'm crazy?"

"No, ma'am."

"OK, then. Well, maybe you need to know first that I never have thought I was your client in any way."

"You haven't?"

"Doctor Barlow," she sat back in her chair, nursing her latte again, "if I thought I was your client, I would have spoken about a need for your services. I don't recall ever doing that. Wherever did you get the idea I was your client?"

"Uh, sorry. OK then. I guess I didn't understand something."

"I guess not," she concluded with mild disapproval.

"I think I might have written a note at some point that you were seeking services from me. But I'll see it's changed. You have never sought my services."

"No. And thank you for fixing that . . . now . . . tell me about any dreams you've had."

I told her my dream.

"That little squirrel, she's your connection, your bloodline. You're afraid of her but you're following her anyway.

She may be little but she's very important. She's led you across the street to your Indian side."

"Oh. I thought she was a . . ."

"Don't interrupt me." She reached in her bag and brought out her beading. "Listen now. Along come your ancestors to take you away from the arguing-over-ideas conference hosted over at our money pit, the Casino, where everybody eventually loses. The dream tells you you're too caught up with Dominia and Dr. Fitzsimmons and your big doctor's ego."

I was taken aback. "That's kind of harsh, *kála*. I didn't know you knew Dr. Fitzsimmons."

"Sure, a *walak'ikláama* psychiatrist. You might have gone another way toward the meaningless arguments with Dominia and people like her. But you got in the car with those ancestors and they took you to a little house and the white picket fence, the fence inside you between white and Indian. Where the bear shits."

She laughed. "A bear never sleeps where he shits, you know."

"Trick said something about *ta*," I added, quite ignorantly.

"Better to not pretend to know anything about that, doctor. Trick's a good Rock Creek boy. That bear in the dream isn't your *pawaat'ła*. He's your laziness. You been sleeping in your own shit behind your picket fence like so many white people. Hiding behind your comfort and security, taking and having and holding all you can. But baby panther knows better. She wrestles with you so you'll wake up. But you keep kicking and hurt your wife." She chuckled.

"*Kála*, I've never thought about dreams like this. Do you mind me asking where you learned to think this way?"

She paused as she held her beading and looked ahead momentarily. "Oh, I suppose from my grandmother . . . and school."

"*Kála*, are you . . . *twáti*?"

Her eyes went wide for a moment before she hooted, "Hah! Me? No, no. I'm not *twáti* . . . didn't I tell you? There aren't any *twáti* anymore."

Then, a knowing look passed over her face. "But my grandmother was."

"Ah . . . and you mentioned school. Did you go to college?"

"Of course I did."

I was astonished. "I never knew about that."

"Well, you never asked, did you? I got a masters in guidance studies from the University of British Columbia."

I gaped at her.

"There were a couple Jungians there," she said. "I liked Jung the best because at least he visited the Hopis. I could relate to him more. Don't look so surprised. I don't brag on myself. Besides, that's forty years ago. I lived with family up there near Kelly Lake. Then I come on down to Vancouver and took my degree. Don't think bad of yourself now, doctor. Most psychologists assume we're all feeble-minded."

"I never thought any such thing . . ."

"But you're not most psychologists."

She set down her beading. "I told you I spent some years at Chemawa. You're not the first psychologist I've known. There was a white man visited there who had a name like Barth or Carth; I never was quite sure. He was likely one of your forerunners. You heard of him?"

"No, Elisi."

"That time you fell asleep in class, maybe." She enjoyed this remark. "BIA had all these Indian children captive in the boarding schools. He believed Indian kids would be inferior on his IQ tests and did most of his studies in those schools. They thought he was a magic scientist who'd tell them how we should be educated and what would be a waste of time."

She shook her head, "Anyway, he tested me and told me I was a 'very rare Indian' and I should go to college to make my people proud. I talked to my grandmother about him."

"What'd she say?"

"She said he was a trickster and not to cooperate next time. In Yakama words, I mean. When I got on into my high school years, my counselor, Mrs. Ames, said I shouldn't 'aim so high' and Indian people were better suited to 'vocational school.' Think on that, doctor. Dr. Barth's studies infected her mind so bad with ugly ideas. Even he stopped believing them but it was too late by then. They're still infecting us today. You really should look him up."

She opened her bag and brought out a little baggie, pouring several berries into each of our hands.

"Here. You cannot domesticate the huckleberry, you know. Blueberries, yes. Huckleberries, no. Huckleberry is clearly sweeter and tastier, right?" I nodded.

"Bring me some water, please."

I brought a little cup from the faucet in my office, which used to be an examination room.

"I grew up without running water. Most white people think water comes from a pipe and their meat comes in a package. They think their milk comes in a carton. . . They are not *alive* to the gifts provided to them. I know this *chíish*, this water from your faucet, comes from a stream somewhere up near White Pass. I was raised to know this."

She held up a huckleberry and then popped it into her mouth.

"I didn't make these huckleberries and I can't domesticate them. White people can't create anything; it's all been given to us, all this beauty and nourishment. We should be thankful about that every single day. This is the Indian way, being grateful. I can't make these huckleberries, but I can pick them."

And she set the baggie in front of me. "For you."

"Thank you, *kála.*"

"You know, I'm always going to be a huckleberry in the way I think of it. And you're a sort of blueberry. I'm glad to have been born a huckleberry. I don't want to be a blueberry. I enjoy blueberries, but I'd rather be a huckleberry. That's who the Creator made me to be. I can't be domesticated..."

She laughed again.

A knock came on the door; it was Deborah.

"I'm sorry to interrupt," she said, a look of worry on her face.

Elisi gazed up as if she were working on me. And she was.

"No problem at all," she said.

Deborah turned to me. "It's just your wife called up front. She said she needed to reach you."

I glanced at my phone and could see I'd muted the ringer. "Oh. Did she say what about, Deb?"

"She sounded stressed out..."

"You better call her," said Elisi.

"Do you mind?"

"I'd mind if you didn't. Do you want me to leave?" She started to get up.

"No, no. You're fine. I don't have anyone until 10. Just hold on." I called home.

"Ret?" She didn't even say 'hello.'

"Ruthie?"

"Ret... someone put a dead cat on our porch."

"What do you mean? How do you know someone put it there?"

"Ret, I found a dead black cat on our porch."

"When?"

"About a half hour ago. Ret, I'm scared. It wasn't there when I went inside. I stopped by to pick up some stuff for parent conferences. It was there when I walked out the door."

"Where?"

"Right on the doormat. Ret, it scared me; somebody put it there. I can tell."

"Ruthie, did you call the cops? I'm coming home."

"Yes, I called them. They haven't gotten here yet."

"Shit. When did you call?"

"I just called them and then called you. Ret, I'm afraid somebody knows I'm here and is watching."

"I'm on my way. Call the cops again. I'm on my way."

"OK." I hung up and turned to Elisi.

"I've got to go. Somebody put a dead cat by our front door . . . a dead black cat."

"And she has the cops on the way?"

"Yeah, I'll talk to you later."

I picked up the huckleberries baggie and tried to hand them back to her. She cocked her head at them and me.

"Doctor, is that what you mean to do?"

"Sorry."

"Take them to your wife." She opened the door, "She's put up with too much from you lately. Call me."

"Thanks."

I was still putting my coat on as I started into a run. Passing Deborah, I yelled, "Cancel my appointments. Family emergency."

There were two Yakima squad cars out front, one black with dark-tinted windows, unmarked, except for the words "Gang Interdiction Unit" and the other just a regular cruiser. Ruthie was in the living room, sitting with a plainclothes officer. A uniformed officer was standing in our kitchen talking on a cell phone.

"Dr. Barlow?" said plainclothes.

"Yes . . . you OK, darlin'?"

I sat down next to her and put my arm around her shoulder. She doesn't usually go for public display. Uncharacteristically, she hugged me back tightly. She was trembling.

"I'm OK. They just got here."

This pissed me off since it takes me more than twenty minutes to get home, and she'd already been waiting.

"I'm Detective Rankin with Gang Interdiction."

"This is gang-related?" I asked. "Why does it take you guys twenty minutes to get here?"

"The call wasn't life-threatening."

"Nice. Somebody just put a goddamn dead cat on our front porch . . ."

"Ret, calm down," said Ruthie.

"Scary," he sighed, "but no imminent threat. Dispatchers stack our calls and we're short 130 officers, doctor. So ask City Council. I just came from shots fired down by Garfield School and, before that, a body over by the water sanitation plant. It's 10:30 am—so good morning to you. That's how it is."

"OK, fine, I get it," I said. "What makes this gang-related?"

"Well, I don't know. Williams here called me over after spotting a pair of tennis shoes on your power lines over the back alley. That can mean somebody bought the farm, or it can be just kids horsing around. Do you have some relation with gangs in your work?"

"I work sometimes with gang-involved kids on the rez."

"Lower Valley rez gangs don't usually move around here. That'd start something with crews in town. Do you know of anyone wanting to put a scare in you? I've been asking your wife the same thing, and she can't think of anyone."

He wrote some notes in a little memo book.

I could've broken confidentiality on the situation with Tessa and Parker at that point. She was doing so well, I decided not to. I had no reason to conclude it was him.

"I can't think of anyone, to be honest."

"Your wife says you're a psychologist with Indian Health. Nothing going on with a client suggesting someone is angry with you or wants to scare you?"

Ruthie looked at me long and hard. She wanted me to say something.

"I can't think of anything," I lied and she glared over at the window, irritated I wasn't saying more. "Does this sort of thing happen often?"

"I've seen pets poisoned, dogs shot. This is the first time I saw a cat's head on somebody's doorstep."

"A cat's head? Just the head? Ruthie, I thought you said a dead cat."

"It's a cat's head. That's what I meant. I was scared . . . A black cat's head," she said. She shivered.

"Well, we don't know where the rest of the cat is, or if it's somebody's pet. Williams put the head in a little bag out there if you want to have a look."

We stepped out on the front porch, and I saw the baggie on the ledge. It was a black cat's head. Its eyes were open and the tongue stuck out. It was gross. He asked a few more questions before asking us both to sign his report.

Sergeant Williams, the guy in uniform, finally stepped outside too and introduced himself just before they both left, apologizing for being on the phone the whole time. He was a shift supervisor and would have his officers keep a closer eye on our home for the next week or so.

By the time they pulled out, Animal Control had stopped by and picked up the cat head. That was a minor miracle because we only have one Animal Control truck in the entire city.

"Well, that's it, I guess," said Ruthie as I pulled her in close again. She looked up at me suspiciously. "And I sure know you didn't tell them the whole story. Which I think is completely stupid—Ret, what is going on?!"

"I'm buying a gun."

"Oh no, you're not!" she pushed back hard and glared at me. And we were off and running for a while before I backed off on the idea. Even so, things stayed chilly for us—we were both shaken up. She went back to school about an hour later. I didn't know how she was going to do parent conferences from there.

I stayed home the rest of the day, checking window and door locks, buying double padlocks for the two backyard gates, and fabricating a couple of creative Ninja-type traps for the basement—several sections of two-by-four with nails driven through and the points turned upward, nailed into the inside window frames, and two small pails filled with broken glass on the sills. You scrape hell out of yourself trying to climb in and make a bunch of racket too. Ruthie might not like it but it was a compromise in relation to our discussion. I wouldn't have wanted to try crawling through.

An alarm salesman I'd called stopped in and gave me an exorbitant quote in the early afternoon. I scanned his company's logo off the quote sheet he gave me, mocked up "Protected By" across the top with a photo-editing application on our desktop, and printed several copies off in living color, using rubber cement to place them on conspicuous doors and windows. They looked convincing to me. I'm on a government salary.

## Twelve

> Next to the sunset, before you reach the bridge,
>    up against the bluff there's a big rock.
> On it are prints of horse feet, one large and
>    four small ones. The large was the stallion
>      and the small are a mare
>    of about three snows and her new colt.
> These tracks give the law that Indians
>    will raise horses all over this country.
> The rock may still be there or maybe lost.
> Maybe the whites used it for something.
>      *-Chief Saluskin*

   The day was gorgeous, bright, and beautiful. Buds were beginning to burst on the old apple trees and wildflowers were popping up. All the colors held the benefits of late afternoon light. The steady buzz of the early yellow jackets grew louder, but I now knew how to park well away from them. I could hear them in the distance, yet I was quite comfortable.

   I'd been invited to come out for a 'session of sorts,' according to Elisi. Tessa and I would normally meet up at school at that time, but she had a half-day. Her siblings were not so lucky, and Arnold got more work down at the fishery. I rendezvoused with Edward, Elisi, and Tessa near Ámashitum's corral and spotted the filly grazing at the far corner of the pen.

Elisi greeted me gripping a small plastic pail of apples. Edward was getting something from his truck. Tessa leaned against the railing and watched her horse.

"We've been doing this for about a week and today's a special day, doctor," Elisi noted. "That's why I got so many apples. This filly loves apples."

Edward strolled up, wearing copper-brown overalls and heavy, laced boots.

"Tessa! We're ready," he called, and she walked over, greeting me with a silent wave.

"Same thing as yesterday only today," he instructed her. "You whistle as you set the apple down for her, not before like we been doin'."

Elisi tapped me lightly on the shoulder. "Doctor, you and I got to move downwind from Ámashitum or this won't work. We're an unfamiliar scent to her and she won't come if she senses we're here. I suggest we move over behind that sycamore."

As we watched, Tessa climbed over the railing and with Edward's whispered encouragement moved in toward Ámashitum. Ámashitum raised her head immediately from grazing, clearly sensing Tessa's presence. Tessa carried Elisi's apple pail and moved forward slowly.

When she was about thirty yards from Ámashitum, the horse started slightly and swung sideways, rearing slightly but playfully. Tessa lowered an apple down on the ground and whistled loudly. Ámashitum's ears sprang high, and she became very alert.

Tessa backed up slowly, perhaps about half the distance she'd approached. Minutes passed. Ámashitum began to graze again, but as she did, she circled a bit closer to that apple. Occasionally, she'd raise her head sharply and cast a sidelong glance at Tessa who stood very still.

"Just wait right there," Edward whispered loudly, coming up behind Tessa.

He kept himself about twenty feet behind Tessa. Ámashitum circled forward more, grazing, raising her head, closing in on the apple.

"We could've tried carrots," Elisi whispered to me. "But this filly loves apples. She can't resist. Juicy, red Yakima apples, that's her weakness. I went out and bought them, actually. Honeycrisp. Try one."

She pulled one out of her shirt coat pocket and handed it to me. I bit into it and was surprised when it burst crisply and spit juice on my cheek.

"I never had an apple like this," I observed.

"Won't find them just anywhere," she said. "Now watch. That's a taste this little horse is after. We've been working to get her to this point."

Ámashitum was within five feet of her goal and suddenly, playfully, pranced forward, leaning down and biting into the apple as she raised her head back up. She stood staring at Tessa as she chewed.

"Pretty fearless, I'd say," Edward whispered. "She's a strong spirit, ain't she?" Tessa nodded slowly. "I think she's ready Tess. Do like I said; let's try it."

Tessa set the pail down slowly, pulling out another apple, and then holding it out in her hand. She let loose another loud whistle.

Ámashitum started from where she was, stopped, and stood gazing at Tessa holding the apple out in her hand.

"You see what it is," I heard her whisper. "Come on, baby, and have another."

Ámashitum continued staring. Tessa whistled again, this time shorter. Minutes passed. Ámashitum grazed a little, looking up occasionally at the proffered apple in Tessa's held out hand.

"Getting tired," Tessa whispered.

"Hang in there," Edward encouraged. "I think she'll go for it."

Another minute passed. Ámashitum walked slowly closer to Tessa. She didn't graze; she just stopped and stared at her and the apple. Stopping and staring must have happened several times. Tessa stood like a statue. Suddenly, Ámashitum closed the gap and nibbled on the apple while Tessa held it.

The wind blew lightly over both of them and the sun burnt both their shadows vividly into the ground as Ámashitum munched on the apple held out in the flat palm of Tessa's hand. When she finished, she nodded her head up and down at Tessa and immediately burst into a cantor all around the pen, stopping back in the rear where she began.

Tessa turned toward Edward.

"That was awesome!" she mouthed, her eyes wide, a look of utter delight on her face.

"Happiness," Elisi whispered to me.

"Come on out for a minute, Tessa," said Edward. "I want to try something else."

He had her set down the pail next to him and then take just one apple.

"In your pocket this time, Tessa. It's a stretch but I want to try it."

Again, Tessa climbed back in. She moved back to where she had been standing.

"Whistle," said Edward. Tessa's whistle was loud and piercing. I can't make that kind of a whistle, but I've always wished I could.

Ámashitum's head shot up from her grazing, and she looked sidelong at Tessa. She began prancing around, playfully.

"You're family, Tessa, I think," said Edward. "I'm not going to try a halter today. I just want to get your whistle in place."

Ámashitum stopped prancing and shook her head. Then she strolled all the way over to within ten feet of Tessa and eyed her. Tessa pulled out the apple and held it out.

"Good girl," Tessa purred at her. "What a beauty you are."

Ámashitum stood eating the apple before her.

"That filly, she's like any young woman," Elisi whispered behind me. "She wants to be courted. Especially with sweets."

I believe Tessa must have summoned Ámashitum ten more times after that and each time, the horse got braver.

As the sun went low, Ámashitum moved from wild horse to a friend who'd come for Tessa anytime she whistled.

Several weeks later, I'd coaxed Ruthie into taking an afternoon off, driving out with me, and stopping at Cougar Den on the way. She thought I was being charitable at first. I had to work to persuade her that I really did get it and wanted her along with me. I even ordered a salad, mostly just to please her. I also wanted her to witness what was happening with Tessa and Ámashitum. I needed to do something to include her.

"I know you're making a big sacrifice," she noted as we ate.

"How?"

"Because you eat bacon burgers out here whenever you can."

I shifted my head lightly and noncommittally.

"I'm not hassling you," she reached out and touched my hand. "I just want you to be able to talk to me. I don't want you to keep stuff from me anymore."

"Including excess bacon cheeseburgers."

"Oh with cheese too, huh?" She shrugged. "Whatever, Ret, it's your body," she said. "Just don't have a heart attack."

After we parked at Arnold's place, Leila's look cautioned us to walk up slowly. Tessa stood next to her with both hands gripped tightly on the top rail, not moving or apparently even breathing. Some extra fencing had been added behind Ámashitum, making the space in her corral tighter. We could see Leon standing in the middle of the pen and began to watch him work.

He approached Ámashitum for a moment, and when she started and quivered, he slowly backed up, crouched, and held out a clump of alfalfa in one hand as he stayed down low. He looked toward her, then away, but kept his eye on her movements.

He talked softly with words such as 'sweetheart' and 'little girl.' I couldn't make out most of what he said. Each time he moved back and forth and spoke like this, Ámashitum, seemed to me, well, to be surprised.

"She's pretty curious," Leon proclaimed to Edward.

Suddenly, she bolted to the left and then right, but Leon boldly stepped over and cut her stride. Then he backed away a little, turned and crouched down again slightly, and this repeated the effect of causing Ámashitum to stop in her tracks. She snorted and whinnied, but you could see her gaze and how she was interested in him. He repeated these same behaviors several times over.

With all his patient, slow movement and posturing, Leon eventually noted a little louder, "She wants some . . ." and Edward nodded in agreement, standing at a nearby rail.

Miraculously, Ámashitum, moved in, sniffed his hand tentatively as he stood still, and then took a quick nip of the alfalfa. He slowly backed away, continuing to posture but holding the alfalfa toward her now, as though offering it.

"You want a little more, don't you sweetheart? Here's some more I'll give you."

I glanced over at Elisi, smiling at us while Ruthie stood close to me, watching.

"Everything OK?" she mouthed quietly. Yes, I signaled thumbs-up.

And the filly came in again, slightly less tentative. I think we were holding our collective breath as the interaction repeated itself for the next few minutes with Leon upping the ante first by gently touching her on the forehead and then elsewhere as she nibbled. At first she would start, and he would maneuver a little; eventually, she seemed to acquiesce. I don't know how else to explain the transition; it seemed surreal how soon she was standing next to Leon, looking more relaxed, eating right from his hand as he touched her neck, back, sides, and legs very gently.

"I learned this way from Diné friends," said Leon, looking back at us. "She's not aggressive so don't get mixed up and fearful yourself, if you're here to help. She's kind of skittish, and so we're going to start with a very wide circle."

Edward asked, "Are you ready, bro?"

"Yeah, but get folks in slow."

"OK," Edward strolled round to us. "Doctor, you and Ruthie both helping us today?"

Ruthie looked at me inquisitively.

"That's why we're here."

He turned toward the whole group. "Before you all come in, a few instructions." He kept his voice low, and we gathered in.

"Yes, that's better. She'll get used to shouting soon enough, but she spooks easy now. So . . . I'll be bringing you in one at a time. There are some rules in how we do this. First, I want you all to keep your attention on this filly and don't take it off her for a moment. That said, do not pay attention by looking her in the eye or staring at her. That's impolite; it's aggressive in the animal world. Everyone understand?"

We all nodded. I had no idea the plan was for us to get inside the pen.

"Leon calls the shots. He's our leader and hers too for now. Do what he says, exactly what he says, and only what he says. When you do a movement, do it quiet, slow, and in a coordinated manner. Does that make sense to you, doc?"

He looked with mock inquisitiveness at me, and Ruthie, Arnold, and Leila tried unsuccessfully to suppress laughter.

"Yes, coordinated," I responded, "I'll pay attention."

"So," continued Edward, "The key to this is you will not approach the horse. The horse will approach you. If she gets more jumpy, just back up a bit and if she seems to be getting real agitated, slide back through the middle rail space there. Everyone see that?" We looked where he pointed. "That's nearly one thousand pounds of animal we're working to reassure. If she gets to feeling unsafe, we're going to need to give her some room."

I was noticing a slight twinge of anxiety emerge in my chest.

Leon offered Ámashitum a little more alfalfa as she approached him again, and then she just stood there looking at us for a moment, bent down, and sniffed some blossoms on the end of a stalk before consuming them.

Edward walked over to his pickup for something. Elisi sat down in a lawn chair and watched; she was not interested in participating. That left Leon, Edward, Arnold, Leila, Tessa, Emily, Eloise, Ruthie, and me to work with Ámashitum.

Edward returned holding a large beach ball. "We're going to play horse volleyball to start . . ."

Tessa's eye widened, "Are you kidding?"

"Awesome . . ." said Emily.

"Won't she get spooked?" asked Ruthie.

"Not if we do things right," he smiled. "Arnold, suppose you and the good doctor here swing under the middle rail real slow, and we'll start that way."

As we did so, I concentrated on staying fluid. Even so, my boot dinged the rail, and it rang. Ámashitum started back suddenly.

"Easy, easy," said Leon.

"Sorry . . ." I whispered.

"No problem," Edward reassured, "She's going to have to get used to humans, including human noises. Don't worry about it. She's still doing fine. Just stand here."

Arnold and I took up positions at opposite points of the radius.

"Now Tessa, Ruthie, and Leila . . ."

They made their way in, and Edward placed them at points diagonal to Arnold and me. He pointed to Emily and Eloise. "When you girls come in, I'm coming in with you. All of us are going to have to even out our circle around the horse."

"Now, let's start our game."

Edward held up the ball then rolled it gently to Tessa. Ámashitum immediately pranced backwards from Leon, who crouched slowly, murmuring, "It's OK, sweetheart. It's OK, just a game."

Tessa rolled the ball back to Edward—quite beautifully.

"Good. Now Ruthie." Another perfect roll toward me. "OK, doctor."

I did not blow it. I took the ball and gently rolled it to Arnold. He sent it to Emily. Soon we had the ball moving around our circle, Leon talking and murmuring, Ámashitum kept well away, watching, sometimes wild-eyed, other times seeming fascinated by the movement.

After maybe ten minutes, which seemed very long, Leon said, "She wants to play, I think."

Edward then rolled the ball very slowly toward Leon. He stopped it with his foot and bent down low and sniffed it. Then he picked it up, held it, and slowly lifted it higher, sniffing it. Ámashitum stood near his right shoulder. He held it up to his nose and stood upright, sniffing it. She leaned in; he leaned away. It was almost like a tease.

"Now she really wants to play," said Leon. He sniffed it again, slowly leaning back toward her as she leaned forward.

Eventually, Ámashitum was leaning all the way over Leon's shoulder, trying to sniff the ball like he was. This was so amazing to me, I missed the ball when it came my way, and it rolled under the fence. Elisi struggled up from her chair and rolled in back in.

"Pay attention, doctor," she scolded in a whisper.

It was my turn to roll to Leon. As he caught it, he repeated the same explorations, but then he finally lifted it and shared it with her, holding it toward her sniffing nose, while simultaneously giving her another bunch of alfalfa. Now both Leon and Ámashitum were included in our rolling of the beach ball.

"Keep it up! A little faster . . ." Leon said louder, but Ámashitum did not react to his raised voice. She was too involved in watching the ball. Sometimes, Leon would catch the ball and before he would roll it, he would touch it to her nose or gently on her chest. Soon, Ámashitum would follow the movement of the ball physically, darting a little back and forth, still staying behind Leon.

"Remember, keep your eyes on her at all times. Don't stare. She's getting braver. Keep your movements a little slower but still smooth and confident."

Leon rolled the ball to Tessa several times in a row, back and forth. Ámashitum darted at one point very close to her, and Tessa started a little.

"Don't worry, Tessa," said Leon, "She's been very curious about you for a while." He rolled the ball to her, and Tessa rolled it back. "She's going to try again. I'm sure of it."

Ámashitum darted forward and stopped as Tessa held the ball in midair, coordinating with the horse's movement forward, but ignoring her, and getting ready to roll it back. Ámashitum leaned in and sniffed Tessa's hair.

"Good," said Leon, "Very good. You obviously got some horsechaser in you."

He turned to Edward. "She seems least afraid of Tessa."

This happened again.

"Now, Tessa," said Leon, "This time when she sniffs you, I want you to touch that ball lightly to her chest before you roll it over to Leila."

Tessa did as she was told, and Ámashitum started backward.

"That's OK, we're going to keep doing things like that with her," said Leon.

On and on our game of horse volleyball went. Soon, we had Ámashitum running more or less haphazardly between all of us. All of us had touched her chest but only that and no more.

"Now one at a time starting with you, Ruthie, I want you to back out of the pen through the middle rail going clockwise. Tessa you stay in here with me."

Slowly we backed out until only Tessa and Leon remained. Tessa stayed on the fringe while Leon was at center, rolling the ball to her. Ámashitum slowed a little on the game, tossing her head side to side and shaking her mane.

"OK, Tessa. Now Ámashitum is losing interest in our game a little. So I want you to pick up a little alfalfa while I back away a bit."

"I'm a little nervous . . ." she admitted as Edward passed a clump to her.

"Not as much as she is," whispered Edward, "I know you have it in you to help her stay calm. Just talk to her. She's just a baby."

Leon stayed about fifteen feet away from the filly, and Tessa stood still at about twenty feet.

"Tessa, first thing is you make your way over by me just like a horse . . ."

"I don't know what you mean . . ."

"Well you saw how she did it, didn't you?" said Elisi, somewhat loudly from the fence.

"Do it that way, just kind of back and forth toward me," echoed Leon.

Tessa tried her best to come to him in a slow, tentative, checking way.

"That's it. You're her big sister, Tessa. She's been watching you and you've been giving apples. Apples are love to this filly. Now we'll try some real food."

Soon Tessa was next to Leon, who was holding his clump of alfalfa outward. He moved her hand with her own clump next to his.

"There you go . . . go ahead and talk to her, Tessa. Whistle soft to her, Tessa. Then tell her to come and have a bite."

Tessa made a soft whistle. "C'mon, Ámashitum. C'mon . . . it's OK, baby."

The filly walked over without hesitation and nibbled on the end.

"That's it . . ." Leon backed away slowly to about five feet behind her. "I'm right behind you. You're feeding her yourself. She's liking it too."

And Ámashitum was eating from Tessa's hand with Tessa in a sort of trance. Leon turned toward Edward. "Did you see how she come right up on her like that?"

"Yeah, that was crazy."

"Never seen anything like that before."

"What do you mean?" asked Arnold.

"Never seen a wild horse being gentled come up so early on and confident with someone. We only been working with her for a few weeks, you know. I've never seen a horse just move forward after a human round pen exercise to one person like that."

"She's her sister," said Elisi.

"Must be . . ." remarked Edward. "We've worked a lot of horses but never with you, Tessa, maybe you're her big sister. Are you sure you two didn't already meet somewhere before?"

"Try reaching and touching her lightly between her ears, Tessa," Leon encouraged.

As Ámashitum nibbled from her left hand, Tessa lifted her right slowly and lightly petted her head.

"Geez," Edward turned and looked at all of us. "Not a move, not a start, not a snort—must be your baby sister, Tessa."

And Tessa stood hardly moving as the light changed again and her brown filly's coat turned rusty red, Edward and Leon taking turns handing her clumps of alfalfa, urging her to pet her here or there with no visible reaction from Ámashitum other than seemingly greater calmness and self-control.

Soon, Edward and Leon backed away out of the pen themselves, and Tessa stayed, listening to them talk about the halter they would bring back in a couple of days, briefing her on what to expect, how training worked, how to understand certain subtleties of Ámashitum's behavior, the importance of getting the vet out soon, and many other particulars.

The rest of us just watched and listened, transfixed on the two of them, even Elisi. We couldn't shift our eyes when Tessa's hands would pet her horse, her voice humming and uncharacteristically soft, as if they'd touched before and now, like old, close friends reunited after many years, were communicating wordlessly about where they'd been and what they'd seen during all the time they were apart.

As we headed back to our cars, we all remarked on the intensity of what we'd seen.

"It's rare . . . very rare," said Elisi knowingly.

We expected a story, but she said nothing else except for wishing us *shix kwláawit*. She laboriously lowered herself into Leila's front seat and then gazed back at us.

"What's rare?" Ruthie finally asked.

"Not much I could say on that right now," she responded. "Sounds like quite a scare to your place."

Ruthie was a bit confused by this until she remembered. "The cat's head."

"You take care of her," Elisi said pointedly to me. "She's a beautiful spirit and she deserves it. Don't neglect your woman."

How she sensed the healing efforts occurring between the two of us, I have no idea. She turned to Ruthie and spoke reassuringly, "Kid's games. Nothing from our ways in that at all . . . but I still haven't figured how somebody knew how to scare you two."

Then she glanced at me, "You been talking around about your dreams to everybody?"

"What do you mean?" I responded.

"The cat's head. The little panther—your *pawaat-łá*."

"Just a coincidence?" I called out, wanting her to say more.

"Not likely!" she shouted, still waving as they drove out. "Don't talk about dreams with anybody but your wife and me!"

Two weeks later, I heard from Tessa that she and Leon and Edward had gotten Ámashitum through accepting the halter and putting up with a saddle on her back. Leon said he'd be the first on her back, but there was still much to do before then. Tessa insisted it would be her.

There seemed to be only good developments in Tessa's life in the weeks that followed. She didn't object to meeting with me and actually seemed to benefit from our talks. As early summer came on, we had only a few more meetings scheduled before school would let out. Her grades were up, and she was on target at school. She spoke excitedly of wanting to learn to cook professionally after seeing a short-order kitchen in action while working with Leila, moving her hands in pantomime as she spoke, commenting on the often strange eating habits of their customers. Then again, she wanted to become a horse breeder or trainer, brushing them down, leading them, explaining how Leon rode Ámashitum briefly but got thrown. A week later, she'd been on her back and Ámashitum just stood there, tolerating her. Maybe she could be a veterinarian, she said—all this but never a word about Tina, Jack, or the fear, violence, and abuse of her early days.

Tessa was looking toward the future, and if I tentatively probed a bit toward more painful memories, she shrugged or changed the subject. She let me know what mattered, and I backed off completely from her past. She had an orientation toward her future, and this was fantastic.

I had no idea she was still deeply involved with Parker Heslah.

Basketball season was long over and Tessa didn't make the school team, but she somehow got herself chosen for a pickup team in an exhibition game at Blessed Savior Christian School, a fundraiser for intramural teen sports across the valley. She was very excited and so respectful in asking if we'd come watch her play, I didn't want to let her down.

Ruthie and I pulled up to the posh, modern school in Sunnyside on a Saturday night in early May, having finally located it behind the small civic center. The lot was jammed; we parked on a residential street and walked more than a half mile only to find the gym filled to capacity with so many people standing along the sidelines, we couldn't even get inside. We were barely able to see the game through the outside door. I felt bad about arriving so late when the girls' game was almost finished.

I sorted out Tessa in the mix for Ruthie as she sprinted down the court and guarded a towering blonde girl in a white Blessed Savior shirt. She was hard to recognize in her oversized blue and yellow jersey with her hair braided and tied back. Her brown skin contrasted sharply with the bright whiteness of her foe.

A pass flew across the court to her opponent suddenly, and Tessa's hand lifted fast enough to tip it but not enough to stop the grab. She was elbowed in the neck—a clear foul—and dropped to the floor with both hands to keep from falling. I looked for the referee's seeing-eye dog, but no call was made. Tessa jumped back up without hesitation, running down court after the ball, pressuring and cutting the girl off just outside the baseline. This was not enough to stop the shot, unfortunately, which was good for Blessed Savior.

Tessa and her teammates massed a bold and sudden offense, becoming a blue, yellow, and brown blur pounding hard and passing fast and accurately back down court. But the buzzer went off before it could mean anything, and it was too late; they were beaten 65 to 50.

"Ret, some people are leaving," said Ruthie. "There's spaces opening up."

We moved upstream past exiting people and found a little space at the very bottom row. Tessa walked dejectedly back across the court with several girls before she glanced along the stands and in our direction. Her eyes found us both briefly, and I waved at her, lifting my hand off my knee slightly and covertly. She didn't wave back, but she smiled.

"Ret," Ruthie whispered in my ear. "Look . . . check out our side of the bleachers."

I gazed behind us. We were definitely the only white people on that side of the basketball court. Several faces I recognized smiled or nodded in a friendly way back at us. Ruthie shifted her eyes pointedly to the bleachers on the other side of the court, beckoning me to gaze over there. The Blessed Savior crowd hadn't a brown or even an off-white face among them.

"Here we are white and sitting on the Indian side," Ruthie said, wonderingly, and then pondered for a moment. "And I think that's good."

"You do?"

"Yes," she said deliberately. "It's very good."

Under the circumstances, we decided to stay and watch the boys' exhibition game. Our boys' pick-up team came out to face off with the kids from Blessed Savior to thunderous encouragement emanating from our bleachers, but several shouts cut through.

"Hey, Chief!"

"Hey savage!"

I thought I imagined this at first. I heard the 'Chief' comment and then turned to Ruthie, who looked back at me aghast.

"Where'd that come from?" she asked me.

"I don't know," I scanned the other side. "I can't spot who said it."

There wasn't a word in response from our side except for more enthusiastic whoops and shouts. The game started out aggressively. There were multiple foul shots and pushing and shoving on both sides. Our boys quickly moved ahead and were dominating 25 to 10 toward the end of the first quarter. This was impressive—but every slipped pass or missed opportunity was capitalized upon by the hecklers on the other side.

"Can't shoot, savage?"

"Dropped the ball again, Chief."

"Dumb Indian!"

The refs did nothing except remain oblivious. There were no obscenities, but the racist slurs continued to punctuate the air every minute or so. I finally spotted one of them—a young white guy with two little kids sitting next to him.

"Ret, this is making me sick. Can we leave?" she said as I pointed toward him.

"Do you really want to? Given we're the only white people?"

"I can't take the ugliness anymore. These Christians should be fed to the lions. Can we go?"

We got up and made our way toward the door just as the buzzer went off for half-time.

"Back to the rez, savage!"

I turned around and faced the direction from where that shout came from.

Ruthie watched fury cross my face and grabbed my arm—her own face flush with rage.

"Don't get in a fight, Ret," she cautioned me. "Let's just go."

We were going through the door, and I stopped and turned around again. For some reason, there was a lull—the entire gym quieted down for just a moment.

"*Yaych'ū'nal!*" I yelled. "*Yaych'ū'nal!*"

Ruthie pulled my shoulder. There was both embarrassment and amusement on her face. She had no idea what I was yelling. One of the Indian boys on court turned and squinted in my direction.

"What are you yelling?" She pulled closer and whispered in my ear. "Ret, you're embarrassing me. What are you yelling?"

"Sorry," I said while we tried to get outside. "Courage," I explained, "that's what it means."

Someone lightly tussled my hair as we exited through the door, and I glanced back to see Ms. Samuels, our school computer teacher, waving shyly. *Yaych'ū'nal*, she mouthed, and smiled at both of us.

We were still ventilating our anger about what we'd witnessed when I spotted the glint of glass all over the pavement by my car sitting in its parking space about a hundred yards distant. Shit, I thought to myself, I must have run over a bottle or something.

But there were two shadows on the other side, fiddling with something on my passenger door.

"Shit!" I let go of Ruthie and began to run.

"Ret, what the . . . ?" yelled Ruthie. "What are you doing!?"

"Goddamn it!! Get the fuck away from my car!"

They turned and sprinted to the vehicle behind mine, jumping in as I came to within thirty yards. The driver patched out from the parking space; I squinted to read the plates as they sped away but couldn't focus.

Struggling to get my cell out of my pocket, I dropped my keys and a bunch of change scattered across the pavement as Ruthie ran up next to me.

"Goddamn it! Shit!!" I stomped around on the pavement. "Assholes."

"8278E . . . something," said Ruthie.

"You got it?"

"Got that much," she said in a calmer voice than mine. "I'm just glad you didn't pick a fight with them either."

"Bastards."

"Breathe—they're just punk kids. We can't do anything about it except call it in . . . Oh my God, look!"

On the passenger side door, '187' had been spray-painted all over again.

They got the CD deck and six CDs, including my John Martyn "Solid Air" disc and a Fairport Convention anthology, both out-of-print. The female Sunnyside police officer listened sympathetically and patiently to my musical loss, took a report, and then explained how they'd blew the window out by pushing the tip of a sparkplug into the middle.

"Works fast. That's how they usually do it," she said as she shook her head.

She paused for an indecipherable radio call and then reported to us the plates were stolen from a local vehicle. As she drove off, we knew our car prowl complaint would be added to a very long list.

"At least they didn't get my purse," said Ruthie easily. "And I'm really glad you didn't catch up with them. I don't want you to get hurt . . ."

"I could've taken care of myself."

"They might've had guns, Ret. Not worth it," she glanced at me. "And quit trying to be such a hard-ass with these kids. You're going to get yourself hurt. Leave it to the cops, please. We'll get those CDs for you again," she added as she reached over to stroke my cheek.

"How can you stay calm? You amaze me."

"I know." She smiled. I was still very wound up and glad she was driving.

## Thirteen

[She] has made some cry for help at the PHS Hospital within 1 week of the attempt . . . [She] probably was involved in an intense hostile-dependent or symbiotic relationship with this other person. –*Carl Mindell, MD & Paul Stuart, Suicide and self-destructive behavior in the Oglala Sioux, 1969*

I visit Trick sometimes on Wednesday morning to share a cup of his weak coffee and a smudge. He teasingly introduced me to a new chemical dependency counselor, Renee, as "the only shrink to survive at the clinic this long."

He also told me, "Tessa's working her recovery" in the adolescent talking circles he ran twice weekly; "she's into her groups and the other kids, they look up to her."

"Doc here dreams of panthers . . ." he pointed out to Renee.

"Wait a minute now," I said, "Have you been telling people about that?"

"Didn't know it was a secret."

I didn't want to appear to get on his case. I never asked him to keep it private.

"Is that OK?" He sensed my discomfort.

"Fine, Trick. I just didn't know."

"Nice meeting you," Renee nodded as she got up, sensing something was up. "I've got paperwork."

"Still be here when you're dead," Trick offered his usual black twist.

"Thanks for that," she said, "but Dixie will kill me anyway if it's not done . . ."

"I didn't mean anything there, doc. I heard from Wilma about that Cherokee word you dreamt and just thought the connection was pretty cool. We never got to talk about it. I didn't blab it all over the place, I mean . . ."

I told him all about the dead cat.

"Shit! And you didn't tell me."

"God's honest truth, I tried to put it behind me. It was a shock at the time, and the dream connection was weird, but I just wanted to forget about it. I didn't figure I'd ever know who did it. Do you remember who you told?"

"Dixie, Wilma, let's see . . . shit, doc, I hate to admit it. I might have mentioned it to the kids in talking circle."

"You mentioned the panther dream I had in circle with Tessa there?"

"Because I have all these panthers hanging on the walls, you know. They were asking about them, and I was teaching them about *pawaat'la* or whatever."

He looked sheepish.

"Like I said, I never told you it was a secret. Trick, just do me a favor and don't mention it anymore. And don't mention the dead cat's head or those Cherokee words to anyone either."

"Sure. No problem."

At our last session before school ended in June, Tessa admitted to me she still saw Parker against her grandfather's wishes. I knew this might be true but didn't suspect how often.

"He don't want me to talk to you," she disclosed.

"I heard that. Why do you think?"

"He don't like me maybe saying about his business. But I don't."

"Tessa, Parker's still gang-banging. Your grandpa's worried about you having contact with Parker and I am too. Doesn't that make any sense to you?"

Her tone became mildly defensive. "You don't know him and neither does grandpa. Nobody does."

"But you do . . ."

"As much as anybody . . ."

Ultimately, I had to tell her that her "secret was safe with me."

If Arnold found out about Parker, she'd lose privileges with Ámashitum. If that happened, lots of things could come apart.

I still pushed her about Parker and she admitted, yes, he'd sometimes been involved in drugs, alcohol, and crime, but he shared many similarities with her in his painful background. She wanted to help him. She'd gotten her life together; what was wrong with trying to help him? She insisted her efforts were reciprocated—Parker cared about her, loved her, and encouraged her in positive ways. She claimed he'd stopped tweaking and drinking completely. If we only knew him as she did, we'd want to help him too instead of criticize him.

"Look what he gave to me . . ." she said as she pulled a folding knife from her back pocket as evidence. She handed it to me.

"Tessa, you'll be expelled carrying that around."

A look of consternation crossed her face. "Don't you think I know that? I'm not stupid. I wanted to show it to you."

Her statement had just a touch of inquiry, so I nodded reassuringly. I rationalized that it's not my job to monitor knives for the school. There was no implied imminent danger in possessing the knife, I told myself.

I looked it over. I'd never seen another like it—most of the knives sold around the rez looked very vicious but broke easy; they were made with cheap steel by indentured little children in China or India and sold for five bucks at the convenience stores. This knife was well-made. It was a little short of four inches on the blade, which was carbon-tempered steel with a strange embossed emblem that looked like a human figure. It was rounded and tipped like a dagger and had a genuine antler handle with round brass fittings at each end. You closed it with an odd locking mechanism involving a tang you flipped backwards.

"It's called a Navaja, and it's from Spain. It's the only thing he inherited from his grandpa and he wants me to hold on to it. His grandpa got it from a Spanish doctor who saved his life during Vietnam."

"I didn't know Spain had anything to do with Vietnam. Did you say Navajo?"

"No, Navaja."

"Ha. How come he wanted you to have it?"

"What do you mean, how come?" she answered as though this was an obvious link for anyone but me. "It's something precious he wants me to keep for him."

"Well, it's a deadly-looking knife, Tessa. Please don't show it to anybody else." I handed it back to her. "I imagine it must be pretty valuable to him. I don't doubt he cares about you."

I gradually drew her attention to the rumor that Parker and friends were breaking into people's houses and stealing guns.

Tessa became quiet and shook her head, "You don't understand what's up with that. He's all done with that stuff. He's out of it. And you don't know what kinds of people he's been hooked in with—they're not easy to get away from."

She wouldn't say more and changed the subject, closing the knife, and shoving it into her back pocket.

As pretty as that knife was, it made me very nervous.

About a week later, Rena called and asked if I'd stop by the jail.

"Will Tork be my concierge?"

"Come straight over to my office if you don't want to talk to him."

"What about?"

"I have Parker on a release here for a DUI. He wants a word with you before he goes. I have no idea what about."

Parker wanting to talk to me instead of threaten me and paint my car was unprecedented. It was only a five minute walk.

Rena sat behind her desk, surrounded by stacks of paper with several cock-eyed plaques on the 1970s paneled wall behind her and a couple of diplomas. A woman's softball trophy from 1993 lay on its side against one of those bobbing head puppies people put in the rear window of their cars.

Parker slouched very low in a chair across from her desk, peeling a torn fingernail with his teeth, his jet black hair covering the left side of his face.

Rena finished up on the phone. "Come on in."

I sat down next to Parker who didn't look at me or say anything. Rena got up.

"I'm going to leave the two of you alone."

"Fine," I said as she quietly exited without another word, closing the door softly behind her. I gazed at Parker, who stayed silent and still didn't look at me.

"Hey," I said.

"Hey yourself," he said, still picking at his fingers. He didn't look drunk or stoned, just bored.

I waited. I looked more at Rena's office and saw there was even paper on the floor behind her. Probation officer, key-keep, kid advocate, custodian, paralegal, what else?

"I got something I need to say to you," he finally said.

"Shoot."

His eyes glanced at me and then back to his hands.

"I'm only talking to you 'cause I feel I got to."

"I get that."

"I done some bad things."

I didn't comment. He pulled himself up, his eyes met mine momentarily, and now I saw they were more bloodshot than I thought and quite sad.

"Like '187' and '56' on my car?"

"Shit means stay away is all." He eased back for a moment. "You should stay home to your IHS office and don't go around the rez poking into what don't have nothing to do with you."

"Objection noted, Parker. I go where I want. It'll be chilly in hell when somebody fucking with my car and my home keeps me from doing my job. Keep it up though and I'll be sure to make your business mine."

He stared at me long and hard, and I stared right back.

"How come you didn't snitch on me?" he asked.

"Seemed a bad idea to do so and be able to still keep Tessa going in a good direction," I responded. "Otherwise, I'd have had you picked up."

"I've been cleaning myself up . . . I'm getting older and want to do right."

"Yeah, but it takes a while. I hope you keep working at it and stop messing with me. I guess we both care about how things turn out for Tessa."

I could see he was struggling, and he looked away. There was a sudden look of grief, and he tamped it down hard even though his eyes filled. He poked a finger at his eye and coughed.

"My . . . ma weren't much of a mother. She grew up in foster care. She used to hit me and Flo with a block of wood, her shoe, whatever. . . I mean, even when we was real little. I'd fight her. She was a drunk. Flo would hide under the table, and I'd jump on my ma's back when she came home drunk so she'd hit me instead. I took care of my sis. That's one thing I done right."

"I'll give you that," I said.

"Don't want no sympathy or psychology bullshit, doc. I'm not making excuses. I made some bad choices. I been moved all over. I don't trust people like you but I need to tell you something . . . I been worried about my sis."

"OK."

"I remember that circle we had at the school where I wouldn't talk. You need to know I never wanted anything from school or nobody. Only thing I ever wanted was to get the fuck off this reservation and the hell out of here. I been trying to get some money together, buy me a truck, and get to Tacoma. I got a cousin over there. Well, I ain't got shit and I ain't going to get shit. I'm caught up in something. I'm worried about Flo and the money I was going to send her. Now I'm getting no money and she ain't either. Another drunk Indian from White Swan."

"I know a lot of good people in White Swan."

"I hate White Swan and I hate being a fucking Indian. I hate being Indian, being Indian never did anything for me in this world but fuck me up. My own relatives wouldn't take us in when we was in foster care. I hate being a fucking Indian, and I'm not about to argue with no white man about it."

"Parker, this kind of thinking gets you stuck."

"No," he shook his head. "You don't understand, and I'm not telling you more about all that shit anyways. None of this is what I wanted to say. I want you to know that Tessa is the only person I ever really loved besides Flo."

He glanced at me again with that same look Tessa once gave me, as though he was deciding. "And what I want you to know is she's got to have a life."

"Sure. We agree on that," I said gently.

"She's got to have a life, and I'm not really going to be able to help her with that, even if I love her. And don't ever tell her I said that."

"I'm not sure what you mean. I wouldn't tell. But why are you telling me this?"

His eyes took on a kind of desperation.

"Parker," I pushed, "are you thinking of hurting yourself?"

"Fuck no," he gestured wildly, "nothing like that! It's just she's got to have a life and I can't go the direction she needs me to go. I got too much hanging by a thread right now."

"What do you mean?"

"Before today, I wanted you to stay away from her. Now that's changed. I want you and other people to keep helping her. She needs to keep getting help. Things are moving fast, and I can't make life better for her."

"Parker, you've trusted me this much. Tell me more."

He lurched upright out of his chair.

"No," he said, "I said too much already. Most shrinks is fucked up snitches. I'm glad you didn't snitch. Just remember what I told you."

And he opened the door and walked out without another word or glance. Rena came back around the corner.

"Is he gone?" she asked.

"Yeah," I said, confused.

"Can you tell me anything?"

"Not really," I answered. "He's in trouble and he's scared—worries about money and taking care of Florence and Tessa. There's some deep well there, but he wouldn't let me look down it. I think he's in danger."

"Yeah," said Rena. "All his life."

I did not sleep well that night. I did not remember any dreams, good or bad. At least I didn't kick Ruthie. I tossed and turned and got up to pee several times. Since the cat incident, I'd taken to reading a book and then patrolling the house when I couldn't sleep. Ruthie hated it when I was doing this because it invariably woke her up.

"Ret, come to bed!" she yelled down the stairs into the basement as I made my way. I nearly jumped out of my skin.

"Can't sleep!" I yelled back very loudly at her.

"Well, come lie down anyway. You're driving me crazy with this walking around at night. I have to work tomorrow, Ret. C'mon!"

"I'm checking the cellar door."

"You checked it when we went to bed. It's just as locked as it was then."

I checked it anyway and came up the stairs carrying my fish beater, meeting her in the doorway, bleary-eyed and yawning. It's a heavy oak stick with one end banded in metal. Embossed on the side is "Beat 'em before ya eat 'em."

"So what is this for?" She reached out to grab it, and I swung it behind my back.

"To beat down the bogie man."

"Ret, there's no bogie man . . ."

"So you say . . ." I reluctantly climbed into bed and listened to her fall asleep and snore intermittently for the next two hours. I might have fallen asleep about twenty minutes before the alarm went off.

"Gosh, your eyes are red." Deborah spoke to me right away as I walked up to my mailbox with my triple shot latte. "Did you hear what happened out in White Swan?"

"What?"

"Parker Heslah."

"Yeah. What about him?" I sipped my coffee deeply.

"He's dead."

My coffee cup slipped through my fingers and exploded on the floor, spreading across the linoleum like a pool of brown blood. I ran to grab some paper towels from behind her desk.

There weren't enough towels and she got down next to me on her hands and knees with a wad of tissues. Even working together, we couldn't get it all mopped up.

"I'll call George in maintenance," she said reassuringly. "Don't worry about it."

"What happened, Deb?"

"Suicide is what they're saying. He shot himself while he was drunk," said Deborah.

"We need more towels," I looked over at her, desperately. "Get me more fucking towels."

"Doc, take a minute, I said I'll get George; we'll get it cleaned up."

Dominia came out of her office, strolled up next to me on the wet floor there, and leaned over to check her mailbox behind the counter. She didn't look at me or say a word, and acted like there wasn't any mess beneath her feet while I blotted and swished around more brown liquid, and then stood up. Dominia strolled silently back into her office, absently staring at a clump of papers.

"Can I get a government car?"

"Yeah, sure. You can sign one out," Deborah answered with a curious gaze. "I've never seen you use one before."

"That's because people know what they look like and always see you coming. I don't like being associated with the government when I go visiting. I usually use my own wheels."

"And today?"

"I want a government agency car parked where I'm going."

"Why?"

"My own reasons, Deb."

She didn't like it. "There's some sort of trouble, isn't there? That Parker boy was bad company and you know something. Are you going to White Swan?"

"I'll be fine. Come on, Deb, I hardly ever use the cars. I know I'm going to get called for crisis intervention out that way anyway when something like this happens."

"Hmmm." She was still not satisfied. "Take the Impala. Stay in touch. Record your mileage." She reached into her desk drawer, shuffled around, and handed me a set of keys.

"Thanks." I went to my office for a minute, packed up, hurriedly, and left.

Deborah's eyes met mine as I walked past, undoubtedly prepping an urgent wire for the moccasin telegraph.

My plan was to go to the White Swan annex building and hover outside, navigating across the street if I needed to in order to get some talk going with the local kids about Parker. I also wanted to get over to Arnold's. My cell phone rang while I was driving out near Harrah. As a matter of good driving habits, I don't usually pick up. In this case, there wasn't a car in sight so I fumbled until I could get the speaker phone on.

"Hello?"

"Barlow . . ." It was Tessa's voice.

"Tessa, how'd you get . . ."

"He's he . . . he . . . hee . . ." Her voice crackled and sounded high pitched.

I didn't remember ever giving her the number. The reception cut in and out.

"He's, he . . ."

"Tessa. Breathe. I know what happened, Tessa. Stop and look at your breath. Can you hear me?"

"Ye, yes . . ." She was sobbing.

"Tessa, I know what's happened; I'm coming out there."

"I'm trying . . . I'm try . . ."

"What is it?"

"He's . . . he's here."

"Who . . . who is here? Tessa, I heard about your loss. I'm so very sorry."

A long pause.

"Hello, Tessa?"

I can't get reception when I really need it on this goddamn reservation.

"Tessa?"

"Yes."

"You hear me now?"

"Yes."

She sounded distant, not in regards to reception, but in the way she does, in the way she goes away in her mind.

"What's happening, Tessa? Breathe. I'm sorry. I heard."

"Je . . . Jack!"

"What?"

No response.

"Jack Brie?" I said as clearly as I could.

"Ye, yes!!"

My mouth went dry.

"He's there? In the house with you? He's out at your grandpa's? At Arnold's?"

"No, not now. But he was."

"How do you know?"

Silence.

"Tessa, are you there? How do you know Jack was there? Tessa?"

I smacked the cell against the dash. "Tessa??"

The signal cut in momentarily.

"I found uh. . . a note."

"What do you mean?" The line became clear.

"On the kitchen table. It was there when I came in from getting Samuel at the bus stop."

"A note. How do you know it was him?"

"I, I remember. I remember his writing. He wrote a note that said, 'I'm back baby.' It was him!"

"Tessa, I'm going to call the cops."

"No! No! You can't do that."

"Why not? They know Jack Brie."

"But don't you see. He's back. He's come back around. He's Ce Ce's daddy. There's nothing can stop him. There's no court order to stop him."

"He's not to be within 500 yards of you, I know that much."

"That's expired. There's no restraining order, nothing. He can say he just wants to see his kid."

"I think we get some law in on this anyway."

"No! No. He'll hurt my family."

"Tessa, they'll protect you."

"Please, please, please. If you mean you're my friend, if you really mean it, please, don't call the cops. They can't help. They won't help. He'll hurt my family."

"What do you want me to do?"

Silence.

"Tessa! What do you want me to do?"

I turned my cell phone upwards and read 'signal faded.' Goddamn it. I threw the cell onto the passenger floor in disgust.

I drove back to the agency and called Ruthie on her cell from the clinic parking lot.

"Ret, no matter what she says, you have to get the law involved. It's in your license and your ethics code. It's imminent danger. You have to report it."

"I know. But she's right; they won't do shit. And then the relationship and all this work is shot."

"Do what you have to do—it's her life and your career. Maybe the sheriff's deputy out there will step up."

That gave me a thought, mostly because I knew he wouldn't.

"I'm calling tribal police."

"Is that enough?"

"Why wouldn't it be? They're trained law enforcement. They carry guns. I'll have done my duty, and maybe I can get Rena to work with me on whether Tessa needs to know I reported it."

"It's your call. Will you be late?"

"Can't help it."

"I swear to God, Ret Barlow, let the police do what they need to do and stay out of it. Don't make me worry about you. Promise me you won't do anything stupid."

"OK."

"You aren't planning on going out there, are you?"

"I'll call you later . . ."

"Ret, don't go out there!"

"Ruthie, I'll call you later."

I hung up, still hearing her objections, which I knew meant I was going to pay later. I called Rena and had to have her paged. Yes, they still had pagers. She called me back about five minutes later.

"What's up?" she began.

I told her. Then I asked her, "Can you get Officer Whitcomb to go out there with me?"

"Let me check the shift roster. You're saying you want to go out there with him?"

"If it'd be all right."

"Not usually. But this once, probably. Given the circumstances."

I met the 2010 Chevy Yukon with "Yakama Nation Tribal Police" and the arrowhead shield of Yakama Nation as it was pulling up near the backdoor of the clinic. On the upper edge of the front fenders, the words "*Walak'ikláama* since 1855" were emblazoned. I parked the government car and dropped the keys with Deborah who was totally confused by my behavior. I didn't have time to explain.

Whitcomb pushed the passenger door open, and I got in. His speech was smooth but maintained the same formality and distance I felt from him outside the courtroom.

"So we're heading out to Arnold's?"

"That all right with you?"

"Sure. I just came on shift. You asked for me. Rena told me. Worried about Tessa, she said. Is that professional, personal, both?" He framed it well, provoking me to react.

"Blends a little, I suppose, Officer Whitcomb. I'm probably in a little deep with this family, deeper than usual. I had an alarming talk with her over the phone a little while ago about Jack Brie."

"Guy's a scumbag."

"You know him?"

"Oh yeah, lots of years. He's been around here forever. But we don't arrest non-Indians. He and I crossed paths about four years ago when I was an auxiliary officer. He was up to Parker Dam with Tina, Tessa's mom, drunk on Nation property and beating her down. I had him picked up by the county deputy. I got to call this in."

He pressed a button on the dash, and I heard "Dispatch." Tribal police seemed to have better technology than Marta and her crew out in White Swan.

"Flora, this is Whitcomb with a 10-38 to look into a 10-12 at A. Miyanishatawit's place out beyond Medicine Valley, possibly code 40 or 60. Complainant is non-enrolled. Stand-by for 10-27."

"Standing by."

"What did that all mean?" I wondered aloud.

"I need your driver's license to start a complaint. Are you saying she might be in danger? Did Brie threaten her or her family?"

"She told me he left a note on the table saying 'I'm back baby.'"

He glanced sideways at me. "Is there anyone in the house related to him?" The sixty-four-thousand-dollar question.

"Her baby sister, Ce Ce, is his daughter."

"Is there a restraining order?"

"There was. It's expired."

"Oh. Hmm. He may have rights to at least come to the door and ask to see his daughter. Does he have custody?"

"As far as I know, Arnold does."

"The note could be for his baby."

"I doubt it."

"I do too. But I've got to have grounds to do much about it. Simple trespass is all it would be so far. I know the guy's an asshole . . ."

I wasn't sure how far to go. "Tessa and her sisters have a long history with Jack Brie. He lived with Tina and them for a couple of years. It wasn't a good environment."

He glanced sideways at me.

"Would you care to elaborate?"

"It'd be better if you could read between the lines."

He drove on and thought on that for a moment. "He'd be the kind of guy who'd look at little girls the wrong way. Correct me if I'm wrong."

"You're on to something," I allowed.

He handed my license back to me. "We can do all this at some other point."

He pushed on the accelerator and scared the shit out of me. The Yukon's heavy police suspension and big engine smoothly surged to about ninety.

"Be there in about twenty minutes."

I adjusted my belt as we shot down the straight highway and dusk started to come on.

He found the two-track without any trouble. We met up with the same usual barking. As we got out, the dogs didn't even bother with him—in fact, one of them scampered away with his tail between his legs, looking back at him. I had to go through the same ritual I underwent the first time.

The house was dark and quiet. I didn't like it. I started to walk toward it with him.

"Stay back at the car," said Whitcomb.

I held further back but kept up with him. The moon was waning, and a chilly breeze hissed through the outline of the scrub trees. He drew his gun from his holster and held it pointed upwards.

"Stand still or I'll blow your brains out."

Arnold's voice was matter-of-fact, muffled, but discernible. There was no questioning Whitcomb was within sights.

"Arnold! It's Whitcomb."

"Oh. Okay, Charley."

A front porch light suddenly beamed blindingly at us, and Arnold appeared outside the screen door, holding his Marlin 30 odd 6. "I didn't call any law."

"Just checking up on you and your family with the good doctor here. He was worried."

"Good timing then, I'd say." Another light came on inside. "You kids can sit up." I saw all the children get up off the floor. Tessa wasn't with them.

"Are we OK now, grandpa?" asked Samuel.

"We got some police here, Samuel. You get your sisters and you something to drink and some more beans and noodles while I talk to Charlie and the doctor."

I stepped forward from the gathering shadows.

"Hello doctor," said Arnold. "You're probably looking for Tessa. That Parker boy's took his own life."

"Yes, I heard."

Arnold looked at me and then at Whitcomb, who looked at me too.

"Tessa's gone." Arnold's eyes reflected worry while the rest of his face just looked irritated. "I don't know where she is. I haven't seen her since late afternoon."

"She called me, Arnold. On my cell, which I didn't even know she had the number for . . ."

"I might have give it to her," he admitted. "I was talking to her about keeping up with her treatment."

"That's quite all right. But Arnold, she sounded scared when I spoke to her. I had terrible reception . . . She said Jack Brie is back."

"I seen the note he left. I haven't seen him, though." He flipped up his pack of Pall Malls in one motion and pulled a cigarette out with his lips. "If he comes into this house like that again to drop off notes or anything else, it won't be pretty."

"Arnold," cautioned Whitcomb, "let the law take him on."

"All I'm saying is, he comes near here, Charlie, I won't have to aim twice."

"You have his daughter."

"Ce Ce ain't his. Never was. He only thinks that. That little girl don't have a father per se. Tina don't know who her daddy is. I'm her only daddy."

He took a long draw on his smoke, blew out mountains of smoke, and stared at Whitcomb.

"You and I know you can't do shit to a white man out here or anywhere else. He knows it too. County won't come here even if you call 'em. He's a bad man, Charlie." He stabbed his smoke into the air. "I'm going to shoot him down like any other dirty dog if he comes within 500 yards of my kids."

Whitcomb glanced down at the Marlin leaning up against the porch wall.

"Arnold? What about the filly?" I asked, trying to ease the tension.

"She's back there."

"Mind if I have a look?"

"Help yourself. I'm staying right here." He would never admit it, but I could see he was scared.

Whitcomb walked with me, "Well, that seemed dangerous," he allowed, letting his breath out. "If he comes back and Arnold shoots first, it'd be cold-blooded murder no matter what you think of Jack Brie. That's how it would be. Then those kids got a mom and a grandpa in prison."

We got back to the corral, and although it was dusk, we could see it was empty.

"Either she took her horse or it ran off," said Whitcomb.

"She took it. I have a feeling," I said.

We made our way back to the house. Arnold was sitting on the front porch, and the kids were eating inside at the table. He had the Marlin laying across his lap. We told him.

"Goddamn it." He stood up and spit onto the ground. "Goddamn that girl."

"Where would she go, Arnold?" asked Whitcomb.

"God knows where. That filly is unpredictable. She ain't trained yet. Tessa only got riding her around in the fields here two weeks ago. She don't even hardly know how to ride. Goddamn stupid." He spit onto the porch.

"You've no idea where she might go."

"No." His gaze looked distant; he was thinking but not saying.

"Anything you can think of, Arnold, might help," said Whitcomb. "She lost her boyfriend today, and she's probably all mixed up. She called the doc here and he says she was scared about Jack Brie . . ."

"She was here when I come back from White Swan," said Arnold. "She showed me the note, and I recognized the writing. I told her wait here while I catch the gates closed. She was all upset about Parker and crying. She kept saying she had to go, and I kept saying 'where you got to go right now?' And she wouldn't say where. I ordered her to stay here, but she'd run off when I got back in. I thought she just walked out to blow off steam."

"She's still a kid, Arnold," I offered. "She's probably not sure what she's doing, things being as they are."

"I'm going to thank you to stop messing in my business, doctor." I stepped back at his words. He was on fire with fear and anger and not to be reasoned with. "I need that girl home right now safe with her family. That man Brie is a dangerous son of a bitch. There's no good reason she should run out on her family now."

"Well, Arnold," said Whitcomb, "I'm going to stay patrolling out this direction tonight because of all this." He handed up a card. "This is my cell number and I have reception. It links right into my car, and I'll be out here within five minutes. Do not, I repeat, do not take the law into your own hands. You'd be the one doing time, Arnold."

Arnold stared at him. "Somebody's got to do something about Brie."

"We're all agreed on that," said Whitcomb. "How about letting me be the one to take him on if he comes around?"

Arnold said nothing. That was as much as we were going to get.

I got home late, and Ruthie was really scared and angry. She hadn't gone to sleep early this time. I told her how things went down.

"So you are now a cop?"

"No, I just knew I could talk to her if she was there."

"Why did you have to go out there? You could talk to Tessa at the police station or the jail. You could talk to her at school. You could talk to her at the clinic. You promised me you wouldn't try to be a hero."

"I rode with Tribal Police, Ruthie. She was very desperate, and I felt I should check up on her."

"To meet up with a half-crazy old man scared to death pointing a bear gun at both of you in the dark." She crossed and uncrossed her arms, pacing across the room. "Are you trying to make me a widow?"

"I'm sorry."

"I'm done with sorry. Are you going crazy? I think you need help. You're up all night banging windows and doors, carrying around a club like our own private rent-a-cop, kicking the shit out of me while I sleep, and now you're a cop. I didn't know I married a cop. First I didn't know I married an Indian and I've been working on that. Now I'm married to an untrained cop who's never dealt with criminals. . ."

"I've seen lots of clients in jail . . ." I protested weakly.

"Oh, that's how you got your training. You're in too deep with this girl and her family, Ret."

She paused with her mouth open, and then brought her palm to her forehead. "That dead cat head has something to do with all this, doesn't it?"

I just looked at her.

"It does, doesn't it, Ret?" She read my face, although I tried to stay nonplussed. "I've been so stupid! I knew it. Some criminal knows where we live, don't they? Oh my God, this is so scary. Oh my God!"

"Calm down, Ruthie, it was probably Parker who did that."

"Parker and he's dead. Right? Did he really kill himself? How did he come to put a cat head on our porch? And why would he do such a thing except to scare us? How did he know where we live?"

"I don't know. I don't know that he did it. We're in the phone book."

"No, you don't know. Shit, why do we have to have this going on in our lives?" She started moving around the room before swinging around to point at me. "I'd tell you to sleep on the couch, but I'm too scared to be alone in my own room in my own house. Does Jack Brie know where we live, Ret?"

"I very seriously doubt it."

"But Parker did. That's what you're saying. So you can't say absolutely no, Jack Brie, a known violent criminal, doesn't know where we live, can you? You can't say no.'"

I couldn't truthfully say 'no.' "I can't say anyone doesn't know where we live. We're in the phone book."

"No, you can't. And you're right; anyone can look us up. Tessa knows Parker and Parker's dead. Tessa knows Jack Brie.

And she's on the run, and she's scared. So did Parker know Jack Brie?"

"Doesn't follow necessarily, really, Ruthie."

"God, this is so bad," she shook her head. "Ret, don't you understand? I hardly see you; you're not really here when you're home and then this. I can't take this anymore. I was so scared today—scared for you and for me, scared for our home. You're running around pretending you're a policeman—I can't take the worry. I couldn't do any work at school and people noticed—even the kids. Tell me we're not in danger—please."

It didn't look good when I didn't respond.

"Don't try to sleep on the bed."

She stormed off into our room and slammed the door. Then she opened it again to peer out with a scowl at me. "And don't think you're going to sleep out here either."

"Well, where the hell am I supposed to sleep?"

"Sleep on the floor. Sleep at the foot of the bed like a dog, for all I care."

She was right. This was my fault.

## Fourteen

The blundering,
wobbling,
offtimes treacherous
administration of Indian affairs,
conducted from the seat of power
three thousand miles away is the most
sickening,
discouraging,
disgusting
failure
in the history of American government . . .
-*William E. Johnson, United States Indian Service, 1912*

A man accepts what he must. I found myself over my head. After a rough night on a camping pad with a sleeping bag on the floor of my own bedroom, I finally got hold of Elisi. It was my third night with about two hours of sleep, and it showed in my voice. She talked to me from her sister's house near Neah Bay.

"You sound tired."

"I am. And I'm in a lot of trouble with my wife. She's scared."

"You bought a gun yet?"

"I might as well file for divorce as do that. She hates guns."

"You might want one anyway. Don't have to tell her."

"I don't think so. I'm in lots of trouble for what I keep too much to myself. And I don't know much about guns."

"You better try to protect yourself and her. There's more."

"What the hell, *kála*?"

"My sister broke her hip. I've been staying here with her for a few days." She seemed to be changing the subject. "She dreamed of Tessa. She dreamed of a girl on a horse."

"When?"

"Two nights ago. My sister said this girl was lost, lost on her horse. She saw her in a dream."

"Elisi, I can't do this anymore. I'm done."

"You're already involved."

"I can't be this involved. It's not right. I'm going to stay in my office at the clinic. This is something for the police."

"What police?"

"If Tessa runs away..."

"Status offense," she interrupted. "No one gives a hoot."

"If Jack Brie comes to Arnold's house..."

"Misdemeanor trespassing at most until Arnold gets a restraining order."

"So he will, Elisi! I am not a social worker! I cannot fix this!"

"You can help, *kála*."

"I already have," I said, irritated.

"There's more to do." She just wouldn't let go.

"Elisi, I'm just an IHS psychologist, whatever that is. I can't be following clues in somebody else's dreams and having dead cat heads dumped on my porch for my wife to find. And I'm not a goddamned mystic! I'm done, I'm telling you."

"I thought more of you."

"No."

"Doctor Barlow. This is not about Tessa or your wife or anyone else. This is about you. This is about you at a crossroads. You have to figure this out."

"Elisi . . ."

"You called me *kála* for a while."

"I mean *kála*."

The line was dead.

The honest truth is I passed out on the floor of my office. I had a no-show and went to get a cup of coffee. I drank the coffee and caught up some notes. I had the thought "I'm stressed out," my first clue being I was sweating, and I wasn't even moving around. I wanted to call Ruthie for moral support and concluded immediately and with a sigh that this was a very bad idea right now. Then I felt my eyes sink into my head and got mildly nauseated, which are familiar signs that a migraine is coming on. I took four ibuprofen and sumariptan succinate, closed the door, turned the lights out, lay down on the floor, and started progressive relaxation.

I followed my relaxation with some imagery—first, from my childhood, weeping willows blowing in the breeze on a warm summer day, then the more traditional image of my nostrils as great city gates; the gate opens inward, the breeze rolls in; the gate opens outward, the breeze flows out. Next was a river delta meeting the ocean; the river flows very slowly inward, then slowly back out to the sea.

I started to feel the sumariptan succinate coming on and this was very good. It has a mildly-sedating effect, and I could feel a rush over my head, a loosening of unspecified tightness there. I started to feel better. I had the sumariptan succinate buzz. But I was asleep. I didn't dream. I thought instead. I do some of my best thinking while I'm asleep.

I thought. "Where would she go?"

Arnold promised he'd call me if she came back. So did Whitcomb. No word at all. Was she dead? Why would she leave the kids and Arnold? She couldn't go to Parker. Parker was dead. She must be overwhelmed with grief; she was really close with that boy. Where would she go?

I said to myself, "She's gone to kill Jack Brie."

But she's terrified of him, I protested. Still, she doesn't believe Arnold can stop him. I thought some more. She explained how she could manipulate Brie when she was little. She took his note as an invitation to her. She's going to try to talk to him, try to manipulate him, and then she's going to kill him . . . but how would she find him? How would she even know where to find him?

I started to fall even deeper asleep.

"Sorry to interrupt your rest," came Gaillard's voice.

How would he know? What's he got to do with this? I thought some more.

"Ahem. Sorry to interrupt your rest, doctor."

Christ Almighty. I opened my eyes as the lights came on; he was standing in the doorway.

"You all right?" His voice was sincere with a hint of amusement. I struggled to my feet, trying to look nonchalant.

"Sorry, sorry. I had a migraine and decided to lie down."

"Oh," he smiled slightly. "I get those sometimes. They're a bitch."

"Sorry to be sleeping on the job . . ."

He pursed his lips. "Maybe you need to go home."

"No, no. I have clients coming later." I sat down at my desk.

"I stopped by to talk to you about burning sage in your office."

"Sage?" I was still pretty bleary.

"There's been some complaints about you burning sage in your office," he continued.

"Come on in and have a seat." He took the chair by the door, noticing my sandbox on the table. "This is a neat idea . . ."

"Yeah, my wife actually gave me that. Lots of folks play with it while they talk."

He raised the little rake, moved the stones around a little, and started playing himself.

"Therapeutic," he concluded.

"It helps . . ."

His eyes met mine. "Look, Ret. I'm so pleased with things you've been doing lately. There's no question there are people who respect you, whatever the differences of opinion might be among your compatriots." He seemed a little awkward. "I didn't come by to get on your case about burning sage. In fact, I rather like the smell. I know it's a tradition for some folks around here and makes them feel good."

"But you need me to stop doing it," I offered, trying to help him get to his point.

"There've been complaints to the facility management committee. Actually, it's stimulated some debate, too."

"Well, I haven't done it very often. I've had some folks ask me if I could from time to time. You know, they want to bless their tears. I keep a smudge kit around and I . . ."

He held up his hand. "You don't need to explain. I get it. I'd prefer to just say 'go ahead' and do it. After all, if it helps, why not?"

"I don't think it'd set off the sprinkler system," I continued. "I've only burnt the tiniest bit at a time . . ."

"Well, the sprinkler system is not the problem. The complaints have been made by individuals who say they have allergy problems. They say they can smell it all down the hall, and it gives them allergy problems."

He looked again right in my eyes. I could tell he didn't really like what he was saying. Down the hall were Dominia, Leo, Kent, and Eileen.

"Well," I noted, "there is the Native American Religious Freedom Act."

"Which actually came up at the committee meeting . . . I was there, you know. I don't sit on that committee, but they asked me to come by for just this issue."

"If an Indian person asks me to burn sage during the performance of my duties—that is, while I'm doing therapy or consultation with them—isn't that a traditional healing practice they're asking me to incorporate? How is that any different than you or another doc doing some medical procedure that's smelly or unpleasant?"

He raised his brows. "I get your point, and it's a good one. In Winslow, IHS has a healing hogan they've constructed right adjacent to their clinic. No doubt they burn sage or whatever else they want in there . . ."

"But we can't do the same thing here."

"We're just not equipped. If I approve you burning sage and you do it more regularly, I'm going to have Portland personnel office on my ass in no time. There's going to be some governmental environment rule or clause you and I don't yet know anything about they're going to invoke."

"Why not wait until they do that? After all, I don't burn sage that often in here."

"I'm looking for a new pediatrician and personnel are ranking the job definition as we speak. I need them to maximize the duty pay for coming out here in order to have any hope of getting any applications. I can't afford to alienate them over an issue like this."

His explanation rang true.

"So speaking of burning sage, I'm just burning with curiosity," I said. "I'm so aware how little of the sage smoke I've made could actually get in that hallway. And I've never heard a sneeze. There's never been a knock on my door. No one's ever talked to me about it. I just can't help wondering if Dominia or Leo or Kent have developed a new allergy recently."

He raised his hands. "I'd like to comment on that. Believe me. I don't think it's right. But my role has its limits." He got up and started to open the door before pausing.

"You could defy me." His eyes glimmered.

"Sorry?"

"You could just defy me . . ." I thought he might start to laugh.

"What do you mean?" He had an impish look.

"Well, Ret, just because some folks like to waste my time with little games, doesn't mean you need to play along. I'll tell you what," he put his index finger to his chin and then pointed to me. "How about I send you a memo forbidding you from burning sage? In the meantime, why not put a little placard up behind your chair here—it could read something like 'Smudge supplied upon request' or 'Native American Religious Freedom Act supported here.'"

"And have clients prep and burn their own sage . . ." I liked Gaillard a little more.

"Look, I'd have to come at you about the memo, which I would certainly copy to Kent. But I'd expect you to indicate, in writing I might add, that you're following my directives and not burning sage. You might add that some of your clients are burning sage, but it's not you. That would be sufficient for me. I'd just mention to Kent or whoever else wants to know," he paused knowingly, "that you seem to have stopped burning sage, but I hadn't the legal authority to stop your Indian clients from practicing their spiritual beliefs."

"What about the allergies and facility's management committee . . ."

"It'd be a hot potato. They'd all be much less interested in making trouble for the tribe, believe me."

With this, he gave me a mock salute and started to leave.

"Go home and get some rest if you need to, Ret."

As he closed the door, I thought of how very far away the Indian Health Service was from what I was currently involved in, how distant it was from the people I worked with.

I decided to take Gaillard up on leaving early. I was supposed to go home midafternoon anyway to meet the alarm installation guy, now I could leave earlier. On route, I dialed Elisi at her sister's again and set the cell phone in my lap with the little speaker turned on.

"I don't see Tessa running away out of shock over Parker's death. There's something else." I said as soon as I had her on the line.

It was her style I was using. Coming right back at her. I wasn't sure she'd even speak to me.

"I'm glad you've at least decided to try to use your mind," she agreed.

"*Kála*, why'd you hang up on me?"

"You were irritating me . . ."

There wasn't much I could think to say to that. "Fine . . . on a different subject, is there a place for people to do illegal business out near White Swan?"

She laughed. "Is there a place where you couldn't do illegal business is a better question, doctor."

"I'm not asking my question right. I don't mean a place like somebody's home or a drug house or something like that. I mean a place you could do business if you weren't from there, and you didn't want anyone to know. A place where you could lay low without people knowing you were around and still maybe do business."

"Like a hideout. You better let the cops figure that kind of thing out."

"Before you wanted me involved—I'm trying to determine where Tessa's gone."

"If she's gone anywhere and not staying at some girlfriend's..."

"I think this is different. She's not home when everything I know about her would say she would be. We have to figure out where she's gone. Can you think a place like I'm describing?"

"Oh, I surely can."

"You can." I waited.

"I know a place out that way Indian people don't ever like to get near. People say it's haunted. Besides all that, it's not particular well-lit . . ." She laughed. "Probably ought to be condemned too. The gate's always locked up tight and the buildings are set a good half mile off the road."

"Mission Boarding School."

"Yes."

"That's at least ten miles from Arnold's place. Anywhere else?"

"No. That's all I can think of."

"*Kála*, do you think she'd go look for him? For Brie? I mean riding her horse—would she actually do try to find him on horseback?"

"Ahh," she hesitated. "Well, it's hard to know what young Indian girls will do. And she's a Yakama girl. Her family is threatened, and she's a Miyanashatawit. *Yaych'ū'nal* with all those people, like I told it—I meant all that about that family. That's why her grandpa stuck a rifle in your face."

"Arnold told me Tessa only got on her horse for the first time two weeks ago for about ten minutes or so and while Leon was helping her."

"Doesn't mean she wasn't getting on her on her own time when nobody was looking. I suspect that filly would let her ride her anyway. The bond between those two comes from some other place. I'm letting my nieces care for my sister and coming back early. Maybe you should call Whitcomb about her possibly going somewhere particular instead of just running around. But don't call Arnold about the idea. He might go shoot somebody up."

After we hung up, I went inside and ate a homemade ham and swiss sandwich before dozing off until the guy from the alarm company showed up about two pm. Frankly, I thought the new technology might get Ruthie and me back on speaking terms. I signed up for the best system, both wired and wireless relays into the alarm company office and also directly to the cops, window and door sensors, and two motion sensors, too. When she walked in at around four thirty, I eagerly pointed out the fancy chrome code pad to her and the several security features we now had at our disposal. She just looked at me and rolled her eyes. I tried not to be discouraged. After all, she didn't get angry with me about the expense. I tried to stay optimistic.

By afternoon of the next day, I'd already seen four clients and then had a cancellation. I decided to try to get hold of Rena on my landline so she could arrange for me to interface with Officer Whitcomb. My cell vibrated while I was calling her; I ignored it, and Rena's voicemail greeting came on announcing she was at an all-day training. After leaving my message, I reluctantly pulled the cell out of my pocket and gazed with mild displeasure at the unfamiliar number. I assumed this was yet another robocall from an Oklahoma State alumni fundraising campaign. Instead, it was a text that read as gibberish. The return number wasn't an Oklahoma area code either. I googled it—218, Beltrami County, Minnesota. I don't know anyone in Minnesota. I then searched the county name. Beltrami County, Red Lake Indian Reservation—I'd never been there. All this seemed rather strange but then an unexpected client walked in (as they sometimes do) and I forgot all about it.

The same text came again three hours later on my way home—'jnsbnstkgtme'. I stopped at a light and read it out loud trying to make sense of it.

"J-N-S-B-N-S-K-G-T-M-E." What the hell? How do you stop this kind of spam?

I pushed the cell into my shirt pocket. I was driving along First Avenue coming into downtown Yakima, trying to remember Tessa's horse's name after forgetting it while talking with Elisi the day before.

"*Ámashi . . . Ámashitum*," I finally recollected.

I felt worried and preoccupied about her, afraid she'd taken off on Ámashitum after Parker had died in order to try to find Jack Brie. I knew I was crossing a professional boundary but I was trying to be a good therapist. There was no one else in her world who might be able to figure out what she was up to and help keep her out of danger. This fact seemed to transcend the rigors of professionalism I'd been socialized to sustain. Who else besides her overwhelmed family would even care if she got into big trouble? Even they didn't know what I knew.

She had trusted me, this old *pashtin*, with secrets she wouldn't even tell her sisters. She'd taken that chance, and I'd watched her transform herself, grow, and heal since then. I knew what all that took; I'd heard the excruciating specifics from her and other young girls facing off with bastards like Brie. If she was pursuing her own rapist, a dangerous man who might do anything, what kind of person would I be to not try to stop her?

And so I just happened to say aloud during this long thought process, "Jack and his beanstalk." And a shockwave moved through my whole body. I pulled into the parking lot right next to me and sounded the text on my cell out loud:

"J n s bn stk gt me. Jack and his beanstalk got me."

I bumped my head on the edge of the door frame I got out of the car so fast. I was very impressed to find myself now standing in the parking lot of Valley Gun and Pawn. I decided to go inside. I needed to do something; I had to take action. I had to buy a gun.

I'd been in this store before. I'd come here once with the idea I was going to buy a shotgun after a meth addict sat on our front porch swing one late summer night. Ruthie and I were having trouble going to sleep. Our bedroom wall ends right at back of the porch, and we had the small window open wide. I first heard him breathing, which was pretty frightening. I slid up the wall while kneeling on our mattress, peered over the window ledge, and he was just sitting there, staring straight ahead, sweating, and breathing. I had nothing to stop him when he eventually got up and checked to see if the front door was truly locked before wandering off. I would've had to fight a psychotic meth freak hand-to-hand. So the next day, despite Ruthie's vehement disapproval, I checked into buying a shotgun at this very pawn shop. I never bought one. Although the meth addict visit took place a couple of years earlier, the owner recognized me instantly. Maybe he was like that with everyone.

"What can I do ya for?" The working man's greeting.

"I thought I'd have a look at your pistols."

"O. . . 'kay," he seemed befuddled by my lack of specificity. "We have a few." He swept his hand toward two display cases full of guns, "We have a variety . . ."

"Uh. Well, I was looking for something smaller, I guess, easily hidden." Suddenly thinking this was suggestive of some petty criminal intent, I quickly self-corrected. "I mean my wife needs to be able to handle it."

A knowing look came over his face. "Well, I don't know your wife. My ex-wife carries a Smith & Wesson model 29, which isn't exactly lady-like or discreet."

"Yeah, well . . . she needs something she can carry in her purse." I was trying to appear knowledgeable about women's firearm preferences.

"She have a concealed weapon permit?"

"Well, uh, not yet . . ."

He seemed unabashed. "Fairly easy to get. Just bring a photo ID up to the police station and fill out the form. Fifty-five bucks."

"Oh, well. I guess I'll need to do that." This was a case of diminishing returns, and I was looking more and more ignorant. "What do you recommend?"

He reached into his cabinet and pulled out three pistols, all relatively small and all used. I learned about the virtues of the Kel-Tec 32, its double-action-only mechanism and easy trigger. I held a Smith & Wesson 442 revolver, which he had in the "Women of the NRA" version with the Second Amendment embossed on the barrel, and I dry-fired a Seecamp LWS 380, "the smallest 380 you can buy." I nodded knowingly. I liked the Seecamp; it tapped into James Bond fantasies for me.

"That's a nice pistol. How much?"

"Eleven hundred dollars."

I was speechless for a second. "Really? Eleven hundred dollars?"

"If you've got gold bullion. I deal in that too."

"Wow, I didn't know they were so . . ."

My ignorance now fully revealed; he took mercy on me.

"Look, I just took a Taurus 85 off pawn," he said, pulling out another revolver that looked like the Smith & Wesson. "It's a good little gun. Used but not very old. It's .38 caliber. Ultra Light is what they call it. Good for your wife. I could let it go right now for $240."

I picked it up and held it. It fit my hand.

"I'll take it." He still had the case for it and succeeded in selling me two boxes of shells before I left. I got into the car feeling like I'd just had an affair. Ruthie must never know, I thought. I stuffed the entire bag under my seat and drove home.

She had her book circle that evening, so I made homemade chilaquiles and opened a Beck's non-alcoholic beer. She got home about 9:30.

"Hi, Ruthie," I tried the formal approach.

"Hello." She put her things down then stood with her hands on our hips gazing at me.

"So . . .," she said. "Are we getting divorced?"

"I hope not."

"Me too," she said. She turned and strolled into the kitchen.

"I made chilaquiles . . ." I announced.

"Good."

And that was that. We didn't talk about anything else. She came out and sat with me, glaring while she chewed. I smiled and said, "Hi." She did not respond. She just sat staring at me and chewing.

Before we turned in, I went over the alarm system and how to use it. I had her try it out and key herself into the house.

"Can I turn it on when you're not home?" she asked.

"You can turn the motion sensors off," I pointed out how. "And the windows and doors are still armed."

"What do you mean armed?"

"The alarm will go off if anyone tries to come in."

"Oh," she nodded. "Well, that's good." She stood pretty far away from me. "OK, then. I get it."

"Ruthie."

"That's enough for now. We're on preliminary speaking terms. I don't want to talk about anything else right now."

"OK." We went to bed. At least I got to sleep in the bed.

The next day I called in sick. I had an idea and I was going to follow it. I called Rena. She said she'd get a message to Whitcomb. He called me on my cell about eight am.

"Have you heard anything about Tessa Miyanashatawit, Officer Whitcomb?" I was in a hurry.

"Not a word, doctor."

"Can you tell me more about Parker Heslah's suicide?"

"Well, that'd be police business at this point."

"I need to know if his death was really a suicide."

"Something your client say make you think it wasn't?"

"That'd be my business." He knew I couldn't talk about that; I wasn't in the mood for bullshitting.

His voice became icy. "Not if you have information pertaining to a police investigation. I could have the tribal prosecutor work with the county DA to subpoena you."

"Sounds like an interesting legal procedure. I have no reason to believe you need to go to such an effort. Is there a police investigation, by the way?"

Our little conversation was taking on an adversarial tone.

"All unattributed deaths are subject to investigation. Felonies on the rez are FBI business," he added, somewhat curtly.

"Lots of luck. I assumed Mory already ruled it a suicide."

This stopped him in his tracks. "And how would you know Mory?" he asked. Mory Diligu is the best and only coroner in Yakima County.

"When you're involved in youth suicide on the rez, you get to know Mory," I explained. I tried to diffuse the tone between us, telling him I was technically 'out sick' and maybe we could meet up and talk more. He said he had a split shift and wouldn't be back on until five pm. We agreed to meet at Yakamart at four-thirty.

"Mory didn't rule on anything yet," he said as he walked up. I grabbed a French vanilla hi-rev coffee, he settled for the regular brew, and we sat at one of the free tables in the café. "He did the autopsy already but not the report. It'll come back a suicide, trust me." There was sarcasm in his voice. "What I'd like to know is what kind of psychologist you're supposed to be getting all involved in this. This doesn't seem like the place of a therapist—to be asking all these questions about somebody you didn't even work with."

"That remains to be seen."

"Because I would think somebody in your profession would only be interested in Parker's death as another youth suicide and what could prevent such occurrences. After all, that's a boy who clearly had a lot running against him."

I looked him over as he spoke—he wasn't so much unfriendly, just not warm, as though there was something generally missing from human interaction for him, something he was looking for but had never found.

"You think I'm overstepping . . ."

"Just surprises me is all," he said as he jostled his coffee and spilled a little. "Shit." He grabbed a napkin.

"I do think I know where Tessa is, and why she's there."

He raised his eyebrows high. "Go on . . ." the typical cop suspiciousness seemed something of a put-on to me.

"It's not that easy . . ."

"If you know where she is, tell me, and let's go get her and take her home."

He then glanced absently out the window at a passing car as if the matter was not really that important to him. My flags were up at the mix of his responses to me, but I didn't know why. Was he schizoid? Why apply psychiatric labels? Was he making me nervous?

"I believe Tessa's going where she thinks Brie is . . . or maybe knows he is."

"What makes you think that?"

"I was very puzzled by her first calling me and then leaving home. It didn't make sense. I don't believe she would ever leave her family while they were in danger. She loves those little ones and her grandpa. But then I thought hard about that.

She would leave them under one condition—if she thought she could do something more to keep them safe by leaving than by staying around. I think she knows more about Brie and his doings than she's let on. Doesn't it make you wonder why this note she called me about from him comes up so close to the point when Parker kills himself—if that's what happened?"

"Amateur detecting, doctor, and I don't mean to make you feel bad. Whatever that note was all about, which I never saw, by the way, you should know Mr. Brie isn't within a thousand miles of here. I called his parole officer in Minnesota."

"Minnesota?"

"Yeah. I looked him up. Brie just finished a six month stint in Beltrami County jail for felony firearm and forgery. And he checked in with his man last week."

"In person?"

"In person."

I pulled out my cell and showed him the text.

"What about it?" He sipped his coffee, sat back, and lifted his eyebrows. "I can't make sense of it."

"Look at the area code." I showed him, struggling at first with how to access the source number.

"My memory for area codes isn't what it used to be."

Again the sarcasm; why?

"That area code's for Minnesota. Beltrami County."

His face shifted and his eyes narrowed. "What?"

I explained, "This text comes from a number and area code in Beltrami County. It's Tessa. She's got Brie's cell. She's telling me he's got her. I got this text three times yesterday."

"Gibberish. A baby playing with mama's cell. What makes you think it's her?"

He pulled out his own cell and looked at it absently. "Listen, I've got to return a call; I'll be right back."

I nodded and leaned back enjoying my coffee. He stepped out front, and I watched him pace around and talk for a few minutes. His facial expressions became far more animated. I had no idea who he might be calling. He came back and sat down, assuming the same tenor with me as he had left with.

I tried again and held up my cell toward him. "It's not gibberish. Jnsbnstkgtme . . . look—Jack and his beanstalk got me. Don't you see? She knew I'd know what that meant. She's texting me to tell me he's holding her somewhere."

"It's a leap as far as I can see."

"I think Brie's here on the rez, or else why would she call about the note? He's lying low, and she found out where he's holed up, maybe through Parker. I think Brie's got her."

"Well, I'm telling you he's nowhere near here, doctor. I never saw that note and neither did you."

"But Arnold said he did. I trust Arnold. And I wouldn't be surprised if Brie had something to do with Parker's death."

He waved a hand at me dismissively. "Another leap, but it explains why you were asking about all that . . ." He could probably see the frustration on my face. "Well, OK, let's say it's an idea." He set his coffee down. "Let's just go."

"Where?"

"To prove you wrong and get your mind off all this, doc. Call it a mental health intervention on your own behalf." He laughed to himself. "Tell me where you think we should have a look."

"The old Mission Boarding School," I responded readily.

"Fine."

"You don't think we should call somebody, FBI or something?" I guess I thought we needed help.

He sat back and squinted at me again. "Even though I think it's nice to have a new shrink who cares about all this stuff with the kids, I can't look stupid following up on some nonsense from a wrong number on your cell phone. My chief has already been on my ass for straying off patrol in too many directions and missing dispatch calls. But let's go out there and have a look just to prove you wrong . . . and I'd appreciate it if you don't mention it to anybody I work with. I don't plan on calling it in. It just so happens I'm assigned out that way anyway tonight."

I opted to follow him separately. He drove like a banshee. We flew through the thirty-five-mile-an-hour zone at Heritage University doing sixty and by the time we crossed Harrah Road, he was hitting seventy and about a mile ahead of me.

## Fifteen

> Some writers about Indian education have . . .
> claimed that attendance at federal boarding schools
> has a bad influence on the mental health of children and youth,
> and they have implied that the suicide rate
> is related somehow to boarding-school attendance . . .
> This claim appears to have no basis in fact. . .
> -Robert Havighurst, *The extent and significance of suicide
> among American Indians, 1970*

Whitcomb slowed at the Fort Road Extension and waited for me to catch up. It was about six pm, and there were a couple of kids walking back toward town. I didn't recognize them, but one of them waved; he might have been waving at Whitcomb.

The old Mission School is across from Toppenish Creek Longhouse and the Pow Wow grounds. It's not just one building but a central school with several old dormitories surrounding it. Although it's pretty far back, you can see the complex from the gate at the road. Whitcomb stopped in front to unlock it. I always wondered who had keys to that gate. The light was becoming dim, but it wasn't dark yet. We pulled down the driveway, our cars bumbling over the cattle grid and on up the long drive.

The school building itself has an empty flagpole in front of it, and the clanging of its chain in the wind drew my attention. Engraved in the arched stone over the front door were the words "Methodist Indian Mission School, 1924." Whitcomb pulled his

Yukon around behind this building and parked. As I got out, the wind picked up and the trees creaked loudly.

"Careful walking around here. These trees haven't been trimmed in years and they're old elms. Not indigenous to the area," he laughed at his own remark. "The white people planted 'em all around here but the limbs blow down easy. It's not too safe spending time below them when the wind's up."

The sun was down, and I could see a dust devil forming in the field behind us.

"Have you been out here much?"

"Came here all the time when I was a kid," he said.

An old wooden fire escape staircase creaked as it swung back and forth from the decaying brick and mortar. I followed him while he talked on toward the rear of the building.

"I never was scared of this place like some folks. I liked to hang around here and play." He stopped at a grey door with only a little maroon paint left on it and a couple of bent nails holding it shut.

"This is probably the best way in. The front entrance isn't stable. This'll take us through the kitchen."

He un-bent the nails with his fingers and shook the old door open. We stepped through, and the wind immediately died. I couldn't see anything, and he flipped on a flashlight. There was debris all over the floor, broken furniture, empty pop and beer cans, rolled-up orange shag carpeting. Chunks of ceiling tile had fallen, revealing old wiring. There were lots of spider webs. He seemed to sense my fear.

"We got black widows out here . . ." he relished noting. "They don't bother you if you leave 'em alone. They tend to hide away behind stuff and in the dark spaces. Just be careful if you're lifting anything to not let your bare hands get exposed . . ."

He became more chatty, stepping over a couple of empty drawers on the floor. "They still had kids staying out here in the

1960s, learning the white man ways. Becoming more civilized, you know."

As we came into the kitchen, something smelled very badly. "Hmm. Yech," he grimaced. "Dead raccoon or possum or some such." He glanced up at me and saw my nose wrinkle. "That alone doesn't make the place too inviting, does it?" I thought he was trying to discourage me and just wanted to get this over with.

"Satisfied, doctor?" he asked.

The cupboard doors had all been ripped off and the sink was black with filth. The floor, however, was relatively unobstructed, and as we came to the top of the basement stairs, Whitcomb turned and shone his flashlight in my eyes again.

"Can we look down there?"

He smirked. "Look," he said, "It's not safe down there. I've been down there before, and it wouldn't be a good place to hide."

"Can we look anyway? I don't want to have come all the way out here and put you to this trouble but have it nagging at the back of my mind that we never went down and checked the basement."

He stared at me for a very long moment and finally shrugged.

"We're here to help you settle your mind. You have to be really careful of your footing. There's no railing and the floor down there is filled up with junk you don't want to fall on. Probably safest if you move ahead of me and I can shine the light in front of you."

"Thanks..."

He shone the beam down the stairs, several of which were missing. I kept my footing and my balance by keeping my center of gravity low, stooping down as I stepped forward. Soon I was at the bottom, and he was right behind me. I surveyed the area as he moved his light in a circle. There were several couches with the stuffing chewed off sections, numerous old school desks, and a piano lying on its side. Broken piano keys littered the floor nearby. There were some animal feces in various places.

"Careful not to make a wrong step," said Whitcomb.

There were a couple of doors on the other side of the room. I looked back at him inquisitively.

"Have at it. Go ahead." We stepped over several items and made our way forward.

"That's the old coal room," said Whitcomb. "They had a coal furnace back then." I cracked the door; it smelled dank and mildewed. I moved on to the second door.

"Now as I recall, this is the shop. There may even be some old tools still inside there." I grabbed the handle and shook it, but it was locked.

"Let me try it," he moved up, and shook it hard and it popped open.

"There we go," we moved inside. I couldn't make out much at first, even with his flashlight. There were many sheets and tarps over various shapes—a drill press, perhaps, a table saw, what appeared to be an old joiner, and a band saw, several long work tables and shelves. He swept his light back and forth for me but didn't settle on any one item.

Another flashlight abruptly jumped into my eyes.

"Hello, Charlie," came an easy voice.

"Hi," responded Whitcomb. I swung around as I heard him unsnap his holster and slip out his Glock 9 millimeter. I knew it was a Glock from my visit to the gun store. I knew Glocks don't have a safety, which was why I didn't buy one. You just point and shoot.

"Steady there, doc," whispered Whitcomb, waving the pistol loosely in front of the flash while the rest of him stayed in silhouette.

"The famous Dr. Barlow," came the easy voice again. "A pleasure to meet you, sir. I've heard some about you from our girl, Tessa."

At the edge of Whitcomb's flashlight beam, several items shuffled and fell to the floor, and a tall, bearded white guy moved into view holding his light at his side. The stub of a cigarillo glowed in his mouth for a moment before he said, "My name's Jack Brie."

He didn't have a cowboy hat on, which surprised me.

I caught sight of Tessa, standing in a doorway behind him. She didn't look like herself. Her eyes were glazed over. I thought she might be drugged but soon concluded she was dissociating. Brie led her out from the little lit room like he was handling a baby.

"Come on out here, girl. You remember the good doctor, don't you?" he asked. She said nothing.

Brie turned to me as Whitcomb touched his pistol to the back of my head with one hand and slipped a handcuff on each of my wrists with the other. This seemed a clever trick to me, especially when he clicked them tight.

"You're a smart one, doc, I have to say. But you shouldn't have come here. That was a mistake. I figured Tessa's little code might tempt you but I thought it'd take you longer to figure out."

"You put the code in . . ."

"No, that was her idea. I just let it happen."

"How'd you know I wouldn't bring the FBI?"

"FBI don't give a shit, doc," he smiled. "We all know that. But I did figure you might be tempted to come out here yourself. I'm sure Charlie's sorry to bring you out this way, aren't you, Charlie?" Whitcomb didn't respond. "Dirty cops, no matter where you go, they usually feel bad. Not bad enough to step up, really, and in Charlie's case, well, he's already in too deep."

Whitcomb pushed me forward toward Brie and, as a partially-reformed antisocial teen, I didn't like it much. He cracked me hard on the head with the tip of his pistol, and it hurt.

"Nice," I said as I grimaced, trying not to cuss.

"Doctor," Brie continued, "you've been getting into my business a little bit, and I needed to talk to you anyway . . . how's your wife, by the way? Ruthie, isn't it?"

I didn't respond, but I was more angry than scared.

"She's a pretty one, isn't she?" He glanced at Whitcomb. "School teacher, Charlie. A good catch for the doctor, but he doesn't come home at night."

He pulled hard on his cigarillo stub. "How do you keep her satisfied, doctor? With all your messing in other people's business, I should think she'd need to find another man."

There wasn't much I could say to that. "Instead of trying to play with me, Brie, why don't you just let Tessa and me walk away? For my part, I don't care about whatever you've got going on."

Tessa stood slightly behind him, not really looking at anything, zombie-like. Maybe he did have her drugged.

"I wish it could be some other way, doctor, I really do. You see, Tessa here come out to see me because she's especially upset about the demise of her boyfriend. I won't mention his name, it not being polite in the Indian way. She was thinking she'd take it out on me in some way. She didn't understand, but I helped her. That young man was not good enough for her. He was working for me, and he decided—on his own, mind you—he would work both sides of the street. No one likes a snitch, he might say, but then he was one. He became what the police call an 'informer.' At least, that's what he thought he'd be." He laughed lightly and slapped his knee. "Except he decided he'd do his informing to Charlie here."

Whitcomb moved across the shop floor and peered into the little room. He flipped a switch and several lights came on. I looked around the room, trying to understand the set-up. Brie watched me.

"No power here," he explained, "but we got a couple of auto batteries rigged up to make these lanterns work."

As the lights revealed more of the scene, I noticed the shop tables were covered with a variety of firearms. Several power cables ran along the floor, and he followed my eyes. "Sure, we got more lights too when we run these outside and tap into the lines. We don't do that until around three am or so. We only work three or four hours a day out here, you see." He motioned to points where the incoming wiring was spliced into the old electrical system. "Tiller rigged that up for us; he's good with that sort of thing."

Tiller Miyanashatawit stepped out through the door and looked me over, snorting slightly in disapproval.

"Now it was unfortunate about that boy of Tessa's because he had a real drug problem. I showed him how to make some money, but he had a drug problem and couldn't be reasoned with. You must know the type, doctor."

I leaned into the metal jig of the band saw with the back of the cuffs, but Whitcomb poked me really hard in the middle of my back with his pistol barrel. Again, it really hurt, and I flinched.

"You probably aren't much for pain, doctor. Too much TV," said Jack. "A word to the wise—it's a bad idea to act tough here. Charlie's a bigger man than you."

Whitcomb then wrenched the cuffs up so high from behind, I was forced to bend down over low. He then kicked the back of my knee hard which immediately brought me to kneel. He grabbed my hair tightly and pulled my head back as Brie walked up, puffing hard on his cigarillo stub. He moved quickly, and pushed it into the center of my forehead.

I screamed.

"Goddamn it, doctor," he shook his head and smirked. "And I don't like hurting people. I'm a lover, not a fighter."

The searing burn hurt more because I couldn't do anything about it—no cold water, no compress, not even a palm free to hold over the pain.

"I hope that doesn't leave a permanent mark. I was trying to explain to you what's at stake trying to be a superhero. The people we deal with, our customers, they're a dangerous group, much more dangerous than we are. If you tried this stuff with them, they'd just grind you up in a butcher shop or give you an acid bath. All we ask is cooperation, nothing more, nothing less."

While he mouthed off, I continued to glance around, watching Tiller pull another tarp off a shop table to reveal a variety of what looked like automatic weapons.

Brie followed my eyes again. "My God, you're a curious man, aren't you? There's no stopping your curious nature. I don't mind explaining because it really makes no difference. . . Here we have an ideal location for the modification of weapons of self-defense. We don't have an FFA license for what we do. We're not interested in attracting the attention of the ATF. Goddamn but there's a lot of three letter abbreviations in the gun business. To summarize, we're a business that's resistant to government regulation, so the remoteness of our location helps us avoid the taxman and other spurious agencies."

Another young native man joined Tiller at the table, undoubtedly James.

"No doubt you've heard of these Miyanashatawit boys? Tessa's cousins. We've got them part-time on our little crew here. They were very unhappy that young man of Tessa's was thinking of snitching on our business and were good enough to have a talk with him about it. They explained to him that the officer he was snitching to I've known since he was a little Indian boy running around with his mama at the Spar Tavern . . .

Charlie was already in this with me, paying off some old debts, right?"

Whitcomb didn't seem to respond to anything Brie said.

"You killed Parker," I spat. Tessa looked at me through glassy eyes for what seemed like the first time since I saw her.

"I did not!" said Brie with mock indignation. "That isn't culturally correct, doctor, for you to say his name, by the way. I for one am sorry he decided to do harm to himself."

"You killed him, no matter how it went down," I kept up.

Brie moved closer again, and I tensed up. "Aw, don't worry. I'm not going to hurt you again. The truth is that boy seemed to get very depressed after Tiller and James explained how he'd hurt our feelings."

He grabbed my face, squeezing my cheeks, riveting me with cold, steel-blue eyes. "I wanted to like you, doctor. The truth is, I really don't. And even if I did, it wouldn't change a thing. It must be hard for an educated man to find out he's not been real smart."

He shoved my head back and paced away. "You present a special problem for us, no doubt about it. We can't have you publicizing what you're seeing here. And I can't accept your word about not saying anything. Your visibility and what you've been up to would make your murder conspicuous. So I'm considering a car accident or a fall. After all, you nose all around this reservation, and it has to make sense. I promise we won't have any gun or knife play involved. And I won't have you just end up missing because it seems unfair to let that cute little wife of yours go through having you disappear and wondering where you are for months on end. I do have a sense of fair play, you see. No, we'll come up with something. Until we figure it out, I think you ought to get some sleep."

Whitcomb pulled my head back again and James and Tiller came quickly around the table. Tessa just stood there watching. Together, they managed to force my mouth open and drop two pills inside. I spit one out and they just shoved it back in. I tried to cheek them, but Brie knew that trick and forced my head back like I was his pet dog, shoving the pills to the very rear of my throat. I tried to cough them up and succeeded with one, but they just forced it down again.

"There . . . that ought to do it," he pronounced with satisfaction. "That's oxycodone, doc, and as you know, your Indian Health clinic is one of our major suppliers for pain relief. They go for up to 80 bucks a hit on the streets of Seattle. So that's a one-hundred-sixty-dollar investment in helping you simmer down and rest for a while."

Whitcomb pulled me to my feet and started moving me out of the shop. When about three feet opened up behind me, I somehow buried my left heel fast and hard into his solar plexus. Despite it having been many years, it was a pretty decent backkick. The trouble was, he had his Kevlar vest on. Even though I launched him up and onto his back, it didn't really hurt him much, just knocked the wind out of him. He lay down there looking up at me, handcuffed from behind and now looking down at him, which gave me a few moments of strange and idiotic pride.

Something metal and heavy on the back of my head launched me into another dimension of time and space. At least I'd already swallowed the opiates.

"Wake up." Someone was disturbing the hell out of me. "Wake up."

I didn't want to. I was all wet. Why was I all wet? Did I wet myself? How embarrassing. I crawled back into the hole I never wanted to crawl out of in the first place.

"Wake . . . up!"

Someone grabbed my nose and held my mouth closed, which only very gradually became uncomfortable. But then I panicked and this ruined everything. The grip on my nose and mouth eased up, and I shot to life, opening my eyes, and watching the world spin.

I did not find this pleasant. I turned to my left and barfed. Not much came up, just bile. What's the Hippocratic humor for a bilious man? I wondered to myself.

"Gross. Wake up!" It was Tessa.

"Where . . . ?"

"You're here. They're gone."

I tried to get up to see where 'here' was and fell forward onto my face, in part as a result of the drugs, but more because my feet were duct-taped together and the handcuffs behind my back were chained to a drain pipe. Several cockroaches on the floor near my face walked right up to me in greeting. I was fine with them visiting at first but then remembered something about me being murdered soon.

"Shit . . ." I struggled to get up.

She helped me back into a kneeling position. The roaches continued exploring around my knees, a couple moving up my pant leg, which as I've said, I don't favor. I couldn't do much about it.

"Where'd they go?"

"To run your car to Yakima and clean it up. They took your keys while you were out."

"Why?"

"Why do you think?" she asked. "They're cleaning it out of any sign you've been anywhere near them."

"Shit . . . I had a gun sitting under the seat." All I could think was that cost two hundred forty dollars and I'd have to explain it to Ruthie somehow.

I started to snooze.

"WAKE UP!" She grabbed my hair and shook it hard. Not that I could feel it but it was disturbing. "Brie had business near Sunnydale. Whitcomb's back on duty. Miyanashatawits are doing your car." She paused. "When everybody comes back, they're going to kill you."

That last part made a kind of sense. But it's hard to panic when your body's made out of chalk.

"Tessa, run for help," I slurred.

"I can't. Whitcomb's on the police frequency. Who comes to help? Brie said he'd kill my entire family. He told you about these people. Mexican Mafia in Tri Cities, Barlow. Surenos--Black Hand. Parker, Tiller, James, and ESPs have been running guns and crank for them. Brie's the money man but then took over." She paused and put her hand to her eyes, trying not to cry. "Parker was trying to get out."

"I know, I know, Tessa." I tried to calm her as best I could while still feeling enormously sedated and dizzy myself. "We've got to get out of here."

"They'll find us. They'll kill us. They have no problem killing."

She reached forward and grabbed my shoulders.

"Wake up!" she shouted. I was very dozy. "Wake up!"

"We have to get out of here." As I said it, I slumped, and she looked pleadingly at me. "Tessa, it's no use staying if they're just going to kill us."

"I have to protect my family."

"Did you lure me here?" The 'r' of my lure was quite prolonged.

"No!" She said vehemently. "I tried to get a message to you! Getting you out here, that was Jack's idea."

"Why did you come here, Tessa?"

"He told me if I came," she paused, and I knew there was more. "If I came, he wouldn't hurt anybody."

"But why did you really come?"

She gazed at me momentarily. "I came here to kill him."

"You already knew he was here."

"He's been out here for the last six months . . ."

"Tessa, where's Ámashitum? . . . Did you ride her all this way?"

"Yes but . . ." her eyes filled up and she choked. "They shot her."

"They shot her?"

"I don't know. She ran away. She's gone."

"And then they had you."

"Yes."

"Well, they'll shoot you too, Tessa." She looked at me. "And they'll kill your family no matter what . . ."

"No!"

"You know Jack Brie better than I do. There's no buying time or keeping your family safe. He holds all the cards. We've got one choice."

"No!" Her eyes flashed.

"I know you're scared. I am too. But that's all we've got. We have to try to get away." She just stared at me.

"Can you bring me some water?"

She got up quietly and walked away. While she was gone, I noticed I had, indeed, urinated all over myself. I smelled like pee. I also noticed how such a thought made no difference. She came back with an old jar with muddy water in it.

"Is this drinkable?"

"It's well water here. It still works. It might have arsenic in it."

"Great." I drank it anyway.

I still had the spins but was able to get to my feet. There wasn't much give in the chains tying my cuffs to the pipe from my standing position.

"Can you get me free of this?"

"No. Not now." This meant she was at least thinking about it. She continued looking at me.

"I've been with them for three days," she said finally, having made a decision. "They come and go whenever they want and leave me here whenever they feel like it . . . they'll be back within an hour, if it's that long. If you and I are gone when they get back, they'll pack this whole place up. Then they'll go and shoot my grandpa and the kids, then drive on to Tri Cities without a second thought. They're killers. There won't be anything to find out here except dead people. Barlow, they leave no traces. They'll come back from Tri Cities when things die down, look for you, your wife, and me and kill us too."

"What do you propose?" I mumbled.

"Wait until they come back. Find a way to run while they're here; get back to my *tíla*'s."

"Tessa, that's impossible. It doesn't make sense. They'll catch us. We need time. It's the opposite of what we should do."

"That's not how I see it, and I know them. If I'm in, we have to go my way." I could hear distant noises above me.

"They're back . . ." She immediately got up. "Here . . ." She handed me a pair of wirecutters.

"Can you get a gun?" I whispered as the noises approached closer.

"Shush! No!" she whispered back loudly. "Plenty of guns all over this place. They keep all the bullets." She said this like it should be self-obvious.

"Oh . . ." I said and could now plainly see in the reflection of a cracked storm window, lying on the floor behind her, my face looking back from inside the coal room. She closed the door and it went pitch dark.

## Sixteen

> This world is the work of Me-yah-wah.
> Of course God is above us and has great power.
> He hears us talk and knows
> if we are speaking truth or telling lies . . .
> -*Louis Schuster, Yakama, 1910*

I shook my head hard over and over to stay awake. I doubted the wirecutters were strong enough to do anything to case-hardened cuffs, but it was a nice gesture. I balanced them awkwardly in alternating palms, worrying away at the chain going to the drain pipe which was made of jack chain and likely weaker than the chain between the cuffs.

I pinched my fingers and hands over and over doing this, and I'm sure I started bleeding. This became more uncomfortable because I felt creepy crawlies of some sort getting on me, maybe on my hands, too. It wasn't easy to determine if blood was dripping or something was crawling on my hands. I didn't want anyone checking up on me to notice signs of blood or struggle against my shackles, so I took to trying to wipe my hands over my butt repeatedly. I must have dropped the cutters a hundred times, scooted down onto floor in the blackness and rummaged along the surface with my face trying to feel where they fell, spitting out dirt and maybe bugs, astonished to finally locate their metallic shape again somehow. Then I'd use the heels of my taped-up feet to scoot them back behind my torso. If I did this just right, I could pick them up and start back at working on the chain. Although they were numb, my wrists were all scraped up, and I was sure my palms were blistered. I felt several odd bites too and wondered what they might be from. While I was getting ready to be executed, I had to think about bugs.

My biggest worry was that someone would walk in while I was busy. This happened twice. On the first occasion, it was Tiller, who didn't seem to talk much. I had my face on the floor and was terrified he'd see the cutters. Instead, he took me for being still lost in an opiated haze. He looked me up and down for a second, then kicked me solidly in the mouth, much like you'd kick a football. My head snapped back, and I tasted blood.

"Are you awake now, white man?" He looked back through the door at the shop as though he had better things to do.

"Wow, you've got balls, kicking a chained-up man; I'm impressed," I responded, but less articulately.

If there's one thing I specialize in, it's knowing what to say. He kicked me again in the face. This gave me a bloody nose. I still had plenty of oxycodone flowing through me, and it didn't hurt that much. I figured it kept him occupied while I tried not to look at the cutters in plain view next to my left knee. I became boring and he left.

I soon managed to navigate the cutters my way, somehow picked them up, and started working the chain again. There seemed to be a loose piece I could keep working at but galvanized jack chain doesn't really bend as far as I could tell.

The second time, it was Jack.

"Howdy there, doctor. How we doing?" I happened to find a means of slipping the cutters into my back pocket as the door opened, just in time. "Shit, you're not looking too good. I'm sorry about that, too. Looks like you irritated Tiller. He has anger management issues. Maybe you could help him with that at some point . . . Listen, I do have a question for you." His tall, thin frame made a shadow over me from the doorway. "I was wondering how much you might have discussed with your wife about what you've been looking into."

"Not at all," I said.

"Not at all . . ." He looked at me. "Well, that's good. That makes me glad. And I know I have your word on that . . ."

"I never said a word about anything to do with this to her, Brie . . ."

"You don't need to go overboard. I pretty much believed you." He pulled out a fresh cigarillo, tamped it, and spoke as he lit it. "I do. The problem I have is this tiny bit of doubt coming in; my personality disorder, you know. It's not even reasonable."

He puffed on his cigarillo a couple of times.

"If you come anywhere near her . . ."

"You'll what, doc . . . haunt me? Well, you go ahead and haunt me. You won't be the first, believe me. I don't sleep well. I got ruminative thoughts. Anyways, as the young people say, I have a proposition. A cash deposit of sorts as a going away gift from you will help you not worry in the after-life about Ruthie." He pulled my wallet from out of his own pocket. "What's the pin number for this credit union debit card?"

I figured he wanted to build a false track of my movements using purchases on the card.

"Fuck off," I didn't have much time left. All I had to work with was my mouth and provoking him might buy time.

"Neither appropriate nor professional, doctor, but I'm going to let it lie, I think. I'll let you think about it."

And the door closed, and I started working the chain more furiously. I dropped the cutters again, and this time I couldn't find them. It was all black in front of me; my face was covered with dried blood; I had bites on my neck and ears, and my hands were lacerated. As I bent down to try again, something buzzed my hair, like a big deer fly or maybe a moth.

But I also felt the chain give a little. I reached back with both hands and felt the weak spot I'd been working at had bent open just a little. I tried leaning forward with all my weight and it bent a little more. I did this about six times, and the chain link popped. I was very afraid of the noise it made and stayed in position... but no one came. So I lied down and curled into fetal position. This was not easy for a man my age who enjoys bacon double-cheeseburgers. I barely slipped my wrists with the cuffs on under my butt. Then I struggled to get my taped-up feet through. This took a while.

Feeling around on the floor, I found the cutters again. I used them to cut apart the duct tape. Then I started working at the cuffs. There was no way in hell they'd ever cut through that handcuff chain.

I decided the best thing to do at this point would be to get out and hide. I knew I was a little ways distant from the shop door and the work room, but I had no way of knowing if anyone was out there. I stood up and placed my palms on the door handle, putting my weight on them, pushing down hard so as to help the door slip from the moldings with less noise. Very gradually, I turned the handle. The door eased open slightly into the darkened room with broken piano keys all over the floor. I eased my way forward, pushing the door handle down again and cringing as it creaked back into place and finally latched.

As I moved into the room, I couldn't see anyone. So I took a chance and sprinted and jumped toward a patch of darkness near the light of the shop room. This made too much noise. But nothing happened.

I could bend to my left from where I stood in front of a stairwell and barely peer into the shop. I leaned slightly inward and had a look. Tiller was filing on a gun at a table. James had a rifle barrel in a jib and seemed to be working with the site; intermittently, he picked up a little Drexel tool, and the buzz of it was probably what saved me.

Behind them both, near the door to the little room, stood Tessa, leaning against the wall, looking passive and quiet. I could hear Jack and Whitcomb talking behind her. Then she saw me. Her eyes went wide, and I was afraid they'd notice her expression. Thinking this would cause them to glance over to where I now stood, I dodged in front of the door to the other side of the room in full view of everyone. She got control of herself, made a slight negative nod at me, and I moved quickly again, this time back to where I had been, only now at a shadowed area right underneath the stairwell.

And there I stood, terrified out of my mind, certain they would hear my heart pounding. I had no idea what came next.

It's funny how you notice little things when you're hypervigilant and panicking. The first thing I saw was natural light in the corner of the room. It wasn't daylight; it was moonlight. But it wasn't coming through windows. It was coming through a big hole. I couldn't make it out very well, but it was a big hole, and if a person could get to it, he or she might climb through it. I had no way of knowing for sure, and I wasn't about to try to make my way over there. It just looked like you could fit a person through it.

The second thing I noticed was a half-full bottle of chlorine bleach turned on its side. That made an impression on me because I already knew how bleach fumes could be dangerous. During last summer school session, Ms. Samuel's students mixed small amounts of bleach with aluminum foil for a 'controlled experiment' in her science class. The school had to be temporarily evacuated due to caustic fumes hovering much more widely and intensely than expected. This was why the fast food wrappings Tiller and James or someone else had discarded near the door to the shop totally fascinated me. Some appeared to be mostly paper and had a couple of roaches on them. Several appeared to be foil; I couldn't tell.

Tessa came bounding into the room. She pretended to take no notice of me. She appeared to be free to roam around the building and obviously knew of some spot to go to the bathroom.

About three minutes later, she came back through. I skulked down low in the stairwell. She moved up right next to me but didn't say a thing. Instead, she pointed at the top of the stairs from beneath.

After she went back into the shop, I stared at the spot she pointed to for what seemed way too long. After all, they were going to come looking for me, and I could either make a run for the stairs or go through that hole, both of which appeared to involve making a great deal of noise. What I couldn't do was stand around staring at the back of that stairwell for a long time.

I finally noticed, however, what she was trying to show me. There were several holes at the top of the stairs where the framework connected to the doorway. My point is there should not have been holes. Tessa had taken all the connecting bolts out. How she'd done it, I'm not sure, but there were several power tools she could've made use of while they were gone. It was clear she had a plan of her own which might or might not interface with mine. Maybe she thought if the stairs fell, it would give her a chance to do something else. We had no way of communicating at all.

I didn't want to risk sneaking over by the shop door and have her seen looking at me. I had to be sure of that hole in the moonlight. So I started to make my move that way. If I'd run up the stairs, I might have made it part or most of the way before the framework came crashing down, and I broke my neck. There was no way out except the hole leading into the moonlight. She must have seen it too.

"Charlie, the doctor is what we call a 'palooka,'" Brie laughed at his own remark as they came around the corner and out the shop door. "I'll take him out on one of those two-tracks near Kittitas River and he can lose his balance there. And you won't say shit about it, son, because you know what's at stake, don't you?"

They stepped onto the stairs and walked up. I was right below them and poised to jump. But they made it to the top and walked into the kitchen. The framework held together with no bolts in it at all—only the force of gravity and being settled into that position for the last eighty years.

I moved gingerly, shifting over what I could see of piano keys and trash to the moonlit hole. I hunched down again in the shadows just as I heard the creak of the floorboards above me. They were coming back down. They were carrying a large box. Jack was still talking.

"Call them Alaskas, as in AK. I've got ten gifted free from friends in Michoacán. I don't have clips so have to figure that out . . . get Tiller started then let's go, I don't have all night."

The stairs now groaned loudly, and I waited for the crash.

"What the fuck?" Whitcomb looked up as Jack lost his footing, barely regained his balance, and yelled back, "Don't push back so goddamn hard . . . these goddamn old stairs; James needs to fix them."

The stairs still held. They continued backing into the shop with the wooden crate.

After being burned on my forehead, beat down, snorkeling through bugs and dust repeatedly while chained up and stoned, and getting free somehow, I stood there with the full moonlight in the corner nearby and didn't feel like I was really there at all. This was disturbing to me, feeling profoundly disconnected at the moment when everything was on the line.

In fact, I thought I was going to start weeping, even out loud. The oxycodone was wearing off; my jaw was aching, and my nose was terribly swollen, likely broken. My forehead was killing me. I couldn't curl either of my hands, and the cuffs were digging in hard to bloody welts on my wrists. My thoughts were near empty, but I felt physically paralyzed with fear. My intellect sprang up and noted 'this is tonic immobility, snap out of it!'

I leaned over to look up through the hole and there were stars. I couldn't climb through, however, with these cuffs on me and the shape I was in. There was no way I could do that, I thought to myself. My mind wouldn't work right; I could not solve this problem. The climb up to and through the hole was clearly impossible.

This caused a new level of despair to settle in. I'll never get away. I'm going to get caught, I thought to myself. I'm going to die. Prepare for death. What about Ruthie?

There are no atheists in foxholes goes the saying. I started repeating, "God help me" in my head, not realizing I was praying. When I realized what I was doing, I thought, yes, pray, pray, because you can't think of shit, can you?

That was all that was left. The Lord's Prayer fell apart over the phrasing around 'trespasses' or 'sins'. I remembered Ruthie sitting with me one evening, patiently teaching me a Bahá'í prayer for when you're in trouble—"Is there any remover of difficulties, save God?" She wanted me to memorize the rest of it. I couldn't remember it. Now I asked my long-deceased grandmothers and grandfathers to help me, standing there in the dark, looking up at that impossible hole.

Of course, nothing happened. No thunder sounded, no lightning struck. No angel appeared. My head dropped in surrender to hopelessness and I stood awaiting my execution.

The moonlight shifted slightly over the trash and debris. A red panther stared back at me.

Now I'm hallucinating, I thought. I kept blinking at it. It stayed there.

On the floor in the moonlight at my feet sat a partially-opened package of Red Panther firecrackers. The face of a red panther was on the label, not having changed much from how it looked in my boyhood. I reached down and picked it up with my cuffed hands, smelling the crackers. They seemed fresh and dry. How did these get here? I wondered. Maybe some kids tossed the lighted pack down this hole. They never went off. I shoved them into my top pocket.

Then, I stepped back across the room gingerly, foraging very quietly, near the shop door. My hand reached across to the foil wrappers on the floor.

"Where's the bolt ejector, Till?" James' voice was within five feet of me, just around the corner.

I slipped three sections of crumpled foil under my arm, deftly grabbed the bottle of bleach, and tried not to trip in the dark as I crept back near the moonlit hole.

"Goddamn it, Till. Where's the bolt ejector?"

"In my toolbox, in the truck."

Immediately, James came bounding around the corner of the shop and shot onto the stairs. They creaked and groaned.

"Woh! What the fuck!" He continued up and through the kitchen. Two or three minutes and he bounded back down. A crack sounded behind him as his feet hit the basement floor.

He walked back into the shop. "Somebody's got to fix those old stairs. They're gonna break on somebody. They're not safe."

I waited. For what, I wasn't sure. It was my greatest hope Tessa would come back through before they came out to get me.

Brie's voice sounded out from the little room. "Tiller—Charlie and I are leaving in five minutes with Barlow! I want him hog-tied and loaded up in the rear of Charlie's truck."

"I'll get him in a minute."

And she came through. She stood there in the dark, feigning heading to the bathroom but trying to see if I was still under the stairwell.

"Sssss," I tried quietly.

She heard me but couldn't see me. She started to come over and tripped, falling on the piano, which made several strings echo across the space around us.

"What the fuck was that?" Tiller's head peered around the corner.

"I have to pee."

"You just went."

"No," she sounded indignant. "What the fuck, Tiller? I have to take care of something in the bathroom." She put her hands on her hips.

He looked at her for a moment. "Shit, you're out of your fog for once."

He turned back into the shop and spoke to James, "She's out of her fog. Now we're going to have to listen to a PMS-ing bitch for the rest of the night." There was a pause and then he said, "Or maybe not."

Then she made me out in the dark.

"Gotta light?" I asked in a very quiet whisper.

"Shhh. What the hell does that mean?" She whispered back, seemingly stunned by the question. She held up something silvery.

"I got this . . ."

"What?" I couldn't make it out.

She came closer, holding the object up so it flashed dimly. It was Parker's Spanish lock knife; I could see the brass at each end of the handle. She had it open and the blade reflected the moon.

"We can use it," she whispered.

"It's good," I tried to sound positive. "But they have guns. We don't have time for that now, Tessa. Put it away."

"I think they're going to kill both of us."

"Yes. That's likely true . . . do you have a light?"

"A flashlight?"

"No!" There was a rustle in the shop as Tiller and James worked, and I thought someone was coming. We hunkered down momentarily.

"Hold this," I handed her the bleach bottle and crumpled up the foil into little balls. "Do you think you can help me get up through this hole?"

"I can try," she said.

"Here, take these." She took the balls of foil in her other hand. "You climb through first. When I tell you to, drop these little balls into the bottle. Put your hand over the top and shake it up real quick. Then I'm going to want you to toss it back in here. Do you understand?"

"Yes," she nodded.

"Now . . . do you have a light?"

She still looked stunned. "Tessa, do you have a lighter or any matches, goddamn it?"

"Yes," she said. And she reached in her pocket to pull out a tiny butane lighter and handed it to me. There was more noise emanating from the back of the shop. I cupped my hands and boosted her up. She was a strong girl, and she pulled herself through to the other side.

"How will you get up here?" she whispered back.

I looked around and saw an old crate. It didn't look very sturdy at all.

"I've got something," I said, moving it below the opening.

"Where's Tessa?" came Brie's voice.

"Get ready," I said.

I moved forward toward the stairs and lit the Red Panthers. I was afraid the fuse was too short. I tossed them up the stairwell into the kitchen and darted back and up onto the crate, jumping up at the hole.

POW, POW, POW . . . Tiller was the first to come running, then Jack and Whitcomb, James was last, all of them pounding up the stairs. Whitcomb had his gun drawn. POW! He fired blindly up into the kitchen as they charged. As he reached the top step, the other three were all on board.

That's when the whole thing came down. CRASH!

"Go! Go!" I yelled to Tessa. The crate started to crack; I couldn't find anything to grip on when I reached up through the hole.

"The edge of the brick. Here," she guided my hands and I held and pulled.

"Come on!" She tugged at my cuffs, which put me in an immediate agony of pain.

"Ow, God!" I writhed. She loosened.

"No, keep pulling." It was agony.

I turned my head and saw the mass of Jack, Whitcomb, Tiller, and James getting up. Tiller caught sight of me. He began to move across the room and then tripped over the piano. The sound of dissonant strings now loudly pierced the night behind me. He got right back up.

"Pull!" and she tugged at my cuffs, sending sharp waves of burning pain up both my arms.

"Get them!"

I heard Jack yelling as Tessa somehow pulled with all her strength, Tiller's hand grabbed my shoe and tore it off and I surged forward face down onto the ground above.

"Now!" I screamed as I struggled upright, Tiller still grabbing at my ankle. She quickly dropped the little balls into the bottle and shook it, covering it with her palm. His head emerged from the hole; he was pulling himself through.

"Now!" I yelled again, and I could make out Tiller's form as he pulled forward to try to get further through the hole.

"Throw it!"

She tossed it back in and I heard Tiller scream as some of the bleach splashed his face. He screamed again and fell back.

"Run!" Tessa yelled.

"This way!" I tripped, stood up again, one shoe on, another off, tried to follow her into the moonlight, but it wasn't easy to see. I tripped and fell again. Behind me, I could hear coughing and yelling.

I ran faster than I have ever run in my life, into the field where the dust devils blew, under the moon with the high winds raging, and Tessa surging ahead of my old man's gait, yelling, "Hurry! Come on!"

Gunfire rang out behind me. I began running zigzag, turned a corner and spun, heard another shot, and felt an instant burning pain in my left hip. I was shot. I'd been shot.

"Come on!" Tessa pulled me into a small grove of trees, both of us hyperventilating, gasping, and looking back.

We could see the Mission School building complex no more than three hundred yards behind us. We could see all of them running outside. A truck started and lights came on, panning the entire field, looking for us.

"I'm shot," I said.

"I know; we have to go." she answered, quite matter-of-factly given the circumstances. Why is this not a big deal? I wondered. I tugged my cuffed hands sideways and back around by my left pants pocket and brought it back up. I was soaking in blood.

Tessa whistled.

"Tessa, hush," I said. She whistled again, quite loudly.

"Goddamn it, Tessa. They'll hear you. What the hell are you doing?"

"Shhh," she said. The headlights began to beam in our general direction.

From behind where we stood, I heard a sound and saw her coming. The filly, she was coming toward us at a gallop.

Ámashitum. Owl Child. She found us fast. I should say she found Tessa.

"Get on," she said.

"But will she . . ."

"We don't have time. Get on!"

I tried to jump up bareback and groaned in agony at the movement. With a bullet in my hip, there was no way. I heard the truck engine revving and saw its lights moving forward into the field directly toward the copse of trees we were hiding in.

"Get on!" she yelled.

But I couldn't do it. She hopped up and onto her back all in one motion and Ámashitum made no protest. Then she slid backwards.

"By those trees!" I heard Brie yell.

"Can you jump up just enough to lean over the other side? Just throw yourself up here like a blanket."

I tried and got part way over. She grabbed the back of my belt like I was just another saddle bag, pulling me hard, and I wiggled as much as I could, balancing on Ámashitum's back. Tessa's legs gripped the horse tight as she grabbed her mane with both hands, her elbows resting hard on my back.

"Tst. Tst."

Ámashitum carried us both. We plunged into the night in an easy canter as the truck was spinning its wheels across the field. I won't even mention how I felt about our gait.

As we entered the foothills, I knew our silhouette must be only more visible. We'd hear the engine rev and the lights of the truck would flash in and out of view, shaping our shadows.

"There!" yelled Brie. And they had us sighted. They weren't more than two hundred yards behind us. They were clearly able and more than willing to come at us cross-country.

"Do you know how to get home?" I asked, listening to the motor revving as Ámashitum climbed onto a narrow trail.

"No," she answered.

"Are we heading in the right direction?"

"I don't know," she said. "I don't know where we are in relation to home. But Ámashitum does." The horse stumbled slightly near a boulder, knocking my hanging left leg. I felt the nerve ends sing to the top of my head and out the tips of my fingers dangling down across the other side of her back.

"She'll take us there," said Tessa.

"How can you know that?"

"Leon told me," she said. "He told me 'she's never lost; she always knows the way home. If you don't know where you are, let her wander, and she'll take you home.'"

"We don't have time to wander," I insisted. I was talking to her from a place of immense pain.

That's about when I passed out completely.

"You have to get off, Barlow," she whispered loudly.

"Huh?" I was lost in a dream of shock and pain.

"You have to get down. They'll see us. We need to get to those trees." I struggled to slide down and instead crumpled onto the ground. My left hip was on fire. Opening my eyes, I caught a sideways view of truck lights—much closer. They couldn't see us—I didn't believe they could see us. But they were much closer, maybe one hundred yards or so away. They were shouting.

"Get the fucking mat out and under the wheel," said Brie.

"I think they're stuck," said Tessa. Ámashitum nickered and blustered suddenly.

"Over there!" Tiller yelled.

The moon held all our shadows in an indent between two foothills. I peered out and saw the headlights and Tiller and James running straight at us. We call these indentations the "Yakima folds," I thought to myself, noting what a useless thought this was at that moment. Should we jump up, run, keep hiding? I hadn't a clue and felt we were about to be caught.

"I recognize this place," she looked around. "Come on. Mathis orchard is on the other side of this hill . . ."

"That doesn't seem the best place to cut through," I suggested.

"It's the only place we've got." she said.

"Now!" She tugged hard and ripped my shirt.

"You go on," I said, exhausted.

"Stop being stupid," she responded. "We're going over. Get up!"

Ámashitum and she shot up toward the ridge as I began to try to hobble up quickly behind them. My hip wasn't holding up, and I fell. I started to crawl.

Flashlights and truck lights came up bright and suddenly behind us.

"There they are!" I heard Tiller shout. The truck revved.

"Go!" Tessa yelled loudly back at me. I hadn't much go left. I struggled forward watching as she and Ámashitum made the top. Gunfire echoed again into the night. Ámashitum suddenly whinnied loudly and ran down the other side.

Was she hit? I lost sight of Tessa.

God, I thought, after all this shit, I am still going to die.

I reached the top and looked back. Brie, Whitcomb, Tiller, and James were scrambling and already part way up. Brie had his cowboy hat on. I heaved myself forward and fell again, this time rolling down, tumbling, getting up and stumbling forward, rolling again, standing up, faint and dizzy, on the verge of passing out again.

Somehow I came to the bottom and managed to settle myself near a small apple tree. I couldn't move another inch. But I was in the shade, shadowed again by the moonlight. I couldn't see Tessa or Ámashitum anywhere.

"Grandfather! *Tíla*! Help!" I heard her shout pleadingly.

"Now Tessa," came Jack's voice in answer conversationally. "You're all mixed up." He was walking down the hill and followed by Whitcomb, Tiller, and James. "You come back with me and we're going to work this all out." He angled a rifle down toward the ground.

"Doctor?" Jack shouted. "Doctor? I know you're out here . . . I want you to think about that pretty wife of yours, doctor, and the agreement we were working toward. Come on out, and let's talk and work our way past all this."

He strolled forward with a crouch and menace to his movement. He brought his rifle up to sight pointing straight at me in one motion. Maybe he was a former Marine. I was sure he had me. Then he swung just slightly to the right. He pulled the trigger and a tree branch about ten feet from me exploded. He was shooting blind. He couldn't see either of us. He stopped to listen as his crew bunched up behind him. There was no sound at all for a few seconds.

"Come out now, goddamn it!" He raised his rifle again.

From behind him, a pistol shot rang out and the rifle jumped out of his arms. Jack spun around and faced Whitcomb.

"That's enough," Whitcomb said. "That's enough."

"Why, Charlie," said Jack in his same conversation tone, as Tiller and James stood frozen between the two of them, "What can you mean?"

And I saw him start to reach into his back pocket as a small figure came flying out from the orchard trees. It was Tessa running faster than I could have thought possible yet her movement was utterly silent. There was no sound at all in her rapid charge. In her hand, I saw a familiar dim flashing. She was tearing straight for Jack and, before he could turn back around, she jumped onto his back, crooking her elbow under his chin.

"Goddamn," he muttered brokenly, struggling to reach back and pull her off him, getting hold of her long hair and wrenching it hard.

She wrapped her legs tighter around his belly, tying her feet together, knocking his hat from his head, using her stranglehold and her weight to pull his chin upward and back. Then she slashed upward with the flashing knife in her free hand, cutting his throat.

"Goddamn!" he shouted.

He finally threw her off and onto the ground and stood writhing at his throat, making choking sounds as the sheen of blood showed in the moonlight, reaching again into his back pocket again, pulling out my pistol, my newly-bought Taurus 85, and pointing it directly at Tessa laying there on the ground. He started to pull the trigger. Strangely, his left shoulder jumped back as the Taurus went off.

I heard the report of a rifle about a tenth of a second or so later. Tessa crab-walked backwards from where the ground had puffed up from Brie's missed pistol round, and Jack grabbed at his shoulder and winced. Blood began pouring from his shoulder. Another report rang out, and the ground exploded just behind him. He seemed to drop the Taurus involuntarily, run backwards, fall, get back up, and run back up the hill, stumbling and moaning.

At this, Whitcomb, Tiller, and James all dropped their guns and fell to their knees, moving their hands to the tops of their heads.

Two figures ran out from behind a distant, moonlit apple tree. I could just make them out. Arnold Miyanishatawit and a man I'd never seen. They were both carrying hunting rifles with scopes.

"Winged him," said the unknown man. "Now he's running."

"It won't help him. He's dripping blood all over. I'll track him," said Arnold.

Tessa stood up and faced them. Ámashitum appeared on the ridge behind her.

"Thank you, *tíla*," she said.

"You got him, Tessa."

"He didn't look dead to me," she said.

"Oh, he's on his way," said Arnold. "I'll go after him. He can't get far."

"No, *tíla,* don't," and she pulled on his arm. Arnold looked down at her, still tightly gripping the Spanish knife. He glanced at it.

"Where'd you get a knife like that?"

"Parker," she answered. And he nodded at her, wordlessly, pulling her toward him as she hugged him.

The unknown man stepped forward with his rifle aimed at the heads of the men on their knees.

"My name's Frank Mathis. This is sovereign Indian land you're on. We're going to have some law. Stay just as you are and don't move at all unless me or Mr. Miyanashatawit tell you to. No offense but if I see one flicker from any of you, by God, I'll blow your fucking brains out."

Arnold moved up and collected their guns. Then he made them all lie face down against the hillside, keeping his flashlight on them.

"That's better," he muttered as Mathis pulled out his cell phone.

Tessa stood by her grandfather, and soon Ámashitum strolled up next to her.

"She's shot," and she began to cry. Arnold took a look.

"Not seriously, Tessa. Not seriously."

That all seemed very nice but, to me, I really liked the part when Arnold made all those guys lie face down.

I decided I should do the same.

## Seventeen

I think there is only one Creator for all different tribes of this world, whites or reds. Sometime after this different languages were given to the different tribes, white and reds . . . We can see ourselves; if we get too bad, something happens. People are killed by fire, or are drowned . . . If both Indians and whites would follow this up, be friendly and not interfere with each other in any way, the Creator would know this, and by doing right, nothing bad would happen to us. *–Nah-schoot*

Ruthie was holding my hand and talking to me. She was in mid-sentence when I started listening. It wasn't that I wasn't trying. I was still pretty groggy and lying in a hospital bed.

"If you ever do that to me again," she was saying, "I'm not going to divorce you." Hopefully not, I said to myself. "I'm not going to leave you either . . . Instead, I vow I will make your life a living hell forever."

Tears were on both her cheeks. She put her head onto my chest, and I patted her back with my bandaged hand.

"You bastard," she continued as she hugged me. "You bastard."

Dr. Stanton walked in, and Ruthie lifted her head up. "Chewing him out?" she asked.

Ruthie nodded affirmatively, wiping her face.

"Good," she leaned in with her ophthalmoscope. "Just checking one more time. He's pretty stupid for a Ph.D." Then she stood up. "You're pupils are equal, and I don't see any signs of swelling back there. Your MRI is negative. Your nose is broken, and you're going to need rhinoplasty because you now have a deviated septum."

"Great," I said. "Does that entail breaking my nose again in order to fix it?"

"Doctor Barlow, that procedure went out with trephining. However . . ." She turned to Ruthie, "If you'd like to break his nose again before I do the rhinoplasty, I'd have no objections."

Stanton's bedside manner meshed well with Ruthie's mood. "You also have a concussion. You're very lucky it's not worse news. By the way, your name is in the paper today." She felt my neck on both sides. "Maybe the kick in the head will cause a personality change, and you'll stop practicing psychology with armed criminals."

"Very funny," I responded.

"You are cut loose from here in an hour."

"Seriously?" I asked. I still hurt in multiple places and liked being in bed.

"I have a bullet in my butt," I complained and this caused Ruthie to laugh involuntarily, then immediately resuming the most caustic expression in her repertoire.

"You no longer have a bullet in your butt," said Stanton. "You're gluteus maximus is so hard, and that bullet was so spent, it didn't go very deep. I got it out easily, and it took only a little suturing to close. You continue to be a pain in my butt in this hospital. You're all cleaned up, and it's time for you to leave."

"My hands hurt," I complained further.

Her demeanor became only slightly gentler. "Your hands will heal—they're just blistered. You won't be able to use them easily for a while. Put the salve I prescribed on your palms and change the gauze every couple of days. You have flea bites on your ankles, by the way."

She spoke this to Ruthie. "I'm telling this for you too because he might forget. He's still a little fuzzy."

"I am not," I protested.

"I see. You may have some headaches later on. If they get bad, I want to know. You're off work for the next week. I spoke to Gaillard. He wanted me to give you this." She handed me a note. "I'm giving you Vicadin for your head."

"No narcotics."

"Take the script with you; I'm not saying you have to take them . . . OK, you've been treated. I'm charting your status." She pulled an ipad out of her white coat pocket and recited as she made her entry.

"You are a helpless, flea-bitten, pain in the ass." She enjoyed her own humor for a moment more before saying, "Rest for a half-hour longer. It's on the house. Then pack up and hit the street. I need a real patient in this bed. I expect to see you about that nose later this week."

I stared and said nothing.

"He's a pretty good psychologist; he's trying to psych me out right now," she observed, turning to Ruthie. "He pretty much stinks as a super-hero."

"I know," nodded Ruthie.

Stanton pressed her shoulder as she turned to leave. "He's going to be fine."

Ruthie looked at me severely but not without pity as I opened Gaillard's note and read—"Glad to hear you and Tessa are OK. For your info, Mory says Heslah death ruled a suicide. DA wants an independent opinion. Western Oregon IHS called. Parker's sister Florence od'd on imiprimine two nights ago, uncertain of possible relation to his death or whether she died before or after he did. Terrible tragedy, G."

Brie was not found. Arnold followed his blood trail with a flashlight, despite Tessa's strong objections. Somehow, he'd stopped the bleeding. At least, the trail ran out. A search team and even the sheriff's helicopter combed the hills and nooks all over the area. Jack Brie was still at large.

Elisi said Jack Brie was Charlie Whitcomb's father. Ruthie, sitting next to me at her house, shook her head in shock and disbelief as she filled us in.

"Charlie's mother, Stephie, was a good girl from a good family. She had been about Tessa's age and Brie even younger, maybe fourteen. It only took the one time and her mother thought it was rape. Probably was. At least, Stephie wanted nothing more to do with him after Charlie was conceived. She worked for several years as a barmaid over at the Spar Tavern before she got killed in a car wreck. The two of them lived in Harrah. Charlie was always underfoot when she was alive. The Spar was one of Brie's hangouts; he'd stop by and harass her periodically. After she died, Brie wouldn't claim him and Charlie went to foster care instead."

"Did Charlie know who Brie was?" asked Ruthie.

"Yes, he did." She eyed her momentarily and grabbed her hand. "You've been very brave, honey." Ruthie smiled. "No, his mother didn't keep it from him," she continued. "I'm sure he grew up wanting Brie to take an interest in him, obviously even more after his mother died. I saw it myself. So did my sister. It's so sad to watch a child long for a parent. I used to drink at the Spar. Stephie was my niece."

She sat back and looked me over.

"How come you never told me Brie was Whitcomb's father?" I asked.

"You don't like calling him Charlie."

"No. He's an odd guy. He's not a Charlie to me."

"Ah," Elisi raised her eyebrows. "Well, I would've told you about that connection if I'd known you were going to try to link up with Charlie in particular while trying to find Tessa. Even had I known, I figured Charlie would hate him and be glad to bring him down. I didn't know Brie had such hooks in him."

"And I'll always believe it was Brie killed my sister," she said. "I can't prove it. No one can. But I'll always believe it . . . She knew him in the old days. Brie used her back then. She knew the street and the connection between Brie and Charlie and she might have tried to get something out of it. Brie was always a lady-killer, everybody said. I always thought he was too— but literally."

"How's Tessa?" I asked.

"Fine—resting and back home. She's had some painful tears over her boy, of course. His funeral was last Thursday. But family have been gathered very close around her since the run from Brie, especially her auntie Leila, and I think you'll still see her this weekend at the Treaty Days parade."

I'd never been to Elisi's home before and was enjoying her couch, holding a cup of some strange and bitter tea she was making me drink. I had a bad cold. My nose was still very swollen. I was pretty miserable. She took an interest in all that and brewed up some roots she'd picked.

"Drink all of that . . ." Ruthie said. I looked at Elisi, and she nodded.

"It tastes awful . . ."

"It's medicine. It don't work if it don't taste bad," said Elisi, and Ruthie laughed.

"So Whitcomb," I pondered, "worked undercover for the FBI and ATF on this gun-running operation of Brie's. But Brie had an emotional hold on him . . ."

"Played him like a fiddle . . ." said Ruthie.

Elisi continued, "All Charlie ever wanted was to be in law enforcement. Brie coaxed Charlie and he became too involved. He crossed the line in several ways. They never really trained him to work undercover. Brie figured it out and set him up as a dirty cop, setting up a false bank account in his name, making it appear he was profiting. He used it to blackmail him. He saw Charlie coming from a long ways away. He's an evil man but not a dumb one."

"Whitcomb came around . . ." I said, gratefully. Ruthie squeezed my hand. "Oww." She smiled knowingly and I wasn't sure but that she meant to do that. I set my cup down on the little folding table next to me. Elisi had a big screen TV, two cabinets filled with little knick-knacks, an oak dining table, a wood-burning insert, and kitchen shelves filled with home-canned salmon and vegetables of all variety.

"You came around too . . . now keep drinking that." She pointed to the cup.

"It's bitter."

"Drink it anyway," said Ruthie. Yes, she was enjoying this.

"Arnold and Frank got their picture in the paper. All it says about me is 'Ret Barlow, an Indian Health psychologist, was found injured at the scene.' I mean, what's that mean?"

"You done well, doctor. Tessa's not even mentioned," Elisi remarked. "Edward Felipez said the real story can't be printed; the feds are still interviewing Charlie and the boys. The DEA and ATF are grilling them and getting a map of the operation. There's more to come. Brie's on the run, and they want to find him."

I must have been gawking at the level of detail she possessed. I sipped the brew again. It tasted like ground aspirin, and I grimaced.

"Moccasin telegraph," she said with a straight face and winked at Ruthie who laughed at my expression.

Her brother, William, opened the front door, carrying a bag of groceries. She introduced us.

He said, "So you're the 'ologist'."

I grinned sheepishly. "Huh?"

"The 'ologist', you're an 'ologist."

"Yeah I guess—a psychologist."

He shrugged as if it didn't matter what kind, "Well an 'ologist' at least. I like teachers, like your wife here. But I'm not so sure about 'ologists. You came out to study the Indian people. Maybe you'll write a book. That's happened lots of times. We had a lot of you come around when Elisi and I were little . . . we'd go without our dinner so there'd be enough for the 'ologist'. They usually eat big while they're studying us."

I smiled awkwardly at Ruthie, who had her hand in front of her mouth and was evidently laughing.

"That doesn't sound too great," I responded.

He carried the bag into the kitchen—"Well, we better get you fed soon or your stomach will start gurgling."

Elisi burst out laughing.

I had other plans, and she knew it.

"Finish that tea," Ruthie ordered. "You better not eat before you sweat."

"I agree," said Elisi.

As I pulled back behind Trick's house along a two-track road near Parker Dam, the sweat was already underway under a blanketed dome of willow saplings firmly lashed together. Arnold was sitting alone outside the lodge. He nodded his head in my direction as I disrobed but said nothing to me. My whiteness proclaimed itself alongside my nakedness, seeming even louder than the prayers and songs I heard emanating from Trick and his sons inside. I pulled up a chair and sat next to him.

I was late but evidently still in time for another round after they got out.

Arnold and I were down to basics, sitting on broken lawn chairs behind a surrounding high wooden fence. Flies were buzzing about, the sun was bright, and I was completely naked smoking a cigarette I filched from Trick's pack next to his clothes.

Arnold was naked too. Flames shot up from a big fire, heating the river rocks. The same sage and scrub trees played out for miles all around us outside the fence. The tan packed earth and bright relentless sun outlined my very white toes as I looked down.

"Just got back from the city," he said, out of the blue after about five minutes.

"Oh," I responded, startled.

"After they interviewed Frank and me, and we got our picture taken, we headed over to Circuit Court. They had that hearing between the Yakama and the Smithsonian people. . . That was today. The judge made them give us back those bones."

"Oh . . . what bones?" I hadn't the slightest idea.

"Those bones. The ones at the Smithsonian. They had to give them back to us. There was a big ceremony near here about three hours ago. We held ceremony and buried them right away."

"Oh . . ." A dawning realization; I'd read about the fight over those bones. I considered the odd fetish white people have had for collecting Indian bones over the centuries. "How'd you get them back?"

Arnold smiled toward the fire. "He was good. The judge, he was a white man. But he done alright, you know? A young white man." He spoke this to me as though it was a new insight for him for a man to be both white and good. "A smart one. He said 'you give them back those bones' and they couldn't argue." He laughed.

I am a white man, I thought to myself. 'You're my Cherokee boy,' my grandmother said to me from a childhood memory. The image of the Red Panther firecrackers label moved through my mind. *Dhladatsi gigage,* repeated Jane Ross to me from inside the dream image, *remember that.* Wilma passed along a message to me through Trick—the Blue Holly clan was also called Panther Clan in English, *Ani'sahoni* in Cherokee, 'people of the blue medicine.' They were a peace clan, and considered 'protectors of children.' She told Trick to tell me my ancestors were trying to tell me who I am.

These must be bones collected from local graves by anthropologists back in the 1930s and 1940s, I thought to myself. Another pause ensued. These were the bones of ancestors—another legacy of the 'ologists'. The Yakama had gotten them back.

"That young white judge, he was real smart. He did things right."

"Those lawyers. At-turn-knees," Arnold chuckled, making this sound like an Indian word, "they were all lined up. He made everybody stand. I don't think they liked that. They didn't want to give those bones back. They weren't respecting what he said. They were going to try to delay it again."

The Native American Graves and Repatriation Act of 1990—the Smithsonian lawyers were trying to get around it.

"The young white judge, he surprised us . . ." another chuckle. I took a drag from my cigarette. A muffled drum and song sounded from inside the lodge. I was hanging in there for Arnold, waiting.

"He leaned over that bench, and he looked right at those guys. He says—'you been in here before and I already ruled on this. Now you're here again.' He was just a young white man, but he was pretty smart. He pointed and said—'you see that man over there?' And those white lawyers, they're all standing because he made them and they all looked a little bit humble, if you ask me. And he said—'that's my bailiff and he weighs 250 pounds. He's a big man.' The bailiff is standing there, looking at them. And then the judge says—'You better give those bones back to these Indian people within 24 hours, or I'm going to have him lock every one of you in my jail cell for contempt of court.'"

Arnold laughed loudly, joyfully. I laughed too.

"That young white judge, he was smart. They didn't expect him to say that. We didn't either. They were all east coast people. They didn't see that coming. They didn't think a white man would go against them. But I liked him."

The sweat lodge opened and out came Trick, his sons, and several others.

Trick kicked my foot and looked brightly at me. "Hey what's up, Doctor Costner? Where's your blue cavalry coat?"

"Ha ha," I responded.

"We heard you fell down the rabbit hole," he continued, "Aaaaaz." When they tease you, they like you, I told myself yet again. He put his hand on my shoulder, covered in sweat, and then he collapsed onto his back.

"Who's been smoking my smokes?" I blew smoke rings toward him, and he looked up and smirked.

"You going in?" asked Arnold. I was surprised—everyone else was apparently done; it would be just me and him. We crawled in—he first.

I have been corrected more than once about how to enter. Arnold said gently, "We don't enter in that way," and instructed me on what to do. "That's the way." I heard the opposite at another lodge. The families differ. Don't assume.

I sat on burlap and packed pine needles. Arnold called out for rocks, the remaining river stones still heated red hot. Trick's son, Jeremy, leaned a pitchfork in with the first rocks to drop into the center hole. Arnold tossed some sage and cedar on the rocks and they instantly ignited into a plume of savory smoke. He called for nineteen rocks. At his command, the blankets dropped down over the opening and it became completely black except for the red glow.

"This is the womb of our Mother—where every last one of us comes from. That's how we think about it," Arnold taught me.

Inside the lodge, it's very dark. It smells like deep earth. Arnold poured ice cold water on the rocks over and over, and steam shot up intensely. I was bathed in heat and opened my mouth slightly, placing my tongue lightly at the roof of my mouth like when I meditate. I can be very still this way; I don't even have to swallow.

I turned inward. The heat was extreme; almost scalding but bearable if you go to the right place in your mind. "It's only a body being cleansed," I told myself. I felt all my pores open, and I itched a little. I began to sweat profusely and prepared myself for song and prayer.

Arnold began to sing and pray in Yakama language. I understood only a little: We are pitiful, Grandfather. Take pity on us. Please hear us.

"This is a Shaker song I want to bring out," he mentioned. He sang long and mournfully. It was quiet for a while afterwards. He began to speak his prayers in English, which he didn't have to do. He was intentionally drawing me in, including me:

"*Púsha. Tamanawashe.* We been through another battle for our home and we need to be cleansed. Thank you for keeping my granddaughter Tessa and me and all of my family safe. Thank you for preserving the doctor for his wife and family and to serve us with his ways. Thank you for making my aim true to protect my family. We need you to take away our anger at bad people and forgive their twisted spirits . . . help us restore peace inside our hearts."

He poured more cold water on the hot rocks, and I was once again bathed in raging heat. He sang another somber song. We stayed quiet as he poured more, and the temperature caused me to start keeling over to lie down on the floor where it was just slightly cooler. But I couldn't remember if this was all right like it was in some family lodges. He coughed as I moved; I sat back up. Arnold kept a very hot lodge. He sang again for a long while before he spoke again.

"*Púsha.* We got those bones. We got those bones. We buried them today so that they can finally rest. I am sorry we couldn't do it right. We had a hard time finding the most easterly spot on that land. I am sorry it took so many years. We've been trying for so long to get our peoples' bones returned to us. We got these and buried them so their spirits can rest now. Thank you for helping us, *Púsha*."

Arnold began to weep openly. I could hear him sobbing softly in the darkness and heat. Tears jumped into my eyes at being included in such intimacy.

Several days later, I would learn the name of the man who first stole those bones—Richard Barth, Jr. He pilfered bones from many of the Yakama and other graves all over the Pacific Northwest in the 1940s. He was just another 'ologist, an anthropologist, I believe and, like many in his day, he meant no harm. Like his father, Dr. Barth, one of the first 'Indian psychologists' and the one Elisi herself had likely met, he meant no harm.

I decided to say my own prayers aloud when Arnold was done. He didn't ask me to; it doesn't work that way in the lodge. It's up to you. I offered my gratitude for being alive, for being preserved, for surviving and being returned to be with my wife. I promised to cherish her. I spoke about how glad I felt that the bones of lost loved ones were returned and their memory could be honored and how very sorry I was they were ever taken. I prayed for Ruthie and for Arnold's family and mine. I even prayed for my enemies.

Now Arnold sang again and invited me to try to sing. I didn't know the words or what they meant but I could grasp the phonemes. We sang together inside our Mother's womb at the intersection of our common humanity and somehow this momentarily cancelled out our deeply-opposed cultural histories. We sang in a shared reality just temporarily, but richly, our voices coming from very different places within a divine equation, Arnold beating his drum, and me singing loudly with him for sake of mutual healing.

After the lodge was done, we crawled back out. Like Trick, I collapsed on my back and the steam shot upwards off my naked body into the blue sky overhead as though I was on fire. No one spoke until Trick started talking about "never saw a naked shrink all shriveled up like that" and everyone broke into guffaws. Trick grabbed the running garden hose from a bed of rocks and immersed himself. I followed suit.

"Goddamn it, doctor, you'll give yourself a heart attack doing that if you're not used to it. Got to get you back over here next weekend for a sweat before Treaty Days, not be dead before then," cried Arnold as I clapped the icy water off my back and shook my hair.

It was at that moment I realized I had become a brother to this lodge. From there, we joked around a bit more, dried off, and got dressed. Nothing was said about what had happened inside the lodge between us. It was completely put away. The lodge was over, and we were clean.

Tessa stood in full regalia holding Ámashitum's bridle. The filly looked brushed down, groomed, and amazingly tolerant as Eloise sat on the ornate Western saddle on her back. We were on the Legends Casino grounds by the parking lot, surrounded by cars, trucks, floats, and people getting ready for the Treaty Days parade. It was the first time I'd seen Tessa since that moonlit night two weeks earlier.

"Why aren't you wearing your ribbon shirt?" she asked immediately, her voice serious but her eyes teasing.

"He forgot to get it dry-cleaned," answered Ruthie, who stepped forward as I introduced them. "Ámashitum looks gorgeous, and your regalia is so beautiful!"

Tessa was completely covered in buckskin and her moccasin boots were beautifully beaded. Her shawl was almost completely covered with complex beadwork, mostly in white with triangular and cross designs in orange, red, and black. On back of the shawl was a gorgeous rose, beaded in red and black.

She beamed as though Ruthie had been the first to notice. "Elisi gave it to me. It was hers, and she fixed it up with all this new beading for me."

"You look great," I tried to add my own compliment.

"Thanks," she said. "Are you coming to the pow wow?"

"We'll be there for grand entry," I answered.

"But not for dancing?"

I glanced at Ruthie. "Which dance?" she asked.

"Teen girl's traditional at 1 pm," Tessa answered.

"Of course, we'll be there, Tessa. We'll definitely be there." Ruthie answered with certainty. Ámashitum stirred a little.

"I'm going too!" said Eloise unaffectedly.

"Get down now," said Tessa. "They're lining up . . ."

Eloise slowly made her descent with Tessa's help. Then, Tessa once more moved effortlessly onto Ámashitum's back.

"See you," she waved as she turned her.

"It still amazes me," I leaned over to Ruthie as we walked away. "That was a wild horse three months ago."

"That's not a wild horse. That's a match made in heaven," she answered.

We took our spots in front of the RV park, where Buster Road winds around toward the clinic. I saw Gaillard in the crowd and waved; he waved back.

I saw Dominia too and waved toward her, practicing being a nicer person. All right—to keep her guessing. She did not wave back, perhaps she didn't see. She stood by herself, and I felt strangely sorry.

The Tribal Police cars and trucks led the way, followed by the fire trucks and fire jumpers sitting on lawn chairs in back. Their sirens and horns blared, and I hoped Ámashitum hadn't thrown Tessa by now. Next were certain dignitaries, Tribal

Council members, a couple of state senate candidates, and the county sheriff deputy who takes naps out in White Swan. At least he comes to the parade, I thought. I pointed out to Ruthie various features of regalia and how only a veteran could pick up an eagle feather if it was dropped.

"I know that!" she exclaimed.

"How do you know that?" I marveled.

"Because you had to have told me that five times," she laughed.

"Oh," I answered, "I don't remember." Post-concussive syndrome, I worried.

A few seconds later, she kissed me on the cheek, which seemed very good, given recent events.

The parade announcer described each passing float, remarking on its attributes, cracking jokes, followed by loud 'aaaaaaz' through an overdriven and antiquated public address system. I couldn't make out most of what he was saying. But I heard him recognize "some of our Yakama Nation elders" and surveying carefully, finally spotted Elisi, sitting with her woven hat and cotton dress with four other women. Ruthie and I waved and waved, shouting "Elisi! *Kála!*" but she is somewhat hard of hearing.

There was a pause as the parade was halted in front in order to bunch up people and floats a little. Then came Ámashitum and Tessa. The sun bore down on the two of them, and it seemed as though Ámashitum danced a little on the pavement, brown and red mixing hues within her thick coat.

"Tst, shh," Tessa leaned down and whispered.

I noticed how quiet the crowd around us had suddenly become. I glanced back and was surprised to notice Ms. Samuel and Mrs. Marshall from school standing right behind Ruthie and me. Ms. Samuel leaned over to Ruthie, who had been transfixed on Tessa and Ámashitum.

"Thank you," said Ms. Samuel. Ruthie looked surprised. "For putting up with this one," she thumbed toward me. Then they both smiled at her tease.

Mrs. Marshall looked at me with mock pity. "Don't worry," she said. "That's how 'thank you' sounds in Yakama language." Ms. Samuels winked at me.

As we walked back to the car, I thanked Ruthie for being so sweet to Tessa.

"Well, of course." She was still a little prickly but kept holding my hand.

"I saw how she lit up when you complimented her. I think it meant a lot to her. More than from me, I mean."

"Ret . . ." She stopped and faced me. "She's such a beautiful young woman and I'm glad for what you did, although if you ever do anything like that again, I'll kill you myself. You helped her, and I'm proud of you."

Then she kissed me, and I mean really kissed me, which was even nicer.

"She's also showing."

"Huh?"

"She's showing," Ruthie repeated.

"Like . . ." I'm slow on the uptake at times.

"She's pregnant." It was a shock to me.

"No."

"Oh, clearly she is. And she has that glow too."

"That glow?"

"Yes, Ret. Tessa's going to have a baby."

I couldn't think of what to say.

"No shit," I kept repeating all the way to the car, sounding dumb.

We were sitting in lawn chairs on the main floor of the White Swan Pavilion on a Saturday afternoon in late June. We'd visited the table merchants, and Ruthie bought a pair of earrings.

We both had huge pieces of freshly-made fry bread, smothered in huckleberry jam and covered in powdered sugar. Elisi had been sitting with us but wandered off awhile earlier to use the restroom and visit.

Tessa was standing about twenty feet away, looking very nervous. She was wearing a jingle dress covered in bells. Her hair was braided perfectly and a beaded band held three eagle feathers, splayed in a deliberate upwards and sideways pattern behind her head. She held an eagle feather fan in her right hand. She looked spectacular.

"That Miyanashatawit girl's carrying that Heslah boy's baby, did you know that? They were an item before he killed himself . . ." The middle-aged Indian woman in front of us spoke loudly to her friend next to her.

I glanced at Ruthie, who looked furious. Then I leaned forward so they could hear me.

"*Itm'āaksha,*" I said. "*Tm'āakni . . .*" The speaker turned around to glare at me just as Elisi came back and sat down. She looked at me and my whiteness, then at Elisi and her brownness, and then spun back around.

"What did you say?" asked Ruthie.

"He told them to stay on the high road and to be respectful . . ." answered Elisi with a slight smile and nod.

"The next dance . . ." began the caller, "is teen traditional. Dancers come to the center." As Tessa moved forward, I could see many familiar faces—Arnold, Leila, Ellen, Eloise, Samuel, and Franklin—all seated in a close cluster behind her at the other side of the dance circle.

"Our drummers will be our old friends from Black Lodge."

"They're the best on the rez . . ." I said to Ruthie.

"You already told her that," said Elisi, and Ruthie laughed.

The caller continued, "I've been asked by Black Lodge Singers to mention to all of you that this will be a memorial dance for Georgina Miyanashatawit . . ."

Immediately the drums began. They went from soft to loud quickly.

"Hoocha! Hoocha!" cried the lead singer as his Yakama words began to form and his brother drummers answered his calls in unison.

And Tessa danced. The drums and voices filled the room as the bells of her jingle dress joined the rhythm. Her knees bent over her beaded, white deerskin moccasins, and she placed her left hand on her hip, raising her eagle fan in front of her. I couldn't get over the dignity of her expression as she began to bob up and down, her feet moving only slightly as they carried her to the left. She lowered her eagle feather fan and turned left, then right in place, then moving again to the drums in a circle with all the other dancers.

Suddenly the drumming stopped. Everything stopped. No one moved. The caller stepped forward and looked at the Pavilion floor.

"We have a dropped feather belonging to Brother Eagle . . ." he announced, "Is there a veteran who can help us out?" The feather had fallen from Tessa's headband. Trick jumped out from behind the circle and into the center.

"Everyone rise as you're able . . ." said the caller. Most of us stood, except for several in wheelchairs and walkers. Trick ceremoniously handed the eagle feather back to Tessa.

The room stood silent, waiting for her to put it back in her headband. But she didn't. She looked at it for a moment.

Now her jingling bells were all that could be heard as she moved out of the circle. The caller watched her, gawking somewhat at her audacity, holding the microphone close to his lips at the ready. She came to where we were sitting together,

Ruthie, Elisi, and me. I could see Arnold's squinting eyes from over her shoulder.

Tessa reached out and handed me the eagle feather, smiling shyly.

For a moment, all eyes were on the two of us. Then she turned and bounded back into the circle, looking back at me. I raised my bandaged wrists and held the eagle feather high for everyone present to see.

The singer shouted, "Hoocha!"

My eyes met Elisi's as Ruthie's shoulder rubbed warmly against mine. The drums came back up, the singer's voice rose above them, and all of us leaned in closer toward the surging movement of the dancers.

But the bells on Tessa's dress sounded so much louder to me, and I held that feather tightly in my hand and up high for everyone to see, while her feet pounded the earthen floor to the rhythm of my heart.

# Glossary

*Ámashitum*: 'Owl Child', Tessa's wild horse
*áyat*: Woman
*chíish*: Water
*chilwit wapasúx̱*: Devil
*Coma ahora, pague después* (Spanish): 'Eat now, pay later'
*dhladatsi gigage* (Cherokee): [refer back to story where the words are defined]
*ishinwáy*: Poor and pitiful
*itm'āāksha*: Cautious and careful in all things; restrained, peaceful, responsible
*kála*: maternal grandmother, maternal grandchild
*kápin*: Digging stick a young woman receives when coming of age
*k'úsi*: Wild horse
*k'usík'usi*: Dog
*mísh nam wá*: 'How are you?'
*Nch'i Wána*: Columbia River
*ni kso ko wa* (Blackfoot Piikáni): 'we are all relatives'
*páshtin*: White person
*pawaat-łá*: spirit guide, guardian spirit
*piitl'iyawilá*: warrior
*púsha*: paternal grandfather, paternal grandson
*shíx kláawit*: good evening
*shix máytski*
*shuyápo*: White person
*Spilyáy*: Coyote-trickster, mythical hero of Yakama legend
*tíla*: maternal grandfather, maternal grandchild
*tmáakni*: Respect
*twáti*: Medicine person
*wak'íshwit*: life, spirit, soul
*walak'ikláama*: 'Ties one up in bondage'; Yakama word for police

x̱áy: man's male friend
yaych'ú'nal: Courage
yámaash: Deer

For more information on pronunciation, the reader is referred to the excellent resource, *Ichishkiin Sinwit Yakama/Yakima Sahaptin Dictionary*, by Virginia Beavert and Sharon Hargus (2009) from University of Washington Press.

(Draft) Excerpt from Chapter One of

# Signal Peak

Sequel to
Tessa's Dance

## David Edward Walker

Spring, 2013

Request to be Notified!
Email
info@tessasdance.com
and Ask to be Put on Our Mailing List

## One

### T'ÚXT'XW
### (Rain)

"Thought I saw a sex offender from that post office mailer coming out your place t'other day."

Alice Neir grew up in Harrah, Washington. She had a missing left incisor visible only when she raised her lip in disgust. She wasn't much on smiling. Little sequins tipped horn-rimmed glasses not seen since the 1960s and offset her salt and pepper hair. She eyed me suspiciously from behind thick lenses as I cautiously eased a mandarin orange Jarrito across her scarfed-up store counter and tried to look friendly.

I was a known sympathizer with the Yakama Indian Nation's attempt to tax alcohol sales on tribal land to help fund addiction recovery. Beer was her major source of revenue. I'd heard through the moccasin telegraph that she was involved with the Stand Down local action committee, fighting what she considered a local Indian uprising. Besides Indians, I fraternized with Mexicans; I may be white; I may be mixed-blood—whatever I was to Alice, I fit a suspect profile. But I had few other choices when I wanted a soda—her store was right across the street.

"I can't really say, Alice."

"Mexicans and Indians got incest in their families. That Rios girl you meet with growed up in a bordello."

I laid my dollar down and gazed back at her lazily.

"In my profession, I can't talk about people who visit me. Sorry but that's how it is."

Her thick-set, unshaven husband, Warren, surveyed me from a stool through all this, leaning back on its two front legs and resting his close-cropped head against a chew tobacco display. Some time back, I'd noticed a tattoo on his left inner arm reading "Lost Soul." He nursed a Mountain Dew, and settled grey, steely eyes into mine for a moment before they flicked back to *Dog, Bounty Hunter* barking from a tiny TV on the side counter.

Alice smirked while handing me my change. "Don't care much for psych—ology, no sir. People come cry crocodile tears to you over bad things they done and ought to be on their knees to their Lord."

She looked back at her husband but he seemed nonplussed by her critique. I stared down at the ashtray by the cash register with the misspelled handwritten note taped above it: "Need a penney, take a penney."

I dropped the two pennies she'd just handed me in there. "Keep the change, Alice."

Her smirk morphed into a scowl. His eyes followed me out the door.

I shrugged the interaction off, screwed off the cap, took a swig, and savored an orange flavor that was more than real. Across the street, the wind hooked tumbleweed into a wound-up clothes hanger barely holding the muffler onto my 1989 Gran Fury. Road burn will have to shave that off, I told myself; I didn't feel like stooping on all fours. The car is on its last legs anyway.

Kids scurried around the basketball court at Pioneer Park to my left. The grass was burnt brown and recent trimmings hung in the air. I sneezed. Some guy grilled burgers and hot dogs under a small pavilion tent near the angled parking spaces. Thunderheads broke apart overhead, and sunlight shot across amber foothills forming a distant perimeter all around us. God lit up one side of the Lower Yakima Valley, while I shivered at the other end, savoring hot dog and mustard scent, sneezing again, and wishing for less edge to the wind.

My eyes lowered and Tessa Miyanashatawit stood next to Elisi's car in front of my new office pondering me. I wondered how long she'd been there.

"How you?" I asked, walking over.

"Alright," she glanced at kids shooting hoops as she spoke, disconcerting me for the umpteenth time with her native tendency to look at space nearby while conversing.

"We used to come play 'round here when I was little." She pointed with an index finger looped with an old silver-turquoise ring at the faded 'Neir's General Store' sign I'd just been standing under. "Used to get wax candy. They don't make that stuff anymore. Alice don't like Indians."

"I noticed." I said, sipping my soda, and held it up to her. "You want one?"

"No thanks."

"How's life?"

"Different away from *tila*'s land, I guess." She gazed sideways at my freshly-laid concrete front steps. Until a week ago, I had to step up two and a half feet in order to go in the front door. "My land, I mean—it's in my name now. I still go out to ride Ámashitum every week or so." She squinted up toward cumulus hovering over the town of White Swan about ten miles westward.

"That's nice. How is she?"

"Frank keeps her watered and cleans her stable and I give him what I can to keep alfalfa and oats for her. It's not good leaving her alone. Leon and Edward said they'd take her but they're all the way to Granger. It'd be harder for me to get over there to ride her."

The wild horse who saved both of our lives, Ámashitum, connected Tessa and me more than any of our past work as client and therapist five years ago. We'd agreed soon after our near-death experience at the hands of 'Cowboy' Jack Brie and her uncle and cousin—Tiller and James—therapy was no longer part of our relationship. We'd fallen into an abyss of suffering together while held hostage out at the old Mission Boarding School. Ever since then, our friendship circled around her family and Ámashitum.

I knew she still kept tabs. About a year ago, she'd mentioned Tiller was transferred to Monroe Prison and James was still housed at Coyote Ridge, both for a long time for attempted murder, kidnapping, and gun-running. Charlie Whitcomb, the undercover tribal cop Jack Brie corrupted, was now an assistant bondsman up in the city of Yakima. He'd visited me after being released early from a short stint for aiding and abetting a felon and literally held his hat in hand while he apologized. I tried to be gracious but the image of him cuffing me and handing me over to Brie stuck. I remained wary of him.

Her black eyes surveyed jack pines hedging the park. Tessa was always observant and I guess we had that characteristic in common. She stroked her waist-long black hair, waited, and then looked back awkwardly at Elisi's car. I knew she wanted to tell me something.

"And how are things at Elisi's?" I asked, trying to fill the lull. Tessa and her daughter had been living there for several months.

"Fine. Chase is going to Head Start. Elisi's teaching her to speak Yakama language."

"Good, good. Uh, would you want to come in and have some coffee or tea? I have a little spot in the kitchen. . ."

"No thanks, Barlow."

The sun broke through on our end of the Valley, and she cupped her hand along her forehead, peering up at me, fighting the wind from moment to moment as it kept pushing hair into her eyes. She just watched me like that. I gratefully soaked in the passing warmth, trying not to be self-conscious, but wondering what the hell she wanted to tell me, and knowing I needed to wait rather than ask. We must have stood that way for a full minute.

"I was hoping you'd look in on Franklin," she finally declared.

"How come?"

"He's not taking his Ritalin."

"I'm not big on making kids take their meds."

"That's not what I mean, Barlow. Emily says he's stashing it. He puts the pills in a jar under his mattress. I'm afraid he's pounding and snorting it like I used to."

"Did you talk to him?"

"Not easy to. He's running around with little gangbangers on Larena Lane, won't do what Leila or I say, won't sit down with us ever since . . . Maybe you'd talk to him, figure what he's up to, and give us some advice."

"Be better if he wanted to talk to me. Does he have extra money?"

She became impatient. "Nobody has money in my family right now, Barlow. I think he and his pals are snorting those pills up. I know a couple of those boys he's in with huff gas for sure."

She kicked dust with her foot and we paused to watch a huge combine pace slowly along Harrah Road, followed by several pickups and SUVs trying to pass. The roar of machinery drowned the ambient noise of the park and any further attempt at conversation for a few minutes.

"I got a lot going on now," she explained. "I can't keep looking after him and all he's up to." She stopped there but I knew there was more.

"What's going on with you?"

She shook her head. "I don't want to go into that right now. Will you talk with him?"

"He's thirteen, right? He can consent to counseling on his own in Washington state. I don't like to go out and solicit clients, Tessa, just because a relative says so. See if you can talk him into coming for a visit on his own. Who prescribes the Ritalin?"

"He's not thirteen; he's fourteen. Leo Aspen, I guess." Her face brightened slightly at the thought. "Oh, yeah—your old Indian Health pal."

"I'm not associated with Yakama Indian Health Clinic anymore. Or Leo Aspen."

"But you can look at medical records over there."

"Why should I make trouble? Bill Gaillard doesn't like it when I come by."

"I just wanted you to find out how often Franklin's getting those pills and how many. That's all I want to know. And if Gaillard don't like you, you should be used to that by now," she teased. "You cancelled his ticket to a job at the regional office."

Maybe she was right but I never saw it quite that way. In the months after having a bullet removed from my left buttock and a rhinoplasty for the broken nose I got from Tiller, I was full of piss and vinegar to sue Indian Health Service. I'd become something of a traumatized insomniac, my mind flooded with involuntary images of Jack Brie shooting and just missing Tessa with the very pistol I'd bought, and then careening off into the darkened foothills, suffusing blood from wounds opened by her last-minute assault with Parker's fold-out dagger and Arnold's miracle shot from the old Marlin rifle.

I held the not entirely irrational conviction that Jack Brie would come back to get me and Ruthie, even though part of me knew the idea that he was still alive or would come anywhere near Yakima again made no sense. Chronic fatigue, fear, and emerging paranoia had made me more suitable as a client than as a practicing psychologist. In my own view, IHS had screwed my life up.

"Dead and eaten by coyotes," Arnold would say reassuringly, responding to my thousand-mile-stare when Trick and I met up with him at sweat lodge.

He seemed to know exactly who was on my mind.

Made in the USA
Lexington, KY
27 January 2013